GUARDIANS OF THE SIXTH GATE

AMY PROKOPIS

Amy Prokopis

amyprokopis@gmail.com

ISBN 979-8-9854601-5-5 (Paperback)

ISBN 979-8-9854601-4-8 (eBook)

Cover image by Lena Yang

Edited by Lucia Ferrara

Published by Amy Prokopis

First printing edition October 2022

www.amyprokopis.com

To my husband, whose Greek heritage inspired many of the fantasy elements of this story.

Alex, thank you for always supporting me and encouraging me to follow my dreams.

This one is for you.

"But if you only knew, deep down, what pains are fated to fill
your cup before you reach that shore, you'd stay right here,
preside in our house with me and be immortal."
-Calypso, *The Odyssey* by Homer

CHAPTER I

O f all the days to start senior year. Not only was I late, but it was raining hard. I tapped the breaks as I rounded the corner, hoping that the cop parked at the Starbucks across the street didn't question it. Burbrook High consisted of a three-story brick building that stood off on its own in a field just outside Burbrook. It was a strange place to build a school, but back in the '20s the town had been bursting at the seams from the railroad traffic. Expansion had been imminent, but all it took was a single discarded cigarette from the conductor's car to blow apart the future of our now silent town.

My tires squealed as I pulled into the lot. It was nearly full, and I let out a groan as I took one of the last open spots at the back. The engine purred to a dead silence as I turned the key and tossed it into my bag on the floor. I slung the bag over my shoulder and didn't look back, running toward the front door. The bell rang halfway there, and my phone buzzed in my pocket, then a second time as I made it inside.

Mrs. McKellen's voice came over the intercom, making my

stomach sink. I was later than I thought. Maybe that's what I get for driving an old VW Beetle with a broken gas gauge. I knew it was my fault, but it made me feel better to blame my aunt's crappy hand-me-down, even though I knew the excuse wouldn't work on Mr. Puck.

I tried opening the door as quietly as I could, but it didn't matter. The squelching of my Converse sneakers gave me away immediately. Mr. Puck hadn't changed at all since I had him for biology in my freshman year. He was the same twenty-something, overly dedicated science teacher. No matter how much nicer his slacks, button-ups, and carefully polished Oxfords were than the other teachers at school, his youth was undeniable. He had only been teaching a few years, but he had already established himself at school as a super genius. Despite being the best teacher most of us may ever have, the only thing the rest of the student body seems to care about is how hot he was.

"Name?" he asked. Not wanting to draw any more attention to myself, I went straight for the first empty seat I saw. It was the only table without a full group, which I knew would be a problem as soon as we started doing labs in a few weeks.

"Victoria Johnson," I said, not sure if he didn't remember me because of all the smudgy make-up or because the last time I had him was freshman year and I was that unmemorable. He nodded for me to sit, and I did, at the opposite end of the table from a boy I only just now recognized. My friend Macy thought about asking him out freshman year before she realized how much smarter than her he was. He was the same boy who spent fifth-hour English last year answering all of Mrs. McKellen's questions. I remember because she asked him in the middle of the fall semester to join the academic team, the only extra-curricular at school that ever won anything.

The entire junior class talked about it for weeks. What 4.0 student would shoot down the opportunity at the only college scholarship Burbrook High offered? As funny as it had been, it wasn't at all weird for him. He came to school every day in the same leather jacket, the kind of casual roughness that easily blended in with the potheads. They didn't seem to like him though. He must've been too straitlaced for them.

Jamie Quinn.

I looked back toward the front of the room where Mr. Puck was busy gathering syllabi from his desk. My phone buzzed against my thigh again and, after making sure Puck was still sorting papers, I slid it from my pocket. All three texts were from Macy.

Where are you?

I saved you a seat in chemistry.

What the hell?

I glanced her way. Macy shook her blonde head, motioning toward the empty seat next to her. I thought about moving for a brief second before Mr. Puck made his way toward my table, handing out packets of paper. I settled for my quiet corner in the back with the school's weirdo as Puck began reading the school rules.

"I don't really have to read all of this to a bunch of seniors, do I?" he asked after a few minutes. "What's the school's attendance policy?"

There was a resounding "ten absences equal a failing grade," as Mr. Puck waved a hand like he was directing a symphony. He flipped to the next page of the syllabus and lifted a remote from his desk to turn on the projector.

"Let's move on to chemistry class," he said. The room was quiet as he explained his rules, how labs worked, and then the supplies we needed to bring to class. I found out that Jamie Quinn and I were the only ones in the class who bought the three-ring binder and dividers. This earned us both bonus points on the safety test we would take on Friday.

"All right," Puck called over the groans in the room, "I'll make you a deal. The students who have their supplies by tomorrow will get bonus points on the test too." The complaints died down long enough for Mr. Puck to explain the first class activity; an ice breaker. I had been hoping for real chemistry homework, anything but an ice breaker.

"I've put instructions on the board. Ask those questions to a partner at your table. When the timer goes off, you have to move to a new table and find a new partner. Go," Puck said. I looked at the board. It was a list of the most generic questions, the same ones I was sure nearly every teacher in the building would have on their own ice breakers. I turned to ask Jamie question number one, what he did over the summer, but he wasn't looking at me. His eyes were fixated on my left wrist. I had nearly forgotten my new accessories along with the argument I managed to avoid with my uncle as I left this morning.

I adjusted the studded cuff around my wrist and sat my hand in my lap, worrying now that my eye makeup looked just as ridiculous. Maybe Uncle Mark was right about it being too much. My stomach knotted and I wished I had just come to school like the invisible girl I had always been. So much for reinventing myself. I opened my mouth to ask about his summer but was interrupted.

"I don't know if I should call you Tori Johnson or Joan Jett," Jamie said with a smirk. I froze for a moment. Was it possible that he knew old-school rockers?

"Well, no amount of leather will make you Axl Rose," I said, only broadening his smile.

"I guess the answer to question number one is that you

grew a pair," he said, nodding toward the ice-breaker list on the front whiteboard. His words made it hard for me to contain my excitement. I'd always been known in school as Macy's best friend. I wasn't sociable or desirable the way she was. I wasn't *not* pretty, but even the guys who were interested stopped looking when I opened my mouth to talk about books and things that actually matter. Uncle Mark always says they're intimidated by my brains. Aunt Becky calls me an "old soul." The boys call me weird, probably because I spent Saturdays at SAT workshops instead of seeing every movie showing at our town's tiny theater. I made solid grades, but even I knew that being near the top of the class didn't always cover the cost of a good college. Macy had that box checked too.

"What did you do this summer?" I asked, feeling the heat radiate through my face. I placed my hands on the table, feeling a little better about my new look. At least someone thought it was cool.

"I fixed my bike mostly," he said. "I didn't have the part to fix it until July."

"Doesn't sound like a very Axl Rose thing to do," I said. He didn't even laugh.

"Not my scene," he said. I found that hard to believe, but then again... He might look the part, but it wasn't Jamie Quinn smoking pot in the bathroom at lunch. Jamie had never been in trouble that I knew of. He was on the honor roll. He was number one in our class, which everyone assumed bothered me more than it did.

"Have you ever... anything?" I asked. I felt my cheeks heating again as all the thoughts raced through my head. Smoking. Drinking. Sex. Jamie shook his head and then returned the question. I had never broken any school rules, let alone any with my aunt and uncle.

Sometimes, Becky and Mark brought home a bottle of

wine, and I mean only sometimes. Uncle Mark kept a stash of beer in the garage that I'd found a few months ago after I'd driven the Beetle into the cardboard boxes concealed under the tarp. Even the mere thought of being caught made me too nervous to do more than cover them again and hope no one noticed the small scuff mark on the bumper.

"No," I said.

"The queen bee doesn't drag you to any parties?" Jamie asked. I didn't need to ask to know that he meant Macy. Macy was one of the few people at school who hosted the parties everyone gossiped about. More often, she went to Sean Peterson's parties with her other friends, hoping he'd notice her. I always made sure to tell Becky that I was sleeping over at Macy's house so I could pick her up when she got too drunk to even approach Sean. It was the biggest lie I'd ever told my aunt.

"Not really. I just don't... I mean that they don't seem..." I let the words hang in the air as I tried thinking of a better way to say that the parties all seemed like a very bad idea. As everyone liked to say in Burbrook though, if you didn't party on the weekends then you probably didn't do anything at all. At least, nothing to be considered a real social life. Jamie nodded and stared past me at Macy's table.

"They feel stupid, don't they?" he asked. His words struck me. Stupid was what I meant but would never say aloud at school unless I *really* wanted to be excluded. I thought I was the only exception to that normal teenage trope long ago; a thirty-year-old trapped in a teenage body.

"Basically," I said. "Well, I thought so anyway." I turned to look at Macy. She was the only one at her table talking, both boys staring a little too intently to actually be listening to what she was saying.

Mr. Puck rang the bell and Macy's head snapped my way.

She was out of her chair and sliding into the one across from me before I could move. Jamie moved to the table in front of ours, his chair scooted almost a foot back from the table.

"What is going on with you?" she asked, running her fingers over the studs on my leather cuff. I pulled my arm back, my other hand fingering the clasp.

"I think I went too heavy with the eye makeup," I said. Macy nodded and reached for the purse at her hip. She pulled out a makeup wipe, glancing behind her to make sure Mr. Puck wasn't watching before she reached over and began dabbing at my eye.

"This is not you at all," she said, setting the black-smeared wipe aside and reaching for my wrist. I did it for her, unclasping the leather cuff and tossing it into my bag on the floor with a huff.

"The whole day is ruined and it's only first period," I said. Macy rolled her eyes.

"The rain brought out the natural texture in your hair. Connor Taylor was scrolling through your Instagram during Mr. Puck's spiel, and your chemistry partner is number one in the entire class. I'm mad you're not sitting next to me, but I wouldn't go as far as to say the whole day is ruined," she said. My brain snapped to attention before she had finished.

"What about Connor?" I asked. Macy lit up, the kind of smile she only wore when talking about Sean. She leaned over the table, clapping her hands over mine.

"Connor had his phone under the table when Mr. Puck was talking about his grading policy. He was looking at that picture of you from homecoming. You were wearing that pink dress. You wore that sophomore year, right?" she asked.

I remembered the picture. Becky made me pose on the stairs before driving Macy and me to the dance. I didn't have a very active life on social media, but that picture was old enough that he had to scroll a little way through my feed to find it. I looked toward the front of the room where Connor sat. He was cute, an athlete with the muscles to prove it.

"Really?" I asked. When was the last time I even talked to him? Macy squeezed my hands harder before letting them go.

"He's having a party at his house Friday," she said. "His parents are divorced, and his mom has to drive to Holston for work. She won't be back until noon the next day. Connor said we can all crash there as long as whoever stays the night helps clean up the next morning."

My usual response hung on my lips, kept from tumbling out by the one memory of Connor I possessed. Summer practice was when our volleyball team shared the weight room with the football team. I'd watched Conner bench press the entire week. Mr. Puck's bell interrupted my thoughts.

"You're driving this time," I said before I realized it. Macy let out a gasp as she stood up.

"I'm holding you to it," she said, pointing my way before reluctantly moving to the next table. I wondered if I would regret it, trying my best to put my worries aside as Ashton Rogers sat at my table. Thankfully, we only had time for one more rotation of the ice breaker before class ended. Not that it saved me from the rest of the day.

We did ice breakers in every class up to lunch, the only thirty minutes of the entire day where I didn't have to talk about myself. I listened as Macy told me all about her vacation to visit her aunt in France. I was already exhausted by all the social interaction, ready for school to actually start so the most I would have to do was take notes and listen quietly as teachers rambled on.

English class with Mrs. McKellen wasn't so bad. I made sure when we enrolled that I would be in her senior AP English as well as her Shakespeare class. Instead of introducing ourselves, we spent the entire hour of Shakespeare class writing poems that described our summer. I was glad that instead of reading them aloud, we simply had to tape them to the wall above her desk before class ended. I knew I was going to like her class.

"I think I already have senioritis," Macy told me as we walked into the locker room for volleyball at the end of the day. She stripped off her shirt as soon as the door swung shut behind us. I was one of the few people on the team who had a locker; most of the girls brought their gear in from their cars each day. With a car as unreliable as the Beetle, leaving my gear at school meant I had one less thing to worry about carrying around if it suddenly broke down.

"Remember when you got yourself locked in there freshman year?" Macy asked me as I spun the knob on the combination lock. I wish I could forget freshman year altogether. The first week of school, a few girls on the freshman team, who could now be found blowing smoke rings out the bathroom windows at lunch, convinced me to try climbing into my volleyball locker. I had been small enough to fit comfortably. Even now, I was sure I could fit in the small space, though I'd learned my lesson the minute those girls decided to lock me inside.

"Funny," I said, pulling out my shoes and kneepads as Macy giggled. It was good to know that despite the makeup, studded leather bracelet, and all the things Jamie Quinn said, the day hadn't been an entire loss. At least, I didn't get locked in a gym locker.

CHAPTER 2

I was glad when my day ended, an entire hour after school let out. Practice ran shorter than it had in the last few weeks thanks to our coach's faculty meeting. I told Macy I'd meet her at Starbucks, making it all the way to my car only to find that the battery was dead. Pushing my wet hair out of my face, I ventured back into the storm.

Traffic was almost nonexistent around the school now, making it that much quicker to cross the road and make it under the awning of the coffee shop. I had given up on my hair long ago and just gave it a good squeeze before going inside. It was colder inside the building than it was outside. The air conditioning made me shiver as soon as it hit me.

"Tori," Macy said. She sat in the corner next to the window, motioning for me to join her with a few vigorous waves of both hands. I didn't understand the urgency until I noticed Connor blending a drink behind the counter. I hurried toward our table, Macy grabbing my wrist to undo the leather cuff.

"I don't even know why you put this thing back on," she said. I took it from her before she could discard it and tucked it into my pocket. I instinctively reached for the coffee cup that wasn't there, so used to our weekly exchange that I hadn't noticed until I sat down.

"I paid last time," I said. Macy pushed her cup aside to unzip her wallet, sliding me a five.

"I know," she said. "You should talk to him at least once before he's all boozy like he will be Friday." I felt panic turn all my muscles to stone. Macy had to reach over and push the bill into my hand before I took a deep enough breath to relax even a fraction.

Connor transferred to Burbrook almost a year ago and fit in so easily that it was like he'd grown up with the rest of our class. I never talked to him— not that I'd ever had the chance to. His friends were always close by, most of the hoard of boys waiting for their own chance to talk to Macy.

"You should know before I embarrass myself that I hate you for this," I said before standing up. I talked myself through my usual order once just to keep from thinking about who I'd have to relay it to. Connor met me at the register with a big smile.

"Venti blonde roast, right?" he asked, already typing the order into the iPad. I could've sworn he didn't know anything more than my name.

"How did you know?" I asked. He smirked, looking up from the screen.

"One of you pays for a cappuccino with a pump of vanilla and two pumps of caramel and a venti blonde roast, no room for cream. You don't need to spend more than five minutes with Macy to know that everything about her is extra. You're simple," he said, looking back at me as soon as the words came out. "I don't mean that in a bad way. Maybe there's more to you than I thought." His eyes roved over my Pink Floyd T-shirt, stopping at my now bare wrist. I shoved my hand into my pocket to retrieve the five dollars Macy had given me.

"I was running late," I said, "I know they're not exactly cool, but it was the first thing I grabbed, so... It's is my aunt's."

Connor shrugged, turning away from the line of coffee pots with a steaming paper cup. He took the bill from me and slid the cup across the counter and said, "No, it's cool. I love Pink Floyd." He took a pen from the pocket of his apron and started singing the chorus to "You Give Love a Bad Name" as he wrote at the bottom of the bill.

I opened my mouth to point out that it was a Bon Jovi song, but I could already hear Macy's nagging. It didn't matter that he didn't know who sang the song, right? He pretended to know because I liked Pink Floyd. That had to be something. What came next only made me squirm more. He slid the five-dollar bill back toward me, a phone number scrawled along the bottom edge.

"I swear I won't look like this... you know, when I get to your party Friday," I said, letting my index finger rub over the ink on the bill as if it would vanish.

"Tori Johnson is actually going to a party. I thought this new look was all for show," Connor said, glancing toward the far side of the counter where the manager was staring back at us with reproachful eyes. I stuffed the bill deep in my pocket and took my coffee.

"You know what they say about the quiet ones," I said as a few men in suits fell in line behind me. If there hadn't been a wait, I was sure Connor would've kept talking to me. Instead, he offered me a kind smile.

"Maybe I'll find out Friday?" he asked. I looked down at the steaming cup, the warmth making my face hotter than it already was. I didn't know exactly how to respond, so I just moved out of the way. The man behind me didn't hesitate to take my place, already rattling off his order.

"See you later," I called out, not sure if he'd heard me. The walk back to our table felt painfully slow and as much as I wanted to close the distance with a jog, I didn't. Macy was beaming and I was sure my smile gave me away before I could reach her. At least she hadn't let out one of her squeals.

"That looked good. What did he say about your shirt? That part made me so nervous for you," she said. I shushed her, making sure that no one was watching us before I relayed the details.

"He thought that I looked cool today, even though he has no idea who Pink Floyd is," I said, pulling my studded cuff from my pocket again and wrapping it around my wrist. Macy shook her head.

"Speaking of, what's the deal with all the black and stuff today? A band T-shirt can be cute with a jean jacket and the right flower crown maybe, but you look like you stepped out of a mosh pit this morning," Macy said, taking a sip of her coffee. I had already prepared for her questions. Macy was the most fashionable person I knew, keeping up with every trend and making sure she was always one of the first people at school to try them out. I understood the appeal of fitting in, but why stress about looking cool when everyone ended up looking the same anyway? I had spent far too long trying to find clothes I liked that were still trendy.

"It was raining. My eyeliner smudged. I promise that I'm not going to trade my Beetle in for a motorcycle and a leather jacket anytime soon. I just wanted to experiment a little," I said. Macy snorted. There would be no wearing the leather jacket Becky bought me for my birthday now.

"Well, it looked like Connor was down for some experimenting himself a minute ago," she said with a wry smirk. I sat my cup back down, sloping enough hot coffee onto my hand to startle me to silence. Macy laughed.

I was the only one in our circle of friends who hadn't gotten more than a little tongue from a boy, not that I cared. I'd heard enough of Macy's post-relationship drama to stave off that interaction for another year or two.

"I gotta go," I said, standing up from the table and backing toward the door. Macy followed me with a groan.

"Can't Becky host a book club without you?"

Every Monday, the public library's Classic Literature Club met for coffee and discussion. Mostly, they gossiped. They managed to read through a book every two weeks or so, talking about the plot for maybe fifteen or twenty minutes. The club had whittled down to a regular group of eight, me included thanks to my barely existing social life.

"We're reading *To Kill a Mockingbird*, which Mrs. McKellen said we will start reading in her class in a few weeks. You can thank me later," I said, holding the door open for her. Macy didn't protest, driving me back down the street to my car so I wouldn't have to walk back in the rain. As much as I tried, I couldn't get the engine to turn over. So, I loaded my backpack into the trunk of Macy's Challenger, and she drove me home with the radio so loud that we had to yell over the music.

Our two-story house sat at the end of a cul-de-sac in Burbrook's historic district. It was once the most coveted neighborhood in town, boasting homes with original hardwood floors and large porches. However, the original plumbing and crumbling foundation meant that the wealthier families in town like Macy's opted for new homes over vintage.

I liked our little neighborhood in our little town though. From my bedroom window, I could see past the city limits and just barely make up the giant houses that sat along the windy road up Burbrook Mountain. Macy lived at the bottom of the mountain in a two-story house, complete with a heated pool. If she lived any closer, I'd make her pick me up on the way to school instead of driving the Beetle.

"I'll pick you up tomorrow?" Macy asked as she pulled into the cracked driveway.

"I'll let you know," I said, getting out. I quickly retrieved my bag from the trunk and ran for the porch, waving on the doorstep as she backed into the street. I was surprised that Emma's Escape wasn't parked down the street like normal. She was usually the first one to come over for book club. The TV was on in the living room when I went inside. I called for Aunt Becky, and she appeared in the kitchen doorway with a glass of water in her hand.

"First day of senior year, how was it?" she asked me, taking a seat on the couch and turning down the TV volume.

"Good. Where's everyone?" I asked, leaning on the banister.

"We canceled," she said. "It's Margot's week to have her kids and she wanted to spend the day with them after school. So, any news?"

My stomach clenched as I thought about Connor Taylor browsing my Instagram, staring at me behind the Starbucks counter, giving me his number... I tried to push the thoughts away before they made me blush. I shrugged.

"Same old."

Becky didn't question me about it any further, telling me all about how much work she had to do this week. I didn't pay too much attention to all the details until she informed me that she would be working late Friday and Mark wouldn't be home from his business trip until Saturday.

"I promise I'll come home with pizza," Becky finished.

"Don't worry about it. Macy and I are going out to see a movie anyway, if that's okay," I said. Becky didn't care, recommending the newest comedy out in theaters. My aunt and uncle were some of the most trusting people I knew, which only made me feel more guilty for what I was planning. Becky had been a kind of hippie in her day, having done far more at my age than I had. It was my mom who was the golden child. That's what made the accident so shocking.

"I'm going to look over some stuff for school," I said, ignoring Becky's request to join her for an episode of *Gilmore Girls*.

"Nerd," she called after me as I reached the second floor. My bedroom was to the left, the last of the rooms containing the original creaky flooring. Uncle Mark called it a "teenager alarm," since it made noise any time you tried walking across it. There would be no hope for me if I had to sneak upstairs late Friday night, one of the many reasons I was glad no one else would be home until then.

I dropped my backpack onto my desk chair and unzipped it, taking out my binder and setting it on my bed. I pulled back the curtains over the large window and sat down to read through all the information. Teachers always threw everything at us the very first day, expecting us to remember all their rules and such the next. I started with chemistry. Mr. Puck's syllabus was thicker than the rest.

I scanned over the school rules, his assignment policies, finally coming to a piece of paper stapled to the back. It was our first assignment, a group project. I could feel the headache forming. It was due Friday, a group proposal for the subject we would present on form the first chapter. I pulled my textbook from my backpack and opened the chapter, thumbing through the pages to scan the subsections. Maybe Jamie would write the proposal for us. Then again, what if he did? Jamie was so smart that he was likely to completely take over our group. I'd spent my entire life letting people push me around at school and I'd vowed I wouldn't let my senior year go that way. I had a leather bracelet to prove it.

Using my laptop, I logged onto our school website and then plugged in the code from our syllabus to get access to our chemistry class. Thankfully, Jamie had the same idea. His email was one of the few listed. I clicked on it and started typing.

Jamie,

I was looking through the syllabus for chemistry and noticed that our first presentation proposal is due Friday. I was wondering if you'd thought about what we should present.

-Tori Johnson

I never heard back from Jamie, and he didn't show up at school the next morning, or the day after that. While everyone else was busy talking about their presentation options at the end of class on Wednesday, I was coming to terms with the fact that I'd have to do the entire thing alone. I picked through every subject covered in the first chapter and I narrowed it down to those that seemed the most interesting. One day later, and after another unanswered email, I decided to ask Mr. Puck if I could move to a new group.

"You know," he started, "I was so worried about getting everyone separated into even numbers, but I think it works better this way. I think you and Jamie will make great partners."

He started back to his desk, the next class beginning to gather in the room behind me. I followed him, a slight panic rising in my chest. The idea of standing at the front of the room doing the speaking rather than clicking through the Power-Point in the corner sent a jolt through my chest.

"If Jamie dropped the class though…" I said, letting my words trail off as Mr. Puck looked up from his desk. I could tell that he was stressed himself, cringing as a loud group of freshmen entered the room.

"The online roster has had Jamie marked as sick all week. I got an email from his dad this morning telling me he should be back in class tomorrow. Maybe you should try emailing Jamie," he said. I opened my mouth to tell him that I already had when he snapped at a freshman boy who had thrown a pencil at the table next to him. Knowing there would be no arguing, I hurried from the room and made my way toward Mrs. Hawthorne's class.

When I checked my email at lunch, I found a reply from Jamie asking to meet before school in the library tomorrow. There was no way he could expect us to draft a proposal with less than an hour before class started. Sure, it didn't have to be long, but that didn't mean it could be sloppy either. I sent him a simple "meet you there."

Aunt Becky drove me to school early the next day since the Beetle had been in the shop for a new battery since Monday. She dropped me off at the door, promising me that the proposal would work out. I walked down the hall, getting warm smiles from teachers on their way to and from the copy room as I went.

The school library was larger than you'd expect for a school our size. It had all the usual sections with a computer lab off to one side and six tables at the other for studying. I found Jamie sitting at one of them, clicking away on his laptop. He didn't look up at me until I plopped my backpack onto the chair next to him.

"I was thinking we could write about matter since it's sorta the foundation of chemistry," he said, turning his laptop so I could read. He had almost a full page drafted, the minimum needed for the proposal. I wanted to argue with him, but it was exactly what I had planned on writing on my own. I didn't ask before typing, adding in the final paragraph at the bottom and scooting the laptop his way.

"You've really racked up absences this week," I said. He smirked, hitting print on the document. I could hear the printer hum to a start a few feet away.

"You don't believe that I was sick, do you?" he asked, going to the printer for our essay before I could respond. Why wouldn't I believe him and why would he suddenly care?

"I did until now," I said when he returned. I took the paper away from him, tucking it safely in my binder. "So, where were you?"

"Sick," he said with a laugh. Now I *really* didn't believe him. I reached over and closed his laptop before he could search in the browser.

"Just so you know, I asked Mr. Puck for a new lab partner, and he said no. If I had it my way, I'd be in a different group with people who care about other people's grades," I said. His eyes went wide for a moment. I could feel my heart pounding in my chest. I'd never argued with anyone I wasn't related to. Before I could second guess myself, I stuffed my binder into my backpack and left the library.

I sat on the front steps of the school until Macy got there. I didn't bother to explain why I was so early, hoping to God that Jamie decided to skip class the way he had the rest of the week. Unfortunately, he came in just before the final bell rang for first period and took a seat next to me this time instead of at the end of the table.

He didn't say a word when I handed in our proposal. Mr. Puck flicked off the lights and began handing around a fill-in-the-blank worksheet to go along with the video he was now projecting at the front of the room. He warned us that the worksheet was due before we left as he started the film. A dorky guy popped onto the screen and a loud electronic theme song filled the room. A girl sitting at the table in front of us immediately opened a game on her phone and began playing under the table.

I shrugged out of my jacket and leaned over my worksheet. I was doodling a pattern of stars in the corner when I noticed that Jamie was looking over my arms. He looked confused, awkwardly shifting his gaze onto his own paper when I slid my arms under the table.

"Are you okay?" I asked, reaching for his arm. He scooted away.

"Yeah," he said, "just not feeling my best." I focused on the video, zoning back out again when a puppet entered the plot as the scientist's assistant. I noticed that Jamie was looking at me again. He looked away when our eyes met.

"What is it?"

"It's nothing."

"Then stop staring at me," I said. Mr. Puck cleared his throat, looking straight at us. I realized then that I'd missed the answers to the last two questions. I sucked in a deep breath and opened my book to the first chapter, hoping I could find them.

"There's something different about you, Victoria Johnson," Jamie said. I looked up at him, but he wasn't staring at me like before. He was sitting so straight that it looked painful, his elbows tucked against his sides and hands resting on his legs as he watched the scientist in the film explain the founding fathers of chemistry.

"You're not exactly a normal teenager either," I said. He snorted, almost relaxing. He took a deep breath as if it would help ease the tension in his stiff posture. It didn't. He snuck a few more glances my way as I focused on my worksheet and pretended not to notice. Once the bell rang, he managed to be the first person out the door despite our seats being at the back of the room. I noticed his worksheet still sitting on the table, every question answered, though I wondered when he'd had the time to even look at it between all the staring. I put it in the turn-in tray with mine on my way into the hall.

Jamie must have snuck off altogether, because I didn't notice he was missing from school until Macy mentioned it to me in the locker room after practice. We only shared a few classes together, but I was fortunate to share a table with him in just one.

"Who cares if he's weird?" Macy said. "I'd put up with two of him if it meant I didn't have to work as hard and still get As on everything."

"I could sit by myself and still make As easy," I said, kicking the locker door shut. Macy spun the lock for me. I slipped my backpack over my shoulder and thought about leaving the room ahead of her, but she caught my shoulder before I could move.

"Speaking of homework, I told my mom I was staying at your house tonight as my cover," she said, pulling her keys from her purse and leading the way into the hall, "If anyone asks, we're working on calculus."

"Okay. Well, Becky will be home close to midnight, so we'll have to be back by then. I told her we were going to see a movie to buy us some time," I said. Macy let out a little laugh, waiting until we were in the parking lot to explain.

"Tori, I told my mom I'd be at your house. She's out of town for a conference this weekend. You're supposed to tell Becky that you'll be at mine. Why would they ever check to make sure?" she said, the locks clicking on her Challenger. "I'm going to have to watch you tonight. Maybe you should drive," she said. I had already been planning to after I thought about all those times I'd seen Macy after parties. I'd never had a drink in my life and the idea of having more than one terrified me. For all I knew, I'd turn into a sloppy monster.

"Does it ever stop raining in this damn town?" Macy asked, her windshield wipers squelching to life as we started toward the exit. I was beginning to wonder the same thing. Every day, just like the last: dark, wet, same green raincoat... I had reverted more and more to my old plain self as the week went on, finally opting for my favorite T-shirt and jeans. After the fiasco with the smokey eye on Monday, I'd stopped wearing makeup entirely.

CHAPTER 3

Macy talked me into going to the party after I'd decided not to on the drive home. She also fixed my mistake by asking Becky if I could crash at her house after the movie, getting the approval we needed without casting any suspicion about our true intentions. I let her pick out my outfit, a dark pair of jeans, free of holes, and a simple purple blouse I rarely wore. To save her from picking out a new outfit when she couldn't find a matching jacket, I slipped my new black leather jacket on and tugged off the tags. It felt a little like I was trying too hard again, but Macy liked it.

"It's cute," she said. "Well, maybe not *cute*. You look older, sexy." I felt myself relax a little, realizing how sore my shoulders had been. The hallway floor creaked and then a knock came at my door. Becky came right in, her hands busy tucking her hair into a bun at the nape of her neck.

"I wanted to give you this," she said, taking a ten-dollar bill from her pocket and tossing it on the bed next to my purse.

"I have ticket money," I said from the mirror, putting a couple swipes of mascara on and a few dabs of blush. I could feel Macy watching me, knowing that she wanted nothing more than to take her contouring brushes to my face.

"I know. That's for drinks," Becky said.

"We're too young to drink, Mrs. Greenwood," Macy said. I turned from the mirror, half expecting Becky to catch us right there. She let out a laugh instead.

"Good answer. You know what I mean. For cokes."

I snorted, sinking onto the mattress next to Macy. "Doesn't sound any better, Becky," I said.

She rolled her eyes, taking the bill and my purse. She unzipped my wallet and tucked it inside before handing it all back to me. "I'm just thankful that this is all a joke and not something I actually have to worry about."

My stomach knotted, but I forgot about it as soon as Macy nudged me with her foot.

"My mom tells me that all the time. I'm the least of her worries," she said. I knew her words dove layers deeper. Macy's parents were rich, both doctors. She claimed that was why they fought all the time. It wasn't until her mom threw a bottle of balsamic at her dad's head that they split up. The liquid seeped into the frame of their wedding picture on the wall like the universe was spreading its own symbolic black stain on their family. The stain was so bad that Mrs. Evans redecorated the entire kitchen, as if a layer of gray paint could hide the ugliness of the divorce.

"How is Tyler?" Becky asked. Macy shook her head.

"He's going to enroll at a community college in Denver in the Spring," Macy said. Becky sent her a questioning gaze. "What about the scholarship at CU?"

Macy shook her head. Tyler Evans had been a lot of things when he went to Burbrook High; popular, a partier, player... smart was not one of those things.

"The drugs turned up on his first physical," Macy said.

Becky nodded. No one would've been surprised if they'd known Tyler at all. The Evans' had spent thousands trying to make their son look good for colleges. They gave him money for SAT workshops, tutors, football camps, and anything else they thought might help him get into a good school. It all went straight to his dealer.

"Well, I have to go. Have fun at Macy's after the movie," Becky told me, leaning down and kissing the top of my head before leaving. We spent the next hour talking about Macy's party tricks. She taught me all the hand signals she used to tell her party friends if she was having a good time or not. We ate some Chipotle, and then we were on our way to Connor's house.

The road was so dark once we got to the mountain that it was hard to read the house numbers on the gates as we passed. Macy passed her own house and we drove on for another five minutes before turning down a dirt road. There were dozens of cars already parked in the driveway, the line overflowing past the iron gates and onto the side of the road. The house was huge, shutters framing every giant window. Both French doors were wide open.

I could see now why Connor's house was the most popular party spot in town. The trees were thick around the property, and Macy and I hadn't driven past another house since turning off the main road. This wasn't going to be any small high school party and that was clear just looking at the mass of people inside the gaping front doors.

Macy pulled into a free spot on the grass and got out, starting ahead of me toward the house like she'd done it a thousand times before. She was already across the packed driveway before I caught up with her on the front steps, calling out for her to wait for me as my nerves grew worse at the prospect of getting left alone, getting caught, seeing Connor...

The music was so loud that I couldn't hear what Macy said before she disappeared into the crowded entryway. I skirted along the wall, walking right into a cloud of weed smoke. I coughed hard, jumping when I heard a yell from the hallway behind me.

"If the house smells like Coachella tomorrow, I swear I'll kick your ass, Jake," Connor yelled. The group started toward the front door, the sweet smell lingering even after they'd left. Connor looked like he'd spent a little more time playing referee than partying tonight. There was a wet splatter across his T-shirt; beer, judging by the smell. A new bruise had sprung up on his left bicep as if someone had punched him, but it didn't seem to wear on his mood much. He smiled at me, leaning against the wall.

"You just get here?" he asked. The long story was that it took forever to maneuver through the crowd before I ran into him, but I said "yes." He put a hand around my shoulders and led me down the hall and into the kitchen. It was far quieter in the large space. Beer cans, red Solo cups, and half-empty glass bottles of vodka littered the granite counters.

"Your house is nice," I said. He pulled a solo cup from the plastic sleeve and handed it to me.

"You don't have to do that," he said, pulling off his shirt next. I looked away when I felt how hot my face was and waited until he came back from the laundry room wearing a new shirt. "I know you don't come to parties and that's cool, but you don't have to pretend to feel…" He struggled to find the right words, taking a beer from the counter and using a spoon to pop off the cap.

"Not weird?" I asked him. He nodded with a chuckle, drinking straight from the bottle.

"Take what you like," he said, motioning around the kitchen. It took me a moment to realize that he was pointing at his beer and not himself. Already, it felt like I was playing pretend.

"I should probably start slow," I said. The only non-alcoholic thing in the room was the orange water cooler sitting on the opposite side of the kitchen labeled Gatorade. I filled my cup as Connor watched.

"Nice," he said, raising his beer in a toast to me. I wasn't sure what to say, so I toasted back. I don't usually like the red Gatorade, but it had been iced and felt good in the hot room. I drank almost the entire cup in the kitchen with Connor as we talked. It turned out that he was only working at Starbucks because his parents were making him pay for his own college next year.

"Your mom's salary alone could pay for four years, couldn't it?" I asked. Connor nodded, shrugging a moment later.

"Well, it could if she didn't have to spend it all paying off my dad's gambling debts. It took them forever to pay off their own student loans," he said. "So, in a way, I'm glad I'll be doing it all on my own. No one can tell you what to do when it's not their money, right?"

I couldn't argue with that. I refilled my cup and we headed to the living room again. The Gatorade had started to make my stomach turn, but the feeling vanished when Connor placed his hands on my hips to guide me through the crowd. We started dancing, which was more like swaying, with the small amount of space left in the sea of seniors. I let Connor refill my cup a few times so I could keep dancing, joining a group of Macy's friends who rarely ever talked to me. They taught me the moves to a new hip hop song that they played on the radio every hour. It sounded so repetitive and electronic that there was no way it was written by anyone with real musical talent, but the beat soon ingrained itself into my body, keeping me swaying and turning with the rhythm the way Macy's friend, Ashley, had shown me.

I thought about Macy when the song ended, and Ashley let out a girly whoop that served like a mating call to all the boys around her. Now, I remember why I don't like Macy's friends. I stopped dancing, turning around to go to the kitchen. I walked straight into Connor's chest, tripping on his feet and nearly falling over. He steadied me by my shoulders, not noticing the red splotch from my drink now seeping into the sleeve of his white shirt.

"I'll be back. I'll be back," I told him. He stepped out of my way and let me go, sliding just far enough into the group of girls to make me regret leaving. I went into the kitchen, downing the last of the Gatorade and taking my phone out to text Macy. The numbers blurred on the screen, making me mess up my passcode too many times and locking me out for a few minutes.

"Tori!" someone screamed from the other side of the room, the closest people wincing at the noise. I squeezed past a pair of girls attempting to uncork a bottle of wine with a butter knife, bashing my hips into the granite counter as I leaned over it to talk to Macy. She sat on a barstool next to a boy from my history class, fumbling with her phone.

"You have to see this," she said.

"I've been dancing with Connor all night."

I noticed the Gatorade sitting in front of her. I lifted the cup to my lips, but the boy took it from my hands and set it aside before I got a chance to drink.

"Who's your DD?" he asked us, his smile replaced with an annoyed frown.

"Me," I blurted, the heaviness settled into my muscles now. How could I be so stupid to believe that someone would put plain Gatorade out at a party? I thought I was going to puke, but Macy didn't seem to notice my panic. She let out a gasp as she finally found what she was searching for. She leaned over the counter and shoved the phone in my face. It was a series of texts between her and her friend Jess. Jess explained that she made Alison's boyfriend drive her home after throwing a beer in Connor Taylor's face. He'd groped her one too many times, not understanding why she complained about it afterward.

"God, this was stupid. I should've stayed home," I said.

"Well, looks like we're staying now," Macy cried out, practically crawling onto the counter to reach a beer on the other side. The boy next to her let out a sigh and turned around, looking down the hall.

"Woah, woah," he called out, hopping off the stool and waving down the hall. "Alison! Alison, tell Noah to drive Tori home too. She's supposed to be the designated driver and she's wasted." I opened my mouth to argue, but a tall blonde had stormed down the hall to join us before I could answer.

"Tori Johnson's here?" she asked, giving me a sideways glance. Next to me, Alison was Macy's best friend, and we couldn't be more different. Alison was a middle on the volleyball team with us, moving in from Texas sophomore year.

"Come on, Alison. It's just one more person and it's not like Burbrook is that big," the boy said.

"He lives down the street from me," I said. Noah and I usually left for school at the same time each morning. Until we turned sixteen, we waited on the bus together. He'd never said a word to me, always using that time to do his homework. Alison motioned for me to follow her with a groan.

"He can take all the drunk girls home he wants, because he's not taking me tonight," she said. My retort stuck in my mouth as I saw two boys helping Jake, the boy Connor had yelled at earlier, out the door. Jake let out a whoop as they walked, only laughing harder when one of the boys keeping him upright told him to shut up. Noah looked nervously after them, turning his concern toward me on the front steps.

"If you think you're going to throw up, please roll down the window," Noah told me, reaching out to take my arm. I pulled it away from him.

"I got it," I said, focusing on walking in a straight line down the path after Jake. The boys pushed him roughly into the passenger seat of Noah's Mustang. I climbed into the backseat, my head starting to throb. Noah plopped into the driver's seat and started the car, nearly backing into the Jeep parked a little too close behind him. Everything I'd consumed in the last few hours was sloshing around in my stomach and I opened my mouth to ask Noah to roll down the windows when Jake let out an ear-piercing woot.

"Convertible! Yeah!" he screamed as he smashed his finger on the button on the ceiling. The top of the car lifted and slowly tucked itself away behind me as we sped down the long dirt road. The wind caught my hair with a whoosh, and I could feel it tangling behind me immediately.

"Stop touching things. Damn," Noah argued. I fought to gather my hair into a ponytail. We swerved to the right a little when Noah reached over to slap Jake's hand away from the radio. "Blinded by the Light" echoed off the trees as we drove. Noah cursed under his breath as he tried resetting all the buttons Jake had touched.

"Keep going. Take the left," Jake said, pointing toward the main road ahead of us.

"Left heads up the mountain," Noah said. "I swear, Jake, I'll drop you off on the side of the road if you don't stop screaming your head off. Every cop in town can probably hear you." Noah didn't bother stopping at the stop sign, taking the right turn. I leaned over the side of the car to puke when Jake seized the wheel. We veered left and I bashed my nose into the car frame, feeling the blood rain down my shirt immediately and my eyes burn.

I was lifted into the air, Jake's cheering turning into a scream of terror as he realized we were flipping off the road. I clamped my hands onto my seat belt and closed my eyes as soon as I saw the drop on the other side.

I let out a scream as soon as I realized where I was. I was lying on the thick grass, staring up at my feet that were still tangled in the seat belt. The car was smashed apart, glass glittering under the stars and twisted metal hanging off the frame. A large boulder in front of us had stopped the plumet, the nose of the car propped up on top. It was the only reason I wasn't crushed into the leather seats. The passenger seat was empty, the door ripped away entirely. I looked away as soon as I noticed that Noah was still in his seat, hanging upside down and not moving.

I pulled my legs free and crawled out from under the car. I scrambled to my feet just long enough to make it a few paces back up the hill before collapsing and vomiting every ounce of red Gatorade I'd ingested. I looked up the hill. We rolled at least five times from the look of the drop. Then I remembered the car, which looked more like a metal pancake now against the boulder. I ran my hands over my arms and legs. How the hell was I alive? That drop should've killed me. I should be dead.

Blood was dried over the gashes in my jacket and jeans, but there were no cuts. Nothing felt broken. My entire body felt more than alive. My heart was racing so fast that my chest hurt. My head ached from hanging upside down. My vision blurred as I fought to control my breathing, not able to inhale fully before the shaky breaths came shooting past my lips again. I scooted a few inches away from the vomit pile before I let my head rest against the grass.

My heart pounded in my chest and my stomach churned when I woke. I leaned over the edge of the leather couch and dry-heaved toward the gray area rug. As soon as I'd recovered enough, I sat up. Where was I?

The living room was large. I sat on a black leather couch, opposite another of the same make. A fireplace lit the entire room, the only other light coming from a room at the back. A large wooden table in the doorway told me it was a kitchen. I noticed the water sitting on the coffee table next to two Aspirin capsules and a large bowl full of red water. A rag was draped over one side of the bowl. I could tell that the rag used to be white only because of the fibers left untouched at one end.

I wondered for a minute if Noah or Jake was in the room with me, but I didn't see anyone. I saw my leather jacket in a heap on the floor. My arms were clean of blood, just a white bandage around my left wrist to remind me of the accident. My jeans were caked with blood as well as my shirt. A fresh pair of jeans and a black long-sleeve shirt were folded in the armchair next to the fireplace. I glanced around to make sure no one was looking before darting over and changing. After finding a hair band at the bottom of my purse, I pulled my hair into a pony-tail as best as I could with my shaky hands.

I noticed the pictures lining the mantel as I worked. The nearest was a family of four standing in front of a train. The man and woman in the picture were young, no older than thirty. They both had dark hair, the woman's wound in a tight braid that laid over her right shoulder. Next to them stood two teenagers. One of them was a muscular-looking girl with dark hair. The other was Jamie Quinn. On each of their left forearms was the same tattoo that swirled from their wrists. Mr. and Mrs. Quinn's tattoos wound all the way to their elbows.

"I'm not a match," Jamie yelled in the kitchen.

"You won't know until you try," a girl said.

"There's not enough of us to carry that right now, Izzy. We know there's more than just the three of us in our circle. There has to be," Jamie said. I could hear the girl grumbling and then she appeared in the living room doorway. She stopped when she saw me. She was the same girl from the picture, dark curls with the swirling tattoo around her wrist. A second later, Jamie appeared at her shoulder.

"How did I get here?" I asked. Jamie went to my dirty clothes I'd left in a heap next to the coffee table. He kicked my discarded jeans and shirt into the fireplace and bent for the jacket. I lunged for the fireplace but stopped as the flames began to lick the fabric.

"We live down the road from the crash site. We'll have to go down the other side of the mountain," he said. I caught his Colorado State hoodie when he tossed it to me and slipped into it, the entire thing hanging loose around my arms and middle.

"I don't understand. You didn't call the cops? What did you do, drag me here? Why?" I asked. I had to follow him to keep talking. He led me down a long hallway, flanked by large bedrooms, a library, and another living room. What did the Quinns do for a living?

"You weren't heavy," he said, pushing open the door at the end of the hall. The light flicked on within and then the sound of a garage door purring to life filled the silence. I followed down the stairs after him, freezing on the bottom step. The room was bigger than any garage I'd ever seen. Along one wall were three sports cars, all in different colors.

"Do your parents collect cars or something?" I asked, feeling lightheaded. Jamie was at a long utility counter on the other side of the room. He pushed up the sleeves of his leather jacket just enough for me to get a look at the tattoo wrapped around his left wrist. He pulled on a pair of leather gloves and smoothed the sleeves down over them before I could make out the writing.

"We have to talk to the cops," I said as Jamie pulled down two motorcycle helmets from the shelf above him. He strode straight toward me and handed me the helmet.

"Believe me, we aren't going back to that mess. Everyone from the party is already screwed, I'm sure. Nobody should have to see that twisted wreck and the..." He stopped, and I was glad that he did. I might keel over again if he continued. My throat burned from the bile continuing to climb its way upward with every reminder.

"I'm not going anywhere until... How the hell am I not dead?" I asked, feeling tears sting my eyes. I tried my best to blink them away. Jamie softened, but his stoic exterior soon returned when his sister spoke up.

"Take the Ferrari. It'll be easier to explain it all in a car than on your bike," Izzy said from behind me. "Besides, the seats recline." Jamie caught a pair of keys and sent them flying straight back at his sister. She caught them easily, leaning in the doorway at the top of the stairs.

"Tori, let's go," Jamie told me. "I'm taking you home." He started for his bike, looking back at me. I didn't know what else to do. I didn't even know what I wanted to ask him, so I let him adjust the helmet on my head and then I was on the bike behind him. I squeezed his stomach hard as we flew down the road the opposite way from the accident. I'd never been this way before, but I didn't spend the ride taking in the scenery.

I kept my eyes on the seams in Jamie's leather jacket the entire trip. I felt like my heart was going to explode in my chest when we turned down my street. Every light was on at my house, but that wasn't the worst of it. A police cruiser was parked in our driveway. My phone was still tucked in my purse; I hadn't thought about checking it until now. Macy probably assumed the worst. Did Becky and Mark know?

Jamie pulled up to the curb, swinging off the bike and turning to face me immediately. "I picked you up after I saw you walking home. You decided not to ride with Noah and Jake. Don't say a word about anything else," he said.

"Wait. Why? I must've been tossed out of the car. I don't know. Why lie?" I asked, tugging off the helmet. Jamie turned my face to look directly at him with one leather glove.

"I swear that I'll explain it all to you, but you have to stick to this story for now," he said. He let me go and swung his leg back over the bike and started it with a loud kick. He was turning at the end of the street before I realized I still had his helmet.

I barely got in the door before Becky and Macy threw their arms around me. The policeman sitting on the couch stood up, fingering the button on the radio at his chest.

"I was so sure you were dead," Macy said, pulling away. I didn't say anything right away and she must have interpreted my panic for confusion. "Noah and Jake, they... The cops found Noah's car down the hill where the turn-off is for Connor's house. You weren't with them," she said. The tears came pouring down my face and Becky only hugged me harder.

It took several minutes for the three of us to calm down enough so I could talk to the officer. I relayed the same story Jamie had given me. Once he'd radioed in that I was okay, we learned that they were blaming the accident on Noah. I knew that he hadn't been drinking at all. He'd been one of the few responsible ones at the party. That part dug a pit of guilt deep enough that I started to cry again.

Once the policeman left, Macy called her mom. Macy's mom was still out of town and wouldn't be back until the morning, so she got permission to stay with us. We tried our best to distract ourselves with late-night TV reruns when no one felt tired enough to sleep. I was the last one awake on the couch. Every time I closed my eyes, I remembered the lurch of the car as we began our descent down that hill. I remembered the torn and stained clothes. Most confusing of all, I knew that despite having been in the car for it all, I hadn't been injured.

CHAPTER 4

I woke up, with my shirt stuck to my back with sweat. My eyes felt heavy and the clock on the wall confirmed why. I'd only been asleep for an hour and a half. I was curled up in Mark's recliner with my knees tucked to my chest. The living room had a ghostly glow from the TV, the message, "still there?" across the Netflix screen. Macy was lying across the couch asleep, and Becky's head was lolling to one side in her armchair. I went to the kitchen and started the coffee maker, catching my reflection in the toaster and remembering that I hadn't come home in my own clothes. I was still wearing Jamie's sister's long-sleeve shirt underneath his hoodie. My head swam as I remembered the accident and the hoodie suddenly felt stifling around my neck.

I knew I was sitting in the backseat of the car. I remember Noah slapping Jake's hands as he tried pushing the buttons on the radio. "Blinded by the Light" was playing. Jake had reached over and pushed the wheel. They were saying that Noah was drinking and driving. I tugged the sweatshirt off and tossed it into the washing machine as the coffee maker finally kicked into go-mode and began heating up. My stomach rumbled, but the idea of eating anything set a sour taste in my mouth.

I couldn't stand there and wait on the coffee, not without letting my mind go to places I was trying so hard to forget. I went upstairs to shower, my stomach churning worse as I undressed. I barely made it to the toilet, spending the next minute dry-heaving into the basin. Once I'd gained control again, I got in the shower. The water was warm, so comforting. The water slid down my legs in streams and I nearly keeled over again as I thought about the blood caked over my arms from the accident.

After more than a few calming breaths, I could hear a buzzing sound. It wasn't until I heard my phone settle on the bathmat that I realized what it was. I turned off the water and pulled back the curtain seconds too late, a picture of my uncle from last Christmas flashing across the screen before fading to black as the call ended. The cold air hit me, and I reached for the towel on the rack. That's when I saw it. A single line of writing was wrapped around my left wrist. I rubbed my thumb over it, then tried washing it off in the sink with no luck. The writing wasn't in English. Maybe it was Italian? Latin? Did Jamie do this? My breath caught in my lungs as I thought about it.

I tightened my robe around my waist and went to my bedroom, the floor squeaking loudly under my feet. I pulled out my laptop and immediately logged into my school email. I sent Jamie three words: *we need to talk*. I waited for a few minutes with my stomach in knots. I didn't know what I'd expected. It was just six in the morning on a Saturday. He wasn't going to reply so soon. The thought only further irritated me. I dressed and went to the kitchen to pour myself a cup of coffee.

Becky and Macy were still asleep in the living room when I

passed. I picked up Jamie's helmet from the coffee table on my way to the kitchen and sat it down on the table. The mug shook in my hand as I took it to the table, hot coffee burning my thumb as it sloshed over the rim. I pushed back the left sleeve of my sweatshirt to look at the mark closer, my heart pounding. It was the same one every member of the Quinn family wore in the family photo on the mantel.

"Did you hurt your wrist?" Mark asked me. I whipped around to face him. He stood with a mug of coffee in one hand, still wearing his suit from his trip. I covered the mark with my right hand but realized a moment later that I didn't need to. Mark didn't seem the least bit fazed by the new tattoo. Mark Greenwood, the man who thought my aunt had ruined herself by getting a Celtic knot tattooed on her hip the year they'd met. I'd heard them argue over it enough to know his feelings. So why didn't he say anything now?

"I think I twisted it. Does it look bad?" I asked him, holding out my hand. Mark sat his mug next to mine to take my arm. He ran his fingers all over the tattoo as if it weren't there at all. Was I going insane? Maybe I had a concussion from the acci-dent. I *had* been there, briefly anyway. I remember extracting myself from the straps in the backseat.

"It looks fine to me, not even a bruise. Did you have fun at the movies?" he asked. I felt my throat tighten and I tried my best to take a sip of coffee. The warmth of the liquid made me feel a little better the same way the hot shower had. My body had started to relax now that I was home, though my mind was even more confused than it had been last night.

"There was a party," I started. My uncle took a seat next to me, his shoulders tensing. "I can't believe I was so stupid to go, but there was a boy and… I didn't know it wasn't Gatorade and I wanted to go home. Noah was already taking Jake home, so I thought I'd go with them, but I felt sick and uncomfortable. I made them let me out of the car and then..." I could see the realization on his horrified face.

"Noah Peterson and Jake Link?" he asked. So, he had heard about the night. I nodded, blinking back tears. He reached for my hands, but I pulled them back. "Victoria," he started. I shook my head, pulling my mug closer to me.

"I'm fine," I said. "Just a little freaked out about it all." I could already hear what was coming next. Mark had a friend for everything. One of his closest was a therapist. Thankfully, he didn't get a chance to speak. Macy appeared in the doorway, eyes still heavy with sleep and puffy from crying.

"There's coffee," I said.

She let out a long sigh and pulled a mug down from the cabinet. I told her the same story about twisting my wrist, but she didn't see anything wrong with it either. Becky came in shortly after, telling us that Macy's mom had asked her to take her home when they got up. Mark didn't even pretend to mask his worried expression, asking to talk with her in the other room. Macy sank into his chair as they went. She waited until we could hear them arguing to speak.

"I bet Alison is devastated," she said. I couldn't help but scoff. Alison and Noah had only been together through part of the summer and Alison acted like they were going to get married after graduation and live happily ever after. Adults already think we're all brainless and Alison Rivers doesn't help.

"It's not funny. People died," Macy said.

"I didn't mean it like that," I told her. I didn't really know what I'd meant. I was getting a headache behind my eyes, but I knew I'd never be able to sleep. At least, not until I talked to Jamie. I had expected the police officer from last night to ask me more about him, but he didn't say a word. It was just like Jamie had told me. Repeat the story. No one will know.

"Macy, it's time to go," Becky said, reappearing in the kitchen. She turned to look at me, her smile barely hiding her nerves. "You should come with me," she said to me. "We can grab donuts on the way home."

I agreed to go only because I didn't want to risk talking with Mark again. Even now, the pathetic way he looked set me on edge. The entire trip to Macy's house was quiet. I felt a little more relaxed after we dropped her off. Becky was never one to tiptoe around anything. She told me how thankful she was that I had decided to get out of the car. She told me that I shouldn't feel guilty and that everyone made mistakes last night, but two of those people hadn't been so lucky. Guilt was all I could feel as I thought about the story that would be in the paper.

We stopped for two Hallmark cards on the way home. I knew a stupid piece of cardstock wouldn't fix this but signing my name at the bottom of both eased some of the weight. I spent most of the day watching TV with Becky, finishing the entire last season of *Gilmore Girls* for the second time. I stayed up as late as my body would let me that night, moving from *Gilmore Girls* to *Friends* without even noticing. I checked my email a desperate ten times before sleep pulled me under. One email reminder about the volleyball game on Monday. One email about a small memorial service in the gym before school Monday. No emails from Jamie Quinn.

I emailed Jamie another time just to let him know I was going to the public library to work on our presentation for Mr. Puck's class. I searched the science shelf for a few minutes for a book about matter before making my usual rounds. I found myself stopped before the science fiction row.

The book displayed on the top shelf had the most mesmerizing cover. Under the title was a muscular boy, dark tattoos winding up his arms and neck. I took it down. The plot was simple, Jared Simpson was a normal boy whose life changed forever after a strange woman saved his life by making him drink from a vial. When he woke up again, the woman was gone, and he was more alive than ever.

The book reminded me of the accident, so I put it back on its perch. The more I thought about it, the more Friday night felt like something straight from the Syfy channel. I wanted to push away the crazy thought, but I couldn't come up with any rational reason for the new tattoo that no one seemed to see on my wrist. I always believed that there was a reason for everything, but did I dare to go so far as to believe in the supernatural? I couldn't believe I was considering the idea.

Jamie had always been the religious guy, the school weirdo; not me. That is, everyone assumed so. Everyone knew the Quinns lived in town, but they'd always homeschooled. Jamie's story was that the only reason for starting at Burbrook High was the AP classes. After that, no one gossiped about the Quinns being Bible-thumpers. A leather-clad, motorcycle-riding teenager didn't exactly fit the mold everyone shoved him into.

I made my way to the second floor of the Burbrook Public Library, which housed a rarely used collection of records that dated all the way back to the town's founding. The elevator opened to reveal nothing but rows of mostly empty shelves. They weren't the same wooden shelves from the first floor, but rows of flimsy metal shelves that only further highlighted how rarely anyone visited the section. A few computers were pushed against the wall to my left, older models of the nice

Dells that were plugged in downstairs. I went to those first, the monitor coming to life the moment I moved the mouse.

A search bar popped up instantly, the words *Verona County Genealogy Department* emblazoned above it. I typed in Jamie's name first and was surprised when the only record that popped up was Jamie's name among the list of students who had made the school honor roll last year. I tried my name, and my birth certificate was the first document to appear along with my parents' marriage certificate. I clicked the latter, staring at the loopy writing. Underneath their signatures were two more, the witnesses: Maria and Jack Quinn. My parents knew the Quinns.

I tried searching for Maria and Jack, but the screen went blank. Nothing.

I typed in just their last name this time and a couple of pages of different people named Quinn turned up before I found one that looked promising. It was a deed to a house. Maria and Jack Quinn were listed as the owners to a large estate that was located just past Connor's house. I noticed the details in the paragraph above her signature that declared the house a historic landmark. A few clicks and I was staring at a massive mansion. It had been too dark to get a good look at the house I'd found myself in on Friday, but I could tell from the long walk to the garage that it was much larger than even Connor Taylor's.

Every inch of it was composed of old architecture. The porch wrapped around the entire house and the balcony was just as grand. It looked more like a stone castle than a house, diamond pattern windows lining the entire front. A metal crest was set into the stone above the door, but I couldn't make it out from the picture. The article under the photo called the house "The Moore Estate."

A man by the name of James Moore had built the house not

long after the railroad boom in Burbrook. Mr. Moore had been the president of the Burbrook Railroad Branch when it took off, amassing billions. The article claimed that he must have passed the deed off to family members, because it wasn't until the explosion that ended the railroad business that the estate went up for sale. It remained untouched for nearly a decade before Jack Quinn purchased it. There was nothing more about James Moore. A quick search confirmed that.

I remembered the picture on the mantle of the Quinn family. Maybe the people in it hadn't been Jamie's family, but relatives from the railroad days? Even then, it didn't add up. What were the odds of the Quinns having a relative that looked just like Jamie? And on that note, what about the girl I'd seen? She looked too much like the one in the picture to be a coincidence.

I jumped when my phone buzzed loudly against the table. I hadn't realized how late it was. I exited out of the pages and threw my bag over my shoulder. I got home much later than I'd promised Becky, her anxious gaze as I entered the kitchen acknowledgment enough. I could hear Mark whispering something to her as I pulled the meatloaf from the fridge. They stopped as soon as I turned to heat it in the microwave, both watching me so closely that it was uncomfortable. I took my dinner to my room so I could check my email. Still nothing.

I only ate half of the meatloaf before I'd devised a plan. I looked up the Moore Estate address and plugged it into my phone. After telling Becky I was going to return Jamie's motor-cycle helmet, I climbed into the Beetle and followed Siri's instructions toward the mountains. The route looked different somehow, as if I'd been gone for months. Everything seemed new; the wheel tracks in the ditch I hadn't noticed before and the way the pavement seemed to dip a little after the first hill. There were two white crosses placed along the road a few feet from Connor's house. My chest ached. Following the voice from my phone more than the curves in the road, I finally came to a stop at the end of a gravel drive.

The iron gate was huge. The lock was firmly in place and the gate was too tall to climb over for sure. I could see the mansion behind the bars; the house still grand in size despite being so far down the evergreen lined driveway. Siri's command to "proceed to the route" only tipped my patience over the limit. If Jamie wouldn't reply to my emails, then at least I knew where he lived, right? That had been the plan before I'd been faced with privacy only money could provide.

"Come on," I said, putting the car in park. I eyed the wall of metal for a low spot, a bend in the bars, and even a way under the fence altogether. That's when I noticed a gap in the space where the two gates met. I turned off the engine and got out. I tried to push the gates apart, the right door swinging a few extra inches before stopping. I tried squeezing through, but my middle was just a little too thick. I slipped out of my jacket and tossed it onto the hood of the car and with a little wriggle, I was able to pass through to the other side.

It dawned on me how creepy it was now that I was just yards from the front door. I thought briefly about going back to the car, but I forced myself into a brisk walk and slapped my hand against the doorbell a few times before I could reason with myself again. I heard it echo beyond. I let the silence fall for a few seconds before trying again. When that didn't work, I pounded my fist on the door and called out Jamie's name.

It was a Sunday night. What were the odds that they really were religious? I stayed a few more minutes in silence even though it made little difference. They weren't home and if they were, they weren't answering. I yelled a few rarely used words at the door, half hoping that Jamie was just behind it to hear the insult. My feet slapped against the pavement as I walked back to the gate, surprised when it flew open with a metallic screech when I pressed on it this time.

I turned the keys and the Beetle shuttered under me before falling into its normal steady hum. Before doing a haphazard three-point turn, I thought I saw a light turn on in one of the downstairs windows.

CHAPTER 5

I was up early Monday morning so I could swing by the florist on the way to school. Macy texted me Alison's plans to turn Noah's All-State football picture in the school trophy case into a memorial. More out of guilt than friendship, I made sure to buy two roses. I would set one under Noah's picture and tuck the other into Jake's locker.

With roses in hand, I joined the abnormally packed crowd in the hallway. Alison was standing next to the trophy case just inside the door. Notes were taped to the glass, creating a kind of shadowbox frame around Noah's picture. Just down the hall, the same was happening to Jake's locker. His sister was standing with handfulls of neon sticky notes, handing them off to anyone who approached her to offer their condolences.

"Look, Tori brought roses," Macy said, pulling my attention back to the trophy case. I pulled the roses out of her reach before handing her a single red one.

"The other one is for Jake," I told her. Macy pressed her index finger to her lips, nodding toward Alison whose fingers stilled on the *We Love You* banner she was taping to the bottom of the trophy case. Macy tucked my rose in with several other flowers in a vase underneath.

"Thanks, Macy," Alison said, adjusting the floral display before standing up again. "I thought you were bringing a bouquet, but I guess it's whatever. More people will bring stuff." I ignored the dig, pointing toward Jake's sister when Macy looked my way. She shrugged and turned back to comfort Alison.

Jake's sister saw me coming and I could see the tears silently falling down her cheeks before I reached her. She threw her arms around me, swiping the tears when she pulled away. "The cops said you were there, but you got out. I'm glad you're okay," she said. I wished I could remember her name. She was a freshman and I'd never been close enough to Jake to know anything about his siblings.

"This is for you," I said, handing her the rose. She took it and pulled me into another uncomfortable hug. Over her shoulder, I saw Jamie weave through the crowd and into the auditorium. I pulled myself from the hug, offered my condolences, and hurried after him as teachers began instructing those who wanted to participate to file in. Of course, their orderly line soon turned to chaos as everyone pushed through the crowd looking for their own friends. I lost sight of him as soon as I started my search.

I settled for a seat in the first section. Minutes later, Macy sat in the seat next to me with her normal posse of girls. I could hear Alison complaining down our row at the simple Power-Point projected onto the screen. The principal was talking with a custodian a few feet back from the podium. I was glad for the modest display. Anything more and I thought I'd explode with guilt. I was already letting the lie go around about the nature of the accident. As soon as this was over, I was going to find Jamie.

The noise level diminished as the last of the crowd was seated. Then, we were welcomed and introduced to Noah's and Jake's family members who were seated in the front row. I zoned out as Principal Thackery read Noah's impressive résumé. He wasn't the brightest, but he was the most athletic and he came from a supportive family. Jake's memorial speech was much shorter and paled in comparison. I felt my stomach twisting with agitation the longer it went. After recognizing both their achievements, Mr. Thackery went on to talk about the tragedy of teenage drinking. I could hear a few snickers behind us when he said that the accident would make us all think twice about our choices.

Someone a few rows in ahead of us stood up and left for the hallway. I just barely caught sight of Jamie's leather jacket before the door swung shut behind him. I grabbed my backpack and started back down the row, apologizing to everyone as I squeezed past.

"She's the only one who survived the accident. She shouldn't leave like that," Alison said when I passed. I was too focused on catching Jamie to bother with her snide remarks. I was glad that all the teachers down the hall were monitoring the assembly so I could run after Jamie. I grabbed onto his arm and the minute he noticed me he tugged it from my grasp.

"Explain," I said, pushing the sleeve of my sweater up to expose the mark on my wrist. He shushed me and moved toward the lockers. He didn't speak until he'd opened the barren locker and took his backpack from the hook.

"How do you feel?" he asked. I didn't understand. How did I feel?

"Everything's peachy, Jamie. I always wanted a cryptic tattoo to just appear on my wrist. Oh, and you know, rolling down the side of a hill in a convertible and surviving is pretty cool," I said. He let out a sigh and looked at me for the first time, annoyed.

"Have you translated it?" he asked. I looked down at my wrist again, not recognizing any of the words encircling it. "When I asked you how you felt," he started, "I didn't mean about the accident. I meant... Do you feel different— stronger somehow?" The confusion must have shown on my face, because his jaw tightened, and he spoke again. "You broke the front gate, you know, stripped the gears out," he said. So, he had been home all along.

"I didn't mean to break your crappy gate and I wouldn't have if you would've let me in instead of avoiding me all week-end," I said. He laughed. I wanted to hit him. The urge was gone as soon as he pushed back his own sleeve, the mark on his wrist identical to mine. Was this some kind of cult?

"Did you do this to me?" I asked him.

"God, no," he said, lowering his voice a moment later. "We all get one after..."

"After what, near death experiences?"

Again, he chuckled. "Meet me after school."

"I can't. We have a game." It was the first time he'd shown any concern at all; his expression nearly panicked.

"You have to skip," he said, slinging his backpack to his front and unzipping the top. "At least until we know for sure." He reached into his bag and pulled out a sheet of paper from his notebook and a pen.

"I'm not joining your stupid cult." I turned and started toward the auditorium again. He ran after me, stepping in front of me to block my path.

"Text me the translation of your mark. Only you will be able to see it, so you can do it during school. Just don't make it too obvious. Like, keep your arm under the table, just in case," he said, handing the piece of paper over. I stared down at the numbers, the memory of the accident and the mark no one could see the only things keeping me from ripping that paper in half.

"I know no one can see it," I said under my breath. Jamie must have heard because he let out a groan.

"Jesus," he said. "I swore I wouldn't be the one to wake you."

I didn't get a chance to ask him anything else. The auditorium doors swung open, and a sea of students engulfed us. A few seconds later, the bell rang. I started for Mr. Puck's class as soon as I saw Macy, not wanting to explain myself right now.

I beat Jamie to chemistry, or so I thought. He never showed up. When he wasn't in our next class together, I decided to follow his instructions. Maybe he'd give me more information after I translated the tattoo. I used my school computer to translate instead of following along on the digital copy of Shakespeare's sonnets. Mrs. McKellen didn't even look my way as I worked, jotting down each word I found in my notebook until I'd translated the entire line wrapped around my arm.

Guardian of the sixth gate. Complete the circle. Find your match.

I double checked the translation in my next class and came up with the same words. Jamie hinted that everyone got a mark after near death experiences, or something like that. By the time athletic period rolled around, I was thinking about skipping. Macy accosted me in the hall before I got a chance.

"First game of the season and we have to play the team that won the state title last year. Good confidence boost, right?" she said, leading me straight into the locker room.

Macy pulled her blonde curls into a ponytail and began taking her gear out of her duffle bag.

"It's my first time starting, and they'll probably block all my shots," I said. I'd been moved from position to position, doing okay in each. I filled in wherever we were weak.

"Put it down the line," Macy said as she slid on her knee pads. "Their setters can't pass." I nodded as I tied my shoe, still thinking about the translation tucked away in my backpack. The silence must've gone on too long, because Macy let out a huff and said, "What's your deal?"

I straightened up, turning to look at her. She'd stopped dressing, a single shoe hanging from the hand on her hip while the other pointed toward the door, probably to indicate Noah's memorial at the end of the hall.

"I'm fine. It's like Alison said, I'm the only one who made it out of the accident alive. I was lucky," I said. I started for the gym, Macy catching my arm when we reached the court.

"I meant, what's your deal with all of us? Alison is upset that you're not stepping up to help her like the rest of us and you completely pushed me away today. Did you spend lunch in the library to avoid me?" she asked, hands crossed over her jersey number. I couldn't believe that she was making me out to be the bad guy. Alison had every right to be upset about Noah, but she had never been nice to me, and Macy was my only friend among her gang of girls.

"Friday was the first time I've talked to Alison in months. Isn't it a bit weird that she wants my help?" I took a ball from the cart and joined the hitting line along the court. Macy followed, bouncing the ball off my back to get my attention.

"She's a part of our group," she said. "Of course she wants your help."

"She's a part of *your* group, Macy," I said, pausing when the rest of the team let out a cheer as Alison executed a perfect hit that landed almost exactly at the ten-foot line. "Alison was the one who told me my skirt made my thighs look fat and then showed up in the exact same one the next day. She always pretends like I'm not around anyway, so why should I be the one to hand her tissues?" I tossed the ball to our setter, coach yelling for me to hit down the sideline. I thought the anger would burst from my chest the moment my hand contacted the ball. What should've been a cross-court shot miraculously went straight down the side of the court, a perfect hit that echoed loudly around the gym.

"That's why you're starting today," Coach cheered. "That's how you keep your spot, ladies."

I retrieved the ball and got back in line, hoping my next shot would be as good as the last. Macy stopped in line behind me a minute later.

"Glad to know you hate all my friends," she said. "What does that mean for me?" I ignored her the rest of our warm-up, mostly because I wasn't sure what to tell her. A part of me had always been jealous of her for how easily she made friends. Everyone liked Macy; she won all the popularity contests like class president and prom queen. I liked going unnoticed— even our National Honor Society awards ceremony made me nervous each year. But it still bothered me that Macy could do no wrong in the eyes of others when everything about her reputation was fake.

Morale among our team dropped as soon as our opponents entered the gym. The shortest girl on their team was almost as tall as our tallest. We would look like dwarves on the opposite side of the court for sure. Spectators started arriving as we warmed up, El Norte High winning the coin toss. I took my position at the net, Macy looking away as soon as our eyes met. I looked toward the scorekeeping table and noticed a dark figure sitting in the stands behind it. Jamie Quinn had come to the game.

The ball came flying over the net. I sprinted into place, calling out for a chance to hit the ball. It came my way in a beautiful arch, the perfect set. I jumped, swinging my arm as hard as I could. The ball should've gone straight into the hands of the two blockers. Instead, it squeezed past both their hands and straight to the floor. Point Burbrook High. Our team started cheering.

It had all happened in seconds, so fast that I was sure I was the only one to notice the abnormality. For a moment, it looked more like the ball had warped to squeeze past the hands at the top of the net, the memory of it seeming cartoonish in my head afterward. I wasn't on top of my game at all. Was I getting lucky? I remembered Jamie asking if I'd felt stronger in some way. What exactly had he meant by that? Was it possible that something else came along with the mark?

"Tori! Victoria," Coach said. The referee held up a hand to pause the game. Coach Webber walked to the side of the court, looking me over nervously. Jamie was on the edge of his seat watching. I held his gaze for a long time. I felt something click into place in my brain and I knew he could see that in my eyes. His sister wanted to tell me everything that night at their house, but Jamie refused. I had been mad at him all weekend until now. He wanted me to figure it out on my own when I was ready to accept it. I wasn't going crazy. Something supernatural was happening to me and the Quinns were right at the center of it.

"I think I'm going to be sick," I said, not feeling the slightest bit nauseous. I felt like electricity was pulsing through my veins and I wanted nothing more than to meet with Jamie now and get the full story. Coach nodded and I ran from the court to the locker rooms at the back. Once there, I let out a deep breath and opened my locker. I pulled on a pair of sweatpants and a hoodie and had just shut my locker door when I heard Jamie behind me.

"You never texted me," he said. I moved past him and into the hallway. I could hear our team's coming defeat in the groans from the spectators as we passed the gym.

"Am I crazy or did the ball just..." I started. I let Jamie lead the way once we reached the parking lot. The rain soaked into my sweats and made them heavy as we walked to the back of the lot. Jamie clicked the remote on his keys and a black Audi came to life, the engine purring and the lights blinding me.

"Get in," he said, slipping into the front seat. I tossed my bag into the backseat before climbing into the leather interior. It was warm already; the seats shaped to fit the body so that it felt more like a cozy blanket than any car I'd ever sat in. He pulled out of the lot before I could get my seat belt on.

"Your place?" I asked him. We started down the opposite way I was used to, heading out of town toward the forested mountains. The gravel road turned to dirt at the end of the school campus.

"No. Not yet," he said. "I want to show you something first. You'll understand when you see." I took his word for it. I sucked in a deep breath and sat back in my seat. I looked over the car; everything inside was top of the line.

"Did something happen the night of the accident?" I asked, breaking the silence. "No one can survive rolling five times in a convertible. I didn't even have a cut." I remembered the blood. It was smeared over my skin as if I had been injured. Who else's blood could it possibly have been? I was the only one in the backseat.

Jamie didn't speak right away, the evergreens whipping past us as we entered a thicker part of the forest.

"Almost there," he said, more to himself than to me. I

waited, heart pounding, as we continued down the dirt road. Fifteen minutes later, we turned off the road and onto the entrance to the state park. We passed the main building. A "closed for the season" sign hung in the front window. We were alone. Jamie pulled into an empty campsite and parked, turning off the engine. It was silent aside from the soft tapping of the rain on the roof. I waited for him to speak first.

"My sister found you down that hill. She called me right away to come get you," he said. "You had already triggered the change, so the most we did was clean the old blood off you."

I remembered waking up underneath the car. The dried blood was itchy, and I remember searching for the source of it all before passing out again.

"I should have died, though," I said.

"You did. That's what triggered the change," he said, looking at me.

My heart skipped in my chest. If I'd died, then what was I now?

"What change are you talking about?" I asked. Jamie nodded toward my arm before pushing back his own sleeve.

"The guardians of the sixth gate. Complete the circle. Find your match," I told him. "That's what it means."

He nodded and looked back at me.

"Let's start there then," he said, taking out his wallet. He pulled out a small square and handed it to me. It was the same black-and-white picture I'd seen on the mantel.

"Everyone in that picture is a guardian of the sixth gate. Our marks give us our instructions. It's our job to contain anything that comes out of our gate and if we can, seal it for good by completing the circle," he said. I looked back down at the tattoo.

"So, guardians guard the gate. What exactly is the gate?" I

asked, trying to keep calm. He took the picture back from me and tucked it away again.

"The gates have been here since the beginning of time as far as we can tell. They are the only link between our world and the Shadowlands. All your classic monsters live in the Shadowlands and sometimes, they find the gate and get out. That's when we step in. We have to kill them when we find them. Some are harder to kill than others," he said. I imagined vampires walking the halls at school before I realized how crazy it sounded.

"So, you didn't just tattoo me yourself and make up some monster story?" I asked. He let out a laugh and pulled out a switchblade. I reached for the door handle before I realized he wasn't going to turn the knife on me at all.

"Watch," he said as he drew the blade across his palm, ripping open the skin. Blood pooled in his hand for a moment before he pulled the lid off the old Starbucks cup. He held his hand over it so the blood ran off in a scarlet stream, revealing the cut again. In a matter of seconds, the ends began to come back together and then the cut faded to a pink line before vanishing entirely. He cleaned the blood from his hand with a napkin.

I was very aware of how cold it was in the car now, my skin icing over and the air escaping my lungs from the shock of what I saw.

"It's a guardian thing," he said, "and it's the reason you didn't die Friday. There's a curse. No one is exactly sure how it works, but we know that when some people die, they become guardians instead. Guardians are immortal by nature. We have immortality until we meet our match. A match is like a soulmate. Once you match with another guardian, you and the other members of your circle become stronger. It's what you have to do to complete your circle like the mark says. The problem is that when two guardians match, they lose their immortality."

I looked straight at him. If he was immortal, it would explain the mystery behind the Moore Estate. Maybe the Quinns weren't related to the Moore family. Maybe they were the original Moore family.

"How old are you?" I asked him.

All the humor left in his face faded.

"I've been seventeen since 1931," he said.

The car was silent, but I could still hear the echo of the words. Jamie Quinn had lived through the Great Depression. No wonder his history essays were always submitted early. I wouldn't have believed him had he not just sliced open his hand and healed it before my eyes.

"Were your parents guardians too?" I asked.

Jamie nodded. I remembered the two adults in the picture. They looked so much like their kids.

"We used to be Moore, not Quinn," he said. "My dad was the president of this branch of the railroad. My parents met and matched at the railroad station. We were taking a trip when a demon set fire to the train car we were in. The whole thing blew up. Since my parents were matched, they didn't have their immortality to save them. My sister and I made the change then, but we didn't wake for about a year. Waking is when you realize what happened, when you understand what the mark means. After you wake, you get your powers."

It was hard to imagine Jamie as anything but the mysterious kid that sat in the back of the class.

"What powers do guardians have?" I asked.

He shrugged. "Lots of different ones. Each guardian has their own, some the same and some different." A smile pulled at his lips, a kind of ornery smirk that made me nervous about what he would do next. "Get out," he said, opening his door and stepping into the rain.

"It's pouring," I cried.

I let out a groan but followed out of curiosity. He went to the trunk of the car and held up his hands for me to see. He tucked his left hand behind his back and leaned down. With his right hand, he easily lifted the back of the car and set it back down again. The sight was so ridiculous and looked so simple that I couldn't help but laugh.

"Catch," he called out, tossing something I couldn't see.

I quickly threw out a hand to catch whatever it was and looked around wildly for the object. A second later I saw his keys glittering a few feet above my hands. I gasped and they fell into the mud. Jamie let out a laugh and bent down to get them.

"That's what I thought," he said. "You have telekinesis."

That's why the ball had gone exactly where I'd intended it to during the game. I wondered how it was going.

"You have to quit volleyball," Jamie said.

My stomach tightened. I had been playing volleyball since seventh grade, even playing on traveling teams every off-season. I met Macy in middle school volleyball. I remember when we could barely serve a ball over the net and how frustrated we both got the first time we'd learned rotation.

"Why? No one saw but us," I said.

He shook his head. "You're still getting used to it. You were lucky you made it look so seamless today. All it would take is stopping a ball across the court to give you away. Besides, another guardian can spot it, which means that a demon could too. We can't let them notice us or they might try attacking us before we can get to them or worse, crawl into hiding places," he said.

I wanted to argue, but his words stopped me. I would be

exactly like Jamie; the quiet, straight-A student at the back of the room. The idea didn't sound half bad, but a part of me that had been suppressed for so long had clawed its way out and I didn't want to shove it down anymore. I had always been the quiet, shy one in the group and not because I was comfortable that way, but because I was so used to being the weird one if I wasn't. Could I really live that life out of necessity now instead of choice?

"What now?" I asked, pushing away the thoughts. I was still processing the reality. Guardians protect the gate of the Shadowlands by keeping the demons trapped there. Guardians are immortal until they match with another. The instructions seemed too simple, summed up in three sentences around my wrist.

"You meet our circle," Jamie said, opening the car door again. "It's time for you to meet Izzy." I climbed in after him, thankful for the warmth now that my hair was dripping cold water down the back of my sweatshirt.

CHAPTER 6

Two white crosses were stuck in the mud on the side of the road where Noah's car began its descent. It felt like a long time ago now as we passed the spot. The entire weekend felt like a dream, a vivid one, but still a faraway dream I'd just woken up from. Jamie turned right onto a short road and stopped next to the gatehouse.

The gate to the Moore Estate was open, the broken door slightly askew on its hinges. Jamie pressed a button above the rearview mirror and the garage door opened. The house was just as stunning as I remembered, even more so now that I could admire it during the day. The front lawn was massive, evergreen trees lining the perimeter instead of a fence. The driveway stretched on forever, leading the way to the huge garage where the white door was slowly rolling upward. One side of the large space was lined with sports cars, the Audi and motorcycles looking almost comical in comparison on the opposite side. Jamie parked next to a yellow Maserati and turned off the engine. I focused on opening my door with my mind, but I felt a headache coming on instead. Jamie opened the door for me.

"You're not strong enough for that yet," he said. "It only worked on the volleyball because you helped it along by hitting it first."

I got out of the car and followed him toward the garage stairs. We took the same path as we had Friday, only this time I could take in more detail. The hallway from the garage was lined with old photos, some black and white and some more recent. It was obvious how the Quinn siblings kept from drawing attention to themselves in their pictures. They had photos next to monuments across Europe, a few of the pyramids, and some on a beach I couldn't place, their clothes the only detail giving away the dates.

"How long do you stay in one place?" I asked. Jamie stopped walking and I took advantage of the moment to look at a few of the higher pictures. There was one with both Jamie and Izzy in front of a stage, The Beatles playing behind them.

"Depending on the story we tell, sometimes longer than others. Here, because our family house is a historic site, we can't stay as long. The last time we were here for about five years. We both look young enough to be in high school, but old enough to maybe be in college," he said. "The last time we were here for about five years."

I looked away from the picture to see that Jamie was staring at them as well. The small expanse of wall at the end of the hall was covered in framed college degrees. Some of them had Izzy's name, just about every medical position embossed in gold or silver on cardstock. The rest of the wall was full of Jamie's credentials: arts, photography, several different types of music.

"So, you really do like school," I said.

He smirked and looked back at me.

"I don't hate it," he said. "We found out fast that it was easier to be invisible among the drama of high school. No one cares to pay too much attention if you're different enough."

I let out a laugh. Jamie Quinn was definitely different enough. No one has been able to fly under the radar at school the way he has.

"Jamie," a girl called farther down the hall. I followed Jamie into the front entryway. Isabella Quinn stopped halfway down the stairs when she noticed me. She leaned over the banister and smiled as if she'd been expecting me all along.

"Victoria Johnson?" she asked.

"Yeah," I answered.

She straightened up. "Welcome to the circle." She started down the stairs again, joining us under the chandelier. "Well, it's more like a triangle right now. We better hope that we can upgrade to a square pretty damn fast."

She glanced at Jamie. His expression was serious.

"How many people make a circle?" I asked.

They exchanged glances before Izzy spoke.

"Not really sure," she said. "Everyone in our circle has to find their match before we can close the gate. At least, that's what our circle guide says. So, at this rate, we need to find three more guardians. That means that three new people in this town need to have their death experiences to change because it's unlikely that there's someone in our circle outside of this area just wandering around."

It was a strange thing to hope for, but I understood her concerns. If we couldn't seal the gate, would it grow? How many monsters were seeping out from it now?

"So, what do we do? Are we looking for more guardians? And what's a circle guide?"

"At least we got an eager one." Izzy laughed, nudging her brother. Jamie didn't seem as amused. "Lighten up," she told him. She formed a circle with her right hand and pressed it to her lips, a single smoke ring coming out the end and losing shape as soon as it hit Jamie's forehead.

"Every circle has a circle guide. It's a book that the members of our circle use to pass on information. You know, in case the entire circle dies out or something," she said. "It confirms everything our marks say from our immortality, our powers, to our mission to seal the gate. We just haven't figured out how to do that part yet."

Jamie waved away the last of the black smoke.

"The only thing we should concern ourselves with is keeping the demon population low in this town. If it rises any higher then we'll attract some real monsters," he said.

Izzy snorted. "We could handle your so-called real monsters if we had a larger circle, or even just one match," she said. "At least tell me that she's shown her powers."

"Not everything is worth rushing into, Izzy," Jamie said before I could inform her about the volleyball incident. He passed me and went into the next room. We followed him, finding him digging through the silverware drawer. He held up a spoon and then tossed it to me. I caught it and looked at Izzy. She let out an annoyed sigh.

"She'll figure it out the minute she hunts her first demon," she said.

Jamie shook his head. "She already did, but that doesn't mean she knows how to use it. She almost gave herself away at the volleyball game. She has telekinesis. She made the ball change direction."

Izzy laughed, lifting herself onto the counter beside him and ignoring his reproachful gaze.

The spoon was cool, perfectly curved to the shape of my palm. I held it out at eye-level, both of them watching me now. I took a deep breath and tried to imagine the metal bending in half. The minute I envisioned it, I could feel the resistance. It was heavy on my brain, the way a headache pulsates as it grows. My vision blurred and everything relaxed. I let my arm hang at my side as Jamie reached into another drawer.

"Focus on pulling the flame to you," he said, taking a match out of the box. With a single flick, a small flame lit his face. I forced myself to look away from his anxious expression and at the match. I had barely pictured the flame bending toward me when the light vanished, leaving behind a single tail of smoke. Izzy gasped, looking at me with excitement.

"Guardians with telekinesis draw their energy from fire and electricity," she said, "We've only ever met one other before and the things he could... He was a total badass." I felt a little better after zapping the match. "Can you do the lights?" Izzy asked. Before I could attempt it, Jamie jumped in.

"No, not yet," he said. "She can absorb all the energy she wants, but it won't make her any better at putting it back out. She needs to exercise her mind before she moves onto bigger things like disturbing electric fields. Putting out a match won't help us kill a demon but being able to throw a knife with her mind might."

Izzy's smile faded as she accepted the fact. I held up the spoon again, focusing on the metal. I tired more quickly this time, Jamie promising me that I'd get better if I took a little time to practice every day.

"I'm sure your head feels like it's going to explode and not because of all the telekinesis," he said.

Actually, I wished he had told me more. I caught Izzy's eye and it must have been obvious in my face.

"I'll take her home," she said, leading me toward the hallway again. I felt a hand on my forearm. Jamie froze when I turned toward him, and his expression changed to embarrassment. He let go of me and let his hands rest behind him on the countertop.

"Sorry," he said. "You should... Don't let Izzy take over."

"I could take care of myself even before I changed," I said.

Jamie's lips pulled into a small smile. My face was growing hot quickly.

"All I mean is that she's stubborn. We've had decades of practice and she forgets how hard it was in the beginning. We both have a few scars from our unmanageable days," he said.

He carefully plucked the spoon from my right hand with his index finger and thumb and sat it down on the counter. Izzy came back wearing a blue baseball cap and carrying a leather jacket. She slipped it on, concealing the mark on her left wrist. She looked at me. I could feel her eyes roving over me and I was suddenly aware of how heavy my soaked sweatpants had become.

"First," she said, "follow me."

I didn't protest, following her back to the entryway and up the stairs. There were more pictures on the walls upstairs, the same theme of rock concerts and urban backdrops. Izzy's was one of the first bedrooms on the left, the walls plastered with professional headshots of a dark-haired girl with a short bob. It took me a second to realize that they weren't just pin-ups cut out of an old magazine. They were all Izzy.

"Are those real?" I asked.

She turned from her closet to follow my gaze to the wall. Izzy's hair hung in short curls around her face that framed her pout. A few were full-body shots featuring plain backdrops.

"Yeah. I modeled for a bit in the forties," she said, pulling out another leather jacket and tossing it onto the bed. "It really wasn't that glamorous though. The sexism was terrible but owning my body like that was great. It was kind of a catch-22. I got my first real sense of self during the war, but I also noticed how screwed up this place is. That was after I'd been fighting demons and staking vampires, by the way. That's saying something." she tossed a pair of jeans and a T-shirt on top of the jacket.

"It's really not that far to my house," I said, eyeing the clothes. She rolled her eyes and shut the bedroom door so I could change.

"We're not going straight there," she said. "You like coffee, right?"

I froze with one arm in the warm sleeve of the jacket. It must have been lined with real fur because it was softer than any jacket I'd ever worn.

"I love coffee," I said.

Izzy opened the door and went into the hall. I followed her, barely keeping up on the way to the garage. The headlights of the yellow Maserati flashed twice when she clicked the remote. The engine hummed to life before either of us had settled into the black leather seats. I'd barely put my seat belt on before Izzy backed out of the garage. She twisted the wheel hard to one side and the front of the car swung around to face the gate. I thought my heart had stopped.

"Sorry," she said, "Heavy foot."

She was lighter on the gas this time as we made our way to the main road. I could see the similarities between her and Jamie in her face. They both had sharp features and a strong jaw.

"What's the age difference between you and Jamie?" I asked as she turned onto the pavement.

"He's stuck at seventeen and I'm stuck at twenty-one, but physical age doesn't really matter when you're immortal. After ten or so years of it, age just becomes nonexistent to us. We don't get any older on our birthdays and our bodies never ache or sag along the way. We're just exactly as we have always been. Well, aside from all the demon hunting stuff," she said.

I nodded as we turned onto the main road at the bottom of the mountain. Maybe she was right. The last three years of high school, I'd been sitting in class next to a boy in his eighties. It didn't matter then, so did it matter now? Would I feel any different in another eighty years when it would be me?

"Izzy," I said as we pulled to a stoplight. She looked at me, the excitement in her eyes dimming a bit. "What am I supposed to do now?" I hadn't thought about the future until then. What would things be like in another year? Could I really move away to college with both of them in Burbrook? What about Becky and Mark? What would happen when they notice that I'm not aging?

"You're one of us now," she said. "You're part of the circle and we only grow stronger with each new addition to it. So now, we help you figure out how to use your powers. You're a guardian of the sixth gate and that's what we do. We guard it until there's enough of us to close it entirely. We are family. Jamie and I need you just as much as you need us. Until the time comes, we stay here and train you."

What would training look like? Me staring at a spoon for the next month?

"Jamie thinks that you need time to settle into this," she said, scoffing. I remembered what Jamie told me about Izzy being stubborn and tending to take over things. I wondered if he realized that he'd inherited the same traits.

"It's nice that he's looking out for me, but I think I'll feel better the more I know," I said. I wasn't sure that I would feel better anytime soon, but the idea of sitting around and thinking about the whole thing only sounded worse. I was tired of planning my future and never really investing in the present. Izzy reached into her pocket and pulled out a spoon. She tucked it into the pocket of my jacket.

"When do I start?" I asked.

I saw the smirk on Izzy's face when she pulled into a parking space. She sat back in her seat and turned to look at me.

"I think we should forget about my brother and get a damn good cup of coffee," she said, getting out of the car.

I was late getting to school the next day on account of practicing all night on the spoon. It had taken me until nearly 3 a.m. to move the metal at all and even then, I could only put a small bend in the thinnest section. I was exhausted, but the progress was energizing.

The bell rang as I darted into Mr. Puck's room, getting a warning gaze from him as I made my way to my table. Mrs. McKellen's voice boomed through the space, jabbering on about homecoming king and queen nominations. I heard one of the boys a few tables ahead whispering and when I looked, I caught Macy's gaze. She seemed just as surprised to catch me staring as I felt about being caught. She'd sent me texts since the accident asking to go out again, and then about my disappearance at the volleyball game, and then the insults came. I knew she was more hurt than mad. No one had ever denied Macy anything, least of all the attention she wanted.

"So, this being late all the time is new," Jamie said.

I forced my eyes back on him and was glad to see he was smiling.

"You never answered my text," he said.

Jamie had asked me if I felt nervous or overwhelmed about

all the new information. Izzy and I were still at Starbucks when I got the text. By the time I got home, I'd forgotten about it and was more focused on the spoon than anything.

"I got busy," I said, looking down at his pencil on the table. I focused on the wood until it was spinning in a slow circle. Jamie sat his hand over it, forcing me to stop.

"You have to be more careful," he whispered.

I knew that. Becky and Mark had argued with me about quitting volleyball senior year, but in the end, they let me send the email to Coach. I told them I was joining a study group to raise my SAT score; I was just a few points shy of a full ride to college. They took this as a jab at their finances, which I knew would do the trick before I'd said it. Becky and Mark never had trouble providing for me, but I knew they didn't have the savings for law school. If I wasn't careful about hiding myself now, then there would be no chance at law school at all.

"I'm not doing anything more than I know I can control. I figured out my limits pretty fast last night. It's why I quit volleyball."

He looked at me for the first time, his expression relaxing in surprise.

"I'm a library aid seventh hour now," I said.

The intercom clicked off and Mr. Puck started collecting homework at the front of the room. I opened my binder to take out my work, ignoring Jamie's stares.

"Just like that?" he asked. "When I told you that you had to quit, I didn't think..."

"You were right about it being too risky, but you're not right about everything," I said, passing my homework his way and nodding for him to take out his own.

"All right, Mindfreak. I'll bite," he said, finally opening his own binder and adding his homework to the stack. "What did I get wrong?" He only looked more confused when I laughed.

"I might not be the class valedictorian, but I'm no dummy either," I said. "I know how to study. Some say I'm a fast learner."

I pointed a finger at his binder, and it shifted off the table, taking our homework with it and landing with a loud slap against the tile floor. Jamie scrambled to pick up the mess as the table in front of us turned to look. Jamie cast me an annoyed glance, but that didn't suppress my snickering. After nudging his foot with my own, he cracked a small smile and turned his focus on Puck as he approached. We didn't talk until we were back in the hallway for passing period. He stopped me just outside the door.

"My next class is upstairs," he said, "but we should talk about that new party trick of yours. Lunch?"

I nodded and he smiled before joining the crowd. I hurried down the hall toward my locker to get rid of all the extra weight in my backpack. I had just tossed my backpack inside when someone knocked on my locker door.

"What are you doing?" Macy asked.

I pulled out my English textbook and notebook and grabbed the door out of her hand to close it.

"What do you mean?" I asked.

She let out a single laugh as she tried to keep up with my pace.

"I mean, what are you doing with yourself? You never texted me back after the game you just walked out of. We got smashed and we could've had a chance if you had sucked it up and came back to serve," she said.

"I quit the team," I said.

Macy surged forward, stepping in front of me and forcing me to stop walking. Her eyes were wild, and people had started slowing their pace to listen in.

"You've been playing for seven years, and you just quit your last season? What the hell? I don't get it, Tori," she said. I tried shushing her, but she wasn't listening.

"I don't want to play anymore," I said. "I don't understand why it matters so much."

"It matters because you've been weird ever since the party — before then, actually. You come to school the first day looking like a cheap hooker and then the first time you go to a party with me, you go crazy and get two people killed."

"I didn't kill Noah and Jake," I said, taking a step toward her. Macy held up both of her hands and took a step back as if touching me would give her some disease.

"So now you're some badass too?" she asked. "Alison is right. Everything always goes to shit when you're around. You're either the goody-two-shoes that can do no wrong or you're the wannabe, leather-wearing rockstar who thinks a little extra mascara will make people take you seriously. I tried helping you. All of us were nothing but nice, but you're still starting drama like we're still in middle school. Grow up, Tori."

The surrounding students had started to ooh and ahh with every word she spoke, and I saw Mrs. Hawthorne walking toward us.

"Macy, you're the only one who ever acted like you even liked me. Maybe I really am the stupid one for believing you could possibly be my friend. Just go put your name on the homecoming election ballot and when you win, know that that tiara, like everything else around you, is fake," I said.

Mrs. Hawthorne didn't get a chance to yell her threats. I was already walking toward the classroom.

"Get to class!" she shouted at the remaining students. I passed her and went straight into history without saying a word. I made sure to sit at the back, but that didn't keep people from craning their heads to get a look. It wasn't until halfway through class that they all stopped stealing glances.

English class went just as history had, except Macy was in this one. Mrs. McKellen had a shoebox sitting on her desk that she'd decorated with construction paper to look like a football. The words *Homecoming Nominations* were pasted across the front. Macy stopped on her way into class to write her name on a slip of paper, purposely not looking at me as she walked to her desk. It was a painful day, and it was only half over.

I was glad for lunch, but not happy about the whispering. Macy's table was listening intently to her retelling of the entire ordeal. Alison made sure to tell the entire group that they should've listened to her last year when she said I was too weird, speaking just loud enough so I could hear as I passed. I stopped next to a table of freshmen to look for Jamie. I felt like the only predator at the watering hole.

A hand squeezed my shoulder. Jamie took my lunch tray in his left hand and started toward the corner of the room. There had always been three tables pushed into the corner, the benches broken, or the tops cracked. He sat both trays on the only one without a broken top and motioned toward the bowing bench opposite him. The wood creaked and the screws squeaked as I sat.

"This your usual spot?" I asked.

He shook his head. "If you go out the back," he said, nodding toward the green doors just past a line of broken chairs, "you can make it to the parking lot without being seen. Sometimes, I just eat in my car with the radio on. Sometimes, I make a trip to Del Taco down the street." He pushed my tray toward me before spearing a hunk of chicken with his fork.

"And you wanted to talk about party tricks over cold cafeteria chicken and canned peaches?" I asked.

Jamie smirked, taking a bite. I noticed Alison pointing our way from her table. She said something and the entire group laughed.

"Ignore it," Jamie said.

I looked back at him. He cracked open the Dr. Pepper with a hiss and took a drink. I felt a pang of guilt settle in my gut as I realized it wasn't that long ago that I was part of Macy and Alison's group, pointing and whispering about Jamie.

"Did it ever bother you, the way we all talked about you?" I asked.

He shrugged. "We have more important things to worry about than a bunch of petty teenage girls. There are real dangers out there that could hurt people."

I let out a sigh and took up my fork.

"But I did take all the nominations for Macy and her friends out of the homecoming box during passing period," he said with a smirk.

I gasped. They would all be furious. Macy always pretended that these kinds of elections were cheesy and stupid, but that didn't keep her from voting for herself. She had single-handedly nominated herself as senior class treasurer and only because she'd promised not to run against Alison for the presidency.

"They're going to think it was me," I said.

He shook his head. "You came to lunch with the same class Alison was in, right?" he asked.

I opened my mouth to reply but stopped when I caught on. There was no way they could blame it on me; even Alison would know that. The realization must have shown on my face, because Jamie only smiled wider now. I reached over and slapped his arm, making him drop his chicken nugget on the floor.

"You wanted to talk about party tricks, right?" I asked. "Since you didn't like mine, tell me how lifting cars makes for a better unobtrusive party trick."

Jamie took the spoon off his tray and glanced over the cafeteria. All the teachers were now gathered near the double doors like they always did the last ten minutes of lunch. People had stopped staring at us. He twisted the metal once to create a kind of wavy design through it and then motioned for my hand. I laid my arm on the table and he bent the metal into a bangle around my right wrist. When he was finished and returned to eating, I pushed on the metal to test how strong it was.

"Maybe I am a little..." he started.

"Uptight? Overly protective?" I asked, pushing my untouched tray to one side.

Jamie smirked. "I was going to say I was a bit of a jackass for the double standard, but I like your version better," he said. "Izzy discovered her powers when she dropped her lighter in a glass of water. Got so pissed off she nearly blew her face off lighting the cigarette. I just assumed you would bypass control for utter chaos like we both did."

"Izzy smokes?" I asked.

"Cancer can't kill the immortal, fortunately," he replied, pushing my tray back in front of me.

"Neither can starvation," I countered.

He smirked again, stacking the trash on his tray.

"You're right," he said, "but that doesn't mean it doesn't hurt."

I relented and took a bite of the near tasteless meat. The bell rang, and I tossed more of my lunch than I had eaten. Jamie walked with me to drama class on the second floor. We agreed to meet at Starbucks after school and then I watched as he walked back downstairs.

"New boyfriend?" Connor asked on his way into the room. I ignored him and took my seat. Mrs. McKellen read off the nominations for homecoming queen and king on the intercom and I tried not to smile when none of Macy's friends were called. I almost wished that at least one of them had been in drama with me so I could see their reactions. The rest of the day got much better now that people were too busy talking about homecoming in a few weeks to bother reminiscing about my fight with Macy that morning.

I found Jamie sitting at a table in Starbucks just minutes after school ended. He had already ordered, two cups of coffee before him and a plate with a blueberry muffin.

"I wasn't kidding about the starvation thing," he said, pushing the plate toward me. "I wasn't sure what you liked, so the coffee's just black." He took up his phone and started typing.

"Which is exactly how I take it," I told him. I wanted to hold out on eating the muffin for effect, but I was hungrier than I thought I'd be. It was still warm. My phone buzzed on the table, and I saw Jamie's name pop up on the screen just before it went black.

"Just making sure it works," he smirked.

"You didn't actually think I gave you a fake, did you?" I asked.

He shook his head. Maybe he was worried that after everything he told me yesterday I'd be running by now.

"So, tell me about yourself, Strongman," I said. My new bracelet clinked against the plate as I tore a piece off the muffin and popped it into my mouth.

"What's there to know?" he asked.

I pulled his coffee out of reach before he could use it as an excuse to keep from talking.

"You're number one in our class. Your family was the richest in the county and the railroad station was named after your dad. You have a sister. Keep going," I said.

The look of annoyance he sent my way confirmed my assumption about him being the quiet type.

"I don't know. I like the color red. In May, I'll have graduated from Burbrook High twice. I have a bachelor's degree in music, business, and journalism. Now, it's your turn, Mindfreak," he said, motioning for his coffee. I pushed it across the table to him. It was my turn to feel uneasy. I hated talking about myself just about as much as he did.

"I also like red, but more of a maroon red. I have read every Stephen King book. I lost both of my parents when I was too young to remember it and I've lived with my aunt and uncle ever since," I said.

The humor faded from his face now. It made me uncomfortable, like I'd said too much or reminded him of some terrible event from his own past. I was just about to apologize when he began talking.

"I had always hoped that when I died, I would just go. Izzy felt a little better about it all when we woke. She would've stayed behind in Burbrook if I hadn't left. I told her we needed to keep looking for others, you know, so we could close the gate for good."

When I finally raised my gaze, he was looking down at his own cup.

"I'm assuming that wasn't really the plan," I said.

Jamie shook his head but didn't say a word. He didn't have to. He was an escapist, the quiet type that always knew the reality when others thought they were doing such a good job of hiding it. I was sure of it only because I was so good at doing it too. It was so much easier to just look the other way than risk confrontation, pretend things were fine when they were slowly unraveling. He took a long drink before changing the subject.

"So, just how far did practicing last night get you?" he asked.

I wished I could tell him that I'd made enough progress to make my own bracelet out of a spoon with my mind.

"I put a dent in a spoon," I said. "And I feel different than when I tried back at your house. It's weird."

Jamie nodded. "When I first came into my own power, each day I could lift more weight. I just kept getting stronger and I grew so fast that I forgot about what was normal. I would smash things even when I didn't mean to. What I'm trying to say is that I'm glad you're getting stronger in your powers, but don't forget to learn control. It's great if you can throw an object across a room, but don't forget to learn how to make it float across one," he said. We stayed and talked for another hour and a half before it started getting dark. Jamie drove me back to my car and made me promise to answer his texts.

"Paranoid much?" I asked. I was glad to see him smiling.

"I won't worry as much after you've fought a few demons," he said. "And I don't mean to seem creepy about knowing where you are. It's just that it's been a while since there were three of us." I saw the pain in his eyes for a mere second before his usual smirk replaced it. I promised to let him know when I got home before starting for the Beetle.

I got into my car and gave him a final wave before he started down the road ahead of me. I took the long way home this time, even though it was much later than when I usually got home. My bracelet shimmered in the sunset, which had sunk out of sight by the time I pulled into the driveway. I didn't see either my aunt or my uncle when I got inside, just a note with the time they'd get home and a twenty for pizza.

I scrolled through Instagram as I waited on the delivery. Most of the pictures were of homecoming dresses. I stopped at a picture of Macy wearing a volleyball T-shirt. She was turned just enough away from the camera to showcase the word *Captain* across her shoulders. I knew I shouldn't have, but I went to her account anyway. Macy always took pictures whenever the opportunity arrived. I remembered almost every picture throughout the feed because I had been there with her, but not in the photos. I was most often behind the camera.

The doorbell rang. I exited the app and tossed my phone onto the couch next to me. The bell rang again and then another time. I called out that I was coming and hurried to get the twenty from the kitchen counter. As soon as I opened the front door, a weight hit me hard in the chest. My vision blurred and the air was knocked out of my lungs when I hit the floor. Something smashed my nose, blood rolling hot down my cheeks. The dark figure smashed the back of my head into the floor once before my hands found its shoulders.

I brought my knee to my chest, finally getting my foot under the body enough to thrust it off. I scrambled to my feet and turned to fight. My skin went cold, and it felt like everything had stopped. It was bathed in a black robe, a hood framing the dark hole where a face should've been. It lunged at me, and I screamed, clawing for eyes that weren't there. We tumbled onto the kitchen floor, my elbow smashing the tile hard enough that my arm went numb. I grabbed a hold of the chair legs and slid it his way hard. It bought me just enough time to climb to my feet again.

I pulled a knife from the block on the counter and threw it straight at its face. The blade went through the center of the hood and out the back as if the monster were made of smoke, sinking into the wall with a thunk. It stood there, facing me.

"What do you want?" I asked. "Who are you?"

It raised two bone-white hands to the hood.

"Ferryman," he said in a ghostly whisper. He pushed the robe from his shoulders, but they weren't shoulders at all. There wasn't even a body to be covered. The black fabric dropped to the floor, vanishing in a plume of black smoke around my ankles. I ran to the couch when the last of the smoke disappeared and immediately picked up my phone. There were three texts from Jamie.

You make it home?

If you don't answer in two minutes, we're coming over.

On our way.

CHAPTER 7

I waited for Jamie and Izzy on the porch, too weirded out to be in the dark house by myself. The pizza came just as they pulled up in a black Audi. They both ran across the lawn, slowing their pace when they noticed the delivery boy getting back into his car, the Dominos light flickering when he shut his door.

"You didn't answer. You look pretty freaked out." Jamie glanced over the blood I'd missed on the front of my shirt. Izzy passed me and opened the front door, a dagger appearing in her hand as soon as she was inside. I sat the pizza on the coffee table and Jamie flicked on the lights. There were bloody spots over the hardwood from that first blow to my face. I heard Izzy dislodge the knife from the kitchen wall. She came back with it in her right hand a minute later.

"What attacked you?" she asked. "Did it have claws or fangs?"

I shook my head. "It didn't even have a body. It was wearing a robe and a hood, like the Grim Reaper. It felt solid when I hit it, but it didn't have a face and it vanished when it took the hood off. He said something about a ferryman."

They both looked straight at me now, no longer inspecting the damage.

"What about a ferryman?" Jamie asked, taking a seat next to me.

"I asked what it wanted and who the hell he was. He just said ferryman and then took the hood off and was gone," I said.

Jamie and Izzy exchanged questioning glances, as if each thought the other would have the answer.

"I know we've never left them alive long enough for introductions, but I've never met a demon with a name before," Izzy said.

Jamie's right hand was in a fist in his hair.

"I don't think we're dealing with demons anymore." he said.

Izzy let out a string of curses under her breath and tossed the knife onto the table next to the pizza box.

Jamie opened the box and pushed it my way. "It's been quiet around here lately."

"You think this ferryman is the one who's been stalking us and keeping the smaller demons away?" Izzy asked.

I froze with a slice of pizza halfway to my mouth. Neither of them told me anything about a stalker. Jamie hadn't wanted to tell me about the demons they hunted at all.

"All we know is that something has been watching us. We figured it was something big since we hadn't seen as many smaller demons like normal," he said.

Izzy crossed her arms and plopped down onto the armchair before looking to her brother. "We found blood in the forest and a deer ripped apart. Do you really think this ferryman hunts and kills like a vampire or werewolf?" She turned to me again, asking me for the second time if the figure had fangs.

"He told me he's a ferryman," I said, "So, what does that mean? He's like the bringer of death or something?"

Jamie let out a single laugh and shrugged.

"Yeah. Probably," he said.

Izzy groaned.

"Before we jump to conclusions about a dark entity we've never encountered, we should just read through the circle guide," she said.

Their house had a library nearly the size of Burbrook High's. If the gate and guardians were as old as they said, then there was bound to be an answer somewhere among the shelves. Jamie chewed on his bottom lip for a moment before nodding. He picked up his sister's knife from the table and held it out to her by the blade.

"You're right, but you should go by yourself. I don't feel good about leaving Tori alone," he said.

I felt a twist of annoyance in my gut. I held my own without any experience. I kicked the ferryman out of my house and got information out of him. I was the only one who knew what he looked like.

"My aunt and uncle will be back in an hour. I think I'll be fine on my own until then," I said.

I heard Izzy murmur something that sounded like "It's the meadow all over again." I noticed the glare Jamie sent her way.

"I'll text you if I find anything related. Don't get too comfortable, big brother. There's work to do," she said, pointing toward the globs of blood smeared in the entryway before she pocketed the knife and left. Jamie went to the kitchen and came back with a bowl of water and a rag.

"Was this your blood or his?" he asked.

The slice of pizza in my hand had gone cold. I set it aside and wiped the grease on my jeans.

"Mine," I said. "He punched me in the face. I tried stabbing him with the knife, but it went straight through his hood like there was nothing there."

I stood up to replace the kitchen knife as Jamie sat on the floor to clean. There was a long slit in the kitchen wall, barely noticeable thanks to the sharpness of the blade. I ran my fingers over the spot as if it would suddenly disappear before moving the corkboard down a few inches on the wall.

Jamie was bent over the floor, scrubbing the rag across the wood to get all the scarlet spots. I retook my seat on the couch and forced myself to eat two pieces of pizza as I watched him. He rinsed the bowl and rag once before making a second pass over the floor. I remembered every moment of the fight as he removed the evidence.

"If he's been stalking you two for weeks, then why did he decide to attack me when I only just made the change?"

Jamie straightened up with the bowl in hand and shrugged, disappearing into the kitchen again. The Grim Reaper was a kind of ferryman for the living, wasn't he? The folktales told of a hooded figure appearing just before a person died, a kind of mythical figure who sent people into the afterlife. Maybe this ferryman was the same? The only problem was that I wasn't mortal anymore.

I went to my room for my laptop, changing out of my stained shirt and settling onto the bed to research. I typed in *Grim Reaper* and clicked on the first article that came up. It was just like I remembered. The personification of death. The dark figure responsible for collecting the dead. The article linked to Greek origins, and I stopped halfway down the page when I saw the word *ferryman*. Like the Reaper, the ferryman guided the souls of the dead into the underworld.

Jamie cleared his throat in the hallway. He took the silence as permission to enter.

"Your aunt and uncle won't be the wiser," he said, setting the pizza box on the bed between us. I pushed it behind us and scooted his way, turning my laptop so he could see.

"If the ferryman is a kind of guide for these souls into the Shadowlands, then why isn't he on the other side of the gate now?" I asked.

"Jesus, Tori," Jamie said under his breath. "The thing just beat the crap out of you and you're already ready to fight it again?"

What else was there to do now— wait for it to reappear?

"If there's something more going on than normal demons like you say then it can't wait, can it?" I asked.

Jamie let out a sigh and pulled his phone from his back pocket. He took a picture of the screen before closing the laptop and setting it on the side table.

"I'll have Izzy check it out," he said, his phone pinging as he sent the message.

He looked around my room for a moment and just as I was sure he was going to comment on the dorky pictures tacked above my desk, he took a pencil from it instead.

"You're no help to anyone without a little practice," he said.

I practiced everything from making the pencil roll across the desk to snapping it in half until Mark got back. Jamie stayed hidden away in my bedroom as I made small talk with Mark. Becky came home not long after and they both had such stressful days that they were content to sit complaining together in the kitchen over glasses of wine. I used the distraction to gather blankets for Jamie. After making a pallet for himself on the floor, we both settled in for the night.

"Try turning the lights off with your mind," he said when I

moved to get up. I took a deep breath and focused on the light switch next to the door. After a few seconds and a slowly building headache, the switch flicked off and the only light came from the window behind us. It was quiet for a long time before the floor squeaked. Jamie rolled on his side so he could look at me. I could just barely make out his face in the dark.

"I don't mean to come off overprotective," he said. "It's just been such a long time since it was anyone other than Izzy and me and... I had given up on the idea of closing the gate the last time we stayed in Burbrook. I'm just glad there's finally more of us and of all the people in this stupid town, I'm glad it was you."

My stomach clenched. I was glad for Jamie and Izzy too. I felt like I belonged than I ever had growing up. Even with Becky and Mark things had always felt a little disconnected.

"I know," I said, "Me too."

I could just barely make out a smile on his face before he rolled onto his back.

Jamie snuck out my window the next morning, leaping down to the ground like some kind of superhero. I stopped a block down the street to pick him up. He said that Izzy was bringing his school bag, so we went straight to school. A couple of girls were in the halls early to hand out posters for homecoming voting in a few weeks. It was fun to watch them tape their glitter-encrusted poster boards to the walls, most of them girls who would never have been nominated had the more popular ones not been removed early from the race. Maybe we'd be voting on merit and kindness for once, not looks or money.

Jamie walked with me to my locker. He placed a hand on my arm when I tried shrugging out of my jacket.

"You have to keep it covered," he said, nodding towards my left wrist.

I had almost forgotten about it. What did it matter when no one at school could see it but us? I noticed small groups forming in the hallway, several students pointing toward the entryway. Coming up the hall with a backpack slung over each shoulder was Izzy Quinn.

She was dressed almost like a student. She wore a pair of comfy looking deep-green joggers with a yellow T-shirt. It was a V-neck cut that hugged her waist, the detail that was drawing most of the stares from students as she walked toward us. The Burbrook High School logo was stamped over her heart, the green silhouette of a baying wolf with the words "Burbrook High School Athletics" surrounding it in a neat circle. The only thing setting her apart from the sea of students was the staff badge hanging around her neck.

Jamie let out a long breath and slipped out of his leather jacket, adjusting the sleeves of his shirt to make sure they were all the way down his wrist. He held the jacket out to Izzy before she was close enough to reach it. Her eyeroll said it all.

"Going somewhere?" I asked her, eying her backpack as she handed Jamie his.

"I thought it was time I discovered what's changed about schools since the eighties," she said as she slipped his jacket over her bare arms. "The athletic trainer agreed to let me shadow her for my college class."

"You're taking college classes right now?" I asked. Did she not have enough degrees?

"Physical therapy," she said with a laugh, "I get bored, okay?"

"Anything to report?" Jamie asked.

Izzy stared right back at a group of boys who eyed her as they passed.

"Apparently not," she said. "Same old building, same nosy kids."

"He means about my visitor," I said, closing my locker door.

She nodded, following as we started toward Mr. Puck's class. I was starting to wonder if I'd ever go unnoticed again as Izzy sorted through her phone. She turned the screen our way, displaying a picture of handwritten notes in a leatherbound book. We both read in silence as other students joined us outside the door to wait for the bell.

The ferryman really was like a reaper, but he could only operate within the Shadowlands. He ferries the demons to the gates of the Shadowlands where they are bound to the Gatekeeper. They serve her alone and it's by her powers that they are allowed to pass through the gate again and back into the mortal world. The more powerful the gatekeeper, the more demons she could release. No matter how many demons the guardians fought, it was this Gatekeeper we were really fighting against. To close off our gate, we needed to grow stronger than her. That single fact filled me with dread as I realized that the ferryman was doing exactly the opposite as the book dictated.

"He's working backward," I said, looking at Jamie.

He nodded, jaw tight.

The bell rang and Izzy pocketed her phone before darting into the crowd. I followed Jamie to our chemistry table, thinking about the attack the night before.

"He has a job," Jamie said, his voice hushed. "The only reason he'd leave his post is if he had new orders. Demons don't need anyone to ferry them back to our world, just an open gate."

"So, what does?" I asked.

Jamie shook his head and sank into his seat. I barely sat down before Sean Peterson turned to talk to me. It caught me by surprise, and I bashed my knee against the table painfully. Sean didn't care that the tables around us were staring; he had other ideas.

"Who was that girl you were talking to?" he asked.

I could tell Macy was listening, her head snapping back our way after the others had turned their attention to the discussion question on the front board.

"She's shadowing the athletic trainer for college," I said. "Mr. Puck keeps looking."

Mr. Puck was still busy taking roll at the desktop, clearly not aware of us. Sean, of course, knew this.

"Oh, a college girl," he said. "I guess that means she doesn't have a date for the homecoming dance." One of his friends snickered next to him.

"You promised Macy you'd go with her," I reminded him. Macy had spent most of high school pining after Sean Peterson, for a reasons unknown to me. While nice enough to most people, Sean seemed to think that no woman was in his league. I was a little surprised he was interested in Izzy at all.

"I'm not her boyfriend, am I?" Sean asked.

I reached out and pushed the back of his blond head, forcing his chair to land on all fours with a pop. Mr. Puck stopped mid-sentence to stare at me in surprise, the entire room going silent. I felt all the color drain from my face before I remembered what Sean had said. I'd never been in trouble in my entire life, but even someone as shallow as Macy deserved better than Sean.

"Victoria," Mr. Puck started. "Is there a problem?"

"No, sir," I replied.

I could hear a few snickers to my left. Mr. Puck's eyes

remained on me for a few seconds longer before he continued with his explanation. I kept my eyes glued on the front of the class, taking notes when called for. I jammed my books into my bag as soon as the bell rang, making me the first one out the door. Jamie caught up with me with a laugh.

"Stop," I said. "It was embarrassing."

My mood lightened when I noticed his smile. Something about his expression was infectious, making me forget the stupid argument.

"You always have been a goody-two-shoes," he said.

I stuck my tongue out at him, stopping at my locker just long enough to retrieve the thick Shakespeare textbook.

"And you aren't, Mr. Valedictorian?" I asked.

He opened his mouth to reply but closed it a second later. A wry smirk pulled across his face.

"That's fair," he said, the smile fading.

I followed his gaze, noticing Sean farther down the hall, talking with his friends. I noticed after a moment what they were all whispering about. Izzy was standing nearby, talking with Mrs. Hawthorne who coached the girls' basketball team. The entire group of boys were gawking, but Sean looked especially gross. He was staring at Izzy as if deciding how to ambush her the way a lion stalks its prey from the tall grass before it ever makes a move.

"I told Macy three years ago that Sean was a womanizer," I said.

Jamie let out a groan. "Yeah. Well, Macy's not the one I care about," he said, closing my locker and turning the dial.

We went our separate ways at the end of the hall. Just before I went into Mrs. Hawthorne's class, Mr. Puck stopped me. I felt my entire body freeze as he asked Mrs. Hawthorn to count me present, explaining that he wanted to talk to me about class.

"I'm sorry, Mr. Puck," I started as the door closed and the bell rang. "I was just telling Sean that you were talking and…" I let my words trail off when Mr. Puck shook his head. He rubbed his forehead with his right hand and let out a long sigh. I could just feel the disappointment.

"I would've kept you after class except you left before I could catch you," he started. "Tori, you're in the top five of the senior class. Your record is spotless. But I've noticed some changes in you and I've been letting them pass as senioritis. I heard you quit the volleyball team even though you're good at it. Your grade in my class has been great, but your other grades are low, at least they are low for you. Today, you disrupted class and it's just not like you. So, I wanted to make sure that you remembered how important this year is. Senior year is not something you can just cruise through."

"I understand," I said, wishing I could sink into the tile under my feet. Mr. Puck was studying me and I half-expected him to continue his lecture before he nodded.

"I really hope you do," he said, "because you are far too smart to let a few new friends ruin your chances at a good college."

He started back toward his classroom. I couldn't help but think about the reality of it all. I might not even go to college. Sure, Jamie and Izzy both had, but they also had to fight demons and try sealing off the gate. I couldn't even bend a spoon in half.

For the first time, I didn't care that people were looking at me when I went back to History. I sat down and searched for the page Mrs. Hawthorne was currently reading from. By the time I found the right page, I had zoned out and missed the source of our class discussion. I pretended to listen as she droned on. I was glad when it was all over.

"First day of school and I already have a date," Izzy

announced when she joined Jamie and me at our dilapidated table for lunch. "The art teacher, Mr. Howard, asked me out to dinner."

"You're not going," Jamie said.

Izzy looked up from her tray, sending a gaze my way as if daring me to side with her brother.

"I can take care of myself," she said. "I have like, sixty years of experience."

"So, he should be the one thanking you, right?" Jamie said, stabbing a chicken tender with his fork.

Izzy froze with her spoon halfway to mouth, lowering it a moment later.

"After eighty-something years, I don't think you can exactly play the big brother card when it comes to me dating guys," she said. "Especially when I'm four years older than you and I'm not the one who's afraid to find a match. Sometimes, it feels like I'm the only one in this since we woke who even gives a damn about expanding our circle. Get over it, Jamie."

She stood up with her tray between both hands. I felt like I'd missed half the argument, stuck between the two of them.

"This is the whole reason I didn't want her at school with me," Jamie said, standing up from our table and picking up his tray. He started in the same direction as Izzy, who was making a beeline toward the staff table near the lunch line. Sean leaned into the aisle after Izzy passed, looking back at her. He turned and said something to his friends that got a roar of laughter. Macy, sitting at the opposite end, turned bright red with anger.

I didn't have time to act. By the time Jamie tossed the last of his lunch onto the floor and raised the tray like a bat, I was too far away to do anything. I raised my hands and called out his name as he braced for a swing. The tray froze mid-air as if someone had grabbed it from behind, suspended behind Jamie's right ear with his muscles tensed.

The surrounding students began to cheer and gasp as Jamie straightened up, lowering the tray, and glancing back at me in awe. Sean rose from his seat and shoved Jamie's chest. Before a crowd could form, Mr. Puck appeared next to Sean to separate them. Jamie turned and made his way toward the back door as Sean yelled after him. Mr. Thackery had joined the scene now, yelling for the roomfull of students to head to class even through the bell hadn't rung yet.

I squeezed past the students on my way toward the back door, getting there after Izzy threw it open and stormed outside.

"You idiot," she hissed, pushing Jamie's back hard into the metal dumpster.

"He called you—"

"I heard him," Izzy said, "and I told you before that I didn't need anyone looking after me. When are you going to let go of your stupid, sexist desire to protect women who don't need it?"

Jamie sucked in a deep breath, his knuckles going white before he relaxed his fists.

"I'm sorry," he said. "I know, but like you said, the last time you went to Burbrook High scrunchies were cool and every girl had a can of hairspray in her locker." He pulled his phone from his pocket, checking the number and letting out a groan. "It's the office," he said, answering it. Before he could raise it to his ear, Izzy had snatched it away and introduced herself as Maria Quinn.

"My son did what?" she asked, sticking her tongue out at Jamie. "I understand completely. I would come rip him a new one myself if I didn't have a meeting at one-thirty... His sister will pick up his assignments for the rest of the week. Tell him he's grounded, and he needs to be home as soon as school is out. Yes. Thank you, Mr. Thackery."

Izzy hung up the phone. She moved so fast that I didn't realize she'd slapped Jamie until his hand was clasped against his left cheek.

"Dammit, Izzy," he groaned, lowering his hand to reveal the pink splotch over his cheek.

"You're suspended for the whole week, genius," she said. "And the principal is on his way to get you, so you'd better go wherever you're supposed to be."

Jamie's right hand came down on the side of the dumpster. The motion seemed calm, but it was still powerful enough to put a small dent in the frame.

"That's okay," he said with a sigh, "I'll be at the house looking for anything about the ferryman." He made sure no one was watching before darting back into the cafeteria.

"Mom is probably cheering me on from her grave about that," Izzy said, shaking the hand she'd slapped Jamie with. I was still in shock. I'd never been involved in a fight before and now I was late to my first class of the afternoon. Izzy wasn't worried at all, leading me around the side of the building.

"Well, cafeteria food is just as bad as it was in the eighties," she said, "Do you like Del Taco?"

I wasn't at all surprised when I got home and was immediately met with Becky and Mark's reproach. I listened to them repeat the same lecture for at least thirty minutes before they turned on each other. It took them a few minutes to decide that I should be grounded for the rest of the week. Turns out, Mr. Puck was more concerned than he'd let on, especially after finding out that I was involved with Jamie Quinn, the new bad boy at school.

I managed to text both Izzy and Jamie about my being grounded before Mark thought to take my phone away as well. Neither of them remembered that I had a whole laptop at my disposal, not that I ended up using it for anything but homework. I was halfway through rereading what I'd missed of *King Lear* from Shakespeare class when I heard a tapping on the window.

Jamie had pulled himself up on the windowsill, motioning for me to let him in. I thought about letting him hang there all night, but I knew enough about guardian powers to know he'd be able to do just that. I unlatched the window and let him in, reminding him to be quiet as he lowered himself into my room.

"I'm sorry," he whispered.

I closed the window after him with a sigh.

"It's not your fault," I told him. "My grades are slipping. Bs aren't that bad unless you've never had one and your aunt and uncle don't think anything is wrong until your dumb teacher thinks you're messing up."

Jamie snorted, picking up the abandoned math book on my bed.

"This is my fault," he said, pulling the book out of my reach when I tried tugging it from his grasp. "Did I mention that I have a teaching degree?"

I couldn't help but snicker, a smirk spreading across his face.

"I didn't see anything about math on that wall of degrees in your house," I said.

He shrugged.

"Right," he said, "but I have taken calculus four times. Come here."

I relented, taking a seat on the bed next to him. He explained everything I'd missed from that afternoon, helping me finish my homework for the next day. After just an hour, I was ahead again in all my classes.

"You should go home," I told him, noticing the clock on my bedside table now read A.M.

He carefully moved to his backpack in the corner, pulling out a fresh set of clothes. He held them up for me to see. I nodded. I liked the idea of him staying.

"Turn around," he said. After a moment, I agreed. I could see his shadow tugging off his shirt against the wall before me. He'd said that he didn't mean to be so protective, yet here he was. I wished I could kick him out, but I remembered the cool voice of the ferryman. Unless Jamie had found anything new, we weren't any closer to figuring out why the dark figure was in the mortal world instead of in his own.

"Did you find anything out about the ferryman?" I asked, turning around when Jamie's shadow signaled the okay. He dragged the same blankets out of the closet that he'd used the night before, careful not to make a sound as he spread them over the floor.

"Nothing new," he said. "What happened at lunch was new, at least it was for you."

If we hadn't turned off the lights earlier, he would've seen the pride on my face. I knew it was me who had really stopped Jamie from throwing that punch. I'd felt the tug just as he had, holding him back.

"Don't test me, Jamie Quinn," I said.

I could hear a small hum of a laugh. It was quiet for a while. I rolled onto my side, letting my hands wrap around my pillow so I could see him better on the floor.

"You're still wearing that?" he asked.

It took me a moment to realize he meant the spoon bent

around my wrist. I turned it around my wrist so that the moonlight gleamed off the metal. I wasn't sure what to tell him. The fact that I hadn't taken it off since he clasped it around my wrist somehow didn't seem like a good option.

"I don't know. I think it's cool," I said. It was quiet. After a while, I thought maybe he'd gone to sleep.

"You're not practiced enough to bend one with your mind," Jamie said, "but I bet you could still use your hands to turn one into a bracelet." He rolled onto his back after he'd said it. I wasn't sure what he'd meant exactly. I tested the metal again, pressing against it until I worried that I would actually be able to bend it like he said. I slipped it off my wrist to avoid the urge and set it next to a glass of water on my nightstand. I wanted to ask him what he was going to do now that he was suspended the rest of the week, but his eyes were closed.

CHAPTER 8

When I woke up for school the next day, Jamie had already left. Becky reminded me to come straight home. The fact that neither her nor Mark would be home never came up. I agreed, planning to head to the Moore Estate first. Before I had even made it to the Beetle, Izzy pulled up to the curb in the yellow Maserati. She rolled down the passenger window and called for me to hop in.

"I thought we could go homecoming dress shopping after school," she said as I got in. The seat was warm when I settled into it and curved so that it fit my body, almost like it was made for me.

"I can't," I said. "I'm grounded because Mr. Puck called Becky about yesterday and then they found out I skipped the last half of the day."

Izzy groaned, leaning back in her seat. I hadn't thought seriously about homecoming until now. After Macy got mad at me, I didn't really think I'd be going.

"You're really making me question why I decided to go

back to high school in the first place, Tori," Izzy said, pulling away from the curb as I mumbled my agreement.

I wasn't even sure where the homecoming dance was this year. All I knew was that the homecoming king and queen would be someone unexpected considering the usual popular posse had been taken out of the running early on. I'd never found myself dreading school as much as I did now. Maybe I did have senioritis. Whatever it was, I had it bad.

"As much as I'd like to drop out to stake vampires or whatever, I guess I should graduate," I said.

After a moment, we both laughed. It was strange to me how real the statement was. It was the first sunny day since school had started. Despite Jamie's suspension, things had gone back to normal. Macy, while still clearly sore about everything, was even nice enough to me. After agreeing to a jerky ride to school in the Beetle, Izzy forbade me from driving my aunt's hand-me-down, deciding it was better to pick me up each morning.

By the end of the week, Mark and Becky had forgotten about my being grounded and let me go out with Izzy on Friday so long as I replied to every text they sent. Izzy let me drive the Maserati the thirty minutes to Holston. Holston was a tiny town nestled between two mountains. It was known for being a vacation spot for rich people, home to a luxury ski resort, and several expensive boutiques. The more well-to-do families in Burbrook would spend their weekends shopping in Holston. Girls like Macy would show up to all the dances in overpriced dresses bought at the very same store we were planning to visit. Thanks to volleyball, I'd never really had lots of time for a job, so I hoped the fifty dollars Becky had slipped me would be enough for something on the clearance rack.

"This car is so touchy," I said as I pulled into the first parking spot I saw, ignoring Izzy's complaints about being so far down the street. I tossed her the keys when I got out. She tucked them into her purse, the yellow car clicking as it automatically locked the doors the moment we started down the sidewalk.

"You're going to love this place," she said, leading me down the street toward the tiny Italian restaurant. It was surprisingly busy; small groups of people gathered outside under the lights strung across the street. Izzy walked into the building, telling the hostess her name. After consulting with a list at the podium, we were led through the dark front room and to a booth in the back.

"Enjoy," the woman said, setting a menu on the table before both of us. I noted the time on my phone before tucking it away in my purse: nearly seven o'clock.

"Relax," Izzy said. "Like your aunt said, if we're running late, you'll just let her know."

I scoffed. Becky didn't know we were in a whole different town. For all she knew, we were shopping the single street of boutiques in downtown Burbrook. Thankfully, Izzy didn't say anything more and busied herself with the menu. I scanned the entire page before deciding to order my usual; spaghetti and meatballs.

"So, looks like I won't be going to the homecoming dance after all," she said.

I groaned. "I can't be the only one shopping tonight. Is this because Jamie got so overprotective at school?"

"I'm still bitter about that," Izzy said as she turned the menu over to look at the back. After a moment, she looked up at me and added, "Jamie is infuriating sometimes. He lectures me all the time about keeping hidden and not being too obvious in public. Where was all of that when he ambushed Sean?"

She was right and the protective side of Jamie was one that

annoyed me a bit. On one hand, it was sweet. Still, I didn't like the assumption that I needed someone looking out for me.

"More water?" the waiter asked, pulling me out of my thoughts. I handed her my glass, and she began taking our orders, no notepad needed, as she filled out glasses. Izzy waited until he moved a few tables away to talk.

"I hate to say it, but I may have to spend the whole homecoming dance staking out the parking lot." She stuck her tongue out in disgust.

"Why?" I asked. "I didn't think homecoming was important to you at all."

Izzy hesitated with her glass raised halfway to her lips, long enough to reveal the real reason. She took a drink and motioned for the waiter to come over before I could launch my cross-examination.

"Izzy," I said, firm enough that the waiter took her order for a glass of red wine and didn't bother to stick around to check her ID.

"So, Jamie has a point about being concerned."

"I thought you didn't like it when he went into over-protective big brother mode."

"It's not being over-protective, and it wasn't his idea," Izzy said as the waiter made his way toward us with a wine glass. "Not entirely anyway."

I waited until the waiter left us again to ask, "What part was yours then?"

"Jamie wanted me to enroll at Burbrook High, so I was with you during school, but I told him that was weird and kind creepy. Shadowing the athletic trainer for a semester of college was my contribution."

"Was keeping an eye on me his idea?"

"Tori," Izzy said and let out a long sigh. She turned her wine glass in a circle by the stem once before looking up at me again. I could see her weighing the words, trying to decide how to put what I already knew as delicately as she could. "You're the newest member of our circle. You are just getting used to your powers and the Shadowlands spit out a serious figure after you. We'd be on high alert if it was any of us, but…"

"I get it," I said and groaned, "but that doesn't mean it's not annoying." I reached for her wine glass, and she slid it closer to her with a surprised but amused expression.

"Excuse me," she said with a laugh. "Are you twenty-one?"

"Excuse me, but should a woman in triple digits be drinking?"

Izzy's jaw dropped and she laughed. She slid the glass back to me and I took a sip before sitting it in front of her again. I'd never had red wine before. It was dry, bitter. It was in the same vein as my black coffee order at Starbucks. I thought about taking another sip, but the waiter returned with our dishes.

"So, back to how the hell I'm going to get into the homecoming dance," Izzy said as she twirled pasta around her fork, "Going with a high school boy is out. That's so weird. What BHS staff members are single? Maybe I should've just told Jamie to deal with it and gone out with Mr. Howard."

"Why not just volunteer to chaperone?"

"Good point," Izzy said with a shrug and took a bite of pasta.

"That's why I'm the salutatorian," I joked, splitting a meatball in half.

"Valedictorian," Izzy said past a mouthful of pasta.

"No, salutatorian. Jamie's valedictorian."

Izzy swallowed and lifted her water to her lips, saying, "You really think he's going to take that from you?"

I stopped with my fork still stuck in a meatball. Izzy sent me a knowing look. Ugh. She was right. I'd have to talk to Jamie about that later.

"So," Izzy started with a wry smile on her face that made me nervous. "Are you taking a date?"

I never went to dances with anyone other than Macy, her date, and her friends. I usually danced with whoever was free, whatever single boy hung around Macy's friends, until they all paired off. I wasn't outgoing enough to go about the pairing process, just politely stepping aside whenever one of Macy's friends asked if they could dance with whatever guy I had been with at that moment. It must've shown on my face, because Izzy started mentioning the various boys she'd seen in the halls at school.

"I'm not really interested in that, especially now with everything going on," I explained.

"How about that cute brunette girl whose locker is next to yours?"

"No, I mean I like boys, but I just don't see a point," I told her and sat my fork down. "I know all the boys in our class and none of them really interest me and in a few months..." I stopped when the thought of after high school filled my head. Was that even an option anymore?

"Have you ever dated anyone?" Izzy continued talking as I shook my head. "Kissed anyone? Got a little handsy? One night stand?"

"No. I'm as new to that as I am to this whole guardian thing," I said, feeling my cheeks flush. Thankfully, Izzy didn't tease me about it like Macy usually did.

"Well, it must be because you give off uninterested vibes or something, because you're totally hot."

"I spent all of high school standing next to the most coveted girls."

"Because you look just like them," Izzy said in disbelief, "except for the whole blonde part." We both laughed and we stopped talking so we could finish our meals.

The boutique was small; the heather gray exterior stood out from the rest of the red-bricked buildings. The punchy red Hollywood-style lights spelled "J & J" over the door. I was starting to worry about my budget as we crossed the street. Izzy led the way in. The entire store was glowing from the patio lights strung above us. It looked like prom, the nearest rack of ball gowns glittering as we passed them.

"Welcome to J & J," a petite blonde woman said, stepping around the counter, "We have dresses for all occasions, but the most formal are on that side of the store." She pointed to the wall lined with heavy-looking prom dresses and wedding gowns. I awkwardly thanked her before ducking behind a rack of simple A-lines.

"Long or short?" I asked Izzy. I draped a long light-pink dress over my right arm, Izzy returning it to the rack a moment later.

"You want a dress, not a nightgown," she said, holding out a long red dress. It looked simple in the front, a slit down one side of the skirt worrying me about the amount of thick volley-ball thigh I'd be putting on display. The back was low, two straps from the left shoulder holding it firmly in place at the lower back. "This one's for you," Izzy said, handing it off. "It checks all your boxes. It's about as simple as you can get, struc-tured, and it's on sale."

I took the dress from her and held it to my front as she continued her search. Just like I feared, the slit was going to be inches above my knee. Sure, I'd spent the last six years in a pair of volleyball spandex shorts that were shorter and tighter than this, but they had a purpose I understood. Macy would've taken the dress for herself and attracted all the male attention in the room wearing it. A pit was forming in my stomach. I knew that the dresses I wanted were just like the first I'd picked, long and flowy. It was easier to disappear in them. That last thought sent a pang of annoyance through my gut.

"I think I'm going to try this on," I said.

Izzy had her arms full of dresses as she followed me to the dressing rooms. I picked the door closest to the mirror at the back. I stared at the dress for a long time before I even moved to try it on, getting my shirt off before I decided to check my phone. Becky had sent me a text a few minutes before asking what we were doing. I told her about the dress, taking a picture before deciding not to send it. Before she could reply, Jamie called.

"Hey, what's up?" I asked, tucking the phone against my ear as I shimmied out of my jeans.

"I was just wondering where you two were," he said. I could hear the rustling of paper at the end of the line. Jamie had spent his entire week of suspension in the library of his house. Every time I'd heard from him, he had moved on to a new book, rarely finding anything more than a mention of the ferryman.

"We're at J & J. It's a store," I said, quickly slipping the dress over my head. "Find anything new?" I could hear more pages turning on his end.

"Yes, well, I think it's important," he said. "We know that the ferryman is supposed to remain in the Shadowlands to ferry souls into it after they die, not the other way around. I'm not exactly sure how it works, but we know that demons don't need his help to get to the mortal world. They just cross the gate. So, from what I've read, the ferryman never leaves his post at the gate because he's ordered not to."

I untwisted the strap at my shoulder as I listened, shivering as I remembered the ferryman's empty hood.

"So, you're saying that whomever he works for ordered him here for something. He's looking for something," I said. The rustling on Jamie's end stopped and I thought for a moment that he had hung up. "Jamie? Tell me you know more than just that." We had assumed as much just days ago. After a beat, I heard him sigh.

"It means there's someone bigger and badder pulling the strings. Promise me something,"

he said. I felt my skin go cold. "Sure," I said, "What is it?"

I heard a door snap shut and an engine.

"Stay where you are and don't hang up until I get there," he said.

I didn't understand. I already had one guardian with me. Did I really need another?

"Izzy's been with me the entire time," I said.

"Tori, please," Jamie said. "Just do this one thing for my sanity."

"Tell me if you know more. No sane person would watch someone while they sleep or follow them around unless they knew something. Say it," I said.

It was silent for a long time aside from the hum of the engine.

"Just stay where you are," Jamie said.

I hung up and tossed my phone onto the pile of clothes on the floor, ignoring it when Jamie called again.

The dress made me look different, unlike the graphic-tee wearing ponytail girl I normally was. It hugged what few curves I had, and the slit highlighted the muscles of my right leg. I turned back to the small mirror and gathered my hair on top of my head to get a better look at the back. I noticed the tiny buttons at the bottom left gaping. I tried my best to fasten them, my wrist aching the more I twisted. A knock came at my door a moment later.

"Need any help?" the store clerk asked. I opened the door and turned back around.

"I can't get all the buttons done," I told her. "But even without them, I think this is the one I'm wearing to homecoming. Izzy, you need to see it. I look..." I wanted to say sexy, but the word stuck in my throat. I heard Izzy's door stick in the frame, the entire wall between our cubicles shuttering as she shook it.

"Tori, open my door," she said.

"I'm not close enough," I told her, feeling the woman's hands sweep my hair over my left shoulder.

"No, Tori. Focus on the lock and open the damn door," Izzy said.

I looked toward her stall, catching sight of myself in the mirror. Where the blonde store clerk should've been standing was just empty space. A glass vial was pressed against my neck and a dagger was floating just above it.

"Demon!" I screamed. The woman shoved me hard against the wall, my forehead smashing the clothing rack. I saw Izzy's head rise over the cubicle as she pulled herself up.

"Vampire," she said. "Stake her!"

The woman turned from me to swipe the dagger at Izzy, forcing her to drop into her changing room again. I kicked the woman in the gut when she turned toward me, forcing her back into the door. She swiped at me, the dagger emitting a high-pitched squeal as it dragged across the mirror. I ducked when she swung her fist at me, the mirror shattering into chunks of glass and raining down my back. I grabbed a large shard off the floor and rammed it upward, feeling the sharp edges cut and pull across my palm as the point sank into her gut.

"I stabbed her," I said, the door opening a second later. The woman turned just in time to seize the wooden clothing hanger Izzy jabbed her way, breaking it in half as easily as I could snap a pencil.

"A wooden stake, Tori," Izzy said, letting out a groan when the woman grabbed onto the front of her dress. She pulled hard, forcing Izzy against the doorframe with a bang that shook the whole stall. I took the hanger down from the rack behind me and tried snapping it in half, dropping it instead and watching as it slid into the next cubicle. Izzy had the woman's head between both of her hands forcing it downward, her knee smashing into her face.

"Get out of there," Izzy said, nodding toward the space between the changing room and the ceiling. I snatched as much of my stuff from the floor as I could and tossed it over the wall before leaping. I used the little arm strength I had to drag my body over the top, my hips banging painfully against every edge of the wall. Izzy kicked the vampire into the spot I was just standing in before raising both hands. I watched just long enough to see the flames erupt from her palms, dropping to the floor as they rose to the ceiling.

The vampire's scream echoed loud and high-pitched through the building, shattering every mirror in the dressing room to tiny fragments. I felt a few glittering pieces pierce my arches painfully as I ran from the room, Izzy right behind me. I skidded to a stop when I saw the dark figure just inside the doorway.

"Ferryman," I said.

Izzy stepped in front of me. She flipped back the hem of her skirt with one move, letting out a gasp and feeling for her middle next.

"Shit," she said. "I left it in the stall."

I followed her lead, taking a dress from the clothing rack and pulling the hanger off it. The ferryman walked our way, small, slow steps that made it look like he was floating.

"I know you want something from us," I said. "Tell me what it is and maybe we can make a deal."

The ferryman kept coming, a dagger sliding out of one sleeve and a vial from the other. A scream drew our attention toward the changing rooms again. The woman ran toward us, her clothes charred and blackened from Izzy's inferno. She charged at me, but Izzy shoved me into the rack of dresses and took my place. I watched as the vampire drove her dagger deep into Izzy's chest. They both fell to the floor, the vampire landing with a final scream on the broken point of a hanger. The woman slumped to the ground as Izzy's head rolled to the side, eyes open and lifeless.

As the weight of what I'd seen iced my skin, the ferryman settled on top of me. He raised the vial and the dagger, but I batted both of his arms away before he could bring them any closer. The vial slipped from his hand and broke in two jagged pieces next to my ear. Before I could grab one, the ferryman gathered a fistful of my hair and brought my head down hard against the floor.

CHAPTER 9

It felt like my head was splitting in two. I could hear waves to my right, the soft sloshing easing the pain at the back of my head. I opened my eyes, but I couldn't see anything except black shapes, a wall of darkness to my right and what felt like wooden planks underneath me. After some furious blinking, my eyes adjusted. I took a deep breath and pushed myself from the ground, able to make out the lake before me... or was it a sea? I looked behind me. The water faded into the darkness of the cave. It was pitch black above me, not a single star speckling the darkness. I could just make out the tips of a few stalactites directly above my head. The only light came from flames ahead of me, casting eerie shapes over the water.

I turned around. The wooden dock stretched on for yards, lined with iron torches all in the shapes of wriggling tentacles. At the very end, I could barely make out an iron gate. On my right, was a short dock where three wooden dinghies were tethered by chains. On my left, was a larger platform. It was draped in a black veil, transparent enough so that I could see the outline of the furniture within.

"Hello," I said. It stayed silent aside from the rhythmic waves. I stood up, feeling my head spin for a minute and half-expecting to be lying on the floor of J & J when the dizziness subsided. So, I wasn't dreaming after all. I walked toward the platform, remembering that I was barefoot and still wearing the red dress as soon as I took a step. I peeked past the flap in the veil to make sure no one was there before I went inside. The room was simple. In the middle was an onyx throne, the back of the chair tapered upward into a point. Black velvet-cushioned benches surrounded the perimeter of the room aside from the stone table at the back. I skirted the large throne to reach it, noticing the mirrored tabletop.

I let out a gasp when I looked down and saw Jamie instead of my own reflection. He had just gotten out of the Audi down the street in Holston. He ran toward the flashing lights. A firetruck and several policemen were parked outside of J & J. Before he could reach the police tape, a dark-haired girl snagged his arm. I let out a deep breath when I saw Izzy's face, remembering only then that guardians were immortal until they found a match. She pulled him back toward the car, their heads bent in conversation. The mirror must be able to show the viewer whatever they were searching for. I thought about Aunt Becky and Uncle Mark and just as I predicted, the scene changed. Becky was leaving the kitchen, two glasses of red wine in her hands. Mark was in their bedroom upstairs getting the TV set up. I thought about the ferryman, but the scene remained the same.

"Show me the ferryman," I whispered. Mark and Becky disappeared, and my own reflection replaced them. The breathy voice echoed in my head.

Those dead or alive are less than
The one who is the ferryman
Look inside and you shall see
Whatever it is that pleases thee
However, dare not demand or ask
For giving orders is not your task

I felt the pressure building in my head until I thought it would explode. A sharp pain replaced it, spreading through my entire body and growing as I felt my knees smash into the floor. I pressed my forehead to the wooden planks, grinding my teeth together against the burning.

"Please," I barely spoke.

The same breathy voice replied, firmer this time.

Obey the Ferryman. Fear the Shadow Mistress.

The pain vanished, leaving me a shaking mess on the floor. I took a few minutes to focus on controlling my breathing, amazed that I wasn't cut or bruised at all.

"Hello!" I heard a woman yell.

I forced myself to my feet and hurried back to the dock. About fifty yards into the sea was a dinghy with a long-haired figure sitting in the center.

"Hey! Can you pull me in?" she asked.

I looked around for rope, more chains, anything I could try tossing out to her. The boats tied to the doc were padlocked into place.

"Do you have a rope or something you could toss me?" I asked her.

She pointed to the front of the boat where a long chain sunk into the water.

"I must be anchored here or something. There's gotta be someone on the dock who's supposed to pull me across, right?" she asked. That was probably the ferryman's job. For all

I knew, she'd be stuck there until he came back to the Shadow-lands. I was sure I was the last person he'd want to see on his dock.

"I'm going to try pulling you across," I said, holding up my left arm and pointing to my mark. "Stay sitting."

She nodded her head, and I took a deep breath. If this didn't work... I focused on the front of the dinghy, feeling the weight of the chain as if I were holding it. Maybe it was the supernatural environment aiding my efforts, but it felt almost easier than practicing in the mortal world. The woman began to glide toward me. I was panting by the time she was close enough to leap to the dock.

"Guardians retain their powers in the Shadowlands after they die," she said, "and using them here is easier if you're still mortal. Guardians are like gods here, stronger." She had green eyes and long hair that hung past her shoulders in soft waves. She zipped her jacket up when she joined me, shivering.

"So, I'm not dead?" I asked.

She smiled at me. "No. You may not be able to tell, but the dead can, and I know for certain that I died back there." She thrusted her thumb back toward the sea. I was struck by how casually she said it. She made it sound like it was normal for mortal beings to be in the Shadowlands. Jamie and Izzy had never talked about the gate working that way before.

"How can I be here?" I asked.

She started toward the arch at the end of the dock.

"You don't know?" she asked me.

I shook my head. Why did every supernatural being seem to understand this place as if it were a second home, some-thing to embrace after death rather than fear it the way I did?

"I woke about a month ago. There's three of us in my circle and we were attacked by..." I stopped, unsure about mentioning the ferryman. I didn't even know this woman's name, much less who she was associated with.

"After the attack, I woke up here. I checked behind the veil and someone called the ferryman is supposed to help us across the sea. He's not here," I said.

The woman nodded her head slowly as if she were thinking through my story a second time.

"Wherever you were fighting must be the entrance to the gate then," she said. "I was in a car before I woke up in that boat."

I thought back to the fight. The ferryman had knocked me out rather than stabbing me. He must have taken me to the entrance himself, which meant I couldn't be sure where that was. Why drop me into the Shadowlands instead of leaving me alone in the woods or injuring me? Jamie had told me over the phone that the ferryman was in the mortal world on orders to find something. That's why he seemed to follow me everywhere. This time, he and the vampire both had vials. Were they after my blood? Why mine?

"If you're at the sixth gate, does that make you a member of our circle" I asked her.

She smiled, clearly holding back a laugh.

"I'm a witch," she said. "I don't know why I ended up at this gate, but I can promise you that I'm no demon. I'm as supernatural as you. You could say that we have different jobs is all."

I was still stuck on the first bit. Was there no limit on what supernatural beings existed?

"Maybe I should stay at the dock," I said. "I didn't mean to come here, and I just want to get back."

She stopped and turned to look back at me. The fear in her eyes was chilling, her entire stance seeming to shrink in size.

"Please, come with me," she said. "At least for a little while.

Guardians have some authority here and I think I broke a law passing the dock without meeting the dock keeper. I think that's why the gate is still locked and if I'm caught, I'll be damned to the Shallows for eternity."

"The Shallows?" I asked.

She nodded vigorously, her eyes going back to the sea yards behind us.

"After you die, you come here to the Shadowlands. It's like heaven here. If you don't abide by its laws, you live in the Shallows forever," she said, pointing to the sea.

"You mean, there are dead people floating around in there?" I asked her, feeling my stomach churning. She nodded. I wanted nothing more than to go back to the dock now and pray that the ferryman would let me out.

"Because you're a mortal guardian, your powers will work on the gate. The rules here don't apply to you because you aren't dead. Mortal guardians can travel the Shadowlands however they want, but you have to pay the dock keeper to get back to the mortal world. That's how demons make it to the mortal world, so that's how you will," she said. "But please, help me through the gate first."

She was asking me to do something illegal. Had I already broken the law by helping her across the sea? It was like all the rules she'd just told me were mixing in my head. I took a deep breath. All she wanted was to get to the gate at the end of the dock. That's it.

"I'll help you," I told her.

Her entire body seemed to relax, and we began to walk again. As we got closer, I could make out the buildings behind the gate. They were all dark. Everything dead, from the activity in the streets to the trees lining the gate. To the right of the gate was a dark castle, figures in armor pacing the walls. It was massive and angular, as if someone placed shards of obsidian along the top of the castle walls.

"Are you sure we're in that heaven you mentioned?" I asked.

The woman nodded. "If you come to my side," she said, motioning for me to join her, "I can show you."

I did, following the direction she was pointing. Down the street just past the castle was another gate, illuminated at the end of a cave by sunlight. The words *Free from Darkness* stretched in iron above the gate. The Shadowlands were a kind of purgatory then and the Shallows were their hell.

"You think you broke a law, and you want to just walk through the prison?" I asked her.

She let out a single laugh." Looks that way," she said, offering me an apologetic smile.

If all of these gates worked the way the ferryman's dock seemed to, then she would be allowed through the last gate if she really hadn't broken any laws. If passing the ferryman without his knowledge was breaking the law, then she'd never make it past the third gate. Either way, I wouldn't be in the Shadowlands to find out.

"Okay," I said. "Once I let you in, I'm going back to the dock,"

She nodded, stopping a few feet from the massive lock. I stared up at the sign for the Shadowlands, noticing the plaque hanging underneath.

Those who owe will serve their time, those without debt will pass.

"I think you have to do it," the witch said.

Where a key should've been was the shape of a hand. I hesitated a moment before matching my left hand to the spot. There was a metallic groan and the gate swung open slowly. I felt both my shoulders tighten the way they always did before a big test or a state qualifying game. The witch girl let out a sigh of relief and a small giggle that relaxed me a little. She grabbed onto my arm and led me through.

"I was sure there'd be a guard or something," I said, feeling much more relaxed now. I felt a twinge at the back of my head again and remembered the attack. I turned to head back to the dock, but the gate had settled back into place.

"Something's wrong," the woman said.

I looked toward the castle. The guards there had all stopped pacing, calling out to each other.

"Bring me the guardian," a woman's voice echoed throughout the space, causing stalactites to fall from the cave ceiling and smash into the street yards away.

"That's why you got dropped here," the woman told me. "She wants you."

I felt the bile burning the back of my throat. I ran back to the gate and pressed my hand to the padlock. The moment I felt the cold steel, the pain exploded in my skull and the iron turned hot against my palm. A scream burst from my lips as it felt like my entire body was engulfed in flames. My face was pressed to the grass before I realized it and the same voice echoed through my head.

Obey the Ferryman, fear the Shadow Mistress.

I woke up with a shiver, my entire body aching so badly that it took much of my strength to prop myself up. I noticed the witch across from me first, sitting on the floor in a small cell. I was trapped in a similar one; a hunk of bread and a small paper cup of water were on the floor by the door. A loud groan made me jump. In the cell next to mine was a gaunt man with a gray beard. Unlike the woman and me, his arms were shackled behind his back and around a ring bolted to the wall. A heavy-looking metal mask was locked around his mouth so he couldn't talk, although he looked like he wanted to desperately based on the way his eyes widened upon seeing us.

I noticed the plaque mounted above his head. It said he was a werewolf and was set for transfer to prison block 4A, cell 50 in two days. I looked behind me for my own.

Guardian (mortal)
Meeting with Shadow Mistress at sunrise

I turned back to the woman across from me.

"Who is the Shadow Mistress?" I asked. "What the hell is that?"

She held her finger to her lips, crawling to the bars and glancing down the hall. I followed her gaze. There was a single guard at the end, a thick man that had to be near seven-feet. I focused on the padlock above me, but as soon as I did, I felt that same burning sensation crawling over my skin. I gave up before it could grow any worse.

"I made you a promise," the witch whispered.

What was she going to do behind bars? If my powers set off the Shadowland's mind control, then her powers would have a similar effect. I let my body sag against the bars, watching our guard for the next half-hour until he shifted positions. Clearly, he was imprisoned by his job just as we were. At least he got to go home at the end of the day.

I was half awake against the bars when the guard came. The girl held her hand outside the bars just long enough for my guardian senses to pick up the movement, pulling me from my thoughts as I realized her plan. The guard stepped onto the icy patch she'd conjured, and his feet flew out from under him. The sound his head made against the concrete made me wince, but it didn't slow the girl's pace. With more strength than I thought her capable of, she tugged the man closer by his belt and unclipped a set of keys from his hip. Before I could congratulate her, she slid them toward me so that they stopped at my knees.

"Wouldn't it be easier to do your own first?" I asked her.

She shook her head. "They'd find me no matter what," she said. "It could be centuries before you're ever back here to be caught. You go."

I froze for a moment, before the werewolf's groans reminded me of how little time I might have. I twisted my wrist through the bar and plunged the key into the lock. The door swung open loud enough to make my heart skip.

"Wait," she hissed, motioning for me to go to her cell. I drew close to her. She tugged a beautiful gold bracelet from her wrist and slipped it onto mine. "To pay the dock keeper off," she said.

I nodded, moving to the guard next. It took all my strength, but I made sure to push him into the bars of my door to make it look like I'd escaped alone.

I was surprised to find the rest of the dungeon empty of guards, sneaking past the only and last pair at the main door. I was in a long hallway filled with tattered tapestries. The first I passed was of the ferryman, standing at the bow of a boat with a passenger seated behind him. The next were rows and rows of prisoners, some of them busy building more cell blocks off to one side in chains. The third depicted a lake with trees surrounding it and a small dock. In the center of the lake was a kind of green whirlpool.

The last depicted a dark figure at the center, standing on what appeared to be a pile of bodies. She held a ceptor with a half-moon in one hand, a sword in the other, and an antlered crown on top of her head. A second, smaller figure stood farther down the pile, the hood a dead giveaway for the ferry-man. The last figure had long hair, the curvy outline telling me it was a woman. There was almost no light in the picture to make out her face, the glow of the painted moon leaving her face covered by the shadows of the antlered woman.

I paused before the tapestry for a moment. We were being followed by the ferryman and Jamie and I concluded earlier that he had been sent after me on someone else's orders. The tallest figure had to be this Shadow Mistress. So, who was the third woman and what was her part in all of this? I forced myself to focus on finding a way out of the castle. The dark passages were mostly clear of guards, the only pair I encoun-tered too engrossed in their conversation to notice me slip by in the shadows.

I was back on the path within twenty minutes of wandering the castle. I stopped at the guard tower on my way out to pull on a dark cloak. I thought my heart would burst in my chest as I crossed the grassy path between the castle and the main gate. I felt my heart sink when I saw the guards posi-tioned along the dock. There were dozens of them, all armed and spread out nearly halfway down the path. They wore dark uniforms, and I wouldn't have noticed them if I hadn't caught the glint of one of their spears. I froze a yard away from the gate when one of them spotted me.

"Let me see your face," she called out. I had no choice. I

was quick to adjust the hood to hide my hair, fastening the clip high on my neck. I approached the gate as she did. The woman had green scales over her skin and shark-like teeth that were visible only when I stopped just a foot from the gate.

"I'm from the castle," I said, trying my best to make it sound obvious, "to see the ferryman."

The longer she studied my face, the more worried I became. I wasn't sure how much longer my poker face would last. She looked to the two men standing just behind her.

"Um, there was a form about the mistress sending..." The man didn't finish. The woman holding her hand to the padlock and the gate creaked to life. I stepped back just enough so it could swing past me.

"Bow before the noble lady," the woman called, "The Shade of the Shadowlands."

A cry of "All hail the Shade of the Shadowlands!" echoed through the dock as I started forward. Every dark figure bowed my way, not rising until I'd passed. I wanted to run, sure the Shadow Mistress herself would come barreling down the dock after me. I kept my stance tall and my breathing even until I'd passed all of them, letting myself walk a little faster the closer I got to the dock.

The hooded man was standing at the end, his back turned to me. I froze less than five feet away, unsure if he knew I was there. After a full minute, I called out to him. My stomach plummeted as he turned to face me, that eyeless hood staring back.

"Ferry me back," I told him, adding, "It's your task, right?"

After a beat, he surged forward, stopping inches from my face. I kept my eyes on the dock ahead, trying to ignore the rotting smell inside the hood. I heard him breath once before he moved back, holding one bone-white hand up. He rubbed his thumbs against the rest of his fingers before opening his palm out to me.

"I can pay," I answered, holding out my left wrist so that the light caught the metal bracelet. I let out a small squeal when he seized my wrist, holding it close to his hood, inspecting it. He nodded his head.

"Take it," I said, moving to unclasp it.

He held my wrist tighter and shook his head. He pointed to the bracelet and then to me. He did this twice before I thought I understood.

"F-for me? You want me to keep it?" I asked.

He nodded, leading me back toward the edge of the dock. I could just barely make out thin human forms silently floating through the water underneath, making my stomach turn.

"Will you ferry me back to the mortal world?" I asked, a little worried that I hadn't been clear enough.

He nodded his head once. He took my left wrist in his other hand and before I could even suck in enough air to scream, he shoved me over the edge and into the water.

CHAPTER 10

T pulled my head above the surface and opened my mouth to scream when I noticed the difference in my surroundings. Trees circled the entire lake, and it took me a moment to realize why it looked so familiar. It was the lake just miles past Burbrook High in the national park. It was the same lake depicted on the tapestry in the castle, it had to be. I was so excited about finding the sixth gate that it took me a moment to realize how far out from shore I was.

I was out of breath by the time I reached shallow water, taking my time to trudge over the rocky bottom. My feet were sore from the last few hours, forcing me to take a seat at the first picnic bench I found. My new red dress was soaked through, making it heavy. I looked around for the off chance that I'd find a payphone, not surprised when I didn't. Izzy and Jamie had gone almost a hundred years without ever being caught or suspected of anything. Surely, they thought to grab my things before leaving J & J.

I looked down at the gold bracelet over my mark. It was

half a thin bangle, clasped together by a gilded chain. Upon closer inspection, I could just make out the initials in cursive. *E. L. M.* I took it off to get a better look at it, finding an inscription on the inside.

I love you forever- Jay

Who was Jay? It made me think about Jay Gatsby from *The Great Gatsby*. It was one of the few novels we read in school that didn't have the rest of the class groaning the entire time we were ordered to turn to a new chapter. Just then, I remembered how close I was to the school. It was maybe three miles away. It hadn't been that long ago since I quit volleyball. Even without any shoes, I could make it three miles, right?

I hadn't even passed all the campsites before it started raining. As embarrassing as it would be, I hoped someone would drive by and see me. No matter who it was, a ride back to school would be better than walking in the rain, in my homecoming dress, without any shoes on. I gathered fistfuls of sopping fabric in my hands to keep the mud from further ruining the dress as I went. I was panting by the time I made it to the empty parking lot.

I tried all the front doors before I found the single open one, slipping on the tile with my first step. It was weird. The entire entryway was dark aside from the backlighting in the trophy case. I noticed the memorial still clinging to the glass around Noah's football picture. Alison's vase of roses was long gone now, but the remnants of green wolf-shape notes littered the glass. What was once an organized ring of mascots was now a smattering of simple paper, a few littering the floor underneath where they had become victims of the mob of students rushing to make it to class on time.

I rubbed the mud off my feet the best I could, mostly collecting dust from the dirty rug, before I went to look at the notes. Just a few short weeks ago, I was climbing out of the twisted metal of Noah's convertible. I barely knew the Quinns and yet it felt like we shared a tighter bond than anything I'd been a part of before. My stomach sank fast as I thought about how little time Noah Peterson had had and how much longer a life I was destined for. I could live another century or more before I found my match. It dawned on me then that it didn't really matter that I'd found the gate. The marks on my wrist bore the instructions. There was more to our circle than just the three of us and we all needed to find our matches before we could ever seal the gate.

A light flicked on to my left and when I looked, Mr. Puck was standing in the door of his classroom with his cellphone raised to his ear. His mouth was parted in shock as he took me in. I looked down at myself, feeling my face heat with embarrassment at the grimy spots I'd left on the white tile around me. He'd already called Becky once about my slipping grades and he told me he was concerned that I'd quit volleyball and changed friends senior year.

"Um, no," he finally said into the phone. "It's just one of the custodians leaving. I'm sorry I interrupted your evening, Mr. Thackery." The screen of Mr. Puck's phone went black as he lowered it and shoved it into his pocket, still staring at me in awe.

"The door was open. I just walked right in," I said, unable to keep the awkward laugh from tumbling out.

He sighed in disbelief and looked down the dark hall. I was

beginning to wonder now why he hadn't turned me in to the principal.

"What are you doing here?" he asked.

"I lost my phone and I need to call for a ride," I said, hoping he wouldn't comment on my attire. He looked over me another time, his expression changing from shock to serious so fast that I begun to realize how cold it was.

"I don't understand," he said under his breath, letting the door close behind him. I waited for him to speak again, but he didn't. Mr. Puck let out a sigh and adjusted the tie around his neck and then both cuffs of his shirt.

"I know it's late, but I just need like one minute to call Jamie Quinn," I said.

He scoffed again, propping open his door.

"I've already called your aunt once, Victoria," he said. "And I don't know what the hell you were doing to show up in a ball gown with no shoes to school, after hours, and practically breaking in to do it. We talked before about how stupid it is to risk it all as a senior, but I'll make you a deal just this once."

I felt my heart leap in my chest. A deal? It had to be near midnight now and he was going to just let me off?

"Thank you, Mr. Puck," I said. "I swear I won't be in any more trouble at school. I'm going to go to the tutoring sessions before school and I swear I'll be back to an A next week." He opened his mouth to speak and pointed a finger at me. He froze like that for a moment, not making a sound. His eyes roved over me again and he lowered his arm. He grasped his left wrist and gave it a squeeze so that his knuckles turned white.

"How many noble gases are there?" He finally asked. I had been prepared to defend myself, ready with a fake story about leaving my phone at home and my car breaking down. I had been working on the reason for the fancy dress when he'd asked.

"What?" I finally asked.

"I won't ask again, and you won't get another pass from me," he said. "How many noble gases are there?"

"Six," I said, listing off two before he started back into his classroom. I stopped talking and followed him. He opened the top drawer to his desk and took out his school ID. He fished in his pocket for his phone, unlocking it and sliding it down the first table toward me.

"I'm going to grab you some clothes from the donation pile in the office. If anyone finds out you were here, I thought you called your aunt," he said. "Am I understood?"

I nodded, waiting until he'd left the room before I typed my number into the keypad. I hoped they had my phone on them to feel it vibrate and I prayed they didn't mute the unknown number the way I so often did. After several seconds the ringing stopped, and I heard Jamie's voice on the other end.

"God, Jamie," I breathed. "You won't believe what happened."

"Are you okay? Where are you?" he asked. I could hear Izzy asking in the background and the sound of a car door slam shut.

"I'm fine. I'm at school and I need you to pick me up. Mr. Puck let me use his phone and said he wouldn't get me in trouble," I said.

Jamie went quiet for a moment, and I was sure he was just as shocked as I was.

"We're still in Holston. Damn it," he said. "Stay there. Izzy's going to stay here to clean up. I'm coming to get you."

I felt like I was going to throw up now that I checked the clock above the desk. It was well past my curfew.

"Becky and Mark are going to lock me away the rest of the year," I said.

"We've been texting Becky since you went missing. She

called once and Izzy told her we got a flat tire and that our mom is coming to fix it. She did a great job mimicking your voice," Jamie said, letting out a forced laugh. I could tell he was keeping his cool only so I would— not that it was working.

"How did you get into my phone? I never told you my password," I said.

"It's volleygirl9," he said. "It's all over the cork board over your desk. You were half-asleep when you told me about Becky not letting you use your name when you made your Instagram account. You used that instead. You're a volleyball player. Your jersey number is nine. You're not as invisible as you think."

I didn't reply. I didn't remember telling him that story at all. I think Macy is the only person who ever knew my old screen name, because I was with her when I'd made it. Even now, I didn't think I could remember what was tacked above my desk as well as Jamie seemed to. The classroom door opened.

"This will be a lot warmer," Mr. Puck said, holding up a folded pair of sweats and a cheap pair of flip-flops I could already tell would be too big.

"I'll see you in a bit," I told Jamie, hanging up and setting the phone down on the table. Mr. Puck let me use the staff bathroom down the hall to change. I squeezed as much water as I could from the dress before I pulled on the new clothes. They were old basketball sweats, the back of the hoodie bearing the names of the senior players from six years ago. Aside from the flip-flops, it was all a perfect fit.

I was surprised that Mr. Puck hadn't waited for me outside the door. I turned off the light like he'd asked and started back down the hall toward the sliver of light from his open classroom door. I could hear the clinking of glasses coming from the room as I grew closer. He was at the back of the room, setting small stands of test tubes at the tables for Monday's lab.

"Thank you," I said.

He turned from the box, studying me for a moment before speaking.

"When did you start seeing Jamie Quinn?" he asked.

I nearly tripped over the leg of a chair at the first table, bashing my knee into the corner.

"We aren't..." I let the words hang in the air as I felt my body heat again.

He nodded his head, but his expression remained curious as if he didn't believe me.

"Okay," he said, "You've been very distracted since you and Jamie finally started to get along in class and I noticed that you and Macy had a falling out. Whatever fight you had with her doesn't seem to bother you though." I wanted to ask how he knew, but I stopped myself. With a teacher in the hall every ten feet, they were bound to hear and see more of what went on than we thought.

"It's sorta complicated. You could say it started that night of the accident," I said. My stomach started to churn again. Mr. Puck abandoned the box and moved around the table, stopping to lean against Jamie's and my usual spot.

"I've always thought Macy was a bad influence for you, but Jamie Quinn..." he shook his head. It was the same unsure expression that Becky and Mark got on their faces whenever I mentioned spending time with Jamie.

"Jamie's not the reason my grades dropped or that I quit volleyball, or the reason Macy and I aren't friends," I said.

"Why did you quit volleyball?" he asked.

I felt an ache of frustration in my gut at his questions. The last thing I needed was anyone thinking that I was having any kind of trouble.

"I wanted to focus on my grades. I love volleyball, but I'm not good enough for a division one school and I want to get into the best college that I can. Without practices and games, I can focus on the next SAT," I said, repeating the same excuse I'd given Becky. The room was painfully quiet. I tried to keep my expression even so he wouldn't ask any more questions.

I turned my attention to Mr. Puck's desk, noticing how much empty space there was. It was like he'd just moved into the room. Most of my teachers stuffed their desks with family photos, organizational trays in matching themes, or coffee mugs. He had a lesson plan binder open next to the desktop, a single pencil, and a dwindling stack of sticky notes sitting in the corner.

Mr. Puck started teaching at Burbrook High my freshman year. For a while, he'd been the most popular teacher in the building. He was in his twenties, just starting his career, straight from an Ivy League university. He also dressed like a model and looked the part, so that alone captivated every-one's' attention until they realized how strict he was. After getting nothing personal out of him, the student body went from pining after him to dreading his class.

"Are you always here this late?" I asked. "It's a Friday."

He straightened up, checking the clock.

"Put out the rest of those test tubes. Every table gets one rack," he said and pointed to the box. He passed me for his desk, taking up the pencil and bending over his binder. I did as I was told. It was a small price to pay to keep him from turning me in. When I finished, I sat at the table near the door. After a few minutes, Mr. Puck's phone rang. His mouth pulled into a frown when he answered it.

"Don't come in," he said, "I'll walk her out."

He hung up and gathered his things into a tote bag. I could see the muddy spots over the tile in the moonlight as we crossed the entryway. Jamie's black Audi was parked next to the curb. Mr. Puck stopped outside the door to make sure it was locked behind us. I gave him an awkward wave goodbye before I settled into the Audi's warm passenger seat. I balled up the red dress and sat it on the floorboard.

"I knew I should've gone," Jamie said, shifting into drive and turning away from the curb.

"I don't need a babysitter," I said.

Jamie let out a sigh. He relaxed a little in his seat.

"I know," he said. I could hear the reluctance in his voice. It almost sounded pained, chasing away every bit of anger I felt toward him for his protectiveness. He's lived through worse things than tonight's attack. He was immortal and he'd spent the last decade defying death with his sister. So, why did he act as though I was made of glass?

"Even though I wasn't, if I had been injured it would've healed within minutes," I pointed out.

"Tori, please," he said.

"If I died like Izzy did tonight, I'd just wake back up again. I'd be totally fine."

"Stop," he snapped. He took a deep breath before he spoke. "It's not fine. I have a pretty good idea what happened to you based on where you ended up. Guardians don't just get sucked into the Shadowlands and find their way back out again. You don't just... I can't face that again. I need you to be more careful."

I wondered what he'd meant by "again," but I didn't want to ask. I was the one who'd been trapped in that cell, not Jamie. Why was he so much more frightened by the ordeal than I was? Had I missed something in that castle? I thought about the figures in the tapestry: the Shadow Mistress, the ferryman, and the third woman. Was that mystery woman the reason for the extra fear I was seeing now in his eyes, the piece to the puzzle I had seemingly missed?

"You knew the lake was the entrance to the sixth gate?" I asked.

He just nodded, barely pausing at the stop sign before pulling onto the gravel road.

"What else did you know?" I asked him.

He didn't speak right away, his expression tightening as if he was still trying to decide what to say.

"We all knew that someone ordered the ferryman to the mortal world. I wasn't sure that it was because of you until..." He didn't need to finish. I could feel a headache coming on, reminding me of the sharp pain of the echoing voice.

Silence filled the space, my eyes catching the sliver of gold on my wrist. I pushed the left sleeve of the hoodie back just enough to look at the bracelet. I wish I had asked for her name. The witch could've escaped with me, but she chose to stay behind and gave me a priceless gift by the looks of it. I wondered what the story behind the gilded bracelet was. It looked expensive, the rain not tarnishing it at all. She knew so much, so much more than I do. As much as I hated Jamie's worrying, maybe there was more validity there than I knew.

"I won't stay if you don't want me to," Jamie said.

I hadn't realized we had stopped outside my house until now. I could tell he wanted to talk. His expression had softened, much different than the serious manner I was so used to.

"Wait for me to open the window," I said, grabbing the dress and stepping back into the rain. He pulled around the corner like he always did as I went to the front door. I heard Mark stop speaking mid-sentence as soon as I shut the door behind me. Both my aunt and uncle came into the living room in their pajamas.

"Did they get Izzy's car fixed?" Becky asked, pulling me into a hug and stepping back to look at my new clothes. Mark remained in the doorway to the kitchen, the scowl on his face telling me that he didn't believe a word of the story Izzy and Jamie had told them.

"Izzy and I got the tire changed before her mom got to us. We took the car to a shop to get the dents and scratches out," I said.

Becky let out a sigh of relief. She'd been easy to worry since the accident and I was glad that she hadn't thought to drive to Holston herself.

"What's with the clothes?" Mark asked, pointing to me.

"We got caught in the rain changing the tire. Mrs. Quinn keeps extras in the back of her car," I said, looking down at the oversized flip-flops.

"Take those off," Mark said, his tone so sharp that even Becky jumped at it. "You're going to track mud all through the house," he said. I slipped off the flip-flops, the cheap foam squelching under my fingers. Becky took a deep breath, the kind she usually did whenever she wanted to tell off Mark.

"Is that your homecoming dress?" she asked, trying her best to look excited as she took the wet fabric from my hands. She held it out, Mark letting out a mumble when she shook it and muddy drops flecked onto the floor from the hem. I was surprised at how well the fabric kept its shape and glad that I'd chosen a more structured dress over the flowy tulle I'd first picked up.

"I accidentally dropped it in a puddle when we took Izzy's car to the shop. Do you think we can save it?" I asked, again hearing Mark grumbling something about the value of a dollar. Becky took a closer look at the mud around the hem, checking the tag at the back for washing instructions.

"It should all come out easy enough," she said. "I'll toss it in the washer, and we'll see." Mark moved from his spot at last, taking the dress from Becky's hands.

"No," he told her, holding the dress out to me with a

reproachful look on his face. "It's your dress. Your aunt and I are going to bed, and you can stay up and try and fix it yourself. If it's ruined, then you can earn the money for another."

I took the dress with a nod, noticing the annoyed gaze Becky was sending Mark. They both wished me goodnight and went upstairs.

I went through the kitchen to the sliding laundry doors. After scrubbing as much of the dirt and grime from the hem of the dress as I could, I started the washing machine. The light was off in Becky and Mark's bedroom when I went to the bathroom. My hair was a tangled mess from the rain, making it painful to brush through. When I looked down, I caught sight of the bracelet. I unclasped it and dropped it into a drawer with the rest of my rarely worn pieces before going to my bedroom to pull on a pajama set Becky gave me last Christmas.

I sat by myself for a while in the room. Just as Jamie had described, my desk was full of old volleyball pictures and handwritten notes from Macy with my not-so-secret screen name written on them. I tugged everything from the cork board. I cleared my desk of everything related to volleyball and Macy, leaving only a few honor student certificates and first-place ribbons for contests I no longer remembered pinned to the sparse board.

I had been so set on making senior year special. I was tired of being invisible. The words Jamie had said over the phone rang in my head and stopped my work. *You're not as invisible as you think.* It was never the attention I really wanted. I just wanted to feel like a part of the group, invisible or not. I blinked back the tears before they could fall and focused on rearranging the certificates above my desk, accepting the stretches of empty space after I grew tired of reattaching my honor roll letter.

I pulled back the blinds and slid open my window, spotting

Jamie looking back at me from the base of the oak tree. He always made it look so easy, jumping to my window and pulling himself inside with strength only he possessed. I could tell his mood had lightened a little since the tense conversation in the car before. He had a backpack with him this time, which he shrugged out of and sat gently to the floor. I noticed his eyes go to the cleared-off desk area before he looked back at me.

"You came prepared," I said.

He sat the clean clothes from his bag aside to look at me.

"It's like I said earlier. I don't care if I've made my bed and changed clothes, I'll leave without a single word if you ask. I don't want you to feel like I'm hovering or make you feel uncomfortable about..."

I thought I had imagined it at first, but Jamie was blushing. He hid it well, tucking his bag into his designated corner of the room. I went to the nightstand and tugged open the bottom drawer where I stashed my volleyball spandex and club jerseys.

"Jamie Quinn, you are a tightass old man trapped in the body of a controlling seventeen-year-old. I'm a part of this circle now too and you won't treat me like I'm going to fall apart if you're not around. I don't need some boy to catch me if I fall, mostly because guardians can't die and they recover fast, but also because I am strong enough to handle the reality. I'd rather know the truth and face the worst of it all than be a burden in a fight. Izzy says I only make the circle stronger, but I can't do that if you won't let me," I said, emptying out the contents of the drawer onto my bed before I looked up at Jamie. His cheeks were tinged pink, making my stomach do somersaults.

"Tightass, huh?" he asked, scratching the stubble on his chin. "Sure you don't mean my literal ass?"

I threw a pair of spandex shorts at him, smacking him

square in the face.

"Your ass might be the only nice thing about you, Jamie," I said, feeling the heat rush to my face immediately. I was glad that he didn't reply, refolding my shorts and sitting them back on the bed. "This drawer is for you. I do my own laundry, so no one will ever know you leave stuff here." I gathered my volleyball clothes in my arms and took them to the closet, dropping them into a heap on the floor and closing the door.

"Thanks," Jamie said, staring into the empty drawer for a moment. "You're right though, about me. I am uptight and too protective and controlling. My power is strength. I forget that sometimes strength of mind is way more valuable than strength of body. Izzy puts on a good face, but she was pissed when she lost you tonight. We almost got pulled into it all when the police got there; she was so mad at herself. You're the most level-headed of us all, Tori, and I don't give you enough credit for that."

We stared at each other for a moment. I wasn't sure what to say to that. A simple thanks seemed stupid, but anything more than that would have left me a blushing mess.

"Why won't you train me?" I asked, watching his shoulders tense. "I don't mean helping me learn to use my telekinesis at night like we've been doing. I mean teaching me to fight like Izzy did." Izzy was clearly trained in self-defense. She searched herself just before I blacked out as if she was used to carrying a weapon.

"It has nothing to do with you," Jamie said, going back to the corner for his backpack.

"This is what I mean, Jamie," I said. "You can't close yourself off to the world just because you have a secret to keep, least of all shut Izzy and me out." Jamie let out a long breath and straightened up. He turned to look at me.

"Learning to fight is very physical and it's rough and with

my powers," He paused to take another calming breath. "I'm afraid I might hurt you."

I let out a laugh. I'd taken enough volleyballs to the face to know I could take a punch. There were still marks on the inside of my lips from the braces I wore for a year when I started playing.

"You taught Izzy, didn't you?" I asked. I could tell my assumption was right when he struggled to reply right away. He let his hand fist in his hair before he'd calmed down enough to speak.

"I trained her right after we woke, but that was different. It's different taking a few swings at your sister," he said.

"I'm a part of your circle. If I can fight, then there would be three of us to take on whoever attacks us instead of just two," I said. He knew he couldn't argue against that. There was no way we could seal the gate if I didn't educate myself. Just like any sports team, you can't win unless every member on the court is ready to play.

"You're not just any member of the circle, Tori," he said.

The words hung heavy in the air. I felt my stomach squirm. I wanted to touch him, reach out and take his hand until I found the right words to explain why he felt so important to me. A larger part of me wanted to keep arguing with him, but something about that felt a little like pouring salt onto an open wound. I'd gotten everything I'd wanted so far. I didn't have to press for Jamie to know I was right.

"If you want to use the bathroom, now would be a good time. I have to go downstairs to switch the laundry," I said.

Jamie followed me into the hall with his toothbrush and toothpaste in hand. I was glad for the subtle hum of the washer and the privacy. It felt like I hadn't relaxed until the moment I made it to the kitchen. There was still five minutes left on the cycle, sparing me a little time to compose myself.

Why was I so embarrassed? Normal people didn't usually blush whenever they stood up for themselves or demanded things.

The dress looked exactly as it did in the store when the spin cycle ended. There wasn't a single stain anywhere on the fabric, easing my guilt about the money Becky had given me to buy it. I started the dryer and went back to my room, finding Jamie sitting at my desk. He didn't look up from the cork board until I closed the door.

"You don't have to erase your past to make space for the future," Jamie said.

I switched off the overhead light, the lamp next to the bed the only source of dim light in the entire room. I flipped back my comforter and settled in.

"I can't believe I ever thought Macy was actually my friend and I'd like to forget that," I said.

Jamie snorted and rose from the chair.

"Forget Macy," he said, straightening the blankets he'd laid over the floor while I was gone. "You aren't Macy, and she doesn't determine who you are. You should wear Pink Floyd T-shirts and leather cuffs, if that's what you want. You should keep all your volleyball stuff where it is, if you want to. Just because a few things about you had to change, like your mortality, doesn't mean that anything else needs to. Frankly, all that stuff you had on the first day may not have been your style, but the way you acted was more you than I'd ever seen."

I couldn't hold back the smile, feeling it tugging on the corners of my mouth. He smirked back at me, pulling the blanket over himself and laying down on his side so he could see me. I leaned over for the switch on my lamp and the room went dark. The springs in my mattress gave a small squeak as I laid down.

"Goodnight, Tightass," I said. I didn't need any light to know he was smiling.

"Go to sleep, Mindfreak," he replied.

CHAPTER 11

I noticed that Jamie was gone as soon as I woke up. His blankets were folded and replaced in their spot in my closet. I managed to sleep better than I had since the accident, yet I was up hours earlier than I usually was on a Saturday. I showered and dressed before I noticed that the bulletin board over my desk had been redecorated again.

My certificates and academic ribbons were still tacked along the left edge as I'd left them, a plaque for the year our volleyball team won the tournament at team camp leaned against the wall. My MVP medal was draped over one corner of the board, the sun glinting off the gold surface. There was a very detailed drawing of a spoon on a pink index card, pinned next to a small picture of Mark and me holding up the single fish we'd caught on a camping trip when I was seven.

Three rectangular photos, all printed on one of those tiny phone printers, were pinned next to the drawing. The photo pinned closest to the drawing was one Izzy made me take with her. We were standing in front of the Maserati just seconds before we went into the Italian restaurant in Holston. Izzy's hand angled her phone slightly downward, just enough to give my usually thin and gangly body a little more shape at the waist.

The next photo was pinned on top of a green notecard, forming a kind of frame around the picture of Izzy and me talking on the couch in the Moore house. The third picture was pinned dead center on the board, clearly meant as a focal point. Jamie had written *Mindfreak* on the white space at the bottom of the photo paper. The picture looked like it had been taken by a professional with high quality equipment. I was sitting on the porch of Becky and Mark's house, leaning against one of the white posts. It was raining, providing a kind of ghostly glow. *King Lear* was propped up on my knees. He'd somehow managed to blur my surroundings, making me stand out in the photo. He must have taken it when he picked me up one morning.

I added the spoon bracelet to the collection, letting it curve around the top of the board, before I went downstairs to retrieve my dress from the dryer. Becky and Mark were having breakfast, both still dressed in pajamas. I shook the dress when I pulled it from the drum, the structured fabric releasing any wrinkles it had from being crumpled all night.

"That looks like new," Becky said as I held it up to inspect it. There wasn't a single stain anywhere on the fabric, easing my worry about affording a new one.

"It looks like half of it is missing," Mark said, setting his coffee cup down. Becky and I both snorted. I held the dress to my body, letting Becky pull on the fabric at the waist so that it stretched around my stomach.

"It has an open back," I said, turning the dress so he could see.

"There's so much missing that you're gonna show off more

than a little back," he said. "You're gonna have a little crack peeking out, if not a whole damn cheek."

Becky gasped, telling him to calm down. I took the dress upstairs and hung it in the closet. Their voices only grew louder with each exchange about teenage girls being too sexualized in society and Mark's comments about letting me run around half naked.

"It's on you when she gets herself pregnant," Mark yelled.

"You say that like it doesn't take an equally-as-stupid man to get her there," Becky called back.

I checked my phone, a text from Izzy asking me to come over to talk about last night. I didn't hesitate, grabbing the first pair of shoes from my closet and slipping them on.

"I'll be at the Quinns house," I said as I went downstairs. I could tell by the look on Mark's face that he didn't like the idea, but he handed me the keys to the Beetle nonetheless and looked to Becky as if I'd somehow just proved some point he'd just made. I sent Izzy a quick text that I was on my way before I pulled out of the driveway.

The gate to the Moore Estate was still pulled open from the day I'd unknowingly broken it. The garage was open, and Izzy's yellow Maserati, Jamie's black Audi, and his motorcycle were parked down the long driveway. I parked at the end of the line and got out, spotting Jamie next to his bike with a sponge in his hand. The hose was curled over the concrete. I focused on the handle of the sprayer and within seconds, water shot from the end. The hose lashed around, drenching the front of Jamie's jeans and T-shirt with water. I lost my focus immediately, shutting off the stream and leaving Jamie dripping.

"I'm getting better," I said with a laugh, pulling my phone from my pocket. He looked my way, smirking. I snapped a picture once he was in focus and pocketed the phone. "At least I tell you when I'm taking pictures of you," I said.

He snorted, dropping the sponge into the bucket at his feet and taking up the hose.

"The best photos are taken when the subject doesn't expect them. Real moments," he said, squeezing just enough to spray the concrete just feet from me. I wondered just how many "real" moments he had collected on his phone. He flashed a smile before turning to wash the bubbles from the motorcycle.

"I'll be inside with Izzy," I said.

"I'll be a bit," he said, motioning to the line of cars behind him, "but I'll meet you in there."

I went through the door in the garage and called out for Izzy, hearing her yell something back from upstairs. I checked her bedroom first, but she wasn't there. I noticed the next door was left open, finding Jamie's bedroom.

It was a large space, bookshelves covering the wall on the right. They were full mostly with classics, the binding in pristine condition considering how old they were. After checking a copy of *A Tale of Two Cities*, I concluded that most of them were collector's editions. I carefully put the book back on the shelf and took a step back. Some shelves held collections of records and CDs, framed pictures interspersed throughout. Most of Jamie's pictures were of scenery, lots of trees and plants.

I found the tiny iPhone printer sitting on a low shelf. After looking over the sleek box, I figured out how to use it. I plugged it into my phone and within seconds, Jamie's picture was sliding out from the printer. He looked relaxed, reminding me of how open and honest he'd been last night. I was used to the business side of Jamie Quinn, focused on finding more guardians and sealing the gate, the same serious boy who'd argued with his sister when she accused him of being a killjoy.

I almost hated how photogenic he was. All he'd done was turn my way and smirk, and yet the photo looked like the ones printed on glossy magazine pages. It was as if he'd strategically wetted his T-shirt rather than me surprising him with a garden hose. The jeans looked like they had a dark acid wash now, the extra weight from the water making them sag on his hip bones, perfectly outlined thanks to the T-shirt sticking to his chest.

I slipped the picture deep into my pocket and sat the printer back on the shelf when I remembered that Izzy was waiting for me somewhere in the house. I continued my search, finding her in a large room at the end of the hallway. There was a pool table in one corner, ping-pong, foosball, and other games scattered throughout the space. Izzy was sitting on a squishy couch at the back, the chess table covered instead with mugs and a half-full pot of coffee.

"Jamie told me you were in the Shadowlands," she said, straightening up and motioning me over, "What the hell happened?"

I hurried across the room and sank into the couch, pouring myself a cup of coffee as I recounted all the details. I told her all about the series of gates, the castle, the girl who'd saved me, and how the ferryman tossed me into the lake, and how I swam to the surface to find myself back just miles from Burbrook High.

"I thought Mr. Puck was going to turn me in for sure," I said.

Izzy didn't look as shocked as I anticipated, her expression more like confusion.

"Mr. Puck didn't even give you a lecture or think it was weird that you were in a dirty dress?" she asked, sliding her hands down her waist and onto her hips.

"Don't say it like that," I said. "You make it sound weirdly sexual."

She made a face at me as if that was exactly what she'd meant. My stomach knotted tight, and I felt myself go faint.

"No," I said. "I told you, he let me use his phone to call for a ride. Nothing happened between then and when Jamie picked me up, I swear. He asked me all kinds of questions about why I quit volleyball and my grades. He's been on my case about college stuff since the accident."

"He knows something, Tori," Izzy said.

Jamie had entered the room seconds before, asking me who we were talking about. I recounted exactly what had happened after I got to the school, including every annoying question Mr. Puck had asked me. Izzy laughed when I told them Puck thought Jamie was a bad influence.

"If he thinks you're a badass, wait until he meets me," she said, pointing from Jamie to herself.

"There's no reason for you to meet him when you're here shadowing the athletic trainer," Jamie said.

Izzy rolled her eyes.

"Well, I think he's up to something and I'm going to find out for myself," she said, "What if he's a demon and he's working with the ferryman?"

I wasn't even sure if the ferryman was still following us. What was the point of pulling me into the Shadowlands after all? I had escaped the Shadow Mistress and he didn't seem to care that much. He just let me go for free.

"Then he would've taken Tori's blood last night when he had her alone instead of covering for her," Jamie said. "Puck could've gotten her suspended or even arrested for breaking and entering, but he agreed not to even call her aunt and uncle."

"Which is why he's up to something," Izzy argued.

"Let's go back to the fact that the ferryman wants my blood, or someone does at least," I said, glad that the question put an end to their fighting. They exchanged nervous looks. "The vampire had a knife and a vial with her. Instead of sucking my blood, she was trying to collect it," I said, jump-starting the conversation again.

"We just don't know what they want it for," Izzy said, "or, why the ferryman didn't take it when you were unconscious with him."

She had a good point. Why didn't he just take my blood then when I was unable to defend myself? Maybe there was some kind of stipulation on how he had to get it? Jamie stood up, balling his hands into tight fists before relaxing. He wore the same pained expression he had when he picked me up the night before. He looked back at me.

"Follow me," he said and started back across the room. Izzy and I had to jog to catch up with him in the hall. Jamie led us down a second set of stairs at the back of the house, giving a view of the stone waterfall that emptied into the pool in the backyard. Instead of taking us out the back door, he opened one just before the kitchen to reveal another set of stairs. He turned the lights on and started down ahead of us.

"What are you doing, Jamie?" Izzy asked.

"Keeping a promise," he answered from the bottom.

The basement was almost completely empty. One wall was covered in large mirrors, racks of weights sitting in front. A few benches were pressed against the wall at the back and a few bars for deadlifts were propped in the corner. I noticed how squishy the floor was when I stepped farther into the room, looking down at the gray padding under my sneakers. I understood what promise he was so intent on keeping now.

"You're going to teach me to fight," I said.

Izzy looked my way, mouth open.

"Now you think she should know how to protect herself?" she asked. "You know, only after you couldn't do it yourself."

"It's not about gender," I said before Jamie could answer.

He gave me a nod in agreement and Izzy relaxed a bit to look at me.

"I was worried about her not being ready," Jamie said. "and I thought we could keep the ferryman away until we found more guardians for our circle, but we can't take that chance anymore. Tori wants to learn, and I promised I'd teach her."

I didn't understand why Izzy was so surprised. I thought she'd be excited that Jamie had stopped playing protector and realized I was capable of everything he was. She gave us both strange looks, as if she thought there was more to the promise than just some sparring.

"Okay then," she said with a laugh, "As much as I want to watch her kick your teeth in, I have pretend homework to do."

I could tell Jamie had wanted her to stay, but Izzy was already halfway up the stairs when he moved to stop her. The door closed behind her, and the room went silent. Jamie turned to face me again. His expression had changed, face blank and eyes flicking from mine to the rest of the room and back again. I could tell he was out of his element, and it was funny to watch the normally prepared boy scramble for ideas.

"Let's start with the basics," I said. "Like, what's an athletic position for this?" I asked.

He looked up at me as if I'd spoken another language.

"Athletic position?" he asked.

I shrugged, widening my stance and bending my knees into a squat.

"Like this," I said. "An athletic position for volleyball would be low so you can pass the ball. What would a base position be for a fight?"

He let out a sigh and nodded his head, turning red in the face.

"So, you want to keep your legs apart like you just did," he said, waiting until I stood just right to continue. "Keep on your toes in case you need to lunge quickly or even make a break for it. Keep your hands up and ready to strike or defend your face," he said, pausing to raise my hands a little more and warn me about keeping my fingers spread too far apart. "Wide hands lead to broken fingers." He stepped closer to me to explain the best way to incapacitate an opponent.

"You hit these points, you make it harder to be attacked," he said, raising a hand to my face so his fingers just brushed the bridge of my nose. "Eyes." He slowly brought his right fist forward, flattening his hand so the heel of his palm just barely touched the end of my nose.

"The nose," he said, switching arms again. His left hand went completely flat like a blade. He brought it around in one smooth swoop, letting it rest at the side of my neck. I felt his hand soften a little, the pad of his thumb grazing my skin once. "The neck. Chop like I showed you, or an elbow here can stun an attacker." He ran his index finger lightly down the spot, from my chin to collar. He took a step back and I let out a breath.

He bent down on one knee, patting my right calve twice before wrapping both arms around them so they laced together. "A kick to almost any part of the leg is good," he said. "You can sweep them if you kick here." He ran his left hand farther down my calf, gently squeezing the spot where my Achilles tendon was most prominent. He drew his hand to the back of my knee, nearly shifting all my weight backward with a gentle push. He smirked and looked up at me. "That will send anyone buckling. Aand a kick here can really hurt someone, but it's less likely to imbalance someone." He brought his hand around to my kneecap. He used both hands this time, sandwiching my knee between both palms.

"A kick on either side of the knee will imbalance an attacker and easily break the joint," he said. His hands stilled on my leg, and he scooted back and got to his feet. "Kicking the groin will definitely keep someone away," he said.

I could still feel his hands over my skin, taking me a moment for the rest of my body to catch up to what he'd said.

"You don't need to be the Karate Kid to know that one," I said.

He smiled, relaxing a little more as I did. He showed me the best ways to attack next. I repeated the arm swings, punches, and jabs as he directed, needing a little longer to get all the kicks just right. We walked through different possible attacks carefully, stopping each time when Jamie subdued me. After I successfully swept his legs out from under him, I took a step back in surprise.

"Are you okay?" I asked.

He propped himself up on his elbows, rubbing the back of his head.

"Don't stop. Don't ever just stop," he said, checking his pockets before fishing a pair of earbuds from the right. He tossed them to me. "What are those?" he asked.

I held them up so he could see, doing my best to untangle the knot that had formed.

"A pair of earbuds," I said with a laugh.

He shook his head. "That's a weapon," he said, his tone sending a shiver over my skin. "Anything and everything can be used as a weapon. Find it and use it however you have to in order to keep safe."

I wrapped the cord around my hand, feeling the tension grow the more I tugged. I couldn't imagine myself taking it that far, but I had never seriously thought I'd have to prepare for that moment.

"I was stuck in a dressing room with that vampire," I said, remembering the moment. "Izzy couldn't get to me."

Jamie's jaw tightened.

"I tried using a clothes hanger to stake her," I said.

He nodded his head. "Good. That's good." He got to his feet. "And now you'll know a few more tricks for next time."

He took a deep breath and told me to run through the moves again. He taught me how to escape some holds after he'd captured me a few times, not letting up for a break until I got good at them. After working up a sweat, he helped me strengthen my powers. I focused on lifting a five-pound dumbbell off the mat. It shuttered a few times, but I finally gave up when my head began to ache.

"I had the opposite problem when I first woke," Jamie said, helping me off the floor.

"I'm imagining you hulking out each time Izzy made one of her jokes at you," I said with a laugh.

Jamie smiled, picking up the dumbbell with his foot and replacing it on the rack before the mirrors. I thought about the spoon he'd bent into a bracelet at lunch, one of the first times he'd used his powers in front of me. The spoon had become part of the new collage above my desk. I remembered the tiny photo tucked in my pocket that was surely creased now after all the kicking and lunging.

"I should go home and shower," I said, sliding a few fingers into my pocket to make sure the picture was still there as I started up the stairs.

"Tori," Jamie said. I turned to look at him. He opened his mouth to speak but closed it a second later. I wondered what he wanted to ask, feeling a pit form in my stomach. "Keep your mark hidden," he said, nodding toward the black writing curling up my forearm. I nodded and went back down the stairs to take my jacket from a rack of weights. Izzy waved at me from the living room couch as I passed for the front door.

The Beetle looked funny parked halfway down the long driveway. The walk to it felt long, giving me more time than I'd wanted to think about all the training. I knew I still only had a slim chance of making it out of a real fight without a scratch, but it was a start and even more than just being able to protect myself, it gave me a boost of satisfaction to know that Jamie had willingly relinquished that role. I settled into the seats as I remembered what he said when he picked me up from school after the attack. Our circle had lost someone in the Shadowlands before. He'd said that guardians don't just walk into the Shadowlands without their match and walk back out again.

I jumped when I heard my phone buzz in the cupholder, rattling loudly against the faded plastic. I wondered how long I'd been sitting in the driver's seat as I answered the call, hearing Izzy on the other side.

"Is something wrong with your car? You've been sitting there for a while," she said.

I thought about telling her that it just took a bit to get it to turn over, but I stopped myself. Izzy would try driving me herself and I wasn't sure I wanted to go home just yet.

"I'm fine," I said, finding my keys in the passenger seat and jamming them into the ignition. "I was answering a text from Becky." The engine screeched to life before fading to a hum.

"I wish your aunt and uncle wouldn't say anything and let me give you the Maserati." Izzy said, "Even the Jeep is better than that thing you drive."

I loved driving Izzy's yellow car in Holston and would've taken the car the first time she offered it to me if Becky and Mark wouldn't throw a fit about it. The Beetle had been Becky's first car and she still loved it despite how banged up it was. Mark had sold his motorcycle and 2008 Honda, now driving his work truck, so that I would have the Beetle when I turned sixteen. They were still paying for the Ford Escape Becky got when I took her car.

"If only," I said, putting the car in drive. I promised to text her later and hung up, turning around and starting back down the winding mountain road.

After driving a few miles, I decided to go back to the lake. There were so many thoughts swirling through my mind that the drive felt short. My heart sank when I saw the silver chain stretched across the entrance, pulling onto the dirt shoulder behind a silver Toyota. I got out and walked to the entrance to read the sign attached to the chain.

Campsites closed for maintenance.

Assuming the campsites were the only closed portion of the park, I ducked under the bar and followed the dirt road. At the very end was a large building, the entire front composed of tall glass windows. The Burbank Community Center was a popular venue for weddings and dances, the very place homecoming would be held in just a few weeks. The road forked there, a paved section leading toward the parking lot for the building and the other heading toward the campsites. The latter was blocked by a large utility truck.

A dog's bark made me jump. A jogger dressed in spandex apologized as she stopped on the trail to my right, using the sign to balance as she stretched her legs. I passed her on the trail, finding the lake minutes later. It was completely still. Boating season was coming to an end and no one swam in the chilly water except during the hottest days of July. I was alone, exactly like I'd hoped.

I traced my path as I'd taken it the night before, not sure what I hoped to find. I stopped at a picnic table to look over the lake. I don't know what I expected to see. It wasn't like the entrance to the sixth gate was labeled. All I knew was that the ferryman had tossed me back into the sea in the Shadowlands and I'd surfaced in the middle of the lake. Was it possible that the entrance to the gate wasn't at the lake at all? Maybe the water worked as a kind of portal to spit me back out. What if the entrance wasn't stationary and it moved around? I let out a sigh as I thought about it.

I went to the bank, falling into the dirt when my heel sunk into a hole. I wouldn't have thought anything about it if I hadn't seen the trail of indentions in the mud. I got to my feet for a better look. At first, I thought they were bear tracks, but the toes weren't right. I'd gone camping every summer as a kid and Mark kept me entertained by looking for animal tracks on hikes. We almost never found anything exciting, just a few deer tracks and dogs. The tracks on the bank were in the dog family, but they were much too big to be that of any dog or even any wolf I'd ever seen.

I took a step back and felt my body go cold. The tracks weren't just walking by the water, they were leaving it. I pulled off my shoes and socks and waded into the cold water. I followed the tracks as far as I could see without letting the water rise any higher than my shorts, making out a couple more a few feet under the surface. I couldn't believe it. What kind of beast had the gates tossed out? Was there more out there than the demons and vampires Jamie talked about? Were there monsters too?

I staggered from the water as my stomach turned, keeling over and nearly vomiting onto one of the tracks. I took a few deep breaths to calm myself before I pulled my shoes back on. I wished that jogger and her dog were still down the trail as I stood there.

I snapped one picture of the clearest track before running back down the trail. I didn't slow my pace until I'd reached the main road, passing a family of three on their way for a picnic. It took everything in me not to scream for them to turn around as I passed them for the entrance. I ducked under the bar and settled back into the car. I looked at the picture of the track, glad that I'd accidentally gotten my left foot in the frame. The beast's paw was the size of my foot, sunken deep enough into the ground to put the thing at around a couple hundred pounds. I sent the picture to Jamie, startling when a motorcycle zoomed past me.

After nearly five minutes and no reply, I decided to go home. I tried my best to zone out to the pop songs on the radio, but it still felt like my heart was in a sprint. Mark noticed my panic right away.

"I just remembered that tomorrow is my chemistry presentation," I said, not entirely lying. Jamie and I had finished the PowerPoint days after we'd submitted the proposal to Mr. Quinn, but I had forgotten about it until Jamie had brought it up earlier.

"I swear, it's like I don't know who you are anymore," Mark said, standing up from his chair. "Becky and I have worked overtime to pay for the SAT classes, and I go on the weekend work trips for the extra cash for your college fund, not because I like riding with Terry and listening to his stupid country CDs. Your grades are going to be the difference between good scholarships and lots of student loans."

"I know," I said, my voice barely carrying across the room.

"No, you don't," Mark said, pointing a finger at me. "And you never have because we didn't want you brought up around that stress. We barely make it some months, but we've never taken away your allowance that you spend on dresses you drag through the mud and volleyball camps you decide to... You had a chance at a sports scholarship, and you blew that too in one night."

"What about all the money my parents left me then?" I said, my words punctuating the air in a way I never thought myself capable of. I had never raised my voice at Becky or Mark before, and I know he'd never yelled at me the way he was now either. "That money belongs to me. There's enough of it to pay for four semesters of college and more, I'm sure. You don't have to pay for college or law school or any of it." I wanted to tell him that I wouldn't be going to either of them anyway, but I knew I'd open myself up to a whole new level of grounded.

Mark stood there blank-faced. I had never seen him so stunned and it only made me feel worse about the things I'd said. I turned on my heel and went straight for my bedroom. I waited to see if he'd come after me but heard the front door slam shut minutes later. I checked my phone, but still no text from Jamie. I tugged the picture free from my pocket. The bottom corners were wrinkled, but it was otherwise untouched. I pinned it next to the picture of myself in the middle of the cork board and wished I hadn't. I reached out to take down the picture, but I stopped with my hand raised. It was one of the only pictures I'd ever been in that made me really look like myself.

I left the board to check my phone again. Just before my fingers reached it, the phone buzzed twice, and the screen lit up with a new text from Jamie.

Izzy covered them just now. We need to figure out what this thing is and why it's here. Tonight.

CHAPTER 12

Jamie and I stayed up well past midnight searching through the circle guide for any descriptions of large dog-like paw prints. Werewolf tracks were as close as we got but judging by the size of the toes and the spacing between them, we concluded that they definitely didn't belong to a werewolf. It wasn't until Izzy texted us *Google supernatural dogs* that we began any serious search. We slowly narrowed down the results until we were left with hellhounds.

Hellhounds are sometimes called "the guard dogs of the underworld" in mythology. They were tightly bound to the spiritual world and often lurked just out of sight of those marked for death. Just when I thought I'd left the ferryman in the Shadowlands for good, a hellhound is ordered after me.

Jamie and I stayed up trying to come up with reasons why someone would want my blood. Again, we scoured the circle guide for answers and came back with none. From what we could tell, there wasn't anything particularly special about guardian blood. The circle guide had noted that a vampire fed on a member of the sixth circle decades ago and nothing came of it other than the guardian walking away with a sore neck.

The next morning, I was surprised that Jamie was still with me. I was so used to him ducking out early to bring the car around or to run back to the Moore Estate for more books. He was barely dressed, just wearing a pair of blue checkered boxers. He picked up a pair of jeans off the desk, slowly stepping into them to keep from making any noise. He did a funny little wiggle as he slipped them onto his hips and sucked in a gasp when the floor creaked loudly under him as he buttoned the pants.

I rolled onto my back and propped myself up on my elbows, trying my best to look surprised. Thankfully, he bought it. His face flushed when he caught my eyes, turning back to the zipper on his jeans and tugging it upward.

"I didn't mean to wake you," he said, slipping the gray T-shirt over his head and flattening it down his chest. I giggled.

"I can see that," I said. "You know that there's a bathroom next door."

He turned to look at me and nodded his head in the direction of Becky and Mark's room.

"They were up early," he said. I could tell from the serious expression on his face that they had been fighting. They had been fighting more often since the car accident, and I knew it was because of me. It was stupid to think that the shouting match I'd had with my uncle would be kept between the two of us. I noticed after a moment that Jamie was still watching me and I hoped that the truth wasn't painted on my face.

"I have to go," he said, shrugging into his leather jacket, "but we should meet later. See you at Starbucks in two hours?"

I sat up a little straighter. My back was sore from stooping over my laptop most of the night. I pushed my palms against the spot in a stretch.

"Sure. I want to know everything you find out. It's *my* blood this demon dog is sniffing out, after all," I said.

Jamie froze, conflicted. He looked as if he wanted to spill something big right then, but he kept quiet.

"Actually..." he started, struggling for a second to find the words. "I think I just want to talk and you're the easiest person to talk to since... forever ago." His lips twitched into a brief smile before the conflicted look settled over his face again. I could tell that there would be more to this meeting than just small talk. Jamie had started opening to me the minute I'd nearly trapped myself in the Shadowlands. What else was I going to get out of him?

"Okay. Starbucks at ten," I said, deciding not to point out how busy our Starbucks typically was midmorning. That was the last thing I cared about.

After a brief pause, Jamie nodded his head and went to the window. He pulled it open and slung his backpack over his shoulder. Without giving me a second glance, he leaped out, not making a sound when his feet met the ground.

I checked the hall for Becky and Mark before I went into the bathroom to shower. I decided to wear the black combat boots I'd bought mostly because they were the edgiest shoe I could find, styling them with my favorite baby-pink long-sleeve T-shirt and jeans. I took the extra time I had to sweep my wavy hair into a low side ponytail, spraying a little sea salt onto my dark locks so that they'd keep their shape. I was glad I didn't run into Becky or Mark so I wouldn't have to see the reality of their argument in their sullen expressions on my way out the door.

It looked like it would rain at any moment, the sky dark and a distant cloud illuminated by a sudden flash of light. I ducked into the Beetle and with two attempts, got the engine started. It was misting when I parked outside the tan building, glad that the ugly weather had chased away most of the crowd. I took my backpack inside with me and claimed my usual table near the windows at the front.

Connor Taylor was wiping down the front counter when our eyes met. He offered me an apologetic smile. I unloaded every item from my bag one at a time. After stalling for as long as I could, it was clear that he and the manager, who was busy in the back stocking shelves, were the only two working all morning. I sucked in a breath and went to the counter.

"What can I get for you?" he asked, punching a few buttons on the screen and looking up.

"Nothing from you," I blurted.

He recoiled with a snort and pointed to the mermaid on his green apron.

"I just work here. I'm talking about coffee," he said, glancing toward his oblivious manager. I could feel my face growing hot, but I didn't budge. I wasn't going to let him talk over me or let my embarrassed nerves keep me from telling him off for what he did at the party.

"Jess told Macy what you did to her," I said.

Again, he balked.

"I don't know what you're talking about. I haven't talked to Macy or her minions since the night Noah and Jacob died," Connor said.

I felt my anger wane as I saw the concern in his expression. He hadn't been that drunk, had he?

"Jessica Harper?" I asked. "She texted Macy that you groped her at the party when you were dancing. She tossed a beer on you. It was the reason we were in the kitchen together."

His eyes widened as he remembered. He began stuttering, pulling a large cup from under the counter.

"We were all dancing in a group together. Jess was drunk

like she always is at parties and Sean grabbed her ass like he does every time she's drunk and I was in the line of fire. She passed out before you even left, which is why I was in the kitchen. If you had stayed at the party just an hour longer, you would've seen my fist fight with Sean in the backyard," he said, pulling the cap off a Sharpie with his teeth and scribbling my name on the side of the cup.

"If there had been a fight at the party, everyone at school would've been talking about it the next day," I said.

He laughed. "Not when an All-State quarterback takes a tumble down the side of a mountain in a convertible," he said, turning his back on me to fill the cup. I wanted to smack it out of his hands, even if his lazy manager saw. Who cared if I could never step foot in the shop again if it meant being the second girl who tossed a drink on the school's biggest playboy?

"Prove it," I said.

I was surprised when he slid the drink across to me, my usual order exactly.

"Fine," he said, pulling his phone from his pocket after making sure no one was looking. After a moment of scrolling, he handed it to me. I hit play on the video and cheers erupted. Sure enough, Connor was facing off with Sean Peterson. Sean said something about Jess I couldn't quite make out. Connor called him a pervert, accusing him of trying to rape Jess each time she got too drunk to remember. At that, Sean lunged, tackling him around the middle. After just a few exchanges of punches, I could hear sirens in the background. The video began to shake as the director backed away, blurring for a few seconds before it ended entirely.

"Who filmed that?" I asked, handing the phone back to him and reaching for my wallet. He pushed my hand away when I offered my card.

"Tasha James," Connor said. "She's the first chair flute in the band."

I let out a laugh, nearly slopping hot coffee over my hand.

"Since when are you friends with anyone who isn't a top athlete or has parents who make thousands weekly?" I asked.

He looked angry, but not at me.

"Since I stopped being friends with people like Macy and Sean. They've been using everyone else just to piss each other off forever and I was tired of people like Jess and you getting stomped on in the process. Tasha was one of the only people who followed us outside and when she filmed it all... I thought it was going to be all over YouTube and I knew Sean would sue me for assault or something if it got out. He's getting a full ride to basically any D-1 college he wants. Tasha asked me for my number and sent the video to me instead. She told me that it wasn't her war to wage and that I should have the video as my ticket to something better." All the anger faded from his voice, then he smirked. "She deleted her copy and I told Sean to make sure no one bothered me or else I'd let the video out. He was pissed enough at me for the fight that it wasn't hard to get him to agree."

"So, you and Tasha..."

"No," he said, "Tasha's actually going somewhere."

He shrugged and glanced at the elderly couple that just came in. I wanted to argue that he had just as much of a future as Tasha did, but I remembered what he'd said about his family's debts while we were drinking in the kitchen. Maybe what they said was true and Starbucks really did send their baristas to school.

"You meeting someone? Study date?" Connor asked, pointing toward my messy table a few feet away. I remembered my meeting with Jamie and checked the time on my phone. He was running late. It was almost ten past now.

"A little of both, I guess," I said. "I'm meeting Jamie Quinn. I need to finish a few things for our presentation for Puck's class tomorrow too."

Connor nodded. The slight nervousness in his eyes told me he needed to do a lot more than we did to prepare for tomorrow.

"You'll still be the best in the class," he said, "God, I wish you were my partner. Mine don't do jack shit."

I heard the old woman grumble something to her husband behind me as they joined us. I went back to my table to wait while Connor took their orders. After checking my phone, no messages from Jamie, I opened my laptop to work on our chemistry presentation. I went through our slides, making sure that we'd properly cited each one. Jamie had promised to do all the speaking, easing some of my nerves about doing a project like this for every other chapter of our chemistry book.

I lost track of time, only realizing I'd been sitting for two hours after I'd made the final adjustments to our project and finished the last paragraph of my essay for English. Still no text from Jamie. I felt a pit form in my stomach as I realized that he wasn't coming. Even Macy never stood me up. My eyes burned, only furthering my frustration.

"Can I ask you something?" Connor asked, slipping into the seat opposite me.

"Sure. What is it?" I asked.

He leaned his forearms onto the table.

"Well, I know that you got the best grade on that sonnet thing for Mrs. McKellen, so I thought you could help. I need a word that rhymes with flute," he said. I opened my mouth to start my list but closed it when I realized why he was asking. "I know. I couldn't think of anything good. Maybe a poem is too cheesy for a homecoming proposal," Connor said.

Before I could reply, he was out of the chair and on his way to the trash can, fiddling with the stack of napkins. I noticed that the manager had appeared, looking around the room until he noticed Connor. He scowled before going to the counter, pouring himself a cup of coffee and heading back into the storage room.

Jamie never did text me back and I kept my window locked that night. I ignored the sound of pebbles pinging off the glass pane and the single phone call that lit up the room. It took what felt like hours to calm down once the screen went black again. I was up early the next day just so I could drive to school before Jamie tried picking me up. The Beetle struggled to start thanks to the rain again, but I was glad when it did.

I was the first one in Mr. Puck's class. I double checked the presentation on my laptop as more people entered. My heart leaped in my chest when the bell rang. Every minute ticked by like seconds, speeding up my anxious heart the longer I sat by myself. When the final bell rang, Mr. Puck ordered everyone to put their phones and computers away. The intercom clicked on and Mrs. McKellen greeted us with her usual, "every day is a new day at Burbank High, and you can make today a great one." We stood for the pledge, listened to the growing list of announcements about homecoming tickets, and finally a short lecture from Principal Thackery about staying safe on the night of the dance.

Mr. Puck projected the order in which each group would present, Jamie and I set for the second slot. He warned us that our individual grades would be affected in part by how well we listened while other groups took their turns. I turned my attention to my notebook as the first group got set up, their title slide sending an orange glow over the front of the room as they each awkwardly took their places in a line next to the board. I scribbled along the margins of my notes on noble gases, hoping that Puck would notice Jamie's absence and forget all about me slouched in the corner.

When the weak applause died out, Mr. Puck called me to the front of the room. I took a deep breath and started toward the Smartboard. He exited out of the first group's slide show and found Jamie's and mine in the submission folder. The blue background was ghostly. I waited until Mr. Puck had retaken his seat at the first table and had given me a nod to begin. I kept my eyes on the white tile as I explained why Jamie and I had decided to do our presentation over matter. Just as I started into the next slide, the door opened, and Jamie stepped in.

The class followed my gaze when I paused. Jamie joined me at the front, nodding for me to continue as he sat his bag on the floor. I cleared my throat and continued with the definition of matter. I went through each slide, my voice sounding more and more distant as I read, verbatim, from my notes. I hadn't fully realized that I'd finished until I heard the disjointed clapping. Mr. Puck stood up again and passed me on his way to the computer. I went straight for my seat as the next group took their places.

"That went well," Jamie said, keeping his voice low.

"If my powers were stronger, I'd snap you in half," I said.

Jamie looked back at me in shock, as if I had no reason to be angry with him at all.

"I was ready to jump in the moment I heard your voice waver, but it didn't. You did great. You sounded confident even," he said.

I ignored the compliment. "That's not what I mean," I whispered.

He shook his head.

"I'm talking about yesterday, Jamie." When he didn't answer, I said, "Starbucks."

Jamie let out a long sigh and turned in his seat to face me. "I wanted to tell you, but it's just complicated and... Tori, I didn't mean to leave you waiting," he said.

Macy stopped speaking so Mr. Puck could talk. He stood up and looked over the room, his eyes landing on us last.

"Just because your group has presented does not mean you are finished. Don't forget about the grade for participation," he said. He aimed his warning at Jamie and me, doing one last scan of the room before sitting again. Macy picked up where she'd left off, indicating where metals were located on the periodic table. She flashed the room a beauty pageant worthy smile when her group finished, the clapping even weaker now than it had been for the groups before.

"I'm sorry," Jamie said. "And I know I can't expect you to just forgive me so easily."

"I'm tired of fighting," I said with a sigh.

The room went quiet again as the presentations continued. I was beginning to feel the whiplash. One day, Jamie lowered his emotional guard and talked with me. The next, it was right back up and it was business as usual for our circle. If I wasn't a part of the circle, I'd probably keep my distance from Jamie altogether. However, there was still something redeeming about him, but I didn't know what that was. It was something I could only feel deep in my gut.

"It's complicated," Jamie repeated.

I didn't reply. I did my best to focus on the last of the presentations, grading them myself in my head as they all went. To my surprise, it was Jamie who was the first one out the door when the bell rang. I had been preparing for him to follow me down the hall, begging for forgiveness. I wasn't sure how I felt about it going the other way around. I went into the hall, realizing that it had been weeks since I'd walked to my locker myself. I had just opened the door when it was slammed shut again. Izzy drew in close to me, holding a newspaper between us.

"A whole research team found the tracks," she said.

I took the paper from her. The article was dead center on the front page, two pictures set side-by-side the size of my palms. The left picture was of the lake, the paw print in the bottom of the frame. The next was just the track in the mud, a metal ruler lying beside it measured it at six inches long and another smaller ruler at the bottom indicating five inches in width.

"I thought you covered them," I said.

Izzy threw her hands up, nearly smacking a girl in the face as she passed.

"I thought I got them too. I walked the whole bank. The water must have receded more. Look how close to the water that one is," she said. I should've told them how I found them coming out of the water. I had seen a few just below the surface before I bolted from the park. I unfolded the paper to reveal the title, "Monster Wolf Stalking Burbrook National Forest."

Saturday, the Bradshaw family decided to have a family picnic by the lake to take advantage of one of the few sunny days in the last few weeks. Mary and Tim Bradshaw have a five-month-old, Tatum, and a six-year-old, Toby. Toby was playing in the shallow water when he stumbled in a hole and fell in. When Tim went to help him, he discovered the giant wolf paw print set deep into the mud.

"I couldn't believe it," Mr. Bradshaw told us. "It was just so big. I'd seen prints by the lake before and even a few wolves, but nothing

of this size." The family alerted nearby forest rangers who were the first on the scene. After concluding that the paw print did indeed belong to a wolf, they called Dr. Peter Sampson, a wildlife researcher who focuses on the wolf population of our state, to come and investigate.

The rangers took photos, including the two pictured above, before they left to meet Dr. Sampson. When they came back that evening to make casts of the print, they had been washed away. The research team did a thorough search of the surrounding area but have not found anything indicative as of yet. Dr. Sampson said that for now, the pictures will be enough to try studying the overall size of the animal and make an estimate on its age.

Burbrook's rangers are urging park visitors to be aware of the wildlife in the area and know the proper procedure for securing food items and keeping safe while hiking in the forest. That and more can be found on the park's website. As for now, Dr. Sampson and his team will remain for the next six weeks to further study the forests for any more signs of wolves. The exciting find has energized the community of Burbrook overnight.

Burbrook High School will have their annual homecoming dance at the event center located in the middle of the national park. Principal Tom Thackery, a former science teacher and wolf enthusiast, says that rather than taking on the usual themes for such events, the dance will carry a wolf theme to honor the recent find as well as celebrate the school's mascot.

"I think any excuse to inject a little extra school pride should be taken advantage of and this is definitely a big opportunity," Thackery said. The school's student committee is already working on ordering a pair of wolf ears for every student to wear at the dance. Dr. Sampson noted that as exciting a find as the paw print is, we shouldn't take it as confirmation of a new species of wolf.

"Any animal or person who steps in mud is going to leave a larger print behind than their actual foot," Sampson told us. "It is

possible that this wolf is not as enormous as we estimate. There are some abnormalities I noticed about the print that will be hard to study without a cast of the paw. So, until the animal is actually discovered, this 'monster' wolf will remain a Burbrook legend."

"We have to find and kill this thing before Sampson does," I said, refolding the paper and handing it back to her. I opened my locker again and switched my chemistry book for my Shakespeare text.

"Maybe it went back to the bank after you were there," Izzy said. I froze with my hand on the door for a moment before closing it. Jamie and I had figured that the hellhound had been sent after me, so it would make sense. Just how far from the cover of the trees would this beast venture though?

"No matter what Jamie said, homecoming is exactly where we need to be," I said. "Let the monster find me. That's the only way we'll be able to kill it and put an end to all of this." I closed the locker door, noticing the curious gaze Izzy was casting me.

"What's going on with you two?" she asked.

I shook my head and started toward the end of the hall. I wasn't sure how to answer her. I felt strangely close to Jamie, despite how weird he'd been. I didn't understand it, but it felt like we were constantly orbiting each other, like whatever it is that Jamie wanted to tell me at Starbucks was the very wall he kept placing between us. I was a little worried about what it meant to break down that barrier.

"Ask him," I said, "because I don't have a clue." I left her in the hall to go into Mrs. McKellen's class. The bell rang as soon as I sat down. She spared no moment.

"Today, your essay over *King Lear* is due, so pass those in now. I'll keep talking while I collect them. We have lots of exciting news." She was practically bouncing on the balls of her feet as she went from row to row.

I tugged my finished essay from my folder and passed it to Jessica in front of me. Mrs. McKellen finished taking up the stacks and set them aside on her desk. She turned on her projector, and last year's homecoming theme slowly appeared on the screen. It was a picture of a wolf dressed in tie-dye with a peace sign hanging around its neck. The slogan *Peaceful till' Game Time* written underneath in alternating colors.

"As some of you may know, I am the homeroom teacher for all the senior class. Everything from homecoming week to your graduation paperwork goes through me. So, it's my duty to help in the planning for homecoming week," Mrs. McKellen said. "Here's a highlight video of last year's homecoming cele- bration." She hit the play button on her computer and "The Twist" boomed loud from the speaker, forcing her to adjust the volume as pictures began fading in and out on the screen. There were pictures of students in Beatles T-shirts, lots of tie- dye shirts, and several short clips from the pep assembly. The song ended with a photo taken from high above of the home- coming dance, the room decorated with rainbow streamers.

"That was last year. This year's theme is in honor of the recent find at the national park," McKellen said. She switched the slide. In the center was a picture of a cartoonish wolf, muscles exaggerated along its body. Underneath was the slogan *A Howling Good Time at Burbrook High*. I heard a boy behind me snickering.

"So, everything is just wolf themed?" the boy asked. Mrs. McKellen didn't reply but switched the slide to a schedule of events. She picked up a stack of green paper from her desk and began passing them out to each row as she spoke.

"This is the schedule for homecoming week, which is next week. The game is Friday night, and the dance is Saturday night at the event center in the national park. It is a formal occasion so wear dresses and blazers, please. The student committee, which I am also in charge of, will be handing out wolf ears for everyone to wear at the dance and this year's ticket sales are going to the national park's research center," she said. I took one of the flyers and passed the stack behind me before I got a look at the week.

Monday:
   Dress-up theme: dress like a teacher day
   Event: teachers vs. students'volleyball game (starting at six o'clock)

Tuesday:
   Dress-up theme: dress like your favorite storybook character
   Event: 1st hour door decorating contest

Wednesday:
   Dress-up theme: dress like a zoologist
   Event: Dr. Tom Sampson research lecture in the gym (all science classes)

Thursday:
   Dress-up theme: dress for your future job
   Event: Burbrook's Got Talent Show (afternoon assembly)

Friday:
   Dress-up theme: school colors day

Event: pep assembly during school. Football game at six.

Saturday:
 Dress: formal attire
 Event: homecoming dance at the national park event center (seven o'clock)

"They axed the basketball tournament for a science lecture?" a girl behind me moaned. I was glad for the switch. It would give us a chance to see if Sampson found anything new. I hoped the answer would be no.

Much of the morning was consumed with homecoming. Teachers continued to remind us to prepare for the dress-up days, most of them offering extra credit points to those who participated each day. A sign up was placed outside the lunch-room for the volleyball tournament next Monday, two teams of teachers already signed up on the first sheet.

I took my usual seat at the back of the cafeteria, Izzy joining me a few minutes later with news that Jamie had checked himself out of school, making her call in as their mother to tell the office he wasn't feeling well.

"It's because of our fight this morning," I said. I had calmed down a little since our presentation.

"I know that much," Izzy said, peeling a banana. "And I think I'm half to blame."

I sat my fork down. "Why you?" I asked.

Izzy sat her banana aside and looked up, her expression falling.

"The thing is, well..." she started, fiddling with the peel. "Tori, guardians can't just go into the Shadowlands. At least, they can't go into the Shadowlands without having their match with them. Fifteen years ago, we had another member in circle. She was pulled into the Shadowlands during a fight, and she never came back out. Jamie didn't meet you for coffee yesterday because we were together trying to piece together what happened differently this time," she said.

I felt my heart sinking. That's what he'd meant when he picked me up that night when he said that he couldn't let it happen again.

"I'm here though," I said, "It was a close call, but it's been fifteen years since then and this time was different. What does it matter now?"

Izzy shook her head. "It matters now because there are hellhounds searching for you, not all of us. It was you the ferryman attacked, not all of us. We don't know a lot about the Shadowlands aside from the circle guide telling us that we need our match in order to survive passing into it. You didn't need that. It defies what we thought we knew. It matters because something about you is different," she said.

When I didn't respond, she started eating again. I didn't feel much like finishing my sandwich. I waited until the nearest teacher on duty had passed us to text Jamie. I asked to meet him at the Moore Estate later to train again, getting a *yes*, a minute later in reply.

The rest of the day passed like normal. I drove straight from school to the Moore Estate, beating Izzy there. Jamie opened the door for me before I'd even gotten out of the car. I decided to leave my bag in the front seat. Jamie waited for me at the front door.

"Dresses don't exactly make good workout wear," he said.

I hadn't thought about changing. I had forgotten about the training part of our meeting.

"I didn't think about that," I said, "I think we should talk, and I mean *really* talk."

I could see the nerves in his face, but he nodded.

"You're right," he said. He led the way to the stairs, taking me into his room. I remembered all his photographs well from the first time I'd snuck in, but this time I noticed more. On the wall left of the door were racks of instruments. There was a flute, a couple of guitars, a few string instruments, and a keyboard set up on a stand in the corner. A short shelf lined the wall next to his bed, but instead of photography equipment, this one held an organized collection of sheet music and records. Pushed into a tiny corner was an amp, a messy stack of cords, and a metal music stand.

"You should play somewhere," I told him, moving closer to the keyboard.

The sunlight from the window fell over the keys and I could just make out the layer of dust coating each one. I looked back at Jamie. He shook his head and shut the door. He took a seat at the foot of the bed, leaving space for me beside him. I sank into the mattress, already feeling his nervous energy buzzing in the room.

"When's the last time you played?" I asked.

"Ages ago," he answered. My guess was fifteen years.

"I've never played an instrument, not that I haven't tried," I said. "Becky made me take piano lessons when I was in grade school. The teacher tried to teach me to read music, but I never got it and she would get so frustrated with me that she'd just give up and we would spend the rest of the lesson doing my homework or baking cookies."

Jamie smiled a little, finally looking from the keyboard at me.

"My mom loved jazz music when I was little," he said. "I heard so many records at home. She used to make up her own songs and hum them when she was doing the dishes. I started making up my own after that when dad would let me play the piano they kept in the train station. He was okay with a little boy playing for guests in the corner because they'd leave tips. He said he put them away in a trust for me, which I found out wasn't true after he died." He was rubbing the back of his left hand with his right thumb hard enough to leave behind a pink mark from the pressure.

"I'm guessing he didn't like that too much when you got older," I said.

He noticed that I was watching him and stopped rubbing his hand, wiping his palms on his jeans and leaning back on them on the bed. He shook his head.

"As I got older, guests would think I was a beggar who had wandered in or some poor orphan looking for a little pocket money. They would pay me like I was too, drop a couple coins in the jar instead of the dollars like when I was little. Dad thought it was debasing to the family and myself and that I was at the age where I should want to be a real man and study business or some labor job. It didn't keep me from playing though," Jamie said, wincing a little as he said it. "He'd smack the back of my hands with the leather strap on his pocket watch when he'd catch me at it, told me that if I didn't want a real job to rough up my hands that he'd do it for me."

I imagined Jamie's father, the smiling man in the picture on the mantel, slapping away at him. It made my heart skip in my chest. I wanted to tell Jamie that his dad was a terrible person for hitting him for doing what he loved most, but I remembered the way he'd talked about how close the four of them were.

"I thought you considered your parents such nice people," I said.

Jamie smirked again. "It sounds harsh by today's standards, but in my father's defense," he started, shrugging out of his leather jacket, "he was just worried about my future. I was nearly seventeen by then with no real drive to go to school anymore than I had to. I wanted to take the train to the big city once I turned eighteen to become a jazz pianist and I had already spent the money they'd given me for tutors and my college fund on instruments I had yet to learn how to play... Back then, I was every bit the loser troublemaker that the stoner kids at school are now."

He tossed the jacket behind him and showed me his right wrist. There was a leather cuff around it held in place by a gold, tarnished clasp. The leather was cracked in some places from wear and time, the letters JLM stamped into the middle. Jack something Quinn.

"What's the L for?" I asked.

He let me touch the old watch strap.

"Louis," he answered. "I share my dad's middle name."

"What made you change?" I asked. "You know, from that loser piano player you thought you were?"

He thought for a minute, the space over the bridge of his nose wrinkling a little.

"I've never really thought about it," he said, looking back at me curiously, as if the question I'd thought obvious to ask had been some kind of SAT question. "I guess, after they died, I just needed to do something that took some work. I loved playing piano and I did that for a while, but it left my mind to wander too much. Taking college classes and doing things new and outside my usual talents made me struggle in other ways than I had been."

"You were struggling before you woke?" I asked. "You had something you were really good at. Your parents were successful in the railroad industry, huge names in business that earned them millions..." I stopped talking when I realized how bitter I sounded. He had the life I'd never had. I'd watched Becky and Mark struggle financially since I was little. I could graduate with less than they had now. Jamie and Izzy were at least left with something, not that money softened the blow of their deaths. I knew that.

"I struggled with being a guardian. My powers were out of control, and I broke the first piano I tried playing after their deaths. I was constantly scared I'd out myself every time I was in public, and Izzy was the only person I had in the world, and she so easily mastered her powers. She didn't burn down every building we walked into, but I always destroyed something inside. It was frustrating and even on the worst days, I knew there wasn't a way out of it all because I'd just wake up in a few hours like it had never happened," he said.

I chased away the terrible thoughts of Jamie hurting himself before my stomach could twist any tighter.

"I'm sorry," I said. "How did you cope?"

He glanced toward the shelves of photos and camera equipment. I thought he was going to say that photography had saved him, but he didn't.

"I met someone," he said, the words coming out in a sigh. He smiled a little, the corners of his mouth twitching. I felt a pit form in my stomach, suddenly unsure if he wanted me sitting inches from him the way I was, but not able to scoot away at all.

"A girl?" I asked.

He nodded.

"She was ambitious and vibrant. She's the one who did photography, not me. I took pictures, not photos the way she did. There was a goal for everything with her, a purpose for living. The weirdest part was that they were always these huge projects that only she could make feel reachable. I swear she charmed everyone she met, truly bewitching to be around. Izzy connected with her the day we all met, and they were best friends. She knew so much more. She'd been a guardian since the 1700s and she taught me all those things my dad had wanted to: fighting, sciences, and cars." He was smiling wider now.

"You loved her," I said.

He paused before nodding, his smile fading. He looked a little confused and for a moment, I wondered if he'd never told her those words himself.

"Was she... one of us?" I asked.

"She was a guardian of our circle," he said. "But she didn't match with me."

I could practically feel the punch in the gut. He had doted on her so intensely moments before that I'd never had expected her to have rejected him.

"What happened?" I asked, not sure if it was even my place.

"She was sucked into the Shadowlands like you were," he said.

I remembered the feeling of the cold cell and the terror at the strange creatures who guarded the castle gate. The ferryman had seemed almost like an old friend compared to them. Jamie had practically screamed at me, he'd been so scared.

"Maybe she'll come back," I said, already knowing the answer.

He shook his head.

"She's dead," he said. "We can only enter the Shadowlands with our match. Without one, we die and stay there. It's the only loophole to the immortality rule."

I noticed he was watching me, the same curious gaze he'd had moments before. I thought about telling him what Izzy had said at lunch about their research, but it didn't feel like the right moment.

"That must've been hard," I said.

He nodded.

"After the other night, when you nearly..." he started, letting out a deep breath. "I've never wanted to play piano more than I do now."

I felt a knot in my stomach release. Why would he want to play again after a near repeat of the same traumatic event? His expression was just as confused as I felt. He looked away from me a moment later, scooting a little farther from me on the mattress.

"Jamie," I started.

He didn't look up, his eyes remaining on the leather watch strap around his wrist. "Do I seem different to you than other guardians? I mean, like, do you feel..." I wasn't sure how to explain it and my face felt hot at the idea of telling him about the electricity I felt anytime we were close like this. He looked up at last, caught off guard by my question by the looks of it. After a second of recovery, he nodded.

"Yeah. You feel different somehow. I don't know why, but I'm sure whatever it is, it's the reason why the Shadow Mistress wants your blood," he said.

We were both quiet for a long time.

"Now I wish I had worn something other than a dress," I told him, glad for the small smile that crossed his face. Unfortunately, just like everything else right now, it was fleeting and gone seconds later.

CHAPTER 13

*L*oving the new bulletin board. Glad my picture made the *cut.* It was the text that woke me up the next morning. The night had been like every night before it, practicing my powers. I'd grown so used to turning off lights with my mind that I accidentally turned the kitchen lights off after dinner, prompting Mark and Becky to debate how much it would cost to have the entire house looked at by an electrician. Jamie picked me up earlier than usual so we could stop for coffee before school.

"I want a venti Pike Roast and a pumpkin spice latte," Jamie said when the girl's voice came over the speaker. I snorted, a smirk pulling at the corner of his mouth.

"Pumpkin spice latte, huh?" I asked.

"Tis' the season, Mindfreak," he replied.

We pulled around the side of the building to the pick-up. It opened before we were even stopped. Jamie handed over his card and seconds later, passed me my hot cup.

"I swear, cardboard isn't insulated enough for this," I said.

"Drink hot coffee in the winter, iced in the spring and

summer, and lattes and mochas in the fall. You're doing it backward."

I pulled the stir stick from the lid and set it in the cup holder. I hated drinking coffee with any cream or sugar in it. It always tasted too sweet and artificial.

"I'm just appreciating the beans," I said.

Jamie laughed. The car behind us honked and Jamie put the Audi in drive.

"If I had known I was taking a hipster to school every morning..." he said, letting his words trail off when the car honked again.

"Geez," I said, setting my drink down and craning my neck to get a look. "We're moving. Chill."

I recognized the Challenger immediately, just barely able to see Macy's blonde head behind the wheel. I thought I spotted Sean in the passenger seat, drumming his hands on the dash. He reached over and pressed the horn again, so it blared long and loud, Macy's head tipping back in a laugh.

"Is that..." Jamie started.

Macy stopped laughing to take two cups from the barista at the window, stuffing them into cup holders and leaning on the horn again.

"Let's just go," I said. "We have school."

Jamie, who had started toward the exit, stopped the car so abruptly that I felt my seat belt tighten over my shoulder. He turned in his seat to stare at me, casting a look over his shoulder to make sure Macy had stopped too.

"Jamie," I protested.

He cracked a smile of disbelief as Macy honked again, yelling something I couldn't hear out the window.

"You're telling me that you're still letting this girl walk all over you and you don't even consider her a friend anymore?" he asked me.

"Jamie, don't," I begged when he put the car into park. I knew Sean was bigger than him, but Jamie's powers could smash him flat and then where would we be?

"You tried to completely erase your life because of what happened with Macy and the accident," he said, reaching into his backseat. "You can't tell me that you haven't been dying to do something mean to her, just one thing, to make up for the years of bashing she did to you."

He emerged with a McDonald's sack in hand. I could already smell what was inside before he pulled out the half-eaten bacon-and-egg sandwich. He unfolded the wrapper from around it; the moldy biscuit was oozing with what looked like maple syrup. He split the sandwich in half, setting the top half with the egg in his lap and offering me the half with the sticky bacon and sausage.

"Are there cameras?" I asked, taking the hard bread. I couldn't believe I was going along with it. I'd never broken the rules like this before, especially none this huge. My heart was pumping fast with adrenaline, but nothing seemed as satisfying as launching that sandwich Macy's way.

"Only in the school lot and they're too far away and crappy to see anything," Jamie said, taking his half in his right hand and lowering the windows. Macy laid on the horn, the sound making my ears ache. I unclasped my seat belt and pulled my torso far enough through the window to get a perfect aim. Jamie released just before me, his sandwich smacking the windshield with a hard thud and sending the remaining egg exploding over the wipers and hood of the red car. Macy and Sean both opened their doors as I let the bread leave my hands.

The sausage landed with a wet slap on the windshield and slid across the driver's side and off the car, hitting Macy full in the chest when she stood up. She let out a shriek and Sean froze, halfway out of his seat.

"You bitch," she said, the last of the sandwich flopping off her chest and falling over the door. She sank back into her seat and slammed the door shut.

"I'll never be able to go back to school again," I said, banging my head on the side of the door as I slid back into the car. Jamie rolled up the windows up and we lurched forward. I was quick to pull my seat belt back into place after nearly flying into the door as we rounded the last corner for the far exit. I breathed a sigh of relief when I didn't see Macy's car.

"Shit," Jamie said. He slammed on the breaks as Macy sped past, cutting us off as we turned onto the dirt road. I heard the Audi hum under Jamie's foot and felt the jerk as we sped up. My stomach plummeted when we passed the school parking lot and continued into the cover of the trees after the red Challenger.

"Where are you going?" I asked as we rounded a bend in the road. Macy slowed down, dipping into the opposite lane when we hit an abandoned straight away. Sean's window rolled down as the car slowed to our pace, putting us side-by-side.

"You still think you're a badass now, Quinn?" Sean yelled, barely audible over the engines. He reached out and tapped on Jamie's window three times before letting out a whoop and ducking back into his seat. Macy put on the brakes and turned into the entrance of the national park.

"Asshole," Jamie said under his breath, slowing the car back to a reasonable fifty miles per hour. We'd only gone a half-mile farther before I felt the car lurch under us. The front of the car seemed to dip a little and then we both gasped when we heard a loud thunk and felt the car zigzag.

"You hit something," I said.

"Flat tire," Jamie corrected. He pulled onto the grass and turned off the car. I got out first, noticing the nearly shredded front, passenger-side tire. Jamie shut his door and bent over to look under the body.

"You were right," I said, "It's the tire."

He let out a sigh and straightened up.

"So were you," he said. "I think the suspension might be broken. I've had a few flats before, and it's never felt like that."

I stared past him at the sign directing all national park visitors to take the next right. I got back into the car and called for Jamie to do the same.

"We can find someone at the park," I told him, motioning for him to join me.

He sunk into the seat. "No. If we do, I'd punch a hole in Sean's chest."

"Considering the fact that you can literally do that, I hope they went back to school," I said.

Jamie's shoulders tensed and he kept his gaze on the road ahead.

"We're not driving anywhere. We'll have to walk back to the park and hope that we can get a ride to school from there," Jamie said, checking his phone. I slid mine just far enough from my pocket to look at the time. My stomach sank. We were ten minutes late for chemistry. If we could get to school soon, especially with a ride from someone at the national park, then maybe we'd get excused by the front office. I got out of the car and slung my backpack over my shoulder. Jamie looked up at me, his mouth parting.

"What?" I asked, looking down at myself for any coffee stains.

"Get in the car," he said.

"What do you mean?" I asked.

"Tori, get in the car!" he yelled.

I followed his gaze to the trees behind me, noticing the dark shadow moving between the evergreens. I jumped onto the hood of the car as it launched toward me, rolling across and falling onto the ground next to Jamie just as the creature smashed into the side of the car, front paws crashing through the driver's side window.

"Run," I said and bolted across the highway.

I could hear Jamie right behind me, his feet crunching over the dead pine needles. The monster's paws sounded like thunder on the ground as it chased us. I leaped over a tree root, not seeing the slope of the grass beyond. My right foot came down first, my momentum continuing forward and forcing my ankle to give out. I felt it snap hard and let out a scream that I hardly recognized as my own.

"Lie down flat," Jamie yelled, sliding onto the grass next to me like a baseball player sliding home.

I rolled onto my back just in time to see the hellhound fly over me. I could feel the air whoosh past as its dark body did. It was very wolf-like, only much larger and strangely muscular. It landed hard on the ground, sliding over the browning leaves and brush and into the base of an oak tree. The bark shuddered, sending a flurry of pinecones raining down over its bristled back. I thought for a minute that the tree would give out, crushing the hellhound under it.

"Help me," Jamie said before charging straight for the beast before it could pounce. He wrapped his arms around its thick middle and they both went toppling. Jamie quickly rolled onto its back, holding on like a bull rider.

I focused hard on the tree just behind them, the limbs beginning to creak and leaves rustle as I tried forcing it from the ground with my mind. I heard the roots snap once, twice, and then it gave an eerie moan and fell forward. I opened my mouth to scream for Jamie to bail, but the tree was just barely kept upright at an angle by the remaining roots. Before I could try again, a sickening crack rang out. The hellhound let out a single yelp and went limp in Jamie's arms. He loosened them from around the animal's neck and let it slump to the dirt.

Jamie looked down at me, our eyes locking. Maybe it was the adrenalin. My whole body felt light, my skin heating under his gaze. There was a creak behind us and a final snap that echoed off the surrounding trees.

"Jamie!"

He looked up just in time to catch the trunk of the giant tree, sinking into a squat to absorb the force. The lowest branches bent around us like an umbrella before he shoved the whole thing to one side, catching himself on one arm. He was crouched over my lower body when he looked back at me with concern. I let out a deep breath.

"Are you okay?" I asked.

He let out a snort, wiping the back of his hand across a scratch on his cheek and smearing a line of scarlet over his skin.

"Me?" he asked, "You broke your damn ankle."

I felt like I'd fallen back to earth, my stomach turning as I remembered the useless joint. I could feel it throbbing now, the pain nearly unbearable when I tried moving it even a little. Jamie dropped to his knees next to me, his eyes going to my foot. I didn't dare look and waited until he glanced anxiously up at me.

"You'll heal in about thirty minutes, but I can make it ten if you let me set it," he said. I laid back down and motioned for him to do it, covering my face and bracing for the pain. He told me he'd count but started moving my ankle as soon as I agreed. I let out a single shriek before the pain began to fade again. Jamie kept his hands around the joint, stabilizing it.

"Thanks," I breathed.

"No problem," he said.

I carefully sat up, my eyes going past him to the hellhound. The fur was jet black, vivid orange eyes bulging. The claws on all four giant paws were thick like those of a bear and long. It was at least three times the size of even the largest wolf I'd ever seen.

"What are we going to do about the hellhound?" I asked, "We can't just leave it somewhere for that researcher to find."

Jamie looked up at last. His eyes met mine and he nodded, standing up and walking back to the body. He checked our surroundings before heaving the massive body over his right shoulder. Its paws dragged on the ground as Jamie walked back toward the road. After a few minutes, I couldn't hear his footsteps anymore. I felt my ankle, tested out its movement, and finally got to my feet. It was sore, but I could walk fine.

"What did you do with it?" I asked when Jamie came back.

He motioned for me to follow him, leading the way toward the car.

"It just barely fits in the trunk," he said, "We'll get rid of it at the house."

I almost asked him how he got the massive monster to fit in the trunk of his tiny Audi, but my stomach rolled when I imagined him twisting and breaking the animal's body into a pretzel of shapes.

"At least it's dead," I said, my heart thumping in my chest.

I felt like I'd just downed my entire cup of coffee. The hellhound was dead. There was nothing searching for me anymore. The ferryman would have to leave his post in the Shadowlands again if he wanted my blood. After seeing his place for myself, I doubted he would be allowed to switch jobs again. Jamie smirked and I could barely keep from laughing. Once he let out a chuckle, it was all over. We both started laughing hard, not stopping until I noticed the blood dried over his cheek. He helped me clean it off with a couple napkins from the glove compartment of the Audi.

"It's nearly the end of first period," Jamie said. "I can't just leave my car here. Someone's going to hotwire it the second they see that window."

I followed his gaze to the passenger window that had been smashed out by the hellhound. It would hardly be breaking and entering if the car was vandalized or stolen.

"Izzy?" I asked.

Jamie shook his head. "I don't know anyone with a truck," he said.

I felt like everything had stopped dead when the thought occurred to me. I knew someone who had a truck with a towing mount on the back. I tried thinking of anyone else I possibly could, even debated paying a towing fee from a service before realizing they'd never just let us go without asking for a parent's number.

"Mark can tow us," I said.

Jamie's right hand did a slow pass through his hair, making the front stick up at an angle. He let out a long sigh.

"He's going to kill you," he said, more of a warning than a protest. "And he thinks everything about you so far is my fault anyway."

I remembered the argument we'd had in the living room. He'd be mad enough to find me so late for school, but he'd be furious to know who I was with.

"I don't think we have another choice," I said "I'd call Becky, but she can't tow us at all. Anyone else would have to skip school like we already are. It's the best option we have next to just leaving your car here for someone to take."

Jamie nodded his head, giving the tire a weak kick.

"If we wait any longer, your uncle will think we meant to skip, not just that we'd gotten a flat," he said.

I agreed, already listening to the ringing from my phone in my ear. I was worried for a second that I would have to leave a message, but he finally picked up.

"You know you can't use your phone during school," he said.

I turned my back on Jamie. "I know, but I'm not at school," I said, continuing before he could get too far into his lecture. "It's a long story, but we got a flat tire, and the suspension might be busted or something. Jamie doesn't have a spare and the window's broken."

Mark stopped talking midway through his yelling, the phone going silent. I heard jingling in the background and Mark's distant voice telling someone "we'll pick up in an hour" before his sigh came through the receiver loudly.

"I'll pick you up, but I'm not towing his damn car," Mark said.

He hung up before I could argue. Jamie was busy inspecting the back of his car. It wasn't until I remembered the hellhound concealed in the trunk that I realized what he was looking for.

"He won't know, will he?" I asked, "He can't, like, weigh the car and tell there's something extra in it, can he?"

Jamie shook his head, opening the door to the backseat and pulling out our backpacks. I reached for both coffees and joined him at the trunk. He took a long sip, his eyes focusing on my once broken ankle. I tried not to remember the way it had twisted.

"When he gets here," Jamie said, "let me talk to him."

"Jamie, don't make things worse," I said.

He straightened up, setting his cup on the car. "He thinks I'm bad for you, and it doesn't matter if he's right or wrong. What matters is how I react to it. I can try convincing him I'm not and let you continue taking the blame, or I can pretend to own up to something I may not even be guilty of."

I wanted to argue with him, but I knew he had a good point. I just hated that he was going along with Mark's picture of him. The Victoria Johnson I'd always been was so scared of being wrong and doing wrong that she never did anything at all. Mistakes were something foreign to me and I didn't want to keep pretending that they made me a bad person. Macy deserved to have that sandwich thrown at her and much more than that even. It was time I allowed myself to live out the happiness I deserved.

Jamie turned to face the road and I followed his gaze. Mark's silver work truck rolled to a stop in the middle of the road. After doing a slow three-point turn, he was parked directly in front of Jamie's poor Audi. Mark hopped down from the seat, slamming his door hard.

"You," he said, pointing to me, "sit up front. He can sit in the back." He pointed to Jamie all while keeping his firm gaze on me.

"Thank you so much for the tow," Jamie said.

I felt everything inside me contract. I hadn't told him. Mark stopped halfway back to the door and turned to face Jamie in disbelief.

"Oh, I'm not towing you," Mark said. "It's hardly been two months since you started seeing my niece and you've already dragged her through the mud. I'll give you a ride back to school, but I'm not vouching for your behavior. I drop you off and you drop this game with my niece."

"Mark," I said. I froze in my spot as soon as he shot me the warning glare. I felt the shivers shoot up my skin. I couldn't fight him on this, could I? What if I did?

"It's my fault she's here," Jamie said. "I brought her out

here to ask her out to homecoming. It was a kind of romantic gesture overlooking the meadow."

My heart skipped in my chest as Jamie pointed further down the road where the turnoff was for a popular hiking spot. I'd never gone before, but I'd heard of all the prom proposals made there and senior pictures taken before the lavender field. I'd never been asked out to anything before, the very realization there in Mark's surprised expression. He reformed his stern gaze, the shock still there in his relaxed shoulders.

"I'm losing out on my paycheck to pick you two up," he said. "I work on the clock."

"Let me work to make it up then," Jamie said. "I'll mow your lawn for a few weeks or months. I noticed the paint chipping on the front porch. I'll repaint or go to work with you as an unpaid hand. I can make up for the time and money lost, I swear."

Mark finally deflated a little. He closed his mouth and took a deep breath, keeping his eyes on Jamie.

"Every single evening and every weekend for the entire month, you'll do any labor job?" he asked.

Jamie nodded. "Yes, sir. She's worth it," he said. "And I'm not. I know that."

I felt my heart skip. The shock on Mark's face made it more satisfying. He was turning pink in the face, but not from anger anymore. I could sense the bruise to his pride. Jamie was right. In a way, he'd won the war with my uncle simply by giving in.

"You both get in like I told you," Mark said. "I'll come back for the car after I drop you off."

Mark got in first, turning the engine on and urging us to hurry up. Jamie grabbed our bags, giving me a wink when he handed me mine.

The drive was silent, but thankfully short. Mark walked us both into the office and explained the accident. The secretary wrote us both passes and accepted my uncle's story, switching our absences from the morning to excused and sending us on our way. Mark warned me that we would talk about this later, but the threat didn't carry any heaviness in his voice like I knew he'd hoped. I wondered if this meant things would go back to normal between us. I wanted to go back to the relaxed relationship we had before he'd started shooting suspicious glances my way anytime I left the house.

"We've only got one more class before lunch," Jamie said as the bell rang, following me to my locker. I shoved my bag inside and began gathering my books in my arms, letting Jamie hold them for me so I could better dig through the mess of papers on the top shelf. Maybe Mark hadn't been totally wrong. I'd never let myself get so disorganized before. I hadn't even set up all my class binders this year like I normally did, an old folder left in my bag from last year currently doing double duty between my history and math classes. I remembered what Jamie had told Mark, the thought slowing my hands.

"Did you mean what you said back there?" I asked.

Jamie nodded with a laugh. "Of course," he said, "You're worth every minute of painting or scrubbing or whatever it is Mark comes up with for the next month."

I ignored the compliment.

"No, I meant about you not being worth the same," I said. "Because you're wrong. If it weren't for you, I would still be under Macy's feet every day and I'd probably go off to college next year and do all the right things for all the wrong reasons. I've never really understood how to be true to myself until I met you."

I wished I could tell what he was thinking. He looked almost surprised at what I'd said. His lips pulled into a frown, like I'd said something that hurt rather than gave him a compliment.

"Until now, I've been doing all the wrong things since 1931," Jamie said, brushing his hand against my hair. He held up a single pine needle for me to see before flicking it onto the floor. We must have been standing there for a while, because the one-minute warning bell rang out a second later. I felt myself crash back to Earth and I closed my locker before I could risk any more trouble. Jamie walked me halfway to class, promising to see me at our usual dilapidated lunch table in an hour.

Jamie and Izzy both came over after school, Jamie planning on starting work as soon as Mark got home. Izzy kept teasing him about his agreement, reminding him that Mark hated him.

"He'll probably make you do something unnecessary just to get back at you," Izzy told him, plopping down on my bed. I watched her eyes flick to the collage over my desk and she got up a second later to investigate. Jamie stayed in the doorway, looking over my report card. It was the first of the semester, laying out all my lower-than-expected marks thanks to all the changes that had happened.

"These are still good," he said. I scoffed. They weren't what I was used to.

"I dropped in the class ranking," I said.

Jamie lowered the green paper and pointed to Izzy.

"Only because of everything that's been going on," he said. "You've been studying for the SAT, which means your score will get better. I don't understand why you are so sure that Becky and Mark will be mad about a point difference in your GPA."

I had been on a 4.0 streak all through high school, just

barely shy of Jamie's grades. 3.9 didn't look so good after that considering the trouble I'd been in. The rational part of me knew my grades were fine, but after what Mark had said about money for college...

"Shut up. God," Izzy whispered. She swiped once at her phone and shoved it back in her pocket, looking up to notice us both watching her. She let out a groan and shook her head. "Some guy from the football team emailed me to ask me out to homecoming. I don't even know how he got my email," she said. "And he's the second one to do that now, which is totally tacky. The worst part is that the first one got all sulky when I said no. I told them I wasn't even a student, and they didn't at all think it was weird." She let out a huff and turned back to the bulletin board, running her index finger over the pattern on the spoon bracelet.

"I thought you were going to watch the perimeter the night of homecoming," Jamie said. I caught Izzy's annoyed gaze. She would've been happy just being there to keep an eye on things before.

"Thackery had a spreadsheet open, and I noticed that Puck is on duty at the homecoming dance. He's supposed to be posted on the dance floor and I wanted to keep track of him," Izzy said.

"The night all three of us agreed we'd take off from guardian stuff?" I asked.

Izzy scoffed. "My brother never takes time off," she said.

I looked at Jamie who was looking straight back at me, the gesture not lost on Izzy.

"What are you two up to?" she asked.

"Jamie and I are going to homecoming together," I said.

Izzy looked at Jamie next with a surprised laugh.

"It was the best reason I had after the car broke down," he said. "I told Mark I was taking her to the lavender field before school to ask her out to homecoming. It explained why we passed the school."

Izzy snorted and rolled her eyes. "Okay," she said, "Sure." She turned back to her own backpack, tugging out her laptop and chemistry book. I remembered what she had said about dates just minutes before and quickly changed the subject.

"I don't understand your obsession with Mr. Puck," I said, feeling a strange tingle at the base of my neck as I remembered how tense he had been the night I showed up at school. He was acting a little strange, now that I thought about it. He'd been teaching at Burbrook High for a few years and still hadn't seemed to really settle into his classroom. He never associated with the other teachers, and he always seemed a little preoccupied with something. Still though, that was hardly worth Izzy's scrutiny.

"I just have a weird feeling about him," Izzy said. "I don't know how to explain it, but after he said all of two words to me in the hall... I felt strange, almost the weird buzzing I get when demons are close by."

Jamie sat my report card on my desk and pulled his own folded paper from his pocket; he unfolded it and sat it next to mine for comparison. I stopped watching him and busied myself unloading all my homework from my bag.

"I heard report cards went out today," Mark's voice sounded from the hallway. He stopped next to Jamie a minute later. Jamie handed over the green paper without prompting, getting a suspicious gaze from my uncle who didn't look away until he moved farther into the hallway. I wasn't sure how he'd react considering the way he'd backed down to Jamie earlier that day. A 3.9 wasn't anything to get in trouble over and low grades were never a serious offense in our house— not that I'd ever had any to test the rule.

"You went up," Mark said, "4.0 and National Honors. Number one in the class."

Jamie let out a small gasp and stepped around Mark for the desk. I noticed the difference immediately, my perfectly flattened grades still laying over the top while Jamie's crinkled paper was held between my uncle's greasy fingers.

"That's actually mine," he said, trading out the two papers. "Sorry." Mark's expression fell. Izzy sucked in a deep breath to keep from laughing, turning her back to face me. My uncle looked over my grades, clearly disgruntled that the better marks had been those of the very person he was trying so hard to find fault with.

"You're back at an A in chemistry," Mark said.

"Mr. Puck said Jamie's and my project was the best of the day," I noted.

He ignored me, commenting about my drop in GPA before leaving the room with the paper in hand. "No boys behind closed doors," he called out behind him.

"You did that on purpose," I whispered to Jamie.

He shrugged. "They're both green papers. Easy mistake." A small smirk tugged at the corner of his mouth. "I'm going to go see how I can get started." Jamie left the two of us, Izzy rolling her eyes as she closed the door.

"Has your mark changed?" she asked, pointing to her left wrist.

"No, why? Has yours?" I asked, glancing down at the red sleeve covering the black words winding around my forearm.

She shook her head. "Just wondering."

"Okay. No more guardian stuff," I said, getting a reluctant nod from her, "Three questions: what is your favorite flavor of gum, your favorite school subject, and the job you'd have if you weren't... you know?"

Izzy moved from the desk to sit with me on the bed, thumbing the edge of my planner.

"Cinnamon, science, and a surgeon. I don't know what kind. I've gone to med school for basically all of it," she said, "What about you?"

It was harder for me to decide on answers. I knew what I wanted to say, but college seemed like a strange prospect now. I was still working toward it and stressing over the money Becky and Mark were trying to save, but it felt stupid assuming I'd finish or even go right away. I'd been having dreams of traveling the country with Jamie and Izzy, hunting demons and being stalked by the ferryman the entire time.

"Mint, English, and a lawyer," I said. It went silent for a minute, giving me enough time to log into my computer and pull up the eBook of our math textbook. I had just opened my notebook to my homework when Izzy started again.

"It's hard getting any kind of professional job when you always look twenty-one," she said. My pencil froze over the first question for a moment. Maybe college really was pointless. I started writing out the question, copying the equation from my computer screen.

"Is that why you stopped going to school?" I asked. Izzy had been making comments about stopping her education in the eighties just about any time she found fault with our school.

"Probably. I think Jamie started going for that reason though. He needed the distraction," she said. "I went to school so long because of the way I grew up. I used to play the piano in the train station for guests and our dad thought that it was a wonderful job for me and that it was a perfect way to look appealing to a future husband. I hated that the thoughts in my head had no merit. Jamie was the opposite. He loved playing the piano, but it was too beneath him, as Dad said. Has he ever told you he's kind of a musical genius?" she asked.

"Sort of," I said, "He told me about your dad smacking him for playing in the station."

Izzy let out a laugh. "I wondered why he'd started playing again," she said under her breath. I looked up from my homework. "He hasn't played in fifteen years, and now it's like he never stopped now."

I could easily imagine him in his bedroom, sitting at the keyboard, his fingers floating over the keys in a ballad. I wondered if I could convince him to play for me the next time we trained in the basement. By the time I came out of my thoughts again, I realized I still hadn't answered the first question. With Izzy seemingly finished with her questioning, I focused on calculus.

CHAPTER 14

Things were so quiet on the guardian front that it was almost boring. Classes were slowing down in anticipation for the chaos that homecoming week always caused at school. The football team had their new pictures for the season hanging on green-and-white banners in the entryway. The cheerleaders had decorated posters with all the dress-up day themes for next week, every hall plastered with colorful thin paper and streamers. For the first time, I was thankful for the cheesy distraction. Izzy had reminded me at lunch that waiting for the next demon to try getting my blood would only stress me out.

"We can't do anything about that until it happens," she told me, stabbing a peach on her plate with her fork.

"No, but wouldn't it make sense to figure out why the Shadowlands wants it before then?" I asked. I could tell from the way Jamie's jaw had tightened and the way he continued to mix the gravy with his mashed potatoes that he felt the same way I did.

"We've done the research. There's nothing in the guidebook. I think we have to wait for the next attack," she said. "And that could be weeks or months from now. No matter what you think, I'm going to make the best of this week."

Jamie had mixed his potatoes for so long that it looked like a gray paste now, far from appetizing. He sat his fork aside when I changed the subject to what we were going to wear for each dress-up day. I usually didn't participate in the costumes aside from the school spirit day at the end of the week, but this year they were giving away prizes to the best costumes of each day.

"Members of the student council will visit each classroom first hour and take pictures of the best costumes from each. During the last hour of the day, the winner will be announced and will receive their prize the next day when STUCO comes around again," Mrs. McKellen told us during English, going on to encourage everyone to try their best to dress up every day. This year, most of the prizes were gift cards to restaurants and boutiques around town, far better than the school store credit that we had been offered in the past. You could only have so many green T-shirts, and when they gave you a free one each year for attending the Class Day Bash the first week back to school, dress-up days weren't so special.

Before I could escape the room for lunch, Mrs. McKellen had placed a piece of green stationery on my desk. I recognized it at once, having received one about this time of the semester for the last three years. Each year, Mrs. McKellen invited me to join the school's academic team. The top ten percent of each class was eligible to join and given a formal invite. The green cardstock had a border of wolf heads embossed in gold. The letter was straightforward, congratulating me on my accomplishment of top grades. The rest of the letter listed all the years the team won the state tournament, which was more than any sports team from our school.

"I hope you'll take this opportunity seriously this year, considering it is your senior year and it would be a great résumé booster or even college essay topic," McKellen said, tapping the letter twice with one red fingernail before going back to her desk. I shoved the paper into my backpack, hoping she didn't hear the cardstock rip when it caught on the zipper.

"When will your car be fixed?" I asked as I followed Jamie to his motorcycle after school. Mark had dropped his Audi off at one of the auto shops in town instead of taking it back to the Moore Estate like Jamie had asked. It made disposing of the hellhound corpse in secret a little harder and what would've been a couple days of work for Izzy was turning into an extra week at the shop.

"They said I'll have it early next week," Jamie said, handing me his helmet. I took it and clasped it under my chin as he climbed onto the bike. I settled into the seat behind him and wrapped my arms around his middle before we lurched forward. It was just starting to mist, making my hair curl. By the time we pulled into the driveway, it was raining. We ran to the porch. I pulled off my jacket and shook off the water the best I could.

"It's like it's never sunny here," Jamie said. I laughed, stopping when he reached for my wrist. Instead of taking my hand as I thought he would, he adjusted the sleeves of my shirt, smoothing the red fabric down my forearm to conceal my guardian mark. The front door opened, and Mark moved to one side so we could enter.

"This is the last time you let my niece on that bike of yours," Mark told Jamie.

"Yes, sir," Jamie said. "I should have my car back by Monday if all the parts come in." Mark nodded his head, handing Jamie a spray can of furniture cleaner and a rag. "Since it's raining and you can't finish painting, you can clean the house," he said. He didn't stay long enough for either of us to say anything more, clearly intending that we part ways there.

"See you later," I said. Jamie nodded, popping the top off the can and starting for the living room coffee table. I went to my bedroom and started going through my closet for anything I could use to put together a costume, finding the leather jacket I'd worn the night I'd woken. I remembered how terrified I'd been when I woke up under Noah's convertible and then again in Jamie and Izzy's house.

"Cleaning your closet?" Becky asked. She came into the room, taking a seat at my desk. I hung the jacket back in my closet, taking down the olive-green jean jacket next to it and tossing it on my bed.

"I'm looking for stuff that would work for homecoming dress-up days next week," I told her, "I think that will work for the zoologist day."

Becky let out a laugh. "That's one of the themes?" she asked.

"Only thanks to that stupid super wolf find at the national park," I said over her laugher. "Dr. Sampson is speaking at our school next week to all the science classes. I'm only dressing up because the prizes are good this year."

She stopped laughing, eyeing me suspiciously.

"Don't lie," she said. "You've always thought these theme days were fun. You just never had friends who would dress up with you." She was right, though I hadn't realized it until she said it.

"What should I do for book character day?" I asked.

Becky sorted through my closet and drawers with me for the next fifteen minutes before suggesting I try the second-hand store downtown.

"At least you have something for Monday, right?" she

asked me, gesturing to the outfit laid over the bed. It was the best teacher-like outfit I could think of: a pin skirt I only wore once to a relative's funeral, my nicest white blouse, and Becky's gray blazer.

"It's good enough," I said.

I noticed the way Becky's expression had changed, chewing on her bottom lip as if she was debating on spilling some big secret. It made me think that she hadn't come to help me pick outfits.

"What's up?" I asked her.

"Well, it's nothing," she said, shrugging. "You just seem a lot like your mom these days is all." She pulled me into a side hug. I didn't know what more to say to her, unsure I'd be able to say anything at all after her comment. We hadn't talked about my parents in years, least of all my mom. I knew that it had been hard on my aunt. They were close when they were growing up. I knew now that things must have changed when my mom became a guardian and was forced to be so secretive. Whatever she had told Becky, it was the reason Mark had such mistrust for my parents. I thought about Jamie, Izzy, and myself. I was going to be stuck as a seventeen-year-old me for who knows how long. What would I be forced to do when ten years passed, and I couldn't blame my never-aging on genes anymore?

"Thanks," I said. "I miss them too." I had never known my parents to have missed them, but I felt close to them since the accident. My aunt's expression faltered a little, but she gave me one last hug before using dinner as an excuse to leave.

Jamie went home to shower while I had dinner with Becky and Mark. Becky flashed me an encouraging smile when Mark mentioned how glad he was to finally be getting the house repainted. He'd talked about fixing the flaking paint above the porch for the last four years, but never had any time to take on the project until Jamie was wrapped into it. I hid my satisfied smirk behind a glass of water when Mark turned to ask me about my homecoming plans for the week.

I left my bedroom window open while I finished getting ready for bed in the bathroom, coming back to find Jamie setting up his usual bed on the floor. He finished laying out the final blanket before nodding to the outfit draped over my desk chair.

"Fancy look you've got there, Mrs. Johnson," he said, settling onto his makeshift bed.

"I don't know if it says I grade papers on the weekends or sell cars," I told him, settling onto my own bed and pulling the covers over my legs. We both laid down and I used my powers to turn off the lights. I closed my eyes, but I just wasn't tired enough. There were too many thoughts stuck in my head.

"Did you know my parents, Jamie?" I asked. I could hear him shifting and I turned my head to look at him. He was leaning on his right arm to get a good look at me. The moonlight fell over his face as he turned, highlighting his surprised expression.

"Why the sudden interest?" he asked.

"I've always wondered about my parents since I was old enough to understand how Becky and Mark were related to me," I said, propping myself up.

"I only meant that you'd never asked all this time," Jamie said, sitting up.

I leaned against the headboard and pulled a pillow into my lap. I hadn't thought about Jamie's connection to them until tonight. Of course, his parents had known them, well enough to sign as witnesses to their marriage. The only thing left to assume was that they had been guardians too. Then it dawned on me, the strange missing piece about my parents that I hadn't been able to pinpoint. Jamie's parents had died the night he and Izzy woke. That meant that my parents had married before then, before 1931. How could Becky be my aunt?

"Your parents were Maria and Jack Quinn," I said. "I saw them listed as witnesses to my parent's marriage when I tried researching your family at the library."

Jamie was on his feet and crossing my room to join me. He sat across from me on the bed, not at all concerned as usual by the squeak of the mattress under us. His serious expression cooled my skin.

"My parents' names were Maria and James Moore," Jamie said, keeping his voice low. "My name used to be Jamie Louis Moore and my sister was Isabella Maria Moore. We changed our names after we woke." I still didn't understand how this explained things and I could tell that Jamie wasn't going to continue unless I pressed on.

"So, who are Maria and Jack Quinn?" I asked. He sucked in a deep breath.

"After our parents died in the train explosion and Izzy and I became guardians, I told you that it was incredibly difficult for me. Izzy and I weren't sure if we could just walk around in public anymore. After we woke, we just left the scene, we were so confused by it. We went back to the Moore Estate, our house. We stayed there in hiding for days trying to figure out what to do. Not long after, people started coming to the house. We couldn't stay there anymore, so we just let everyone assume that we had died in the accident, and we left hoping to blend into the crowds of city life," Jamie said.

"And you changed your names?" I asked. He nodded. I thought about all the pictures covering the hallways of the estate. "When did you come back and get the estate?"

"We came back twice," Jamie said, "First, we used our new names, Maria and Jack Quinn. We tried to play up our age by a lot, wearing nice suits and dresses and doing a few illegal things in order to change our identities. We both had finished school a few years ago, so Izzy worked as a surgeon for a while. I worked in real estate, which is how I met your dad."

I felt my chest tighten now, wishing I had more to go off than Becky's "dark-haired and fair-skinned" description she'd given me of my dad.

"What about my mom?" I asked.

Jamie smiled a little. "She was pregnant with you then and teaching English at the high school. You have her curls," he said. "Your dad is the one who told me how easy it is to spot another guardian, which is exactly why I found him so strange when I first met him. He and your mom had matched and were rendered mortal again. They had only woken a few years earlier, after they met. I don't know how they woke, but they had been dating at the time. To put it simply, we compared marks and found out that we were all part of the sixth circle," he said. It felt spooky.

"Do you think this runs in families, then? If both our parents were guardians..." I didn't finish, already seeing the answer on Jamie's face. There was no way we could be positive with so few of us existing.

"Izzy and I only knew your parents for close to a year before they died. Your dad helped get us integrated into the real world again. It was his idea to further our identities. That's why you found Maria and Jack Quinn's names on your parent's marriage license. As much as we hated it, your dad was right. It would only build our backgrounds to help us live in the real world with the estate and putting real income to our names. He sacrificed a lot to help us— they both did. Your mom quit her job mid-year because there were some demons who'd discovered us. She spent most of her time at the estate with us and your dad was on the verge of losing his job thanks to the random sick days and unexplained emergencies. Your mom gave birth to you and almost a month later, they were both gone, killed when the four of us tried taking on the demons at the national park without ever training for it. It was stupid, despite the win. Your aunt and uncle were written into their will and so you became theirs. After that, I couldn't..."

I knew this part of the story had nothing to do with me or my family. I could sense the same barrier Jamie had always put between him and the rest of the world. Just like after his parents' deaths, he'd fallen back into a depression.

"How did you get the estate back?" I asked, glad that the question seemed to pull him out of his memories. Jamie sat up a little straighter.

"When we moved back to Burbrook, we knew that our parents had hidden their railroad fortune under the floor of the house, so we saved up our own money and got a large loan from your parents not even weeks after we'd met them. We used it all to buy the estate and we used the flooring remodel as our excuse for finding the money. Of course, there were no relatives of the Moore family left, so we were able to keep the millions. From there, we invested pieces of it, saved some, and created a business using the names Maria and Jack Quinn. We hired enough people that we barely had to work anymore, just answer phone calls whenever stock dropped a little or some bigwigs quit," he said with a shrug. It all made sense now, how they could afford such a huge mansion all this time without ever needing to work or give themselves away.

"You said that you came back to Burbrook twice," I started. "The second time, Maria and Jack Quinn became your parents, right?"

He nodded, a smirk pulling at the corner of his mouth.

"Did you leave after my parents died?" I asked.

He shook his head, rubbing a spot on my comforter where the thread was pulling apart.

"We stayed long enough to make ourselves known for our money. We slowly stopped making appearances in town. Well, I stopped going to town altogether. That's about the time that I met..." He stopped, letting his eyes go from my face to the window. He was talking about the girl he'd fallen in love with, the one who didn't match with him.

"You left after she died, fifteen years ago," I said.

Jamie nodded. "And when we came back, we were Jamie and Isabella Quinn. I waited a year before I started school at Burbrook High, letting everyone assume that my parents had homeschooled me all this time and that my sister was off at college. You know the rest," Jamie said, finally looking back at me with a sigh. I wondered if he felt like he was a part of one continuous circle. Every time he returned to Burbrook, he found another guardian only to be there when they were killed, squashing their chances of closing the sixth gate for good. I reached out for his hand, feeling his fingers start to slip away the moment I tried lacing mine with his.

"Third time's the charm," I said. I could tell by the quiver in his smile that he didn't find my quip funny. I was just glad he was smiling, trying to be anything other than the stoic Jamie I'd known until recently. He let me take his hand this time, giving it a gentle squeeze.

"I hope so," he said.

It went quiet. We sat holding hands for nearly a minute before I scooted closer to the wall and lay down. He laid next to me, tucking his arm under the pillow so I could make out his face in the dim light. I could feel the tension between us, as if any second someone would mention the fact that the ferryman was still out for my blood. Hellhound or not, someone would find me eventually. We all needed to be ready when they did, a fact I was sure was fresh in Jamie's mind.

"What is your favorite book, food, and board game?" I

asked. He looked curiously at me but humored my sudden change of subject. I felt the mood lighten at last at the sight of the first real smile on his face in hours.

"*Great Expectations*, tacos, and chess," he said.

I didn't reply. I adjusted my pillow a little under my head and closed my eyes.

Mark gave Jamie part of Sunday off so he could check the auto shop for his car. Izzy and I dropped him off at the door and continued down the street toward the only second-hand shop in Burbrook.

"Looks like everyone at school had the same idea," I said as we pulled into a parking spot along the sidewalk. There were more cars than usual parked outside the store, enough Burbrook High sport team stickers on the car windows to tell me who they all belonged to.

"Well, all you need is something for book character day, right?" Izzy asked as she got out of the car. I thought through so many different books, but the few I had clothes for weren't obvious enough for any character. It looked like I was just dressing up a little more that day or changing up my personal style instead of copying someone else's.

"You have all your days figured out?" I asked her, opening the door. A bell tinkled as we walked inside. The room was cold, the white tile and white walls making the room look overly boxy and unfinished despite the several years the shop had been there.

"I have more than enough, I told you that. You could've just looked through my closet," she said. I already had a couple of her jackets. I didn't need to borrow any more of her things. "It's not like you aren't over every day anyway," she continued. "Though I know you're there half the time for Jamie, not me."

She led the way to the side of the room underneath the *Girls/Women* sign where metal racks of clothes were stuffed full. The rows were labeled with handwritten signs, some now taped to the floor after falling from the end of the racks.

"I'm there to train," I told her, picking through the shirts at the end of the rack. "And I kicked your brother's ass yesterday in practice, by the way." Izzy snickered, pulling a black t-shirt with a little lace-up detail at the bust off the rack.

"He told me about the bruises," she said, "and I'm sure he showed them to you." She gave me a wink, making my stomach clench. I looked down the aisle behind me to make sure no one else had heard. Jamie and I had been working on footwork, meaning that both of us had ended the sparring session with sore thighs and calves.

"It's not like that," I said. "And what character dresses like *that?*"

Izzy looked down at the black top in her hands and shrugged.

"I just think it's cute. You wear so many plain shirts and this one would still be comfortable, but it also has a little..." She cast me a devious smile. I reached for the top, but she held it out of my reach. "You were looking at it a minute ago, so I know you like it," she said.

She wasn't wrong. I always saw clothes I liked in the store, but when it came time to wear them, I just never did. Jeans and T-shirts were just so much more comfortable.

"Fine but stop looking at me like you're going to turn me into some kind of sex object," I said. "It's not going to work."

She let me take the shirt now; I draped it over my left arm and continued picking at the rack.

"What did you mean about it *not being like that* with my brother?" Izzy finally asked.

I ignored her as long as I could, long enough for me to venture into the Halloween costumes at the end of the rack. I pulled a furry wolf suit from the section and turned to face her, holding the itchy fabric against myself.

"Big bad wolf?" I asked, letting out a little howl. She rolled her eyes, pulling the hanger from me and replacing it on the rack.

"Please, there is nothing big or bad about you," she said. "And you aren't going to distract me."

I let out a moan. Couldn't we do anything else, but talk about boys for once, especially her brother?

"I don't know." I said, "It's just weird."

I wish she'd stop looking at me with that goofy grin on her face. I didn't know what to think about Jamie. Any time I thought about how closed-off he is I remembered the moments he'd been open with me. He was so easy to talk to and I had just barely met him. It felt like we'd already shared so much between us, but we really didn't talk all that much. It felt like every moment I spent with him was a bonding moment, something deeper than just having things in common or sharing our troubles.

"Different than the feeling you get when watching *Magic Mike*?" she asked with a laugh.

"Yes," I exclaimed, giving her shoulder a gentle push. "It's not just some hormone thing. Why are you so stuck on this? He's your brother."

She nodded. "It's a guardian thing. I'm sure of it."

I stopped in the middle of the aisle to look at her.

"What do you mean?" I asked.

She moved closer to me, making sure the woman with her

four kids a few aisles over was still too busy arguing with them to hear us.

"Jamie said that things felt weird between the two of you for the past few years of school, but he wrote it off as being some kind of GPA thing about him being first in the class and you second. After you woke, I told him he needed to be sure it wasn't something else. If two guardians are a match, they will become mortal when they kiss," she said.

I felt my heart skip in my chest, my mouth going dry. I rounded the next aisle where the last of the costumes were hanging. These were much tamer, covering more skin and made with nicer fabrics.

"It's not that kind of thing, believe me," I told her. "We're going to homecoming together because it's convenient, not because we're a match." My eyes were drawn to the sparkles in the middle of the section. I pulled the dress from between the princess costumes to get a better look. It was a deep-blue colored flapper dress, complete with a feather headband. I glanced at the tag, still attached to the mesh sleeve. *The Great Gatsby: Daisy Buchanan.* I held the dress against my body, making sure the length was long enough for school.

"Mrs. McKellen will love the classic lit theme," Izzy said as I measured. It was almost too perfect, the last of its kind and exactly my size.

"I'd better try it on to make sure," I said, "but this is a winner."

"You better take me with you if you do win, not Jamie," Izzy said as she followed me to the dressing rooms at the back. I promised her half of the gift card before I pushed past the pink curtain. The girl's dressing room was small, just four cubicles concealed by the same pink fabric. All but one was open, none of them containing mirrors. The only mirror in the entire dressing room was the slim one on the back wall, a circle of fuzz pasted to the top corner where a sticker once clung. I chose the nearest cubicle and undid the tie on the curtain.

The flapper dress easily slid over my torso and hips, the fringe at the bottom swishing around my knees. I'd been worried that the mesh on the sleeve would itch, but it was far more comfortable than I'd thought. The costume must have been expensive at full-price, and it was clear from the tag that it was never worn. I finished zipping up the back the best that I could before leaving the room to look in the mirror. It was the most dressed up I'd felt since homecoming dress shopping and it would be the most I'd ever dressed up at school.

I attempted to flatten my curls before pulling the headband over them and adjusting the feathers just above my ear. The curtain to my left opened and I shifted to one side to make space before I realized who it was next to me. Alison froze just feet from me. She wore a blue gingham mini-dress and a white pair of leggings to make the length appropriate for school. Her red shoes matched the ribbons she'd tied around the pigtails that perfectly framed the scowl on her face. She looked over my dress before locking eyes with me again.

"*The Great Gatsby,*" she said. "Very relevant for school. Hoping for extra credit?" She joined me at the mirror, her arm brushing mine as she leaned closer to the wall with red lipstick in hand.

"I think I saw a lion suit in the boy's section if you want to make *The Wizard of Oz* a group theme," I told her as she put the cap back on the tube and straightened up. She was tall and leggy, towering inches above me. She adjusted her blonde pigtails so that they laid over her shoulders.

"I know what you did to Macy before school," Alison said. "And you can bet you won't just get away with it." She stepped behind me and before I could react, her hands were on my shoulders. She flattened the sleeves of my dress before zipping it up the rest of the way. "I'm a real friend, after all," she said, brushing a piece of lint from my hair before going back into her stall.

I changed back into my clothes, surprised that Alison beat me out of the dressing room. I noticed Alison and Macy at the register. Macy sat a fuzzy-eared bear headband onto the table along with a brown pleated skirt and tank top. Alison caught me watching them and gave me a friendly wave. I turned from the gesture, seeing Izzy standing in the corner where the shoes were.

"Hey," she called out, holding up a pair of black shoes with a chunky heel. "These would work for your dress," she said. I joined her in the corner, taking the shoes.

"Did you see that?" I asked her, looking back at the register. Macy and Alison were gone now, the bell on the door tinkling as it swung shut.

"Of course, I did. I've been watching since he came in," she said, "He doesn't exactly look like he shops second hand, does he?"

I didn't understand what she meant right off until I scanned the front of the store and saw Mr. Puck looking through the shelves of men's shoes. Mr. Puck was one of the few teachers in the building who really dressed professionally rather than just wearing a nice pair of jeans and a polo. He always wore a pair of slacks and a button-up, at the very least.

"Maybe he knows some tricks we don't," I said.

For a moment, I was sure he'd caught us staring, but he set down the pair of shoes he was looking at and went about his business without a second glance.

"Are you ready?" Izzy asked.

I double checked the size of the shoes I was holding before nodding. She moved so fast to the register that I nearly walked into the woman with her four children as I followed. Mr. Puck left the store as I finished paying. Izzy took the bag of clothes for me and led the way back onto the sidewalk.

"I know what you're thinking," I told her when I'd finally caught up. She walked right past the Maserati, following Mr. Puck into the bookshop at the end of the street. "Izzy," I said, grabbing her arm before she could continue after him down the fiction aisle. She tugged her wrist from my grasp but didn't keep walking.

"I told you both that I have a bad feeling about him," she said.

"And we all decided that there's no way he's a—," I lowered my voice as an old man joined us in the aisle, "A you-know-what."

Izzy let out a deep breath and nodded. "Let's just get a coffee then," she said. "We're already here." After a beat, I agreed, and she led the way to the back of the store where a small café was. Mr. Puck was the last in the line. Izzy hurried forward, nudging him with her foot.

"Oh, sorry!" she said, feigning innocence in a way only she could. Puck's eyes went from Izzy to me before they lit up with recognition. He tucked his book under his arm.

"Victoria," he greeted, "And I don't think we've met."

Izzy extended her hand.

"I'm shadowing the athletic trainer for my college class, so I'm pretty new to the school," she said and gave his hand a firm shake.

He turned from the line to face her now.

"Really? What major?"

"Physical therapy."

"That's great. Mrs. Chung used to work as a physical therapist before she retired and started working with the school part-time." Mr. Puck folded his hands over his chest, fully invested in their conversation now.

"That's why I asked her," Izzy said with a shrug.

"What did you say your name was?"

"Isabella Quinn, but I go by Izzy," she said.

Puck's expression dimmed a little as he made the connection, glancing at me for a second before looking back at Izzy with a smile.

"I have your brother in my chemistry class," he said. "He's a pretty good student..." He said it as though he meant to follow up with a *but*. It was obvious enough that Izzy, being the brazen woman that she was, commented on it immediately.

"But he's an idiot."

"I was going to say he's too smart for his own good sometimes," Puck said with a laugh, glancing at me as though the same could be said for me now that I'd cast my lot with the Quinns.

"Izzy used to be a model," I said.

Both of their expressions dropped. Izzy's head snapped around to glare at me in warning while Puck looked back at her as though studying the angles of her face.

"I, um," Izzy started, straightening up again and reforming her playful façade. "It was a way to pay for college."

"You were good at it then," Puck said, shrugging like it was the most obvious thing ever. In a way, it was. Izzy carried herself with such grace that it was entrancing. Clearly, the decades of being a guardian influenced her physical prowess.

Izzy blushed. The fact that she was flustered was comical. "Well, there's more to modeling than a pretty face," she said. "Like Marilyn Monroe said, give a girl the right kind of shoes and she will rule the world."

Puck smirked. "So, stubbornness runs in the Quinn family?"

"If you mean knowing what one wants and how to earn it, then yes."

"Hard work," Puck said and crossed his arms, "and lots of time. I came from a blue-collar family. My mom raised my siblings and me by herself after my dad split. I worked a couple jobs to help and thankfully, my grades were stellar enough to get into an Ivy with a couple scholarships to pay for most of it."

Izzy's smile faltered. "You understand then, being stubborn yourself."

"There's a difference between stubbornness born out of pride," Puck said, straightening up, "and stubbornness born from humility."

Izzy's lip twitched, but she remained sweet as before. "You're right," she said, taking a step forward as the line moved so that Mr. Puck had to take a step back. "I attended an Ivy as well before our family circumstances meant I needed to be home with my brother," she said. "And I agree that there's a difference. It's such a shame that women aren't afforded the ability of pride from hard work without being seen as self-absorbed. I earned my 4.0 and degrees the same as any other student."

"Degrees?" Mr. Puck asked, relaxing a little.

Izzy nodded. "Two bachelors, both science fields. I'm mostly finished with my masters, which overlaps with a doctorate program."

"You look so young." Puck deflated, his smile forced.

"I'm twenty-one," Izzy said, "I graduated high school early and started college right away, took extra classes each semester plus summers."

"You must've been taking a lot of extra classes..." I could practically see him doing the mental math.

Izzy gave an awkward laugh and twisted a strand of hair on her shoulder.

"I think you're next, Mr. Puck," I said, pointing toward the register. The man in front of him was still placing his order, but it was enough of a distraction to put an end to the conversation. Izzy's shoulders slumped with a sigh of relief.

"I will see you first thing tomorrow then," he told me with a smile before turning to Izzy "And I will see you around the building. We should talk more about academics, our university experiences, you know..." It was obvious that he didn't believe everything she said, but that didn't keep Izzy from politely agreeing.

Mr. Puck ordered a large mint tea and moved to the pick-up window on the opposite side of the counter from us. I ordered a black coffee, which we were able to get within seconds of ordering and be on our way back to the street.

"Maybe I should stop spying," Izzy said with a groan. "God, that was embarrassing." She sank into the front seat of her car and started it before I had even reached the door. I barely had my seat belt clicked into place when we backed out of the lot.

"We told you," I said with a laugh.

Izzy stopped at the red light, pointing a finger at my face.

"Don't even get me started," she said. "And don't you dare think of telling Jamie." She didn't move through the intersection until I promised her I wouldn't.

CHAPTER 15

Izzy picked Jamie and me up for school the next morning. Even after getting all the parts delivered, the auto shop told Jamie that it would be at least Wednesday before they finished with his car. He'd grumbled about it the entire way to school, not stopping until we parked, and Izzy told him to cool off.

"You'll still have your car before your big date," she said. "At least you have big plans for Saturday."

Jamie slung his bag over his shoulder, both of them waiting on me to grab my stuff from the trunk.

"It's not my fault you decided to make a date watching Mr. Puck instead of getting a real one," he said. Izzy flashed me a warning look as I closed the trunk. I rolled my eyes but kept good on my promise not to mention the awkward conversation between her and Puck at the bookstore.

The entryway of the building was clogged with people, most of them dressed up for Dress Like a Teacher Day. Macy and her group of girls all wore long dresses and wide-rimmed glasses like Mrs. McKellen always did. Like Jamie, lots of the boys wore dress pants and pastel-colored button-up shirts like Mr. Puck. Just as I had feared, my pin skirt and blazer were far from the best of the bunch even Izzy's dorky sweater vest fit the theme better.

"I look like I work at Edward Jones," I said. Izzy and Jamie both laughed.

The bell rang and the sea of students started down the main hall. It took Jamie and me a few minutes to weave across the mass to the chemistry room. Every table was set up with beakers and test tubes with mini bottles of vinegar set in the center. Mr. Puck was too busy in the hall monitoring the traffic to notice Sean Peterson holding two beakers to his chest like a bra.

"All right, everyone in your seats," Sean called out, "We have work to do." His table burst into laughter as he sat the beakers back on their tables. Jamie muttered something under his breath that I couldn't make out. I busied myself taking out my notes and homework from last week as the bell rang.

"All right, everyone in your seats," Mr. Puck said as he came back into the room, "We have work to do." Sean's table laughed again, only stopping when Mr. Puck shot them a glare from his computer as he took attendance. The room went silent as the intercom clicked on.

"Happy Monday, Burbrook High and happy first day of homecoming week," Mrs. McKellen said, "Today is Dress Like a Teacher Day in honor of the teacher versus student volleyball game tonight at six o'clock in the main gym. During first period, members of the media class will come around to each class to take pictures of the best-dressed boy and girl. Tomorrow is Dress Like a Book Character Day, so make sure to participate for your chance to win. First period tomorrow will be spent decorating doors. The class with the best door will get donuts the following morning. Don't forget that only you can make today great! Go wolves!" The football players in the room began howling, not stopping until Mr. Puck threatened to give them detentions.

"When they come in for pictures, I want Jamie and Macy to go," Mr. Puck said before starting straight into his lecture about common chemical reactions. Like he usually did before labs, he showed us a cheesy video from the nineties of a boy and a girl talking about dangerous chemical combinations, each scenario over-dramatized. Just as he finished giving us instructions for the lab, the door opened and a freshman boy with a camera sheepishly poked his head inside.

"Jamie and Macy, you can step out now," Mr. Puck said, motioning for them to follow the boy.

Jamie closed his notebook. I elbowed him.

"He only picked you because you're both wearing the same shirt," I said as he stood up.

Jamie flashed me a smirk.

"The man's got good taste," he said, giving me a wink before he followed Macy into the hallway.

Mr. Puck started passing out the lab booklets to the front tables, stopping when he reached mine.

"I'm going to have to ask you to open your backpack, Tori," he said, keeping his voice low. My stomach twisted. What did he expect to find and why was he pointing fingers at me?

"What? Why?" I asked, wishing I'd kept my voice a little lower now that Alison and a few of the girls at her table had turned to watch.

Mr. Puck let out a long sigh and moved a chair from the opposite side of the table so he could sit. He nodded at my backpack, and I knew I had no choice. I unzipped my bag and let out a gasp, feeling my eyes burn as I saw the plastic box filled with tiny tools, the lock still firmly in place.

"You were the first one in the room and I had to ask. I'd

never have suspected you," Mr. Puck said, taking the box from my bag.

I could feel the tears threatening to spill over.

"I didn't put them there," I said. "I wasn't the only person in the room. Macy's table came in right behind me, and they left their lab books on the back table. Maybe it fell into my bag." I was thankful for my quick thinking, though I was sure this was no accident. Mr. Puck looked at the table behind me. The small boxes sat in the empty space in the table where drawers used to be. There were Sterilite containers on top of the table where we were allowed to store our lab books when we didn't need them. With a long sigh, Mr. Puck looked back at me.

"I don't mean to interrupt," Alison said, appearing next to Mr. Puck. "I thought I knocked something off the table when I got my book, but I didn't see anything on the floor, so I just left. Tori has never been in trouble, and I didn't want you thinking she did something wrong." I could tell she was trying her best not to crack a smile as Mr. Puck thanked her for her honesty. She went back to her table, getting a high five from Sean before they went back to their beaker.

"This would've been a serious offense," Puck told me, tapping the lid of the container. "There are scalpels in these containers. Having a weapon at school gets you in trouble with the police, not just us. You have to be more careful about where you leave your things."

I opened my mouth to thank him for trusting me, but he was already at the back table, moving all the locked containers to a cardboard box underneath it.

I took a deep breath and tried my best to focus on setting up for the lab. Macy and Jamie returned moments later, Jamie's expression falling when he noticed me. I continued measuring out the vinegar into one of the test tubes as he took his seat.

"What's wrong?" he asked.

I shook my head, taking a moment to calm myself the best I could.

"Macy or Alison, probably Alison, put lab equipment in my backpack when I wasn't looking," I told him. His eyes went wide, and his jaw tightened. "Don't look," I told him, tapping his hand with my pencil when he glanced toward their table.

"Did you just notice?" he whispered.

I felt my insides squirming with agitation. Mr. Puck had accepted Alison's explanation, but did he believe it?

"Mr. Puck noticed it missing and asked me because we were the first people in the room," I said. "Thankfully, he believed me when I said that it must've fallen in." I wrote out the measurement in my manual, moving on to the colored dye.

"Like we don't have enough to deal with," Jamie said. Just like that, he was back to serious Jamie. He was right though. We still had no idea why anyone would be after my blood. I ignored him and added the red drops to the vinegar, wishing they were any color but red right now. I added the mixture to the beaker of baking soda, watching it foam up immediately and nearly overflow onto the table. Jamie and I spent the rest of class writing our explanation for the reaction and cleaning up our equipment, never once mentioning the stealing incident until class ended.

"You're welcome," Alison told me as she passed in the hall, getting a laugh out of the group. Before I could stop myself, I used my powers to inch the nearest trash can away from the wall just far enough for Alison to walk into it and stumble into the lockers. She straightened up with an exaggerated laugh and continued down the hall with her girls as if the entire incident only added to the hilarity.

"I don't understand why Alison did that," I said. "She wasn't even with Macy when we threw stuff at her car."

Jamie stopped next to my locker and held my bag as I unloaded my chemistry books.

"You're sure that's why she tried framing you?" he asked.

I paused with my hand on the spine of my history textbook, just seconds long enough to tip Jamie off. He let out a sigh.

"What else happened?" he asked.

I remembered the once-over Alison had given me in the dressing room over the weekend.

"It's not worth talking about," I said.

Jamie kept me from shutting the door, his expression softened.

"It is if it means those girls are going to terrorize you like this again," he said, "I understand wanting to be the bigger person, but you can't let them walk all over you either. If you want them to stop, you have to do something about it. Complacency only makes it easier to attack you."

I almost shot back that I wasn't being complacent, but the truth of it kept my mouth shut. Complacent was exactly what I was, what I always had been. It left a sour taste in my mouth.

"Izzy and I went to a second-hand shop to look for clothes for homecoming week and I ran into Alison in the dressing room. She told me that I wouldn't get away with throwing food at Macy's car the other day," I said, shutting my locker when Jamie lowered his hand. He shook his head.

"What we did to Macy has nothing to do with Alison though," he said as we walked. "Besides, it wasn't like we put a rock through her windshield."

Alison had been pretty mean to some of the girls at school before. Despite not liking me, she'd never gone so far as to pull her usual tricks on me. Macy's friendship with me kept her from that, I was sure. Alison had done everything from keying girls' cars to stealing clothing from the locker room during gym. There were no limits and the idea of being on the opposing side of her games made me nervous.

"It doesn't matter," I said, "I stood up to her and her stupid crew for the first time. They aren't used to people giving them shit."

The look on Jamie's face was one of annoyance. He followed me to my history class. When he disappeared from my side, I looked back to see him staring down the adjacent hallway. Sean was pulling away from Macy, his hands lingering a moment at the back of her jeans. Alison leaned toward Macy to whisper, her eyes directed our way.

"He's doing that on purpose," Jamie told me, not at all concerned with hiding his nod towards the group. Sean kept his eyes on us and hugged Macy closer again, an expression of smugness coming over his face. It was a look of pure loyalty, but also ownership. It said, "don't mess with my girl" in such an old-fashioned way that my muscles tightened.

"Mrs. Hawthorne is coming. Let her take care of them," I said, when I saw the lanky woman walking our way, her maxi skirt flowing wildly around her thin ankles. Jamie stepped closer to me, slipping his hand into mine. I felt my body relax with shock, my stomach doing flips and my face warming quickly. When I looked back at him, he wasn't looking back at me at all. He only had eyes for Sean Peterson, both boys exchanging glares of warning. I tugged my hand out of his, finally gaining his attention.

"You're doing it too," I told him.

He looked back at me with confusion.

"Doing what?" he asked, glancing back at Sean.

I flicked the side of his head and he turned to me again, a hand over the spot.

"Guys like Sean don't think about women as people with needs and legitimate feelings and opinions. By acting all big and tough like my bodyguard, you are lowering yourself to his standards," I said. He still seemed confused, as if denying or not realizing what he'd done. "I don't need a bodyguard. I don't need you to speak for me. I know you want to help, but it's not your place."

"Break it up, you two," Mrs. Hawthorne's shrill voice echoed down the hall, drawing nearly everyone's attention toward Macy and Sean who were now kissing. Jamie sighed, keeping his eyes on me.

"You have a crew too, Mindfreak," he said, giving a small smile.

Mrs. Hawthorne had moved back to her usual post outside the door, carefully watching us now that Macy's group had dispersed.

"I appreciate you standing up for me," I whispered to him "But it's like you said, if I don't do anything, they won't stop. Me, not you."

He let out a deep breath and gave me a single nod.

"Meet me for lunch?" he asked. I always met him at lunch. There was a strange pause between us, as if we were missing a real goodbye. I felt my gut clench as I thought about hugging him, confused by the reaction as soon as it had happened.

"Um, yeah. Sure," I told him, turning and walking straight into the classroom before the redness in my face became too obvious.

Classes went back to normal the rest of the morning, even with Macy and Alison sitting a few rows behind me in Shakespeare. After finishing the grammar assignment early, Mrs. McKellen recruited me to sort a small box of T-shirts at her desk. I used a pair of scissors from a mug on her desk to cut away the packing tape on the top. The box was full of green T-shirts, the school's name and logo across the front with the yellow words *Academic Team* underneath in a sporty font. It was no wonder she'd asked me specifically to help.

"Here are the order forms," she said, setting half-sheets of paper on the corner of the desk with student names and sizes written across the top. "Just neatly roll the T-shirts with the order forms on the outside," she said, showing me a roll of green fabric with a rubber band around it, holding the half-sheet tightly against it. I took the plastic bag of rubber bands from her when she held it out and set to work, thankfully spending the next twenty minutes rolling T-shirts without getting a single offer to join the team.

I glanced at my phone when Mrs. McKellen busied herself telling off a group of students at the back of the room for being too loud. The text I'd felt vibrating in my pocket moments before was from Jamie, asking me to meet him for lunch at the loading dock at the back of the building. All I'd have to do was go the opposite way down the hall, following the traffic toward the music classrooms where the back door was. I couldn't reply before Mrs. McKellen turned back around.

"Your worksheet is due at the beginning of class tomorrow," she said just as the bell rang. The room filled with the sound of backpack zippers and books slapping tables as the room full of students packed up, all eager to escape to lunch. I let out a sigh when I noticed the academic team schedule sitting on my desk. I tucked it in the front cover of my copy of *The Merchant of Venice* and shoved all my things into my bag. I hurried out of the room before Mrs. McKellen could finish thanking me for my help, already halfway down the music hall before I realized where I was. It was too late now to turn around. At least, it was if I wanted to continue going unnoticed amongthe choir students.

I skirted the teachers gathered outside the band room chatting and rounded the corner for the back door. I wasn't the only one planning on ditching; a boy and girl clasped hands as they darted out the door and jogged across the parking lot. I caught sight of a dark car just beyond the doorway in the loading dock. I lunged forward to catch the door before it closed. I slunk through the opening, not noticing until then how fast my heart was beating. It was hard not to recognize the black Audi sports car. The passenger-side window rolled down without a sound and Jamie gave me a single wave.

"Campus police make their rounds just after lunch starts," he said, "and I don't want to add any more time to my sentence." Sentence? I settled into the seat and clipped my seat belt in place just before Jamie rounded the side of the building. He pulled into the street, taking a right turn towards the forest.

"Are you in trouble?" I asked. Jamie shrugged.

"Thackery gave me a Saturday School for skipping second period," he said. "They put two and two together about all my morning absences and he thought a detention was below the offence." Jamie didn't seem to mind at all. It was strange. Jamie had never been known at school for getting into trouble; it was the opposite, actually.

"Maybe you're not the one who's the bad influence," I said.

He let out a laugh. "No, it's definitely me,"

I snorted, taking my planner from my bag to double check the bell schedule.

"You never had a record at school until you got involved with me," I said. "You have a higher GPA and SAT score than me."

"Your grades would get better too if you'd been through high school and college as many times as I have," he said. "It's like I told you, I was a loser when I was mortal. I didn't do well in school, and I wasn't serious about anything except playing music. I was going to write songs and play wherever I could until I got a real music job. I was happy that way. I forgot how that felt, being so..."

"Authentic?" I asked.

He smirked. He didn't need to speak. I knew that's what he meant.

"I thought your car was in the shop till' Wednesday," I said.

Jamie's smile was back, a sly smirk that made me wonder who he'd told off to get the work expedited.

"It's why I ditched this morning— well half of it anyway," he said. "The shop's just a few blocks away, so I walked there. I dropped a few hints about knowing that the manager sells pot to the kids at school there when they ditched. They had it fixed halfway through third period."

I let out a hum of understanding, trying to hide some of my annoyance. There were two auto shops in town and Mark couldn't have driven his car an extra five minutes to the nicer shop? I focused on the road, not realizing that we were going the opposite way we needed to for the nearest drive-through.

"What about lunch?" I asked.

"Just wait," he said. "It's taken care of."

We drove past the national park entrance, going just yards down the road before he pulled off where the tire marks were embedded into the grass on the shoulder. It was the exact spot where we'd seen the hellhound.

"Working through the lunch break?" I asked.

Jamie got out of the car and motioned for me to follow him. I left my bag on the floorboard and hurried to catch up with him before he could go too far into the tree line. We were retracing our steps from the attack, the grass sloping into the small clearing where he'd killed the hellhound. The tree was still lying on its side where I'd uprooted it with my powers.

"This was your first time using your powers in a fight, even if it didn't go as planned," Jamie said, taking a seat on the trunk of the thick tree. He patted the expanse of bark across from him. I crossed the dirt and pine needles to join him, noticing the basket just beyond the trunk. It was filled with tightly sealed glass jars. There were cookies, a spinach and bean salad, and two sandwiches. He tapped the log next to him with a single index finger, pointing out the message he'd clearly etched into the bark with a knife. It read *Homecoming?* with a box for yes and another for no.

"You already asked me," I said, barely containing my laugh.

He took two bottles of water from the basket and handed one to me.

"Technically, I told you to come with me," he said, handing me a sandwich next. "Besides, you may not think all the senior year events are worth it now that you're a guardian, but you deserve to be asked out in a cheesy, teenage movie style at least once."

Jamie reached behind him and tugged a dagger free from his waistband. He took it by the blade and offered me the hilt. It was polished to perfection, Latin inscribed along the flat of the blade.

"This is great," I said. "But I don't know that it's worth spending the morning before the dance in Saturday School."

He let out a groan as he unwrapped his sandwich.

"Don't worry about me," he said, "I can get ready after. Like I said, you deserve to have the whole high school experience."

I used the dagger to cut a jagged checkmark in the box next to *yes*. Jamie took it back from me and aimed it at the closet tree. It whooshed past us, spinning in a blur of silver before it hit the trunk with a loud crack and sank all the way to the hilt.

"My turn," I said, focusing on pulling the dagger from the tree. I felt the weight of it threatening to build into a headache and before Jamie could warn me, I forced all my energy into pulling it free. It shot toward me, stopping a foot from my face when I raised both my hands in defense. Jamie snatched it from the air and tucked it back into his waistband.

"You have to be careful of your limits," he said. "It's like with that tree. You had no control over where it fell. Control is important."

I focused on peeling away the plastic wrap from my sandwich.

"You have to admit that it was cool," I said.

After a moment, he smirked. "Fine," he said, "It was cool and as much as I want to see you try mental knife throwing, I won't let you."

I lowered my sandwich and gave his shoulder a shove.

"Come on," I said. "I bet I could aim better using my powers than you could using your muscles."

He hesitated at the challenge and for a split second, I thought he'd agree. He shook his head and took a big bite of his sandwich. We ate for a few minutes before my thoughts wandered back to the last time we'd talked like this.

"You told me that you and Izzy met a telekinetic once before," I said.

Jamie nodded as he finished chewing the last of his sandwich. He reached for the jar of chocolate chip cookies, taking out one.

"It was right after we woke, the first time we left. He was the first person we'd met who was like us and not related to us," he said. "It was interesting being around him." He studied the cookie for a moment as if remembering something particularly puzzling about the telekinetic boy.

"What do you mean?" I asked.

"Well, his circle was different," Jamie said. "Until then, we just assumed that all guardians were connected and that our circle was just our family unit, not anything special. Our parents were the only guardians in Burbrook, so we didn't know any different until we ran into Ahmad. Izzy and I were chasing a demon we'd stupidly happened upon during a drunken night out. We chased her down and killed her. Ahmad caught us doing it and freaked out. At first, we thought he was mortal and was going to call the cops, but he was just mad because he wanted to be the one to kill the demon. Turned out, she had killed his friend, and it weakened their circle."

"How many people were in his circle?" I asked.

Jamie took a bite of the cookie and offered me one, but I was too interested in the story to be distracted now.

"Twelve," he said, "and most of them were matched. Ahmad was the last one without a match. They had all hoped Izzy would match with him until they found out we were from a different circle."

I didn't understand what was so vastly different between circles. I thought it was just a different gate we were all forced to serve until we could seal it.

"You couldn't just join them?" I asked.

Jamie shook his head. "We helped them hunt demons and such for a while, so we joined them in that sense. Things are different when you're a part of a circle though. I didn't realize just how much of a bond that is until we met your parents later," he said, finishing the cookie and setting the jar back in the basket. I rolled the plastic wrap between my hands until it formed a tight ball.

"What happened?" I asked at last.

Jamie let out an odd laugh and shrugged.

"No idea," he said. "Ahmad started to act funny after a while, said that he couldn't tell us things about his circle like he used to because of a pact they'd made. Members of the circle started to just disappear. Ahmad left a voicemail late one night saying that he was moving on. We went to his place as soon as we got the message, but the entire apartment was cleaned out. The landlord had no idea he was leaving; because she was mad as hell when we asked her about it. His phone was still connected after that, but he never picked up any of our calls. Eventually, we just stopped trying. We left the city not long after."

I wondered why they had all rejected Izzy and Jamie after they'd helped them protect their gate. Even weirder was how they all just vanished as if that was the plan all along.

"Do you think that they were up to something, like maybe someone made some kind of deal with the Shadowlands?" I asked.

Jamie shrugged, his expression thoughtful.

"Whatever the reason for leaving, Ahmad didn't exactly seem to agree," he said. "It was like he understood why he had to stay united with his circle, but at the same time he didn't. When they went underground or wherever it is they went, it was like time slowed down in the city. Demons stopped appearing. It was weird."

Jamie's expression fell and his eyes, though still on me, seemed to be trained on something else far away. I could tell that he would only fall deeper into the past if I didn't say something.

"I'm wearing red to the dance," I said. "I thought maybe you'd want to match your tie or something to my dress."

He pulled himself back to the present with a small smile.

"Red it is," he said, tossing the plastic from our sandwiches into the basket and standing up. We loaded the basket into the backseat of the car and started back to school, sitting in the parking lot until the bell rang. Together, we slipped unnoticed into the throng of people pressed together in the narrow music hall. With a final wave, Jamie turned at the stairs and I started my ascent toward drama.

"It's unfair that they're allowed to compete," Izzy said, handing me a yellow flyer when I joined her in the stands. Most of the school had stayed after the day ended to watch the volleyball tournament. The cheerleaders had decorated the gym for homecoming, green and yellow streamers wrapping the rails around the plastic seats. A couple hand-painted banners had been taped to the brick walls around the room, some already torn at the edges from the constant slapping of volleyballs against them. "They could at least have made the volleyball team split up," Izzy said.

I took the flyer and dropped my bag next to hers. One side of the paper had a list of the teams and players. There were only four: the volleyball team under the name *Wolfpack*, a team of science and history teachers called *Old School*, the English teachers who called themselves *The Big Bad Wolves*, and a team of senior boys simply listed as *Team 4*. The back of the flyer was a bracket of games dictating who would play first: Old School versus Team 4.

"I heard Sean say during English today that they were calling their team Balls," I said.

"You mean Ballers?" Izzy asked, taking the schedule back from me. I shook my head.

"No, just Balls," I said.

She snorted; the beginning of her joke was promptly cut off by cheering. We looked toward the locker rooms. Sean's mouth was open wide, his grunt of a scream echoing around the gym. Several boys followed him, waving for the crowd to yell louder. They were all dressed in green gym shorts, cut short with their white sleeveless shirts tucked into their waistbands. Each shirt had a handwritten number on the front, the back bearing nicknames only the students understood.

"Where's the spandex?" Macy yelled when the gym quieted. The rest of the volleyball team looked up from their bags to laugh.

"Thackery said this ain't Brazil," Sean called back, drawing the attention of the teams of teachers awkwardly stretching in the corner. Mr. Thackery strode across the court toward the boys, already waving for the students in the stands to stop cheering.

"Mrs. McKellen has elbow pads," I said, pointing past the boys to the group of English teachers trying their best to pass a volleyball in a circle. I was starting to regret sticking around for the games when the P.E. teacher stepped to the net and called for the teams to take their places on the court. A couple of freshmen girls from the volleyball team took seats at the table behind the referee stand where a flippable scoreboard read all zeros.

"This is going to be pathetic," I said.

One of the sophomore teachers served, the ball arching high into the air before coming down on the other side of the net.

"Why isn't he playing?" Izzy asked.

I followed her gaze to the double doors that led into the hall. Mr. Puck was leaning in the doorway, still dressed in his slacks and button-up. Out of everyone on staff at Burbrook High, Mr. Puck was the most athletic in appearance. Most of the students had just assumed he'd play, though no one ever asked him outright. Everyone at school knew that he worked out; most of us had spotted him at some point at the gym or running along the side of the road.

"Is that why you didn't want to go to a movie?" I asked.

Izzy elbowed me, getting to her feet. I unzipped my bag

and pulled out my history textbook and opened it to a set of questions.

"Lame or not, this game is still more interesting than homework," she said. "I'll be back. I'm going to buy a home-coming shirt."

She took the last of the steps to the floor in seconds and started for a table in the corner. I watched the game just long enough to see that the teachers would be eliminated easily before going back to my homework. It was hard to concentrate with all the cheering, the insults growing louder from Macy's growing crew across the aisle from me.

"If McKellen actually gets the ball over this game..." Alison started, her words lost amidst the laughter. I looked up just in time to catch her gaze, the smile on her face fading. I shook my head and looked back down at the homework, realizing I'd written the same sentence as my answer for the first three questions.

"Someone come get a drink with me," Macy said.

"I'll go, but it will take something stronger than a coke to get me through this game," Alison said.

I saw my backpack move out of the corner of my eye, the whole thing thunking down the last three steps and falling right into the ball cart. Four volleyballs rolled from the top of the pile and bounced onto the end of the court. A few students began yelling for the game to stop as Macy turned to look at me.

"Tori," Alison cried out. "You better get those before someone trips!"

"You're the klutz that kicked the bag down the stairs," Izzy said, stopping next to the cart.

I noticed Mr. Puck staring at us, clearly still trying to figure out if there was an argument or not. Macy noticed him too; she tugged on Alison's braid and gained her attention just long enough to nod in his direction. Alison turned back to me, flashing a smile.

"I'll fix this problem for you too, just like I did in chemistry," she said. "We all know whose balls you want to shag anyway."

The students just behind me started yelling, the words "heads up" standing out. I looked up just in time to see the volleyball coming down toward me. It was as if the entire room had stopped. I raised both my arms, able to see the golden wolf head embossed on the ball a little too perfectly. I could catch it and end the play, or I could angle my left arm just a little and take enough of a swing at it to deflect it directly at Alison.

I turned my left wrist just a little and opened my hand wide, but my heart jolted when I thought about the last time. I remembered the way the ball squeezed, cartoonishly, between the blocker's hands. Jamie's words echoed through my brain, reminding me that any supernatural being would notice the subtlety. I froze with my arm mid-swing, too late to catch the ball. It popped off my hand and went whooshing by Alison so closely that it moved her braid from her shoulder.

The entire crowd groaned when the ball contacted Mr. Puck's face square on the nose. He raised a hand to his face, a red smear just visible over his chin. Izzy turned to face him immediately as if he might throw the ball right back at me, the only one not in shock or laughing behind their hands.

"Radio a custodian," Mr. Puck said when Principal Thackery came running over. Once he saw that Puck suffered nothing more than a bloody nose, he yanked the boxy radio from his hip and mumbled into the static. I slammed my history book shut and moved down the stairs for my backpack as Mr. Puck started for the hall, hunched over to keep from getting any more blood on the gym floor than he already had. Izzy was staring down at the scarlet droplets just feet from her as if they could finally confirm what she assumed about the teacher.

"Izzy," I said, appearing in the doorway, "Let's go."

I started into the hall ahead of her, my heart racing so fast it hurt. As much as I hated to admit it, I should've just used my powers. It would've been more accurate. The fact that I didn't hit Alison made my stomach burn, and the realization that I'd injured the school's favorite teacher made me groan aloud with guilt.

"Tori," Izzy called as soon as we made it out the front doors and into the parking lot, "Stop."

I felt her hand catch my wrist and I spun around. She didn't look shocked like I figured she would but impressed. She let out a single laugh before clapping a hand over her mouth and looking back to the doors to make sure no one had heard. We were totally alone in the drop-off lane.

"I should've just caught the stupid ball," I said, taking a deep breath.

Izzy began laughing again, swinging her arm in a replay of the event.

"You should've hit it harder," she said.

I could feel the smile pulling at my lips as my body finally began to relax. After a moment, we were both laughing. It felt freeing in hindsight. I was throwing moldy McDonald's sandwiches at my enemies, hitting volleyballs at them... I was finally standing up for myself.

"I got some of his blood on my shoe," Izzy said, lifting her right foot from the ground so we could see the single red drop on the toe of her sneakers. "I can test it to see if his DNA differs from normal humans."

I felt myself crash back to Earth. She still thought he was somehow involved.

"If he was a demon, don't you think he would've attacked us already?" I asked.

She shot me a pleading look. "I have a feeling and I know I'm not crazy," she said. "You sound just like Jamie."

"He didn't react quick enough to block the ball. If your feeling was reliable then it wouldn't have hit him straight in the face, right?" I asked.

She let out a groan, struggling to find the right words.

"You don't get it. You think that we're all fine because you and Jamie got rid of the hound, but I'm telling you that I'm feeling this weird energy around him and it's nothing but supernatural," Izzy said.

Maybe Izzy had a point. Jamie had let his guard down a lot, especially since the ferryman disappeared and we killed the hellhound. What if we had been lulled into a false sense of safety? I knew Jamie wouldn't believe her, but she was my best friend. She had always sided with me about training when Jamie hadn't. She trusted me when I said I was ready.

"I believe you," I said. "We'll keep an eye on him."

Izzy nodded, satisfied. We both relaxed a little and agreed after a few minutes of silence that maybe a movie would be the perfect distraction. Now, however, I wasn't so sure that it would be enough. What would it mean if Mr. Puck was a demon? He'd been watching us much longer than the ferryman or any of his henchmen. He knew us, well even. He would be the perfect secret weapon. Was it possible that the real villain behind everything happening was Mr. Puck after all?

CHAPTER 16

I didn't sleep well that night, the same dream replaying each time I was lulled into a brief slumber. I was using my powers on the incoming volleyball, only this time I launched it straight at Mr. Puck instead of Alison. His body morphed, growing darker, eyes turning a piercing yellow until a giant hellhound stood in his place. I made sure Jamie was still asleep across my room before carefully making my way to the hallway.

I stood in the bathroom, just staring out the window into the backyard far too long, almost as if I was sure I'd see the hooded figure standing underneath the oak tree. After shaking the image from my mind, I decided to get ready for school. I showered, long enough for the steam to fog up the window and leave the room filled with the warm haze. I used the hand towel to clean the mirror, the glass trying to fog up seconds after I'd cleared it.

With my robe tied around my middle, I plugged in my blow dryer and started sorting through the my jewelry box in the top drawer, looking for anything glamorous enough for the flapper dress. I noticed the gold bracelet, the only piece of gold jewelry I owned thanks to the girl I'd met in the Shadowlands. I ran my fingers over the engraving, almost deciding to clasp it around my wrist before I remembered the ferryman tossing me back into the sea.

I put on makeup and changed into my dress while the iron heated, just getting started on my hair when I heard a knock at the bathroom door. Becky peeked her head in, letting out a low "oh" at how hot it was in the room.

"I couldn't sleep," I said, as if that explained everything. She snorted and joined me in the mirror, pulling on her cheeks to flatten out the lines under her eyes.

"Me either," she said. "Maybe it's just the time of year."

My aunt always got terrible allergies in the fall, but it was still a little early for that. I wondered if the arguing she'd done with Mark last night had anything to do with her drowsiness. Mark got mad when I let it slip that Jamie couldn't paint the morning of the dance because of his Saturday school. Mark went on so long about Jamie being a bad influence that the argument ended with me leaving the kitchen for my bedroom, Mark calling after me that any more trouble would leave me dateless for the dance.

"Homecoming week is just long, is all," I said. "There's so much to do."

Becky nodded, taking my small basket of root clips from the sink before I could reach for it.

"You make the best Daisy Buchanan," she said, scooping some curl serum from the tin on the counter and beginning to work it through my hair, "You'll be in the yearbook pictures for sure." She wiped her hands on the towel hanging on the wall and began inserting clips at my scalp.

While my hair airdried, I helped her curl her dark hair and

listened to her talk about how rude her boss had been the last few weeks.

"...I'm sure his wife knows about the affair or else she wouldn't keep her distance from the office all the time. She won't even come in anymore to drop their son off," she said as I finished. The blow-dryer made conversation impossible, so she left the room so I could finish drying my damp hair and getting ready for school.

I wasn't at all surprised to find Jamie already gone. I gathered my school bag and went for the front door, Mark beating me there by seconds. He turned from the door to face me, holding up a finger for me to wait.

"I'll keep out of trouble," I said, repeating the promise I'd made during his rant the night before.

"It's not you I worry about keeping clean," he said, taking a deep breath a second later. He pinched the bridge of his nose before looking at me again. "I'm not trying to ruin your first date with a boy or anything, I just want you to be careful. You've kept to yourself more since you started with this boy, and I don't like the secretive teenage thing. I was your age once and I remember some of the things I did during that phase." I felt my face grow hot with embarrassment, sure he was seconds away from the awkward sex lecture.

"I go to school, come home, do my homework, and sometimes go to the Quinns house to see Izzy *and* Jamie. Jamie and I are going to the dance as friends. The most intense things get between Jamie and me is when I beat him at shooting pool," I told Mark, adjusting my backpack over my right shoulder.

"There are worse things to shoot, I guess," Mark said under his breath, moving from the door to take his keys from the table feet away. I felt the anger flare hot within me, not able to control myself.

"I'm not an idiot," I said. "I've seen enough Law and Order to know that selling is more profitable than shooting up."

I heard him follow me onto the front porch. I was forced to stop when I noticed the empty driveway. Mark, tugged on my arm until I turned to look at him.

"That's not funny," he said. "Ever since… I worry about you after everything you've been through since school started. It's only been two months and it's like you've aged years in front of me." I knew it was his way of telling me that therapy was still an option. The last thing I wanted was to see his therapist friend, or his preacher friend, or any other friend Mark thought could cure me of the "illness" I'd never be able to explain to him.

"I'm fine, I just think you're being too overbearing and judgy about the Quinns," I said, noticing the black car pull around the corner. Mark opened his mouth to speak but closed it when he too noticed Jamie slowing to a stop at the curb. He nodded his head slowly.

"Gatsby's waiting," he said, "and so is school."

He nodded toward the car, patting my shoulder before I could hurry down the front steps. Jamie was dressed up much nicer than he normally did for school, wearing a pair of black slacks and a white button-up with his hair gelled to one side the way Leonardo DiCaprio wore his.

"Anything I should know about?" he asked. I was sure he'd heard the same argument from my aunt and uncle's room that I had last night. He didn't need a replay.

"The usual," I said, "Off to school." He pulled away from the curb.

"Homecoming day two," he said, holding up two fingers as we fell in line behind the yellow school bus at the stoplight around the corner. Knowing that I needed a boost, Jamie turned into the Starbucks drive-through despite how close it was to the first bell. We made it to the parking lot with our drinks just as the bell sounded, following the rest of the late students into the building.

Mr. Puck's smile faltered a little when he noticed me walking toward the classroom, both of us averting our eyes as soon as they met across the crowd. Half of our chemistry class was dressed up as book characters; Sean and a few of the boys at his table were dressed up like the T-Birds from Grease.

"Half of these costumes are movies, not books," Jamie noted as we sat down. Macy and her girls were the last to arrive before the bell rang, all of them dressed in a Wizard of Oz theme. Alison had the gingham dress on that she'd tried on at the thrift shop. Macy was the lion, her blonde locks in tight curls and a set of whiskers drawn on her face with eyeliner. Her eyes stayed on me for a moment before she sat down, clearly impressed with the way I looked. The thought sent a jolt of pride through me.

"Good morning, Burbrook High," Mrs. McKellen's voice boomed through the speaker. "It is day two of homecoming week, Dress Like a Book Character Day! Once again, members of the first hour media class will come around to take pictures of the best costumes from each class, so pick your best-dressed boy and girl. This morning is the door decorating contest, so I hope you all came prepared to compete. All doors will be judged today, and a winning class will be announced at the end of the day and receive doughnuts tomorrow morning. Don't forget to make today a great day. Go wolves!"

The speaker clicked off and the room filled with the chatter of students. Mr. Puck raised both hands, calling for everyone to quiet. Before he could say another word, we heard the intercom squeal to life again, the static filling the room for a minute before we could hear Mr. Thackery in the background making sure he'd pressed the right button.

"Attention, all students. Sorry for the interruption, but there is a very serious matter to address before homecoming celebrations begin today," he said. "During the volleyball game last night, someone stole expensive equipment from the chemistry lab on the first floor. It should go without saying that there are always cameras on every floor of the building that are recording. The offending student is on video going in and out of the classroom. If you present yourself to the office by the end of the day along with the stolen equipment, then no legal action will be taken against you. If the student does not turn himself or herself in, then the video will be turned over to the police. That is all. Go wolves." The intercom turned off again with a squeak and the room was silent for just seconds before it exploded with sound.

"Quiet! I shouldn't have to tell a room full of seniors more than once," Mr. Puck called over us. He rubbed his forehead and took a deep breath when it went quiet. Once he'd calmed himself, he finished taking attendance.

"Jamie and Victoria," he said, making my heart skip in my chest as everyone turned to stare at us. "You two will be in the picture for our class. Today, we are decorating our door. Any extra time we have will be used to work on your chapter projects, so make good use of the time you have so you don't have homework tonight. Now, I'm going to put paper over our door. You all should've brought materials. The winning theme for the door was Super Wolf in honor of the find at the national park."

I exchanged glances with Jamie.

"I still think Pound the Panthers is better," a girl to our left said as we all stood up from our tables. I pulled a package of markers from my backpack and a roll of green-and-yellow streamers. Most of the class had brought art supplies, a girl from one of the front tables even brought a Superman cape she'd redesigned with the school logo.

"I can't wait until this super wolf thing blows over," Jamie said as we followed our class into the packed hall. The science classes next door were already starting on their doors, the freshmen biology door halfway covered with a football field-themed tablecloth. Macy took command of our door immediately, pointing out a couple of girls who said they had Theater Design fifth hour and leaving them in charge of drawing a giant wolf on our door.

"Everyone else can work on gluing the green streamer pieces onto the bottom to look like grass," Macy said, ripping apart a piece of the streamer I'd brought apart and holding up the palm-size piece. Jamie and I volunteered for the group tasked with ripping apart the streamers, taking all three rolls a few feet down the hallway to keep out of the way of Macy's vision.

"I wonder what was stolen," I said, keeping my voice low. Jamie shrugged.

"I don't know, but I do know that the cameras inside the building don't work," he said. I stopped tearing the streamer to look at him, taking a glance at the dark sphere in the corner of the ceiling above us.

"They're fake?" I asked.

He nodded, a smirk pulling at his lips.

"I know that because the school board turned down a request to put cameras in the west stairwell after that girl fight there last year. They said the last security initiative went to putting cameras in the parking lots and in the entryway of the building only. Mr. Thackery is playing hardball hoping the thief gets scared," he said. I wasn't too surprised. That fight was the only one we had last year, and stealing was never a huge issue in our tiny town.

"What if Puck took the equipment himself and the school just found out?" I asked.

Jamie let out a laugh. "Izzy's getting in your head. I stand by what I said about him."

I threw a handful of streamer pieces in his face, watching them fall around us like snow.

"I'm just coming up with scenarios," I told him, setting back to work. I hadn't taken Izzy's suspicions about our teacher seriously until last night when she exploded. There was something off about the man. Demon or not, something serious was going on with Mr. Puck.

"That's us," Jamie said, nodding toward the gangly freshman boy. He held a digital camera in both hands, playing with the wrist strap nervously as boys and girls in costumes followed him. Jamie and I joined the back of the line on the way to the large entry way. We stopped in front of the Welcome to the Wolf Den mural painted on the wall next to the trophy case.

"Just stand there," the boy said, pointing to the painting of the school logo. A boy dressed as Harry Potter and a girl dressed like Sherlock Holmes posed against the wall first.

"Turn the camera so you get the entire costume, Jacob," Mrs. McKellen said from the hall. She waved for the boy to continue taking pictures as she came straight to me, green paper held in her hands that I recognized as the Academic Team schedule.

"Great," I whispered, hearing Jamie chuckle next to me.

"Perfect," McKellen said, straightening her glasses on the bridge of her nose. "I thought I'd have to hunt you both down separately."

"Both of us?" I asked.

She nodded, handing us each a schedule.

"I know I've already given you both formal invitations, but

I thought I would come check in. Of course, you both have spectacular grades, which qualify you to join the Academic Team for the year. The team is great for SAT prep, and it makes for a great college résumé filler. We practice every Thursday before school and we compete once a month. It's really a prestigious organization here and I thought you both should take a look at our schedule before homecoming. We are one of the three teams being recognized at the game Friday," she said, all the information rolling off her tongue so fast that I was sure she'd rehearsed it.

I felt my face growing hot at the idea of shooting her down again. I hated telling people no, but as I thought about what she was asking, joining didn't sound so bad. Jamie had been the one who said that I deserved to have a real high school experience despite being a guardian. It had seemed silly to me before knowing that I might be attending school repeatedly like they both did, but it wouldn't be the same then.

Besides, McKellen wasn't wrong about the team being a great college résumé booster. The thought of college sent a jolt through my stomach. Did it even matter anymore with years or even centuries of guardian stuff ahead of me? I could feel Jamie's eyes on me now. He was waiting for me to answer. He was waiting for me to decide for the both of us.

"We both really want to join," I told her. "We were afraid that the deadline had passed." Mrs. McKellen's expression was just as shocked as Jamie's, though he masked his surprise quicker.

"Th-that's great. I'll get both of you team shirts. You can pay your fifteen-dollar registration fee later," McKellen said, practically bouncing back down the hall. I turned to Jamie, his expression the most excited I'd ever seen him. Jacob called for us to take our places. Jamie pulled me to his side and wrapped an arm around my back as the freshman boy clicked away on his camera.

"You guys can go back to class," he said, awkwardly starting for the stairs and leaving the group of us standing in the entryway.

"What changed your mind?" Jamie asked me.

I almost blurted out that he had, but I didn't want to give him the satisfaction.

"Like I said, I'm not normal anymore," I whispered, "but that doesn't mean that I can't pretend to be. I don't want our marks to dictate every part of our lives any more than I wanted Macy to dictate it. I think being a part of a winning team for once would be fun, so that's what I'm going to do," I said, leaving out the part that he'd be there to share it with.

Jamie smirked. "We," he said, "I'm a part of this too apparently."

"I hope you aren't mad," I said.

He laughed. "I was hoping you'd say yes. I've never been on a team before. God knows I can't risk participating in most of them."

I started to warm up to the idea of Academic Team even more as the day went on, the word traveling through the team to the point that members were welcoming me to the group and giving me their cell phone numbers whenever I ran into them in classes. Mrs. McKellen gave me a T-shirt in English class, telling me again how excited she was to have Jamie and me on the team this year.

"You just compete once a month?" Izzy asked as she watched me shelf books during the last hour of the day. I nodded, pushing the cart after her as we moved to a new section.

"It's basically the easiest résumé booster out there," I said.

She let out a laugh. "Now we can call you Mindfreak for a

whole new reason," she said, taking a few books from the cart and handing them to me. I ignored the comment and continued past her, leading the way into the next aisle. I was thankful for the quiet of the room; few people were using the library aside from the English classes around testing time and a few avid readers before school.

"Do you think Puck took all that equipment?" I asked, lowering my voice a little. Izzy didn't even pause at my questions, continuing to shelf books.

"Yes," she said. "And I slipped away from Mrs. Chung for a bit this morning to try and get as much information from the main office as I could about what is missing."

I froze for a minute, forced to push the cart quickly to keep up with her pace. It was the one detail no one was talking about, despite the entire school speculating about who stole from the lab.

"So, what did you find out?" I asked.

Izzy rose onto her toes to shelf the last book from our cart, glancing around us before she spoke. "A whole basket of blood-typing kits and every first aid kit went missing."

"Blood?" I said with a sigh. "As in, whoever wants mine is gearing up to harvest it?" She shushed me as a couple freshmen teachers came into the room, the librarians clearly glad for the social interaction based on their raised voices.

"The office is working to figure out what was in the med kits. They assume that they had some ingredients to make meth," she said with a small laugh. "I've spent most of my guardian life in med school, so I know the chemical compound of meth well enough to know there's no way some of those hard drugs were in a high school chemistry lab but their search will buy us time."

Buy us time? What did we need extra time for?

"Maybe it really is Puck then," I said, not wanting to

admit it.

"We haven't seen the ferryman since he took you to the Shadowlands, which means he probably overstayed his welcome in the mortal world and can't return for a while. He can't leave his post unguarded forever. You and Jamie killed that hellhound, so there's no oversized bloodhound searching for you. Mr. Puck has been acting strange for weeks and he's only gotten weirder... I know Jamie thinks I'm nuts... This is all speculation, but I don't see any real suspects, not any who have shown themselves," Izzy said.

I couldn't believe it.

"Why the hell me? What is so much better about my blood than yours or Jamie's?" I asked.

Izzy shrugged, glancing toward the front desk where both librarians were talking through the state book lists with the teachers.

"I don't know," Izzy said in a sigh. "You're fresh? You just woke? They need the blood of a virgin? All that matters is that they need it."

I elbowed her for the virgin comment, even though it was true. The bell rang before we could discuss anything more. We gathered our things and started for the front of the building to meet Jamie, students brushing past us on the way to the parking lot.

"Don't tell Jamie about any of this," Izzy said. I nearly stopped walking; her expression unchanging. "He doesn't need to go into brotherly protective mode over things I'm not even sure of. He wouldn't believe me anyway," she added. I promised her I wouldn't tell moments before we met Jamie on the front lawn.

"Starbucks?" Izzy asked.

Jamie shook his head, adjusting his bag on his right shoulder.

"I think Tori's uncle would end me for sure if I missed another day of painting, especially when there's no rain in sight."

No one argued with him, but the mention of Mark made my mood dip. After the fight last night and his comments this morning, I was sure he would be in a foul mood with Jamie no matter if he showed up at the house to work or not.

Jamie drove us straight to my house. Mark was home early, surely trying to catch us coming home later than we were supposed to. He grumbled when Jamie told him that he wanted to stay a little late to finish painting the back of the house, going on about how much more work there was to be done than just the back section of siding. Before Jamie could follow Mark around the side of the yard, Izzy surged forward.

"Give me the keys," she said. Jamie's expression turned to confusion. They were both car fans, but Izzy never touched Jamie's Audi or his motorcycle. She had her own fleet to choose from. "I'll be back in like ten," she told us, holding her hand out impatiently. Jamie fished the keys from his pocket and tossed them to her. Without a second glance, she left us for the curb.

"Did she want Starbucks that bad?" Jamie said, "What do you call that these days? Basic?"

I laughed, reaching out to shove his shoulder. Jamie flashed me a smile before heading toward the gate.

I went inside. The house was quiet with Becky working late and everyone else outside. I practiced turning on all the downstairs lights with my mind and turning them back off again. I was beginning to get a decent amount of control over my powers and Jamie had suggested I try lifting weights using my powers whenever we trained at the estate. I made my way to the staircase but stopped on the bottom stair. I lifted the coffee table, holding it in the air until it began to shutter. When I felt the headache forming, I lowered it back to the carpet.

I went upstairs to change into sweats and tie my hair back in a ponytail when I caught sight of Jamie in the backyard. He was holding a paint roller in one hand and the rung of the ladder in the other. Mark was positioned at the base of the ladder, carefully watching as he worked. When Jamie reached higher with the paint roller, the opposite shoulder of his jacket slid down his arm to reveal the top of his bicep. He flexed as he leaned a little to reach the spot on the wall, making my heart skip.

I moved from the bathroom window, catching my bright red face in the mirror that only turned a deeper shade in the reflection. I wasn't sure why I felt so mad at myself until I remembered his muscles. I remembered every time he'd touched me, that electric pulse that always seemed to spark to life within me. I'd told Izzy it was a guardian thing, but if it was, why didn't I feel the same pull with Izzy? if it was? I felt my eyes burn as I realized I'd been denying it this whole time. I liked Jamie, but there was no way he'd share the same feelings, not after the look in his eyes when he'd told me about the girl who wasn't a match.

I began sorting through the drawer under the sink for bobby pins, abandoning the ponytail I'd carelessly done and restarting with a more distracting idea. I started by twisting the strands that framed my face as I fought back the tears. By the time I'd finished two braids, I felt better. At least, I wasn't crying. I pulled the braids to the back of my head and pulled out what I thought was a hair clip. It was the golden bracelet the girl from the Shadowlands had given me before I escaped. I flipped it over to look at the engraving before setting it aside. I finished clipping my hair up and found myself inspecting the bracelet again. The front door slammed shut and I clasped the bracelet around my wrist for safekeeping.

I heard the stairs squeak. I opened the door as Izzy came up the stairs, not even looking at me as she passed for my bedroom. I followed her, settling onto my bed. She let her backpack fall to the floor and closed the door. She held up a brown paper bag with the words *Avery's Pharmacy* stamped across one side so I could see.

"Don't tell me you're pregnant," I said.

She let out a cry of protest. "I got an IUD two years ago. Who do you think I am? It's for you and no, it's not a pregnancy test." She went to my bed and dumped out two white boxes. The one that landed face up had the brand name across the top and a picture of a card with several red smears across it, each labeled with a different blood type.

"Good idea. Maybe there's a shortage of A-positive in the Shadowlands," I said. Izzy scoffed, snatching one of the boxes from the bed.

"Be serious. You already know your blood type?" she asked.

I shook my head. I hadn't been to a doctor in a few years. The school hosted a free physical night for athletes every year and neither Mark nor Becky got great benefits with their insurance plans. Izzy was already ripping open the box, spreading all the cards and tools over the bed and diving straight into the instructions.

"I already know how to do this," I told her. "We did this lab freshman year in Puck's biology class." I remembered the day well. It was the lab we'd all been dreading. One boy got checked out from school because of it, and another girl fainted during class the moment her partner pricked his finger. I couldn't remember my results, but I do remember Macy being a little too proud about having type O.

"I'll follow your lead then," Izzy said, stepping out of the way.

I double-checked the instructions to make sure I didn't waste the kit, probably the entire reason Izzy bought the second one. I undid the plastic case around the needle and sat the card directly in front of me. I held my breath as I pricked the end of my index finger, making sure to press hard enough to get a small bubble of scarlet at the tip. After leaving red smears over each circle on the card, I cleaned the end of my finger with the alcohol pad, and we waited for the blood smears to change. Izzy searched the box for the key, leaning over the bed to examine each circle herself.

"You sure you did it right?" she asked. "The results are inconclusive."

"Shouldn't you know how to do this, Doctor Surgeon Nurse Quinn?" I asked.

She made a face at me before checking both cards again, confirming that the results weren't clear. We opened the second box, Izzy making sure I did every step right this time. The results were the same.

"I know the last time I got a result. I just don't remember what it was. It was right before the spring blood drive," I said.

Izzy studied both test results for a long time, asking me to stay quiet for a little longer as she worked. Finally, she turned from the bed and looked at me, a curious gaze on her face.

"I know that my blood type is the same as before I woke because of med school," she said. "Same with Jamie."

"So, even as a guardian I'm the weirdo?" I asked.

Izzy shrugged and let out a breath. She was probably the most studied and accomplished medical professional in the entire country and even she couldn't tell me what happened.

"Even if I'm some medical mystery and my blood is super-natural or something, how would anyone in the Shadowlands know that?" I asked. Neither of us spoke for a long time. The vampire was the first person to try taking my blood. That was after my first encounter with the ferryman. I wished I could forget the incident. I didn't even see him until well after he was in the house. I remembered the pain, hot in my nose. Jamie had cleaned up all the blood after he and Izzy got there. Could the ferryman smell it? Had he sensed the abnormality somehow?

"I bled on the floor the first time I met the ferryman," I said.

"He didn't take any, did he? You didn't bleed on him?" Izzy asked.

I didn't know what to tell her. If I had bled on him or if he had taken it with him, then they wouldn't be searching for me now, would they?

"No," I said. "I don't think so, but do you think that he can maybe sense that it was different?"

Izzy went back to the cards, spending the next minute bent over both.

"I don't understand how they know you're different," she said under her breath.

I felt my mood only slip further. Great. I was so used to being the weird one of Macy's friends, the girl that never quite fit in anywhere, the one who was almost too smart for her own good. Why should I be any different as a guardian? I was one of a rare group of people and even among them I was strange.

"We should tell Jamie," I said.

Izzy looked up at me and I could see the hesitation in her face. I knew she was worried about her brother taking total control, going into panic mode to protect our circle. Unless demons started appearing around town or someone attacked us, maybe it wasn't worth panicking about yet. If we changed our habits now, we would tip off whoever stole from the chemistry lab.

It was as if Izzy had read my thoughts. She gave me a single nod and after another long pause, we moved onto math homework as if nothing had happened at all.

CHAPTER 17

As if I was reminding myself of the risks, I didn't take off the gold bracelet the witch girl had given me since I returned it to my wrist. The next morning, Mark didn't stop me at all on my way out to the porch. I only had to wait a few minutes before Jamie pulled the car around the corner. I sank into the seat and clipped the seat belt into place, surprised when we didn't move. Jamie was giving me a strange look, as if I had a giant piece of egg stuck in my teeth from breakfast or smeared mascara down my face.

"What?" I asked.

"Mark gave me the sex talk," he said. I gasped, feeling my face flame up instantly.

"Oh god," I said.

"He told me that if we are going out together and late-night school dances are often romantic events…"

I wished I could have sunk right through the leather, through the bottom of the car, and be flattened by it.

"No! Stop," I moaned.

Jamie snickered. "His exact words. I'm not kidding."

"I can't talk to you anymore," I said. "Let's just go, fast."

Jamie laughed as he put the car in drive, not saying a word to me the entire ride to school. Izzy met us in the packed entryway with a Starbucks cup in hand, wearing one of her white lab coats with her name embroidered over the right pocket.

"You didn't get me any?" Jamie asked.

She rolled her eyes. "Don't you usually go before school?" she asked.

Jamie didn't respond, tugging a safari hat from his backpack and placing it on his head. I had pulled on the most scientific outfit I had that morning, a pair of olive-green skinny jeans and a green jacket. Jamie looked much the same, with the addition of the goofy hat.

After a few minutes, we parted ways for first period. Mr. Puck left a hand-written note on his door for all of us to meet in the gym. Jamie and I followed the slowly forming group toward the gym down the hall. One side of the bleachers had been pulled out; the rest of the empty gym floor being used for exhibits. There were tables full of what looked like casts of animal tracks, a couple more with posters, and even more with small TVs set up with DVDs already paused on images of animals.

"Everyone take a seat in the stands," Mr. Puck said. Next to him stood a tall man, easily over six feet. He was lanky with round glasses and a tie that was almost too short for his long torso. His hair was graying on the sides and despite the overworked bags under both eyes, he looked excited to be here.

"I forgot Dr. Sampson is speaking today," Jamie said as he joined our class in the bleachers. We grouped off as usual, almost perfectly seated by our tables in Mr. Puck's classroom by the time the bell rang. The announcements were much louder in the gym, Mrs. McKellen's voice echoing throughout the space as she announced the freshman biology class as the door decoration winners and reminded us to participate in Dress for Your Future Job Day tomorrow. Principal Thackery came next to warn the student who stole from the chemistry lab that legal action was being taken against them. Once the announcements were over, Dr. Sampson stepped before our section of the stands to speak.

"Good morning, Burbrook High Wolves. My name is Dr. Tom Sampson, and I am a wildlife researcher and preservation activist. You may have heard of me after the find of the specimen we are calling Super Wolf in the Burbrook Natural Forest," he said. "I'm excited to be talking with all of you today about the find and how we can all do our part to protect this wolf."

"Is it a new kind of wolf?" a girl asked, raising her hand after she'd asked her question.

"Well, we won't know for sure until we find it, but it doesn't match anything like the species we are aware of in this area. So, we aren't ruling out any possibilities. What we know for sure is that it is from the wolf family," he said. Just as he started into how he came into the profession, another boy raised his hand, this time waiting to be called on.

"My dad works at the park, and he said your team found another set of tracks on the other side of the lake from the others," he said. "No one has said anything about it yet, so I thought you could tell me if that's true."

Jamie's hand went to my left knee. There couldn't be another set of tracks. We killed the hellhound.

"Well, er..." Sampson started, clearly debating if he should comment or not, "We did find another set of tracks. We haven't identified a species yet, so I can't confirm if it is the same Super Wolf as before. I do have pictures at the far table in the room along with updates of our progress in the park, if anyone is interested in viewing those."

So, they *had* found something. I hadn't realized how hard Jamie was grasping my knee until I felt my foot go numb. I could feel him tense when I raised my hand next. Mr. Puck's lips pulled into an irritated frown. Dr. Sampson called on me next.

"How long does it take to become a wolf specialist?" I asked.

Puck's expression changed to one of almost confusion and I could feel Jamie's eyes turn on me. Sampson relaxed, his kind smile returning as he started telling the story about spending one summer away from college helping his dad chase wolves off their family farm. Jamie looked transfixed, but I knew his thoughts weren't filled with the family farm. He didn't even flinch until Sampson began passing around packets of paper.

"Now that you all have your guidebooks," Sampson said, handing the last couple booklets to a pair of boys in the front row, "I am going to pass around a couple samples. Group off so that everyone can have a look and use your books to try identifying what animal the track belongs to. You have three minutes."

Mr. Puck and Dr. Sampson began handing around plastic casts of animal footprints, some much larger than others. Jamie and I scooted toward a group of girls and a boy, their group known in our class for giving the most hilariously wrong answers when asked. I wasn't the best versed on animal tracks, but I'd been on enough hikes with Mark and Becky to know that the cast was of a raccoon's paw.

"We need to get to that table as soon as we can," Jamie said, nodding toward the table farthest from us. It was the only one without a small TV or a poster taped across the front. A couple file folders were sat over the top and what looked like maybe some pictures next to those.

"And what does your group have?" Dr. Sampson asked our group first.

"A baby bear," the boy said.

"It's a raccoon," Jamie said.

Dr. Sampson congratulated him on his work, handing him a large Protect Our Nation's Wildlife button. He clipped it onto his backpack at his feet as we waited for the man to finish making his rounds, handing out buttons to students with correct answers. Jamie and I anxiously awaited as Dr. Sampson launched into a lecture about the ways we could all help protect wild animals and national parks. Everyone in the bleachers clapped once he finished, the conservationist telling us to follow him to the Super Wolf table next.

"Great," Jamie said under his breath as we joined the line of students on the stairs. We followed Sampson to the farthest corner of the gym where he took his place behind a table stacked with file folders. He began organizing the contents, moving photos to the front and setting a couple of colored flyers from the folders to the back of the table. I raised myself onto my toes, but I couldn't get a good look at the photos.

"I wanted to let all of you know of some new precautions in the national park. A contest was announced in the local paper, and it is for that exact reason I would like to stress some important information that was left out," he said. He split a stack of red paper in half and handed them off to students on both sides of the table to pass around. "So, as this flyer states, the park hours have been changed to accommodate the feeding patterns of wolves so that no one may happen across Super Wolf. There are also some instructions on what to do if you do encounter a wolf: Make yourself look large and back away slowly. Do not take your eyes off it," he said. Jamie took two flyers from the "baby bear" boy and handed one to me. At the top, was a baying wolf with the words "Wolf Watch" in a sharp slanted font.

"So, no one will be allowed into the park until the sun is up and you can't stay in the park after it sets, the only exception will be during your homecoming dance on Saturday, which will be heavily monitored by police and my team of researchers. We will be using that night to launch our evening investigation into the wolf population," Sampson said. "From what I have been told, all parking will be closely watched, and the school and park authorities are working together to get valet parking. I'm sure that will change the ticket price this year." Sampson let out a little laugh, sounding loud among our quiet group.

"So, there really is a Super Wolf, I mean, something new to Burbrook?" Macy asked.

The humor in Sampson's face faded fast and with it went what little security I'd felt all week.

"As this young man said at the beginning of the hour," he started, pointing out the boy who'd outed the new find, "we did find new footprints identical to the first set along a different section of the lake. This time, we were able to get a cast of the tracks along with the pictures. We have spoken to some local hunters who said they aren't seeing wildlife like they used to. Considering the short amount of time between both tracks and where we have found them, we are sure that Super Wolf is using the main campgrounds as his hunting location. We are hoping Saturday night to find a den of sorts, if not the wolf himself."

The front row of students had bent over the front of the table as he spoke.

"There's just enough time to talk about the article and visit tables," Mr. Puck told Sampson.

The gangly man clapped his hands again, startling a few girls in the front row.

"Yes. Exactly. Most importantly," he began, not continuing until we were all watching him, "this morning, the local paper released an article about a contest Parker Hunting Store is hosting. It says that the first hunter to capture the Super Wolf will be awarded a five-thousand-dollar cash prize. While I spoke with the owner, and I gave him my opinion, I can't keep him from holding the contest. So, I must impress upon you not to go hunting outside of the new park hours and never to go by yourself. While I wish those under eighteen would not participate, I am sure some of you spend your free time hunting with Mom or Dad. Please, stay alert and prepared for all possibilities. According to our research, this wolf is easily three times larger than the biggest wolf charted in this area. My team and I never go out in fewer than groups of three, so neither should you."

"All right," Mr. Puck said, "Like I said, we have just enough time for all of you to explore the tables if you use your time wisely. Be aware that tomorrow, there will be a short quiz based on the red flyers from each table."

More than a few students groaned and abandoned the Super Wolf station to collect more flyers. Mr. Puck never gave us or told us anything without a reason, much to our chagrin when science field trips rolled around in the spring semester.

Jamie and I waited while the crowd at the Super Wolf table thinned, slowly making our way forward to get a look at the pictures. There were five sitting on the table. Four of them looked exactly like the picture on my phone, several massive footprints sunk deep into the soft mud of the bank. The fifth picture was much different, a small picture taken on a modern Polaroid camera. The date was handwritten on the white strip at the bottom of the frame with the time scribbled next to that. The picture was dark, the only distinguishable thing in it the dark elms. Just past the first set of trees, I could see the shimmer of the moon highlighting the ripples of the lake. Off to the left, a black shape overlapped with the lake. It was huge, almost bear-like in shape, but too lean to be a large black bear.

"This is after," I said, not needing to point out the obvious. Jamie nodded, still looking over the pictures. I wished Sampson would move so we could talk in private.

"Wolves generally keep their distance from humans," Sampson said, "Don't worry. If you follow the guides I gave you, then the park will stay perfectly safe."

The bell rang before we could collect any more flyers, forcing us to stay late to finish up.

"We can tell Izzy at lunch that there's another one," I said, noticing the change in Jamie's face. He didn't plan on being there. "Jamie, no."

"I crushed it before," he said.

"Only after it found us," I said, "And I doubt it will be that easy to find without the thing hunting me."

Jamie's head snapped in my direction. He opened his mouth to speak, but Mr. Puck reminded us of the bell, and we went back to work. I stuffed the loose papers into my backpack on the bleachers and left the gym ahead of him. Jamie stopped next to my locker as I began stuffing books noisily inside.

"I'm sorry," he said.

I nearly dropped my chemistry book on my toe, barely catching it against my thigh.

"This isn't going to work if you can't trust me to be by myself and take care of myself," I said.

"I do trust you," Jamie said. "You pick up hand-to-hand combat quicker than anyone I've met."

I scoffed, shutting my locker door a little too hard.

"I'm tired of always being the damsel in distress of the group," I said.

Jamie smirked and I wanted nothing more than to slap it right off his smug face.

"Victoria Johnson, I'm fairly certain that you've never in your life been a damsel in distress," he said. "You're crazy smart. You are athletic and competitive as hell, which is why I'm constantly covered in bruises thanks to your cheap shots in training."

"I don't take cheap shots, I take opportunities," I said, unable to keep from smiling after the look of satisfaction that came over his face.

"I just think it's stupid to use you as bait is all," Jamie said. "Let's go find and kill the beast, yeah, but let's put a little more thought into it first." The sincerity in his expression told me that he finally understood how sexist he'd been before.

"Says the guy who was ready to skip school to go crush it with his bare hands," I said.

Jamie blushed, trying to hide his embarrassment behind his serious expression.

"Yeah, well, I kind of lose sight of reason when you're involved." He kept his voice low, as if the words were more for himself than me. I wanted to ask him if that same lack of reason was why he really stayed overnight with me, but I couldn't bear to voice the idea. After a beat of silence, I gathered my things and he walked me to my next class.

Jamie didn't skip the rest of the day. Even before lunch, Izzy had heard about the contest in the newspaper and the new wolf find at the park. In keeping with our agreement, neither Izzy nor I told him about the blood kits stolen from the chemistry lab or the fact that no kit could tell me my blood type. Izzy waited until we met the last hour of the day in the library to tell me she didn't find anything helpful in the circle guide after leaving my house last night.

"Should we even go to homecoming?" I asked.

Izzy let out a single laugh.

"You're going to do everything normal seniors do," she said. "So, yes, we're still going, and you are going to look so good in your dress that it will end this stupid feud Alison is trying to keep alive."

I had almost forgotten about Macy and Alison. We had been too busy during chemistry with the Super Wolf stuff to even notice them.

After school, Izzy drove to the national park while Jamie took me home. Having finished painting the back of the house, Mark had moved the ladder and cans to the side of the house now. I went inside to start on homework like usual but stopped when I noticed Becky in the kitchen. She had dishes sitting out on the counter, a stack of plates and silverware setting on the rarely used table.

"What's going on?" I asked, stopping in the doorway to watch as she pushed a casserole in the oven. She didn't turn to look at me as she went to the stove, lifting the lid off a boiling pot so steam rose into her face.

"Making dinner," she replied. "I can't believe I didn't think to ask him sooner. Jamie is going to eat with us before he leaves. I already called Mrs. Quinn. She said he could stay even later if we wanted. They are hosting a dinner party for a few business guys who are visiting from Germany. Can you imagine that? Of all places to visit on business."

There were so many surprising statements that had casually fell from her mouth that I felt like I hadn't heard them all.

Dinner. Jamie is staying late. Becky and Mark rarely made dinner, at least nothing more elaborate than something simple to eat in front of the TV after work. We'd never had a real family dinner like you saw on commercials aside from the year Mark's sister insisted on coming from Florida for Thanksgiving. Even then, there was an ice storm in the city that halted all incoming flights and left us eating sweet potatoes for the next week.

"Jamie's staying?" I asked.

Becky looked back at me from the stove with a laugh.

"That's what I said," she said. "Mark already knows. I think he's working that boy a little too hard, really. You got off easier than he did, and he isn't even our kid."

She went back to the boiling pot, carefully pouring the excess water into the sink and setting the entire pot on a trivet on the table. She took a potato masher from a drawer and handed it to me.

"Green bean casserole, mashed potatoes and gravy, and brisket in the Crock-Pot," Becky said. The blue Crock-Pot had sat unused for so long on the counter that you'd have thought it was just part of the decor. I didn't think I'd be able to eat a bite.

"And Mark is actually going to go along with all this?" I asked.

"Of course," Becky said, looking curiously back at me.

"So, he's not going to cross-examine him over dessert or anything?"

Becky didn't reply, pretending not to have heard. I helped her finish cooking, setting the table and moving steaming dishes there as Jamie and my uncle joined us. Both took turns cleaning up at the sink as Becky and I took seats at the table. Jamie flashed me a smile as he moved to join us. Mark didn't bother drying his hands, probably so he could beat Jamie to the seat beside me.

"This looks great," Jamie said, sinking into the chair across from me. "Much better than some boring business dinner. Izzy will be so jealous."

Becky let out a laugh, spooning some potatoes onto her plate before passing the bowl to Jamie.

"Do business meetings usually happen at your house?" Mark asked. "Seems strange to fly a couple of business guys from Berlin to little Burbrook."

Jamie finished with the potatoes and sat the bowl on the table when Mark didn't turn to take it from him.

"They're from Munich, actually," he said. "And my parents try to work from home as much as they can, but they have to leave at least once a week or two, sometimes together and sometimes separately."

Mark nodded, finally reaching for the potatoes.

"Jamie and I joined the academic team," I said.

Only Becky looked up from her plate. "That's great," she said.

"It will look good on a college application and all the practices and meets are SAT prep anyway," I said, watching my uncle's expression for the slightest peak in interest. He didn't look up until he'd finished filling his plate.

"The school board says it's the most successful organization at the school," Becky said, "but I heard the football team is good this year now that no one's injured. Homecoming should be a good one."

The last few seasons, Burbrook had been plagued by sports injuries, all to star athletes who started on multiple sports teams. None of them had been state contenders since Macy's brother graduated.

"Speaking of homecoming," Mark said, buttering a slice of bread without looking up, "I heard you got in some trouble at school and can't take Tori like you planned."

Jamie and I exchanged glances.

"I still want to go with her, if that's okay with you," he answered.

Mark still focused on the bread that was now so slathered in butter that the edges drooped around his large hand.

"I'm surprised you're still allowed to go to the dance," Mark said. "I guess Tori didn't tell me what you got into trouble for, but trouble at school means trouble at home in this house…"

I looked straight at Becky who was sending me an apologetic smile.

"Well, I'm not *not* in trouble at home for it, if that's what you think," Jamie said. "I'm still working off the car incident with you, so my parents had to be creative."

I thought about Jamie's dad's reaction to him playing piano, feeling my shoulders tense.

"Really? How so?" Mark asked, finally looking up.

"Don't pry," Becky told him. "It's not our business how they parent."

Mark looked up from his bread, setting it aside so fast that the buttered side flipped onto the table. I felt my face burn as I realized what would come next. Mark would argue that he had every right to know Jamie's record if he was going to be around so often. Becky would stand up for me, saying they didn't need to know every detail of my friendships to keep me safe.

"I'm writing an essay," Jamie was quick to jump in, "about the importance of education. Ten pages."

The kitchen was silent, everyone but Jamie poised and ready for the next fight.

"I'd love to read it," Mark said.

Becky let out a sigh and sat back in her seat, mixing her brisket and barbecue sauce before taking a large bite. I almost wished she would've fired back like the night before. Maybe then, we could end dinner early.

"Yes, sir," Jamie said. "Probably good to have someone proofread it before I give it to my parents anyway. They grade harder than any English teacher at school." Mark didn't question any further, ignoring the rest of us as he ate while Becky launched into stories about homecoming "back in her day." She made us dish on everything that had happened at school that week, thankfully never once mentioning the stolen lab equipment. Dinner wrapped up almost as soon as dessert was finished.

"It's getting close to curfew," Jamie said when Becky complained about him refusing a round of cards. Mark lumbered in the background as he followed Jamie to the door. "Besides," he said, "I have an essay to finish."

As soon as the door closed, Becky turned on Mark.

"Why do you keep embarrassing him that way? You know he's probably hearing enough about it from his parents, he doesn't need another set," she said.

Mark pointed to the window where Jamie's Audi was pulling away from the curb. He'd stop again a block away and walk back to climb through my cracked bedroom window like always.

"Sounds like he needs a new set of parents with the trouble he's causing," Mark said, launching into the list of faults he found in Jamie while Becky continued to repeat that it wasn't their business. I left them in the living room for my bedroom, Jamie pulling himself in ten minutes later.

"I swear they're parenting me more than you right now," Jamie told me. "And now I have homework."

I apologized as I took my school computer from my backpack. It was weird the way things had changed, not just for me. It was like that car accident had messed up everyone's life.

CHAPTER 18

Jamie was still in my bedroom when I woke the next morning, already awake and changed into jeans and a Kiss T-shirt. He smiled from the mirror on the back of the door when he noticed me. He took the clothes I'd laid out from the desk chair and held them out to me as I stood up.

"I'm not kicking you out," I told him as he slung his backpack over his shoulder. He went to the window and easily slid the old pane upward with one hand.

"I think now is as good a time as any. I'll pull around," he said. He held the backpack out the window first, climbing onto the windowsill and sliding down the side of the house. He landed easily, slinging the bag over his shoulder again and sauntering toward the gate at the back of the yard like only a guardian could.

I dressed in the same outfit I had for Dress Like a Teacher Day, only this time I exchanged my normal school bag for a briefcase Becky let me borrow for the day. It was Dress for Your Future Day, the one day Jamie had initially refused to participate in until I told him that what he'd wanted for himself was more important than what his dad had wanted for him. Only, what I actually said was much less poetic than that and had us both laughing so loud that we almost forgot about Becky and Mark sleeping down the hallway.

"Off to court, Mrs. Johnson?" Becky said as I came down the stairs. She pecked Mark on the cheek and went to the door for her keys. I did a single turn so they could get a look at the whole outfit, feeling the lightest I had in days.

"Today, the real judge is the first period media class and the yearbook class," I told them, following Becky onto the porch. She kissed the top of my head and waved toward Jamie's car before going to hers.

"We only have three periods today," Jamie said when I slid into the driver's seat. "The assembly starts after lunch."

The student talent show was this afternoon, which always ended before school, but too late to justify sending students to the last class of the day. Izzy and I already had a date for frozen yogurt with "no boys allowed" as she told Jamie at lunch yesterday.

"I'm glad. I don't have to hear Mrs. Hawthorne complain about the fact that we have to play our hardest game for homecoming," I said. She'd complained all week about the way the athletic director scheduled the games this year, saying that nothing killed school spirit like a very public loss. She'd bummed out some of the football players so much that they'd started a game of hiding things from her desk when she was in the hallway, which only made her more insufferable than she usually was.

We swung through Starbucks like usual and met Izzy in the entryway at school. She wore her lab coat again, pulling me down the hall from Jamie as soon as we came through the door. I had no choice but to follow her until I could pull my wrist free from her death grip.

"Jeez," I said, rubbing the spot. "What's wrong?"

"I don't know," she said. "You've been... weird, both of you." She looked past me for Jamie. I snapped my fingers in front of her face to draw her attention again.

"I haven't told him," I said. "I swear."

She rolled her eyes. "I didn't mean that," she said, she opened her mouth as if to explain, but closed it again. I followed her gaze, noticing Mr. Puck standing just feet away. He leaned against the wall with his arms crossed over his chest as he watched the students waiting for the first period bell to ring.

"Still think he's up to something?" I asked.

Izzy turned back to me.

"We'll find out after the homecoming dance," she said.

I didn't get a chance to ask what she meant before the bell rang and the herd of students forced us apart. I moved slowly across the hallway, making it into class before Jamie did. Macy and Sean were the only two at her table, both dressed in Colorado State T-shirts with their faces painted in team colors. Jamie came in and flashed me a rock-n-roll sign on his way across the room.

"Is real Jamie actually this much of a dork?" I asked him.

He lowered his bag to the floor.

"Real Jamie?" he asked. I guess I hadn't talked to him very much about how two-sided he was. There was the serious, protective, and enigmatic Jamie. Then, there was the vulnerable side, the one that shared vivid stories, the creative and detailed Jamie who was soft and sometimes playful. That was the way I liked Jamie best, the way he seemed most himself.

"Nothing," I said. "Just what I call the way I see you when you're with me." I swore my face turned bright red. A smirk pulled at his lips, and he took my phone before I could grab it, only worsening my embarrassment.

"Well, let me show you how I see you," he said, holding the phone before him for a picture. I covered my face, but he tried pushing my hands away.

"Jamie," I protested, barely containing my giggles. I stopped fighting him when I noticed the boys at the table next to ours staring. Jamie had noticed them too, his stoic expression returning just long enough to flatten the sleeves of his T-shirt over the mark on his wrist. He sank into the chair next to me, sliding my phone back toward me. I didn't understand the sudden change until I heard the whispering from the tables around us.

A police officer had entered the room, looking heavy with her arsenal of weapons around her hips. Mr. Puck looked nervous as he led her to the storage closet at the back of the room. He slid a key into the newly installed lock above the knob before opening it wide. Principal Thackery appeared in the doorway, ordering all of us to continue working, not that we had anything to busy ourselves with yet.

"Has this always been locked?" the officer asked, studying the door first.

"Those were installed after the incident," Mr. Puck said, looking annoyed by the question as if he'd known this would happen all along. "The lock on my classroom door has been busted since I started here and I put in several requests to fix it," he added. The woman nodded and moved into the closet. The intercom clicked on, masking the officer's next question with Mrs. McKellen's too-perky greeting.

"... students will return to their first hour classes following lunch. You will leave all your things there and, when called, go to the auditorium for the talent show. Make today a great day, Burbrook High! Go Wolves!"

The intercom clicked off as the officer emerged from the room, motioning toward the hallway to Mr. Puck. The two left the room and Mr. Thackery stepped to the front of the class.

"Quiet," he said, the authority thicker than ever in his voice. This wasn't the usual principal we knew, the man who always looked busy and stressed out. This was ex-military Thackery, the one who dished out detentions so casually that it was questionable if he even knew what the offense was. He looked taller, he was standing so straight. The entire room was silent for a second, long enough for Thackery to take enough deep breaths to calm himself.

We waited for nearly ten minutes before Mr. Puck returned, looking exhausted. Mr. Thackery apologized for interrupting the class on his way out the door, following the cop toward the main office. Puck paused at the front of the room, and we waited quietly for his usual lecture, but his shoulders sagged after a moment.

"Today is a catch-up day," he said. "Make sure you check your grades online and find all missing assignments. We'll pick up with our chapter tomorrow."

With that, he returned to his desk to stare at his computer screen as if not really seeing any of the glowing icons at all. I looked to Jamie who had already pulled his computer out and was busying himself with the school's web page. How did he not find anything weird about this?

I texted Izzy about the strange introduction to class before diving into my own search for my grades, coming away with straight As. Izzy texted me back near the end of class that she'd keep a closer eye on Puck today, worried that he would try slipping away for a half-day of whatever it was he was up to. The rest of the day fell back into the upbeat homecoming spirit, most all my morning teachers abandoning the day to let us either work on projects for class or play review games. By lunch, I'd played so many rounds of Kahoot that I elbowed

Jamie when he replied to Izzy's inquiry about how the morning went with the game's theme song.

"I never want to play that game again," I said.

Mrs. McKellen still hadn't figured out how to use the game correctly, always making the answers either blatantly obvious or entering them completely wrong. The cafeteria was loud with excitement for the coming talent show. I wanted to ask Jamie if he had signed up, but I was sure he hadn't. I still hadn't heard him play.

"What kind of job is that?" Izzy asked. I followed her gaze toward Alison as she passed our table for the trash can paces away. She wore a pair of navy sweatpants with a matching red and white jacket, USVA embossed on the arm with a volleyball underneath.

"Olympic volleyball," I said. "Alison thinks she's good enough to play for any college she wants."

Alison was the queen bee of the volleyball world in town, the only place where Macy hadn't ruled. She played middle, the tall and leggy blonde that was blessed not to look like a volleyball player. While the rest of us developed thick legs and butts from squatting all the time, Alison remained model thin while still being able to crush on the offense.

"Is she good enough?" Izzy asked.

I wanted so badly to say no. Alison wasn't professional material, but she was tall enough and good enough to play for a state school. Her parents paid for all the expensive traveling teams from our first practice in middle school and she went to so many camps in the summer that she surely already had scholarship offers. It wasn't fair.

"We all know she won't get into college with her brains," Jamie said, squeezing my hand under the table. I gave it a squeeze in return, glad for the distraction. I wasn't sure why I felt different today. Maybe it was the visit from the police officer this morning or the subtle reminder of everything at stake when Jamie smoothed the fabric of his shirt over the guardian mark on his wrist. I gave his hand another squeeze and went back to my lunch, feeling my mood return when the bell rang, and teachers reminded us to return to our first periods.

Jamie and I went to our usual table in chemistry, leaving our bags sitting on the table as the rest of our class began filing into the room. We stayed long enough for Mrs. McKellen to come on the intercom to remind us about the game tomorrow. Soon after, we were all packed together in the slow-moving crowd in the hallway. Izzy saved us seats in the back corner of the auditorium.

"I thought you were skipping," Jamie told her.

Izzy's expression fell. "No, you told me you weren't?" she said.

I looked at Jamie, whose devious smirk told me he had other plans.

"Well, Mrs. Chung locked her door," Izzy said, settling back into the cushioned seat, "so, I'm stuck here for the next hour."

"Let me know how that goes," Jamie said, glancing toward the front of the auditorium.

I paused before the empty seat next to Izzy who merely scoffed at her brother and sank farther into the chair. Alison and Macy joined the front row of students, Sean sneaking a hand up the hem of Macy's skirt before she batted it away and checked to make sure Mr. Thackery was too busy struggling with the microphone on stage to have noticed. I turned away from the stage, catching Jamie's gaze as he backed toward the door in the corner.

"Come with me," he said.

Teachers were beginning to appear at the front of the

room, several talking in a huddle near the stage while the drama class got the spotlights positioned correctly.

"What did you have in mind?" I asked him, already following toward the door. We slipped into the empty hallway, picking up pace as we went. "Jamie," I warned him when I heard someone cough down the hallway behind us. He hushed me and burst into a sprint, pulling me into an empty classroom with curtains over the window on the door. We waited until the shadow of the custodian with his cart rolled by to laugh, the sound loud in the large space.

The room smelled like mold and flowers thanks to the half-empty wall plug-ins spread around the space. The back of the room was a halfmoon of risers, all thick enough for chairs and black stands. Off to one side was a black grand piano, the only thing in the room that looked less than twenty years old.

"The music room," I said. "Tell me this was intentional."

He left me at the door for the piano, pushing his sleeves up to his elbows for probably the first time anywhere but at home.

"I always have a plan," he said. "Even when I don't." He patted the spot next to him on the bench.

"That makes no sense," I said, joining him.

He smiled, positioning his hands on the keys lightly.

"It's called thinking in motion," he said. "Even when things go as planned, I'm always planning for the *what if* moment, that second when something goes wrong and changes the course. All it takes is a moment in time, a single opportunity, a window..." He played a single chord. The sound resonated around the room.

"I find it hard to believe that the resolute Jamie Quinn has ever been even the slightest bit spontaneous," I told him.

He lifted his fingers from the keys, letting the sound fade to silence.

"I can be spontaneous," he challenged, starting into a jazz tune I didn't recognize. "Try me." He lifted his eyes from the keys.

"All right, Beethoven," I said, turning a little in my seat to better watch him. "Play something sad."

The song changed immediately, flowing so easily into the ballad that you'd have thought the song had been written that way. He kept his smile on me through the entire change.

"You can't put a damper on my mood so easily, Mindfreak," he said. "Try again."

"How about some rock then?" I asked.

His fingers didn't slow at all, flowing into the edgy riff I recognized from an Aerosmith song. I let him continue until the end of the song, before I called for a show tune, an upbeat melody I didn't recognize floating through the room. We cycled through genre after genre, each sounding so perfectly like the next verse of the same song. It was like he was a living jukebox, never needing a second to think after I ordered the next song. His fingers moved across the keys as if they were a different part of him.

"Rap," I said. "Let's see you do a rap song."

The song had changed again before I could even finish my challenge. The chords of the new song filled the room and soon, Jamie was singing along. His voice was so smooth it was almost sinful, making me realize just how close I was to him now. Watching him play felt like spying on something private, like he was allowing me to see every bit of who he is and who he could be if he allowed himself to be. I let him finish the song, his fingers finally coming to a rest on his knees.

"Why haven't you played for me before?" I asked him.

He didn't speak, letting the silence hang between us for a moment. Finally, he patted his lap. I hesitated, not sure if he was inviting me to sit until he reached out for my hand. I felt a knot form in my stomach as I sat on his lap, his breath tickling my neck as he let out a sigh. He reached around my waist, and for a moment I thought he was going to hug me, but his hands found the piano keys again and started playing a song I'd never heard.

"I didn't hear the music until that afternoon in my bedroom, when I told you about my parents," he said.

"Hear the music?" I asked.

He nodded, continuing into the chorus.

"You know those moments of time that seem to live forever, the ones that just really mean something, sometimes for no reason at all?" he asked, not waiting for me to answer. "When those moments replay in my head, I hear songs. It's like I'm writing the soundtrack to a movie or something in that second and it sticks in my head."

I laughed. "The soundtrack of Jamie's life?"

He chuckled. "Yeah. The soundtrack of my life," he said. "I like that."

The song changed from the chorus into another verse, making me wonder if there were words. I ached to hear him sing again.

"What's this one called?" I asked him.

He didn't reply right away, his fingers finishing the verse and going back into the refrain.

"You name it," he said. "It's yours anyway."

I felt my mouth turn to cotton. My song? I remembered the very moment he was talking about, the first time I'd been in his room with him. He told me about playing the piano in the train station, getting punished by his father for it later in his life, how he was a loser for not wanting a "real" job.

"The Real Thing," I said finally.

His body relaxed against mine and I could feel the contour of his chest against my back, his arms pulling closer around me. His chin settled on my shoulder, his cheek warm against my neck as he played. The song fell into the chorus again, the sweet melody that felt so familiar, the way Jamie always felt so familiar. It was more than feeling at home, it was like I'd never been home until now. I didn't know the song was over until I felt his hands take mine. He placed them lightly on the piano keys.

"You're turn," he told me, forcing my fingers apart. He taught me the chords to the song, laughing at how badly I managed to mess them up at first. I pushed my sleeves to my elbows and set to work, playing the chords he'd taught me perfectly for the first time and asking for a new one when I felt his left hand cover mine. I stopped playing so he could take my hand in his, his thumb brushing the gilded bracelet at my wrist. With a single movement, he lifted me off his lap and onto the bench. He was on his feet and nearly three feet to my left. I didn't understand what had happened. I played the two chords I'd learned again as he paced from the piano to the desk in the corner.

"Tori, don't," he said.

I played again and he whirled around to face me.

"Victoria, stop," he said, his deep voice echoing around the room and stinging like a slap. The color had faded from his face and his eyes looked different, almost glassy before he turned from me again. Applause came from auditorium down the hall, louder than any we'd heard before. I checked the clock on the wall. It was getting close to release time. Jamie must have noticed too because he left the room ahead of me.

"Jamie, wait," I said, hurrying after him.

He didn't care that we might be seen now as he walked down the hallway. He darted into Mr. Puck's classroom, and I barged in right after. I waited at the door as he grabbed his bag, slinging it over his shoulder and coming back my way. I stepped in front of him, forcing him to stop.

"What happened? What's your deal? Was it the mark?" I asked.

He looked up at last, his expression like stone.

"I'll still take you to the dance, if you want to go," he said, "but I hope you'll understand..."

He didn't finish, slipping past me a second later. I couldn't believe I didn't burst into tears right there, but I didn't. I still wasn't sure what had happened. How had we gone from naming our own song to this? What even was this?

I gathered my things from the back table when my phone buzzed in my pocket, Jamie texting me to get a ride home with Izzy. I pulled my backpack on and left the room, making sure no one had seen me before I went toward the front of the building. I was out the door and walking in the rain before I thought what to do next. I moved to the covered bus lane a yard away and settled onto a cold bench as I waited for school to let out. I texted Izzy for a ride and spent the next fifteen minutes trying to calm down before she found me.

"The best act was a mediocre cellist," she told me when she pulled up to the curb in the yellow Maserati, "Tell me you had a better time."

What was I supposed to tell her? What would Jamie tell her later?

"Jamie and I just talked and hung out, but it still sounds better than hearing the same people sing or dance or do whatever for two hours," I said, letting my backpack settle at my feet. I listened to her talk about all the acts the entire way to my house. I told her I pissed off Mark off last night and wasn't allowed to have people over the rest of the week so she wouldn't follow me inside. She promised to text me when she got home, our circle's one safety rule, and she left me on the curb. I was surprised to find my aunt and uncle both sitting on the couch, looking the least combative all week as they debated over which *Law and Order* was better.

"Where's Jamie?" I asked.

"His dad called and told me he went home sick today," Becky said. "I would've figured he'd told you."

I tried my best not to be surprised. Why would Jamie want to be here after everything that had happened?

"Well, he's grounded from his phone this week," I said. Mark let out a small grunt, thankfully going unnoticed by my aunt as I went for the stairs. "I'll be busy with English homework all night," I called out. "I'll come down for dinner later."

I pulled my bedroom door shut a little too hard and felt the tears burn in my eyes. I tugged the elastic from my hair and started to redo my ponytail, fumbling with it a few times as I struggled to keep from crying. Once I regained control, I tried texting Jamie.

Let's talk.

He didn't text back. I tried my best to busy myself with homework, working ahead in math and English before I realized how late it was. I went to my window to open it like I usually did before Jamie climbed in. I noticed the black Audi sitting just outside the house. I couldn't see anything through the dark windows, but I was sure he was there, watching out for me like always. I cracked my window and finished getting ready for bed, telling Becky that I didn't feel well and asked if I could stay home from school the next day.

"We'll take your temperature in the morning," she told me, her way of calling me on a lie. I brushed my teeth and got straight into bed, surprised to find a text message from Jamie.

. . .

I'm posted at the park all night. You'll have to drive yourself tomorrow. Got some things to do.

Not only did Jamie not pick me up the next morning, but he wasn't at school all day either. Izzy was just as confused as I was. She hadn't seen him since we ditched the talent show the day before.

"I figured he'd told you something he hadn't told me," she said with a shrug and turned back to the bathroom mirror to dot yellow and green paint around her eyes. "He's only my brother, you know. Not like it's life or death or anything."

That's the part that worried me the most. To Jamie, this was all life and death. It was the reason he'd gone back to the old Jamie the minute his fingers grazed the mark on my arm.

"I just hope he's not doing something stupid," I said.

Izzy snorted, twisting the cap back onto the tube of face paint and checking her design in the mirror. The dots wove their way over her left eye, down the bridge of her nose, and around the underside of her right eye. I looked more like a linebacker ready to pounce with the green smeared over my cheeks than the cute cheerleader look she wore.

"Meet you at the game?" I asked. Izzy had offered to drive me to the football stadium, but I wanted to run home. Part of me wanted to drive all the way to the Moore Estate to try catching Jamie, but I knew it wouldn't matter if he was there or not. He wouldn't want to see me anyway.

"I'll text you when I get there," she said, pulling her backpack on as the bell rang for fifth period. I waited a little while before I followed her, the traffic in the hall a thin stream on both sides. I pretended not to see Mrs. McKellen as she gave me an overly excited smile. She was overjoyed that I would join the team at halftime.

I texted Jamie the details at lunch and never heard back. At the end of the first half, all six of us from the team were going to meet next to the concession stands along with the members of the varsity volleyball team and softball team. It was going to be the dorkiest thing. They'd announce the softball and volleyball teams, neither of which had the impressive record that would merit the cheering that would follow. Then, they'd call for us and read out the consecutive state wins and no one would cheer at all save for Sean's boys who only did so to highlight how few people cared.

I almost walked past my fifth hour entirely, not noticing until the hall turned left. I turned around and hurried into class just after the bell rang, getting a warning glance from Mr. Bennett at the desk taking roll.

School was over and I was back in my car before I realized just how little I'd done that day. I couldn't even remember what happened in any of my classes aside from my hour of library aid I shared with Izzy. I listened to her talk about how glad she was that it was Friday and her plans for watching Puck during the dance tomorrow night as we finished checking in all the books from the turn-in bin under the counter.

I felt my phone buzz in my pocket on the drive home, but I waited until I pulled into the driveway to check the message. It was Becky. She told me she was working late and with Mark out of town on business, I was left to piece together a meal with what was left in the kitchen. Becky did all the shopping on Friday evenings. She always said the monotony of checking off lists cleared her head from the week, but it meant that these kinds of nights left me with almost nothing to eat. Mark usually took me out for pizza or ordered in, something I wasn't even sure I had the money for myself right now. She texted back as soon as I sent her my reply.

IOU: One homecoming dance mani-pedi tomorrow morning.

I rarely did anything as girly as getting my nails done, the one thing I never let Macy talk me into. The idea of spending so much money for someone to do what I could do at home, though arguably not as well, always seemed stupid. I knew this was less about having pretty nails for a dance though. She felt guilty about the fighting.

Only if there's Starbucks involved.
    Have I ever starved your coffee obsession?

I tossed my phone and bag onto my bed and went to the closet. I pulled out the academic team T-shirt, thankful that it didn't say anything more than that. I tugged on my nicest jeans and a pair of green Converse, a birthday gift from Macy last spring. With nothing better to do, I spent the next thirty minutes doing my hair and then redoing my makeup. The glistening porcelain of the sink was dyed green from my smeared face paint and no amount of scrubbing with my fingers seemed to get rid of it. What was that stuff made of? I scrubbed my face twice before applying foundation.

After getting ready and trying to busy myself with the little homework I had from the week, I decided to grab whatever ten bucks would get me at Subway down the street. I was so early to the stadium that I had the pick of any spot I wanted. I decided to park in the corner of the lot, just far enough away from the congestion that was the Paul's Valley High School visitor section. The cars had blue-and-white painted windows, the charter bus sporting a black panther on one side as it turned into the lot after the lines of parents.

I rolled down the windows just enough to get some airflow and I started to eat my sandwich. Instagram was full of homecoming pictures. There was a girl I only knew because we were in the same fifth-grade class one year, smiling with a blonde boy and standing outside of a house. They were both dressed head-to-toe in green and yellow, pieces of tulle carefully tied to create a poofy crown around her smiling face. Every other picture I scrolled past looked the same, boys with painted bare chests or girls with green-and-yellow tutus all posing together. I went to my own page, the last picture from a volleyball game last season.

I stuffed the last of my sandwich into my mouth and opened the camera on my phone. After thinking hard, I propped my Converse on the dash with my ankles crossed. I made sure the entrance of the stadium was just visible in the corner. I snapped a couple pictures and picked the best one, throwing on a hazy filter that only highlighted the orange and rose gold in the sunset. I noticed something dart past the car in my rearview mirror just as I looked up. I planted my feet on the floor and thought to lock all the doors with my mind just before a hand slapped my window.

"Ha!" Izzy yelled as my own scream died out.

"Izzy," I said, opening my door and reaching out for her.

She stepped out of the way, my balled-up sandwich wrapper flying past her and landing on the gravel. She bent down and picked it up, unleashing it back into my car where it settled on the dash.

"I swear," she said, "you're the only person in the entire state who drives a purple Beetle."

I climbed out of the car and locked it.

"You're one to talk, Mrs. Maserati," I said.

She scoffed and pulled me toward the entrance. We both flashed our student IDs to the volunteer at the gate who let us by without question. The football team was already warming up on one half of the field, the Paul's Valley Panthers using the other half to stretch. Even sitting down to touch their toes, they looked bigger than most of our varsity. Music echoed off the stands, the growing student section moving with the bass.

"I wish we didn't have to cover it," I said, tugging at my cardigan. It was still hot out and the rest of the crowd was dressed as if it were summer.

Izzy nodded, her hand going to her left forearm.

"Honestly, I don't care if demons find us first," she said, scanning the crowd as we moved to the front of the stand. "I'll still light its ass up." Her eyes stopped moving. I just noticed the group of teachers halfway up the bleachers, a few yards left of the student section, when she tugged me toward the stairs.

"Here," I said, pulling Izzy down an aisle a few seats from the thickest part of the crowd. The pregame activities were just starting. The cheerleaders were drawing everyone's attention as they performed a quick-paced routine, ending with the same old "paws up" chant that was probably invented the same year the school was.

The Burbrook High team ran out of their tunnel howling. The entire stadium filled with enough wolf cries to attract every pack in the region. The team lined up to receive, Sean making hand signs to one of the guys on his left just before the ball went soaring. It was clear from the first few plays that it would be a close game, the Panthers having a hard time catching our running backs.

The game was tied up when I left Izzy to find Mrs. McKellen under the stands. I was the last of our team to join her; the volleyball and softball girls were standing together at one end. I noticed Jamie talking with one of the boys from the academic team, exchanging phone numbers. I wanted to join him, but the minute his eyes met mine I froze. Jamie's smile faded and what was left was forced. I fell in line next to Jessica Harper from my math class, the last one before the volleyball line began.

"Okay, so," McKellen started, scurrying to the front of the group so all three teams could see her, "when the buzzer rings, we are going to the sideline. I'll lead us all on, so just follow in a single-file line. Everyone will have their name read over the speaker, so wave nice and big when they call you. We are taking a group picture for the paper on the field before we go, so make sure to stay in line so they don't get the caption mixed up."

We only had to wait another minute, the panthers pulling away and scoring twice thanks to a bad pass from Sean.

It felt weird following Mrs. McKellen; the woman was easily the shortest one of the bunch. I lost her among the crowd as soon as we dove into it, hoping Jessica just followed the line in front of us to the field. We emerged on the sidelines next to the pom girls, a few of them moving out of line to hug members of the softball team behind us. At last, the announcer introduced us, one group at a time. The academic team went first, all of us following Mrs. McKellen like ducks in a row. I could hear laughter from the student section, but nothing stood out aside from Izzy's cheering. They called all our names so close together we could hardly prepare to wave. I tensed up so much at the sound of Jamie's name that I forgot to wave when my own was called.

The crowd cheered when the volleyball team ran onto the

field. The varsity girls towered over most of the academic team, waving over our heads when their names were called. The entire football team erupted in howls and whistles when Macy's name echoed over the speakers. She blew a kiss to Sean on the sidelines and nearly walked into Alison when she stepped forward for her turn to wave. I caught Alison's eye after the exchange, her smile growing wider. She looked straight at me and blew a kiss. My middle finger was up before I could control it, on full display for the half of the volleyball team that was finished being introduced.

Alison turned to face Macy, whispering in her ear. The softball team ran out next, the procession continuing as if nothing weird had happened at all. I felt my phone buzz in my pocket and pulled it out just far enough to see the text from Izzy at the top.

The entire student section is going on about you flipping Alison off!

I shoved the phone back into my pocket and waited until the last of the names had been called. Mrs. McKellen ducked behind the photographer, motioning for us to smile as he snapped more than enough pictures. We filed off the field just as we'd come except this time, we scattered as soon as we were back to the concession stands.

"Look!" one of the softball girls cried to another. "I'm not kidding!" She held out her phone for the other to see, a few more rushing over to peek. I felt suddenly sick, the blood pounding in my ears as they took turns looking my way.

"Tori," someone said to my right. I didn't realize Jamie was just inches from me until I felt his hand try lacing with mine. I tugged it away, looking straight into his face.

"You don't get to do that," I said, loud enough that anyone within five feet of us had heard.

"It's more than that," he said. "And I need to talk to you. It's business."

"Go shove it up your ass, Jamie," I said.

The girls around us burst into fits of giggles. I started through the crowd, finding my way into the first bathroom I found. It wasn't until after the door swung shut that I realized the entire tiny space was flooded with water. Wads of toilet paper and brown paper towels were pressed into the grate on the floor; keeping the floor was nearly an inch-deep swamp. I went to turn off the sink, but the water continued to shoot from the faucet on high as I felt the rusty handle loosening in my grip. Busted.

"Damn," I said, tugging my phone from my pocket as it began buzzing. Jamie's name lit up the screen. I was just about the answer when the door flew open, making me jump. My phone plopped into the gray water at my feet, the screen going black seconds later when I came down on top of it. Alison shut the door behind her, blocking the only way out of the small space.

"Bet you really think you're a badass now, don't you, bitch," she said, kicking the water so a wave washed over my calves and soaked my Converse. I didn't feel angry anymore, at least not at anyone but myself. Mostly, I felt gross standing in who knows what in a bathroom most of us avoided.

"I'm done fighting with you for whatever this is," I told her. "If you wanted to humiliate me, you did. If you want to make fun of me for being friends with the school weirdo, you're too late, because that's over too. Whatever you want, just take it. I'm tired." I picked my right foot off the floor, the water cascading off it in a cascade and a wet piece of toilet paper sticking to the heel.

Alison lunged forward, pushing me so that I was nearly sitting in the flooded sink. I raised my left hand to force her away, remembering the mark there a second later. I had nearly used my powers on her, the one thing that would really mess things up more than they already were. I froze with my hand raised, Alison's eyes stopping on the bracelet. She seized my wrist and turned it over to get a better look.

"It's real," she said in disbelief. "How the hell did you get that?" I knew her mind went to Jamie straightaway. Even people who couldn't point the Quinns out in a crowd knew their name as the richest family in town. Of course, she thought he'd given it to me and now that we were done...

"Give me that," she said.

I tugged my hand away.

"You really think I'm that stupid?" I asked.

Alison was already thumbing through her phone, her head cocked to one side the way she always did just before taking the cheap shot.

"I don't know," she said, turning the screen toward me, "Let's see how dumb you are."

It was a video. She tapped the screen and I watched myself dart into Mr. Puck's room. The video paused and a few seconds later I came back out, looked both ways down the hall, before hurrying toward the front of the building. It was dark in the hallway from the assembly, but there was no doubt it was me.

"I'm wearing my blazer for Dress for Your Future Day at school," I said. "No one will believe I was there stealing that day."

Alison let out a low hum. "I don't know. That could've been that fake leather jacket you wear all the time," she said. "Thackery will think it's lucky I stepped out for the water fountain at the same time you were stealing from the lab."

I knew she'd do it. She was right about the jacket, there

was no way I could prove what day it was. I'd worn nearly the same outfit for Dress Like a Teacher Day, the night of the volleyball game, the same night all the lab equipment went missing. Even if I could prove it was my blazer, I was screwed. With no other cameras, Puck already suspecting I tried stealing before, and just one witness who hated me...

"Take it," I told her, "And that makes us even."

Alison pulled the bracelet from me as soon as I unclasped it from my wrist. She didn't bother saying anything more, just bouncing from the room with her blonde hair swinging behind her.

My phone worked long enough for me to see the blurry texts Jamie had left, though I couldn't read anything more than a few words of each before they vanished entirely. Sections of the screen were completely scrambled, leaving me unable to text. I did get it to work on a fluke, Facetiming Izzy with a black screen just long enough to tell her my phone died, and I'd be in the car.

"That's where I am," she said, just before my phone died. It didn't respond to my button clicking or me smacking the screen until more pieces of glass flecked off. I shoved it into my pocket again and made my way toward the car, my shoes squelching with each step. Izzy straightened up when she noticed me, but I wasn't looking at her. The windows of my car were covered in green paint, giant penises graffitied on every window.

"Did you see?" I asked her.

She shook her head. "I told Jamie. He's going to come back for your car later. There are bigger problems than some dicks," she said, moving aside. A silver line was drawn down the entire side of the car. I couldn't believe it. After taking a bracelet worth hundreds, she'd still seen fit to key my piece-of-shit car.

"I should've dunked her in the toilet water when I had the

chance," I said.

"No, it wasn't them," Izzy said. "Look!" She pointed toward the bottom of the car, more lines joining the other. There were four in total, evenly spaced and too far apart to be any stray dog. I felt myself shiver.

"We're too far from the park," I said.

Izzy shook her head, already moving around my car for the door of hers.

"Not that far," she said. "It's about three miles away. It probably thought it could drag you into the trees and not be heard because of the game."

I followed her, barely getting into the front seat of her Maserati before she backed out of the spot. She didn't bother waiting for the couple crossing the lot, just weaving around them and going toward the exit at the back.

"Where's Jamie?" I asked.

"He's getting you some clothes from your house. You're going to stay with us tonight. Call your aunt," she said as we pulled onto the main road.

"My phone's dead," I said, "It fell in the flooded bathroom, and I stepped on it."

Before I had finished, Izzy tossed hers into my lap. I took a minute to think about what to say. Normally, Becky wouldn't think too much about me staying with a friend on a Friday night, not even getting upset about me asking at the last minute. Things had been so weird with her and Mark and everything at home seemed so tense. Since the car crash, Mark found something wrong with everything I did.

"Becky," I said when I heard her pick up. "It's me, Tori."

I heard her suck in a breath. "Are you okay?"

"Yeah. I'm fine. I just, well, I dropped my phone in a toilet at the game and it's not working. I wanted to call and ask if I could stay at Izzy's tonight."

She didn't reply right away. I could hear something ring in the background and her voice calling for someone. She was still at work.

"I don't think that's a good idea. Mark's trip got called off and he'll be back in a few hours, and he won't like that you're not home," she said. I felt the panic rising in my throat.

"Mark doesn't like anything I do," I said, "and I'm not drinking or partying or anything. I just don't want to be at home and listen to the fighting." I knew the last bit would seal it, but I still felt dirty after saying it, dirtier than the bathroom water that was soaked into my socks. She didn't speak for a long time, the sound of laughter in the background and another phone ringing.

"Okay. Fine," she said. Another pause. "Are we still on for tomorrow?" she asked.

How could I say no after that?

"I'll have Izzy drop me off in the morning," I said. Becky told me to keep safe and I promised I would. I sat Izzy's phone in the cupholder and neither of us talked until we were driving up the winding road toward the estate.

"What happened to you?" Izzy asked. "Alison?" I nodded. When it came down to it, she really hadn't done that much at all. It wasn't like the bracelet was mine anyway. I couldn't be sure what it was worth, though even I could tell it was real gold. I wondered how the witch would feel if she'd known I'd given it away like that. Maybe it didn't even matter. She had been the one stuck in that prison cell. It could've been me stuck in the Shadowlands, pulled under the veil the way Jamie's friend had been. I had never felt more like an outsider than I did now. Alison's joke was nothing; but a bunch of petty kid stuff compared to everything else.

"Like you said," I told her. "Just a bunch of dicks." She didn't ask me anything more.

CHAPTER 19

Five minutes after getting to the estate, we found out that Jamie wasn't coming back. He claimed to have a lead on the hellhound, though Izzy and I knew that was code for "I don't know where the thing is, but I'm not coming home until I do." The news pissed me off even more and not even showering off in Izzy's bedroom-sized shower could fix that. Jamie insisted he had it covered and that we should hide out at the estate, but we did exactly the opposite.

Thirty minutes later and dressed in Izzy's Calvin Klein sweats, I was sitting in a booth at IHOP ordering the largest stack of pumpkin spice pancakes on the menu. The waitress took our menus and left us with two mugs and a giant pot of coffee, my favorite vice.

"I don't understand what kind of sexist jerk can act like this is okay," I said, pouring myself a cup. "He gets so protective and pushy at the slightest thing and tries to shove me into his stupid gated castle like a princess or something. I have powers too. I've played sports my whole life. I've had injuries. Hell, I even bloodied a few noses last season."

Izzy took the kettle from me and poured some coffee into what was mostly a cup of creamer.

"Take a breath, Rocky," she said. "I know what it looks like, but I know my brother. No matter how much of an ass he is, he's not doing this to be sexist. He knows you can kick ass and he's only doing this because, like us, he knows something more is up with you than just having a demonic target on the back of your head. The estate reeks of guardian thanks to decades of us living there, so there's no way anything is going near it."

I wanted to fire back about the way he always pulled back whenever danger seemed to come about.

"He showed off to Macy's group one day," I said, pointing a finger at Izzy. "You know, he acted like he was my bodyguard or something and could stand up for me?"

Izzy nodded, her eyebrows raised.

"That time he was being sexist," she said, "but did he tell you why? Clearly it pissed you off and knowing you, I doubt you just let him do it."

She was right. I remembered calling him on it and he admitted immediately that it was my fight.

"He knew they'd react to it," I said, feeling myself a little calmer as I sipped on the hot coffee. Izzy nodded. "Macy and her dumb girls are probably more sexist," I said. "Macy always thought that kind of thing was romantic, not possessive. It's a double standard. She wanted to be sporty and tough, but she'd probably refuse to marry a guy if he didn't kneel and ask her dad first."

Izzy let out a laugh and even I felt a smile pull at my lips.

"So, aside from Jamie playing the stubborn big brother as usual," Izzy started, leaning forward and lowering her voice, "any ideas why the demons are drawn to you?"

"It's something about my blood," I said. "I don't match any

blood types and I doubt all of those kits were faulty. I'm not about to go to a hospital to find out for sure."

Izzy agreed. "Maybe you're part demon," she said, making ghost moans and wiggling her fingers.

"Come on," I said, laughing and pushing her hands away, "Is that even possible?"

"That's definitely not it, but you needed the laugh," she said with a chuckle. "But it is something about your blood. We knew your parents from when we came back to Burbrook the first time, so it's not like there was a switch or something weird. Do you have any weird birthmarks?"

I shook my head. Nothing weird had ever happened to me until the car accident. Up until then, I thought I was boring, more boring than boring even. I blended into the crowd so well and went unnoticed by everyone. I had Mr. Puck for biology last year and he didn't even remember who I was the first day of school.

"Think Puck knows?" I asked.

Izzy lowered her mug from her lips, turning it a few times in her hands.

"I think Puck..." she began slowly. She didn't finish and I knew she didn't want to admit why. All Izzy had was a feeling, some weird feeling about the loner teacher at school she assumed was her intuition telling her he was dangerous. Like Jamie, she was too stubborn to just accept that she was wrong. She needed to be proved wrong first, have the evidence shoved in her face and every door closed. It made sense now.

"Do you think Jamie is so guarded because he's afraid it will happen again?" I asked. "Like what happened to the last girl?"

Izzy didn't miss a beat.

"We all are, aren't we?" she asked. "It was traumatizing, especially knowing that it could've been any of us at the time and yet it was her, the bravest and kindest one. She saw the good in everything and everyone and it just really sucked that she was the one to go down. Jamie internalizes everything and after growing up together, I think he's unwilling to deal with the pain from her death, not matching with her, all the way back to us as kids. It's more than being afraid it will happen again, it's not knowing if he can bear anything else being added to the list." She spoke the words as thought it was a simple answer, but the severity was there in her eyes. I'd never seen such worry in her expression, even considering what we were up against now.

"Pumpkin spice pancakes and strawberry waffles," the waitress said, sitting the plates in front of us before going back to her post at the back counter. Izzy and I looked at each other, neither of us moving. We should've just stayed at the estate.

Things felt normal the next day. Becky and I got our nails done, something that was much more enjoyable than I anticipated. The red polish was a glassy surface, and even the silver glitter accent nails felt smooth to the touch. Mark didn't say anything about homecoming, mostly due to spending the day on the phone trying to salvage the canceled trip. I almost forgot about how awkward things had been until the doorbell rang and Becky told me Jamie was here.

I pulled on my heels on quickly and grabbed my bag from my bedroom. Jamie was standing just inside the door. He was dressed in black slacks and a blazer, his tie a perfect match for my dress. His eyes lingered on the dress before finding my face, his smile barely masking the sadness. I forced my feet to move and joined him and Becky in the entryway. Mark had come to watch, standing on the bottom stair.

"You look nice," I told Jamie.

He smiled, holding up a plastic box with a corsage inside.

"And you're as beautiful as ever," he told me, handing a single rose in his left hand off to Becky. "For being so nice to me all the time. I know I can be, well, stubborn to say the least."

"From the way Mark talked about the flat tire incident, it sounds like that's how we got here," she said, pulling him into a hug.

Next, Jamie took the corsage from the plastic box, a vibrant rose paired with baby's breath. He slid the elastic band around my wrist, and I took the boutonniere from Becky, struggling to get the rose pinned just right to his lapel. We stayed just long enough to take more than enough pictures on the staircase for Becky, most of them going straight to Facebook where she said us she'd tag us both.

"I wonder if Facebook will come back around like fashion does," Jamie said, leading me out the door.

"I'm sure soccer moms would love to be ahead of that trend," I said. He smirked and I couldn't help but smile in return. Just like that, it was as if things were back to normal.

Jamie opened my door and waited until I climbed in to close it. I adjusted my dress around my legs, so the slit didn't look as provocative as it did now. I could tell he'd cleaned the car, the leather smelling almost new, like he'd had every inch detailed. I almost felt sorry when some glitter from my heels flecked onto the floor. Jamie settled into the driver's seat and the car purred to a start. A soft rhythm filled the car, a soothing bassline that Jamie turned up just enough so that it seemed everywhere. He pulled away from the curb and started down the street as a man began singing, his voice almost whiney as he rapped over the simple melody.

"Not your usual," I said. He didn't reply but started singing along instead. He started off serious, almost as if he was performing. Then, he drew each note out a little longer, mimicking the way the singer moaned. I laughed as the song ended, Jamie letting the last note bleed into the next song. I felt my chest ache when I remembered what that song left behind. In the end, we were still a mess.

"How did you cover it up?" Jamie asked, breaking the silence. He nodded toward my wrist as he took the next turn.

"Izzy showed me," I said. "It was something for covering tattoos that celebrities use." The tube was the size of my pinky and probably well worth what my aunt and uncle both made in a month. I felt bad using it before I remembered the size of the bathroom we were standing in. It was so nice being able to free myself from tight sleeves and bulky jackets and I wished I could afford a tube for everyday wear.

"I was hoping for a closer spot," Jamie said as we turned into the park.

There were already cars lined down the street, every spot around the circle drive of the community building filled. Boys dressed in their suits crossed the street and girls tottered on their heels. I could hear the music from inside through the windows of the car as we followed the line of traffic down the road. Jamie's grip tensed a little more on the wheel the farther away we drove from the building. He let out a deep breath as we passed the last of the string lights and moved from the nice paved parking lot to the gravel overflow.

"It'll be fine," I told him as we parked near the back row, just yards away from the cover of the trees. "They have security here and Izzy's still on watch, of course."

Jamie nodded and took a deep breath. He didn't move in

his seat, simply putting the car in park and leaning back into the leather.

"You're right," he said, looking at me with sincere eyes. "You always are."

A beat of silence passed as I tried deducing what he'd meant. Was this his way of apologizing? Whatever it was, he didn't say anything more. We got out of the Audi and started toward the big building. I was amazed that I didn't trip on any of the rocks or twist an ankle on the uneven grass as we walked, watching as several girls ahead of me did.

The entire building was surrounded by floor-length glass windows, giving us a spectacular view of the space before we ever walked inside. A modern chandelier hung above the middle of the dance floor, shaped like a star. Hardwood floors led to a grand piano that had been covered and scooted to the side to make way for the DJ and his towers of colored lights. Mrs. McKellen and a sophomore teacher I didn't know manned the check-in table.

"Victoria! Jamie!" McKellen's entire face lit up so much it almost erased the wrinkles around her eyes. "You both look fantastic. Let me find you on the list. Yes, here." She pointed our names out to the man who checked them off. He dug into a box on the floor and passed us both furry wolf ear headbands.

"Thanks," I said, pulling them on and forcing Jamie to do the same.

"It seems dorky," he said, smiling despite the fact.

"It's dorky if you're the only one," I told him once he'd put them on. The room was full of students wearing ears, all dancing around the floor. A pile of heels had already formed in one corner, telling me just how late we'd arrived. I felt the awkwardness settle between us again and, unable to stand another second of it, I pulled Jamie into the crowd of people.

"Hey, you asked me out, remember?" I told him when he

made a face. "What happened to the Jamie who said I needed a real high school experience, the whole shebang?" His face split into a smile and he let his right hand stroke my cheek before he let me link my hands with his. After the first verse of the pop song, we were both fully dancing with the bass. My hips brushed the couple's next to us as the dance floor grew tighter and Jamie moved closer to me to make more space.

The song swelled to the chorus and I pulled my hands from his to keep the ears from slipping off my head. My arms draped over his shoulders, and I felt his hands slide around the small of my back. He pulled me a little closer, putting us just inches apart. I could feel his legs slide along mine as we moved and then his hips when I inched farther. The song ended and a soft ballad replaced it, putting an end to our swaying and leaving us standing still and quiet. I watched the spark fade from his eyes, his smirk pulled into a tense line, and his hands moved from my hips to clasp around my back. Innocent.

"Sorry," I said, the words barely making it past my lips.

He looked back at me in shock.

"No. No, don't be. Don't ever be sorry for..." He let out a deep breath as a woman's voice began singing about wishing the seconds could last for hours. If only. "I like the Victoria Johnson that calls me out on how much of a jackass I am and the Victoria Johnson that is so much more honest than I can ever be."

"What's keeping you from that— being honest?" I asked.

Again, he sighed. It was like he was holding his breath between each exchange, like saying too much, touching too much, or even looking at me the sad way he was now would be his undoing.

"I'm a mess, Tori, and I have been for a really long time," he finally said. "I'm not worth the time or the heartache. I'm not."

I moved my hands from his shoulders to his face, feeling the stubble along his jaw.

"You're not broken," I said.

His hand covered my left, pulling it away from his face and holding it between us. He looked down where the guardian mark should've twisted around my wrist, cleverly concealed with the magic of makeup.

"Hey," Izzy said, pulling us out of our bubble and making my head hurt. "I haven't seen Puck anywhere."

I could see Jamie's annoyance in his expression, but he kept calm.

"There," he said, nodding toward the corner of the room. Mr. Puck was dressed in black slacks and a light blue button-up. He was stationed at the drink table with the rest of the science department, looking very out of place among the old and nerdy bunch. He looked more like he was attending the dance, not chaperoning.

"I think I need a drink," I said, ignoring the warning in Izzy's expression.

"I'll meet you near the entrance," Jamie said.

Izzy nudged my arm as soon as he turned his back.

"Tori, we can't tip him off that way," she said, losing her cool for the first time since I'd known her.

"It's only tipping him off if he's really up to something," I started, grabbing her wrist and tugging her through the throng of people. She let out a groan once we came out on the other side. Mr. Puck had spotted us. There was no leaving now. I let her go and we both walked to the table, Puck tugging his hands from his pocket and forcing a smile on his face.

"Come to spike the punch?" he asked, his annoyed expression not matching the sarcasm in his voice. The rest of the science teachers were sitting at the opposite end of the table, their voices low as they discussed what must have been test scores based on the way the one said... "students just filling in bubbles and laying their heads down after five minutes."

"I think I left my flask in my other purse," Izzy said, realizing the sass seconds after it had spilled from her lips. Puck seemed to snap out of whatever daze he'd been in before, rising a few inches and setting his hands on his hips.

"That's not funny," he said.

"Oh, lighten up," Izzy said, suddenly just as annoyed with him as he was with her. "You know it's a joke."

I noticed something out the window behind them and Puck did a double-take at the same time I did. The windows at the back of the building didn't provide much of a view other than the overflow lot and the trees beyond. There wasn't anything in the lot other than a few cars and a couple of dumpsters with signs warning campers to keep the dumpsters locked down to prevent bears.

"Let's go dance," I said. Izzy was reaching for a plastic cup before I could take hold of it. I immediately regretted dragging her over here.

"What's got you on edge, teach?" she asked, taking the ladle and pouring a helping of red liquid into the cup. Puck hesitated before looking from the window, pointing straight at her.

"How is it that your brother's got straight As, set to be the class valedictorian, and you..."

Izzy lowered her cup from her lips. I wished she'd toss it entirely and go dance with me instead of pressing her luck.

"...are clever? Better at public speaking?" she asked.

Puck opened his mouth to launch into a lecture, but hesitated. He let out a deep breath.

"You're barely older than my seniors and yet you..."

"You were going to assign me detention, weren't you?" Izzy said and sat the cup aside.

"No," he shot back, cheeks red like the punch. "You're not a student."

"But you just said that I look like the seniors here. Why is it that when people form their opinions about women it always starts and ends with the way they look?"

"It's not about the way you look, it's the fact that you think so highly of yourself. I find you very conceited for a twenty-one-year-old who graduated early and went to college fully funded by your parents."

Izzy's cheeks turned pink, and her eyes filled with fire. I felt so uncomfortable standing next to them that I could feel the tension in my shoulders.

"Izzy," I hissed next to her. She ignored me.

"Me? You're so pretentious about how much you know and how you went to Brown and that you had connections with some fancy scientists who work for NASA now. If you are so smart and have credentials that could earn you a high-profile job and make three times what you do now, then why the hell are you in tiny Burbrook teaching idiot freshmen about mitosis?"

I kicked Izzy and her expression fell, realizing exactly what she'd just said now that it was out there. Mr. Puck looked back at her in awe. After a moment, he let out a laugh of disbelief.

"Did I do something, Isabella?" Mr. Puck asked with a smirk. "Or, is there some other reason why you've been stalking me on the internet?"

Crap. I nudged Izzy again with my foot, but she was too busy with her standoff.

"You wanted to talk more about academics and what we both know about the sciences," Izzy said. "Let's do that. Monday morning in your classroom. We can call it detention."

Ugh.

Puck snorted and raised a plastic cup of punch to her. Izzy

lifted hers from the table and lightly pressed it against his.

I was just thinking about going back to Jamie when I noticed the movement again, this time just catching sight of him between the evergreens. The ferryman froze as soon as our eyes met, though I couldn't see them behind his dark hood. He darted to the left, vanishing into the tree line again with just a few steps. I followed him, apologizing to the boy I walked into and hurrying toward the door.

I was forced to take my eyes off the window as I went, slipping past Mrs. McKellen and out the front door unnoticed. It was eerily silent outside, the sound of crickets the only noise aside from a scream seconds later. I pried my heels off and burst into a sprint, hearing two sets of laughs before I skidded to a stop at the back of the grassy parking lot.

"Oh shit," Macy said, slapping Alison on the back twice who was bent over the hood of Jamie's black Audi. They both started laughing when they saw me, Alison holding the mirror to keep from falling over when she stepped on Macy's discarded heels.

"Just the bitch I wanted to see," she said. Macy muffled her laugh behind her hands. The moonlight landed on the hood of the car when she stepped away, making the crude scratches over the surface more visible. The word *slut* was carved over the hood, Alison's car keys still resting next to the word. I heard the crunching of feet on gravel just before Izzy stopped next to me, her expression tightening as she noticed the hood of the car.

"There's security all over the place and you're keying my brother's car?" Izzy asked, "How stupid are you?" She pushed Macy's hands from the hood, causing her to trip and tumble onto the ground. Macy flung herself onto her hands and knees and vomited all over Alison's gold heels.

"Can't you at least aim?" Alison groaned, taking a step back from the car.

"How drunk did you get her?" I asked. I'd seen Macy pretty drunk, having picked her up from a few wild parties last year. I'd never seen her so sloppy though. There was no way she was going to remember keying Jamie's car. I looked around for cameras, but the entire parking lot was free of the black boxes and eyewitnesses. I could hear someone speaking on a microphone from the main building, calling all the nominees for king and queen to the stage.

"She took some pills before we got here and she stole a flask off Sean after he broke up with her," Alison said, suddenly more concerned now that Macy was lying halfway in a puddle of vomit. Izzy pushed Alison back, forcing her into the tall grass behind the car. Izzy dropped to her knees and pulled on Macy's arm, so she was propped up on her side by the wheel of the car. Macy let out a small moan, mumbling something about cramps before lying still on the ground.

"We have to call for help. My phone's in Jamie's pocket," Izzy said, looking up at me. My stomach sank as I remembered my broken phone, still sitting on my desk where I'd left it after the lecture Mark had given me about responsibility. We both looked at Alison, whose face had lost all its color. She opened her mouth to speak, and something slammed into my back. Alison let out a loud scream that was cut off in seconds. My forehead smashed into the side of the Audi, leaving my vision blurry as I watched the black wolf dragging Alison's body into the trees.

"Hellhound," Izzy said, leaving me behind and bursting into a run after the animal. I followed. The forest was quiet aside from my panting and the rustle of the evergreens as I brushed past. I had lost sight of Izzy seconds before. I ran a few minutes more before I skidded to a stop.

"Izzy!" I called out. A black shape shot from the trees just inches in front of me. I felt something sharp slice my collar bone just as the ferryman skidded to a stop a few feet away, armed with a dagger that glimmered in the moonlight.

"Let's make a deal, ferryman," I said, taking a breath to calm the shaking in my voice. I remembered the first time I'd faced him, how violated I felt in my own home, the fact that even now the old house didn't quite feel safe from the Shadowlands.

"Tell me what you want and maybe we can make a trade," I said.

The figure froze, still poised for attack with his knees bent and sword raised before his dark hood. He straightened up and reached within his robes and withdrew a vial. I nearly lunged before I noticed the dark liquid within the glass. He sheathed the dagger at his hip and pointed to me with his free hand and then the vial. He tipped the corked vial to his hood and feigned drinking it. He held up his free hand again and began tracing letters into the air.

"S-A-V-E," I said aloud. He held up a hand for a pause before spelling again. "F-U-T-U-R-E. Drink that and save the future. Who's future?" He traced a circle in the air and then a heart. He reached into his hood and pulled a chain free with a single tug. He tossed it to me, and I barely caught it with my middle finger. At the end of the long chain was a circle pendant, pounded flat and strung onto the chain by a small jump ring. As I turned in under the moonlight, I caught sight of a tiny engraving on one side.

VI

"Save the future of the sixth circle by drinking that?" I asked him, getting a single nod in response. He held the vial out to me. I felt my skin go cold instantly, shivering a little as we stood there. A howl sounded out in the distance, reminding me of how little time I might have. What were the chances this was just a distraction while the hellhound took care of Izzy and Alison? I thought the hellhound had been meant for me all this time. Why play games now and if there really was a threat to our circle, would the ferryman out it now?

"Why this?" I asked him, holding up the pendant. He moved slowly, pointing to himself and then encircling each wrist with his hands and holding them before him as if surrendering, captured, imprisoned.

"You didn't have to be the ferryman," I said, feeling my heart speed up, "I was there in the Shadowlands. You have power. You aren't imprisoned. You can't be telling the truth now." Before I could do anything, the ferryman surged forward in a black blur. I felt my mouth being pried apart and the vial was shoved so far between my teeth that I nearly gagged on it. The liquid felt slimy as it slipped down my throat and I keeled over in a coughing fit. When I looked up again, everything was in a hazy black and white hue. I was in the forest, watching myself run through the trees. My clothes were in tatters, the cuts bloody and chunks of my hair hanging in messy strands from my ponytail.

My vision blurred and then I was staring at myself again. I was wearing my homecoming dress this time, my face and chest splattered with drops of blood. A cut from my forehead down my cheek was healing, knitting together on their own thanks to my guardian powers. There was a thump of something heavy settling on the ground and Jamie appeared in the frame, throwing his arms around me. His lips met mine and the kiss deepened instantly, our grip tightening on each other. My insides squirmed and I felt my body heating in response.

Despite Jamie's faults, I wanted him, and I wanted him

bad. I realized now that the pull I felt between us, the reason I couldn't think of separating from him despite how mad I was at him, was something much more than just the bond of our circle. This was something eternal, a soulful joining that I could feel tugging at my powers as I even thought about it. Jamie Quinn was my match.

The image blurred and I was running through the forest again in the same torn clothes as before. The trees opened and I was standing at the bank of the lake, just able to see the main building across its moonlit surface. In the shallows of the water were three figures. There was a woman standing with a dagger held at her side. I couldn't quite make out her face in the darkness, but her hair was dark and hung in short curls around her face. Her head was adorned with a crown of roses and thorns, all of them wilted, encircled by the magnificent deer antlers on both sides of her head.

The dark liquid swirled in a growing pool of the lake around her and a kneeling figure. The figure was dressed in black robes, the familiar dark hood sending a wave of nausea over me. The ferryman raised his head to look up at the antlered woman, holding up two gaunt hands. A figure floated to the surface next to him, the shock of the recognition sending such a jolt through my chest that the scene blurred from the mangled body back to the green of the trees. I opened my eyes, and I was flat on my back, the ferryman standing feet away.

"He can't die," I said, "He's a guardian. We're immortal." I remembered the earlier scene, the two of us kissing in our homecoming clothes. My heart jolted to a stop, and I felt like my feet had turned to cement. A kiss would match us and undo the immortality curse. Jamie would die if I matched with him.

"Ferryman," the dark figure said, his breathy voice making me shiver. He took four quick steps back from me before smoke began to rise from the hem of his robes. I could hear his panting, the figure throwing his hood back and his body trembling. Flames whooshed upwards, engulfing his body and sending a hot wave over mine. He writhed in silent pain, hood turned upwards towards the moon until the flames finally ate through the black garb. A terrifying scream pierced the air for just seconds, and I caught a look at the figure's scrunched up face before the flames and smoke hid him from view. It was James Moore, Jamie's father. There was no mistaking it even as the smoke faded and not a single sign of the destruction was left as evidence.

I realized my hands were nearly sunken into the dirt when I felt the grass held between them pop from their roots. I let the soil go and wiped my hands on my dress, not caring anymore about the beautiful fabric. I was still trying to process what had happened when I heard a scream, a girl's high pitch wail cut off by a howl. I forced myself to my shaky legs and slowly began to run, only able to by the reminder of the hellhound's attack.

The sounds grew louder the faster I ran and finally, I could see the body of the hellhound racing towards Izzy, the front of her dress smeared with blood. She held out a hand and flames shot towards the giant beast, setting fire to the tall grass. The monster leaped easily four feet above the tips of the flames, descending towards her. I raised a hand and let out a yell, the hellhound sent flying sideways and skidding into the far trees of the clearing. I ran past the last of the evergreens to join her as she knelt to one knee next to the body.

Alison was lying on the grass, her body twisted in ways that made my stomach turn. The grass was splattered with blood before her face, making me fear the worst. Izzy looked at me, her shocked expression reflecting all my emotions. I nearly collapsed, my knees wobbling as Jamie finally joined us. He had removed his blazer, his white shirt still clean.

"You couldn't have called me?" He asked.

"My phone is in your pocket, genius," Izzy said, standing up.

"We have bigger problems right now," I said, looking across the clearing.

"I can't get close enough to it," Izzy said. The hellhound rose from the ground, baring its teeth and letting out a growl that rumbled through the clearing. I took a few shaky steps, then surged forward despite Jamie and Izzy's screams. I could hear Jamie behind me as the hound charged. I held out a hand and waited, forcing myself to watch its feet pound closer rather than the sharp teeth opening towards me. Jamie let out a loud yell and I just caught sight of his shocked expression when I felt a sharp pain slice from my forehead to my jaw.

I lost my breath from the force of the fall, the hellhound settling on my chest. I felt the panic rise as it opened its mouth wide. I held my hands out to protect my face, surprised when the hellhound's teeth snapped shut a foot from my face. He lunged again and I could feel his weight on my shoulders, just barely getting control over my powers to keep him away. Jamie's arms appeared around the monster's back, withdrawing a silvery blade from the back of his slacks and forcing the animal's head back by the scruff of its neck. I turned away before he could slit its throat.

The blood splattered over my face and chest, hot and thick. Jamie held onto the beast until it stopped struggling. He let it fall to the ground, his eyes landing on me. I recognized the look in his eyes, the same shocked expression I had seen in the strange vision from the ferryman. I flashed through all the scenes, Jamie kissing me, Jamie dead, and Jamie kissing me again. I felt my entire body relax at the memory, suddenly feeling hot and not from the blood sticking to my skin.

Jamie surged forward, his fingers finding my face and

pulling it towards his. It took all my willpower to turn my head, letting his lips land above my ear. He pulled back, his expression surprised. I shook my head, swallowing against the lump rising in my throat. I could see the hurt in his eyes, and I felt my eyes burn as I realized how much I wanted to kiss him. I knew I couldn't say the words to put an end to any future for us, so I just shook my head.

"How stupid," Jamie said under his breath and turned to check on Alison. The squelching that filled the air when he touched the back of her head forced me to whirl around. I fell onto my knees, sure I was going to pass out as I threw up. After dry heaving a minute, Izzy helped me to my feet and looked at Jamie.

"We need to get rid of the hellhound and get out of here before anyone can see us," she said. I looked down at myself, feeling my head swim again at the blood seeping down the front of my dress. Jamie straightened up, his clothes still in pristine shape by some miracle.

"Macy," I said, "Macy may have overdosed back there in the parking lot." Jamie looked at me and nodded.

"You two get back to the estate without drawing any attention," he said, "I'll get her to the hospital. Don't use your phones to communicate about any of this. Will Macy remember anything?" I remembered her groaning against the wheel of the Audi, and I felt the guilt of leaving her there twisting deep in my gut.

"No. There's no way," Izzy said. Jamie let out a sigh of relief and burst into a sprint towards the trees. Izzy turned to face me, holding me by my arms. Her expression was serious.

"I need you, Tori," she said, "You can freak out after we finish here. We need you first." I wanted to cry, but I knew she was right.

I used what little strength I had left to levitate the bloody hellhound the ten-minute walk to the bank. We used some old rope Izzy stole from the boathouse to tie a cinderblock to its middle. I barely had the strength to levitate it out to the center of the lake, but I did just before collapsing onto the moist bank and watching the large body sink under the calm waters and back towards the hell hole.

After coming out of a fainting episode, Izzy led me the long way around the lake. She had parked further down the road from the national park, the black jeep concealed easily in the trees. I felt drunk as we drove back, the same dizzy feeling I remembered from the night I'd woken. Izzy cracked the windows for some cool air after noting how pale I looked. She helped me into the house, and I sunk into the leather couch where I'd woken up after the last tragedy. This time, it wasn't me who'd been hurt. Alison was dead, ripped apart by some beast. Macy was on her way to a hospital, possibly fated for the same.

I burst into tears, not stopping until my eyes were sore and I sunk into a deep sleep. When I woke again, a blanket was draped over me, and a set of fresh clothes were lying on the coffee table. I sat up slowly, my head aching from the long night. I checked Izzy's phone sitting on the table before me for the time. It was just three in the morning, just hours after the fight.

I took the clothes through one of the guest rooms and into the bathroom, spending so long under the hot water of the shower that my fingers and toes turned pruny. When I turned the water off, I could hear two voices. I quickly got dressed, pushing my wet hair behind my ears as I went back into the hall.

"Why does it have to be that bitch?" Izzy asked, "After all the shit she did to Tori and the way she prances around school like she bought it or something."

"We can't just erase the mark and pretend to be normal again," Jamie shouted. "This is the way the river flows and we have to ride the rapids or be pulled under. We need a fourth. You know that," he said. I rounded the corner and saw them both standing next to the fireplace, facing off as if in a serious sparring match.

"Don't tell me we have to leave town," I said. They both exchanged glances and Izzy finally let out a sigh, motioning for her brother to explain as she collapsed in an armchair in a huff. Jamie's eyes landed on me for just seconds, long enough for the awkwardness to be palpable. He scratched the back of his neck with his marked hand, the black text flexing around his forearm.

He nodded towards the couch I had occupied months before. I felt my heart skip in my chest, not able to move until I noticed Macy's arm hanging off the cushion. The same dark ink was swirling up her forearm the way it did on mine, and Izzy's, and Jamie's. Macy was waking. She was making the change like I had so many months ago. It was just a matter of time before she woke up, just as lost and confused as I had been.

"It was an overdose," Izzy said. I remembered now the last summer Macy and I had together. We both, along with everyone else in the community, had a silent agreement not to talk about Tyler Evans. Macy used to think a lot of her brother until that summer he overdosed on pain pills he'd saved from a knee injury. It had been minor and easily fixed, but she changed after that, seeming to grow more negative.

I forgot that Macy hadn't always been shallow. She hadn't always been so obsessed with her looks, just fashion. She hadn't always been a follower, but a leader the way Tyler had been at school. After he graduated, overdosed, and fell deeper into drugs, Macy cared less about everything but volleyball. Maybe that's why she had been so mad I quit. Maybe she thought I'd quit on her the way her own brother had given up and allowed himself to just float by. He was good enough. That's what I had been since I quit volleyball and stopped studying, just good enough.

I moved past them both and sunk onto the couch next to Macy's limp body. I took her arm in my lap and traced one swirl of the guardian mark. Jamie and Izzy were both watching me when I looked up, both in disbelief. Izzy had changed into jeans and a t-shirt, Jamie still dressed in his button up and slacks.

"You should get cleaned up," I told him. He paused a moment before nodding.

"Yeah," he said, "I think you can do this on your own now." He stayed for just a moment. I let out a sigh and forced myself to think about anything other than Jamie, the ferryman bursting into flames, Alison's dead body, but my mind wandered back to the visions. I had refused to kiss Jamie, preventing us from matching and effectively ending what we might have had for good. How long will I have to wait to prevent the antlered woman from killing him? How far into the future had he shown me?

"I'm going to call Becky," Izzy said and started for the kitchen, "I don't know what I'll tell her, but maybe I can get you out of at least some trouble." I didn't reply, remembering the pendant the Ferryman had given me. I let go of Macy's hand and went to the guest bathroom where I'd left my dress. The pendant sat next to the sink, the silver somehow unmarred by the blood that had drenched my front. I could hear Izzy on the phone when I returned, taking the pendant to the mantle.

I looked at the picture of the Moore family standing before the train station, keeping my eyes on James Moore. He looked younger than the man I'd seen beneath the ferryman's cloak. I didn't know how I would tell Jamie and Izzy that it was their dad who had hunted me for so long. I believed he really had been imprisoned by the shadow mistress. He wouldn't have helped me if he had chosen his position. A long chain hung around James's neck, though the pendant was concealed by his vest. I was sure it was the same one that was in my hand now.

"Well, Becky says you're grounded, but you can stay here. It took a lot of convincing," Izzy said. I whirled around to face her with a groan. "I had to tell her something to keep her from coming over here, so she thinks you're too drunk to get home right now. I told her she could get you in the morning," she said. I thought about showing her the pendant, but something about it felt private. It was like the moment between me and James had been just for the two of us, no one else. So, I tucked the necklace in my pocket and went back to sit with Macy.

"Tori," Izzy said after a while. Something in her voice was strange. She was chewing on her lower lip. Finally, she sat down on the nearest armchair, scooting to the front and lowering her voice. "That hellhound pushed right past you for Alison," she said. I knew what she meant. If it was my blood the Shadowlands wanted, why had they not attacked me when the chance was there? Why not just drag me back to the Shadowlands and kill me the way Jamie's ex-girlfriend was?

"Maybe my blood is the reason I wasn't trapped in the Shadowlands, like it's the reason I can travel back and forth when I want," I said. Izzy's brows furrowed in confusion. "If I'm right, then the Shadow Mistress wants my blood so she can travel from the Shadowlands," I said, the memory of the antlered woman sending cold chills over my skin.

"Who?" Izzy asked.

"The ruler of the Shadowlands. I saw her on a tapestry when I escaped from the castle," I said, retelling the story of my escape and the generosity the witch had shown me.

"So, there's the ferryman," she said.

"A new one now," I said, remembering the fire, "I killed the old one." I didn't say anything else, telling her how he'd combusted but nothing about the man I'd seen underneath when she asked for more.

"The ferryman can travel between the mortal world and the Shadowlands because he ferries the living to the land of the dead. The shadow mistress is stuck in her own kingdom because she can't leave it without your blood, for whatever reason that is. You said there was another?" Izzy asked. I remembered the figure now, a dark shape halfway down the pile of bodies in the tapestry, standing between the ferryman and the Shadow Mistress. I nodded.

"I don't know who it is or what they look like, but yes. There's someone ranked above the ferryman, some kind of hunter in the shadows. I couldn't get a clear look," I said. She let out a deep breath and we sat in silence for a while.

"At least we know what we're up against," she said. I wanted to point out that we had no idea what to look for, let alone who we were up against. No matter what we might face in the future, there were more important things to face right now. Macy began to move, letting out a groan and opening her eyes. She looked around the room before her eyes fell on me in surprise.

"Welcome home," I said.

Acknowledgments

This journey would not have been possible without the love and support of my family, especially my husband's encouragement. This book is dedicated to him not just because he is a wonderful human and my biggest champion, but because his family heritage helped influence a lot of the themes and settings of this book. I remember loving that part of English class in high school where we talked about Greek and Roman mythology and when we read the *Iliad* and *The Odyssey*. While this book is not a Greek or Roman retelling, those myths did influence my version of the Shadowlands and the characters within their depths.

This book wouldn't be what it is now if I didn't have a wonderful team of people that helped me take it from the early draft to this final version in your hands now. Thank you to my wonderful sister-in-law Nikki Prokopis for being the ruthless beta reader I needed. Thank you to Kayla McGuerty, who I connected with on Instagram and who gave great feedback on my early draft. Thanks to the amazing women I talked with on my YouTube series, Wednesday's with Writers. I learned so much from your experiences and got some amazing advice and help with all things writing and publishing.

My editor Lucia Ferrara played a huge part in helping me make this book as good as it could be. She was amazing and wonderful to work with. And as always, my cover designer created a magical cover, more amazing than I could've imagined. Lena Yang, you are wonderful to work with and your art really elevated this book. Thank you to you, of course, who are reading this book now. I wouldn't be the author I am today without you.

ABOUT THE AUTHOR

Amy Prokopis is a fiction author from Oklahoma who writes books for young adults. She loves writing everything from science fiction and fantasy to contemporary romance. She graduated from Oklahoma State University with a bachelor's degree in English and a minor in German before obtaining a master's degree in school counseling. Besides writing, Amy enjoys distance running and spending time with her husband, their son, and their Havanese, June.

OTHER BOOKS BY AMY PROKOPIS

Kenna Riley is Aldierian, but no one but her adoptive father knows and no one else can. All she wants is to escape poverty in her village. All that changes when her identity is outed, she's branded a terrorist, and is sentenced to death in the arena.

Kieran Grace wants to leave the capital of Gallaterra and get as far away from his father as he can. After speaking out against the war with the Aldierans one too many times, he's ordered to live up to his family's legacy by killing an Aldierian in the arena.

Together they do something no one else has, escape the arena and learn a Gallaterran secret along the way. In their search for help from the Aldierians, they find adventure and opportunity that they never thought they'd be allowed. It makes their mission even more dangerous. Despite fighting together, they both must decide what is worth sacrificing alone.

TURN THE PAGE FOR A
SNEAK PEAK OF BOOK 2!

CHAPTER 1

It would've made more sense if I'd just gotten back from a morning jog, but no. I woke up sweaty with my heart sprinting away from my body every morning since homecoming. I had to leave the bathroom where I was attempting to brush through the damp locks at the nape of my neck to turn off my alarm. This had become enough of a habit that I was contemplating turning my morning alarms off entirely.

The bathroom was already steamy from the shower. I pushed the curtain aside to adjust the temperature, pausing when I straightened back up and found myself staring out the window. The giant tree in the middle of the yard swayed a little in the breeze. In my dreams, she was always right next to it, just staring up at me in the window with blood cascading down her chest from the slash across her throat.

Alison Rivers was still missing, and the entire town had lost their minds about it. I guess it was understandable for many reasons. First, everyone was concerned by the discovery of what they deemed Super Wolf, a larger than ever documented wolf that supposedly prowled the national park not far from Burbrook city limits. It was actually a hellhound sent from the Shadowlands after me and we killed it in the forest, but not until after it attacked and dragged Alison into the forest. Now, everyone was extra scared about the Super Wolf being the possible attacker. No one had asked the truly scary question yet though. Was Alison Rivers still alive?

No. No, she wasn't.

I felt queasy at the memory, but not any worse than the guilt and horror I experienced when I woke up each night from my dreams of her standing outside my bedroom watching me. I threw up the first two nights I'd had the dream.

I jumped when someone pounded against the bathroom door.

"Speed things up, Honey," Mark said from the hall. "I have to get to the job site early."

I let out a deep breath and turned from the window. "Becky can take me."

"No, she had to show a cabin outside town. She already left."

I groaned. If I had known before it was too late that the Beetle needed a tune-up, yet again, I would've asked Macy or Izzy for a ride to school. "On it," I called back, aware of how annoyed I sounded and not really caring.

I could hear Mark's grumbling as I undressed.

I didn't bother washing my sweaty hair and the time that saved, along with the messy bun I pulled it all into, seemed to settle Mark enough when I made my appearance downstairs. He was dressed in his work clothes with his lunch cooler in one hand and keys in the other. He started for the truck outside while I grabbed my backpack.

I hadn't been in Mark's work truck in a long time. Now that

I thought about it, I didn't have my license and the reason for the ride was summer volleyball practice.

"Woah," I commented as I climbed into the passenger seat. It reeked of cherries and smoke. "Since when do you vape?"

Mark adjusted in his seat, casting me a glance that told me he didn't want to talk about it. After a moment of consideration as he started the engine, he decided the explain himself after all. "Terry smokes that stuff all the time. I guess I just got used to it over the years."

He backed into the street and turned on the radio. Old rock. Our taste in music was maybe the only thing Mark and I had in common, and it was how he met Becky. They used to go to concerts all the time before getting married. Becky used to tell me that he wasn't so uptight then. I couldn't imagine it.

"I need to drop off my application at Beans and Books after school, but I can get a ride with Macy."

"I can take you," Mark said. "We should spend some quality time together anyway."

I wanted to resist. I knew that what he really wanted was to subtly lecture me about hanging around the Quinns and warn me about reckless behavior. The unspoken jab at Jamie and Izzy reminded me about why I was dreading today.

"Shoot!" I said. "I have academic team practice after school. We won't be done until four."

"That's fine. I'll pick you up then. Gives me time to talk with Terry about next weekend."

"What's next weekend?" I asked. He barely stopped at the stop sign at the entrance of the neighborhood before pulling onto the main street.

"Terry and I are checking out a new supplier. We'll probably stay overnight in Holston and be back Sunday morning." He was excited. The business was going well. Some new company just moved their warehouse between Holston and

Burbrook and he'd landed several clients wanting to build houses. He told me it helped ease some bills and freed up more money to put in my college account. I was up to two semesters now.

"How about I take you to drop off that application tomorrow morning and we grab lunch?" he asked as we pulled into the school parking lot. The talk didn't come up on the way to school, but there was still tomorrow.